MW00438009

Book of the Month

Also from Jennifer Probst

The Twist of Fate Series:
Meant to Be
So It Goes
Save the Best for Last

The Meet Me in Italy Series:
Our Italian Summer
The Secret Love Letters of Olivia Moretti
A Wedding in Lake Como

The Sunshine Sisters Series:
Love on Beach Avenue
Temptation on Ocean Drive
Forever in Cape May
Christmas in Cape May

The Stay Series:
The Start of Something Good
A Brand New Ending
All Roads Lead to You
Something Just Like This
Begin Again

The Billionaire Builders:
Everywhere and Every Way
Any Time, Any Place
All or Nothing At All
Somehow, Some Way

Searching for Series:
Searching for Someday
Searching for Perfect
Searching for Beautiful
Searching for Always
Searching for You
Searching For Mine

The Marriage to a Billionaire Series:
The Marriage Bargain
The Marriage Trap
The Marriage Mistake
The Marriage Merger
The Marriage Arrangement

Standalone:
The Charm of You
Summer Sins
Executive Seduction
Dante's Fire
The Grinch of Starlight Bend
Love Me Anyway
All For You
Unbreak my Heart

The Sex on the Beach Series:
Beyond Me
Chasing Me

The Steele Brother Series:
Catch Me
Play Me
Dare Me
Beg Me
Reveal Me

Hope you enjoy!

Book of the Month

Jennifer Probst

Book of the Month
By Jennifer Probst

ISBN: 978-1-963135-24-4

Published by Blue Box Press, an imprint of Evil Eye Concepts, Incorporated

Author's Acknowledgements

There are so many people to thank for getting *Book of the Month* into readers' hands.

First up, the wonderful team of Blue Box Press. Liz Berry, MJ Rose, and Jillian Stein: that meeting together where we brainstormed and cried will always be one of my favorite moments in my career. Thank you for not only seeing my vision but loving and supporting my new book baby every step of the way. There are no words to thank you. It's how book publishing should always be.

Thanks to Chelle Olson, Kim Guidroz, and Suzy Baldwin for edits and proofing to make a beautiful, finished story.

A big thank you to all the wonderful book influencers who took part in the contest and helped spread the word about Book of the Month. You are a valued part of this community!

"There is no greater agony than bearing an untold story inside you."
–Maya Angelou

"Blame it or praise it, there is no denying the wild horse in us."
–Virginia Woolf

"With flowing tail and flying mane, Wide nostrils never stretched by pain, Mouth bloodless to bit or rein, And feet that iron never shod, And flanks unscar'd by spur or rod, A thousand horses—the wild—the free—Like waves that follow o'er the sea, Came thickly thundering on."
– Lord Byron

Chapter One

Aspen Lourde looked at the line of readers waiting their turn to get their books signed and wished they'd all go home.

This whole event was a disaster.

She kept her smile pasted firmly in place as the young woman shoved a worn-edged hardback across the table and grabbed from the stack of swag, pocketing a few custom-made keychains. "Hi, I'm Juanita. Oh, my God, I can't believe I'm finally meeting you! This is like…epic."

Some of Aspen's dread faded. This was a true fan who wouldn't disappoint. She pumped up her voice to a higher level, making sure it was filled with warmth. "Thank you so much. It's an honor to meet you, too. Should I sign to you, Juanita?"

"Yes, please."

Aspen confirmed the spelling—she'd once written Kim when it should have been Kym, so she never assumed—and scrawled, *So happy to meet you!* across the page. She added her signature with an *XOXO* in purple Sharpie. Closing the book with a snap, she grabbed her newest release stacked in towering piles to her right and offered it to Juanita. "This, too?" she asked casually, annoyed at her nervous heartbeat.

Juanita shook her head. "Oh, no thanks. I'll grab it later. I just loved *Fifty Ways to Leave Your Lover*. It spoke to me, you know? Like, to my very soul. I cried for days—a true book hangover." Juanita sighed with pleasure. "Are you going to write a sequel? I'd love to see how Mallory is doing with Josh. Did they have kids? Did she ever run into her ex? Is there anything in the works?"

Aspen looked into the woman's eager face and wanted to cry. Not because she was flattered. Not because her book was beloved and well-known and touched readers so deeply.

It was for one reason only.

Juanita was talking about the wrong book.

Aspen kept her smile and nodded with understanding. She did her best sales pitch and smoothly skipped over Juanita's question. "Well, I hope you give *Meet Me at Your Spot* a try! It's a story about two kids who grew up together at a lake and reunite ten years later in Paris to find themselves on opposing sides of an important project. It's very romantic—a mix of first love, enemies-to-lovers, and second-chance romance."

"It sounds wonderful! I'll definitely check it out." She clutched the signed book to her chest. "Are you thinking about writing a sequel then? For your next book?"

"Not right now," she responded. "There are still so many new stories to tell."

Juanita looked disappointed. "Oh. Well, I understand. But think about it. Because I'd buy it in a heartbeat, Can I grab a pic?"

"Of course."

She stood up as the bookstore assistant smoothly stepped forward and snapped a picture using Juanita's phone, which showcased the book she'd written five years ago. Juanita squealed. "Thanks again. I can't wait to post. My friends are gonna freak!"

"You're so welcome. Have a great day!" Aspen said with a tiny wave, sitting back down at the elongated card table covered with a white cloth. The next person stepped up, a woman with tight, gray curls, a bird-like figure, and a cane. "Hi, how are you today?"

"I'm wonderful. I'm Edith. I can't believe I'm meeting you. I rarely go out, you know, too many germs, but when my daughter-in-law said you were coming into town, I knew I had to make the trip. You're my favorite author. *Fifty Ways to Leave Your Lover* reminded me of my own youth. There was this man…"

Aspen smiled, taking the book and listening to the woman's account of her own love history. She confirmed the name spelling between dialogue, scrawling her name in purple marker and offering Edith a keychain. "What a wonderful story. Thank you for sharing it. I think you'll love my new book. It takes place in Paris, and it's—"

"Oh, no, I can't afford it right now. I'm on social security. Can I get a picture?"

Aspen tamped down a sigh. "Of course."

The hour dragged by. She managed to sell one book of her new release to the last person in line, who probably felt sorry for her almost getting killed when the pile tilted and crashed on top of her. Or maybe it was the desperation in her voice as she recited the hook and synopsis like she was a used car salesman hungry for a sale to feed the family.

Did it even matter anymore?

She'd sold one. One book from the one hundred copies they'd ordered and expected her to sell. Usually, they sold tickets, which included a copy of the new book, but her last signing hadn't gone too well, so the bookstore decided to let this event be *open ended.* Aspen agreed to the terms, allowing the patrons to bring a book from home for her to sign, and each one had dragged in *Fifty Ways to Leave Your Lover.*

But Lord, what was she supposed to do? Nothing was worse than her last signing. She'd taken a hard stance on people bringing any personal books in, insisting she was only signing her newest release.

Barely anyone showed. A few friends and casual shoppers peeked at her book and then politely declined. She'd literally sat in that bookstore, surrounded by piles of her latest release, chatting with the embarrassed assistant who tried to soothe her by using the weather as an excuse. Rain had been in the forecast. Aspen agreed as they ignored the clear, blue sky and warm, acrid air.

Aspen turned and met the sympathetic gaze of the bookstore associate, Kellie. Her practiced smile told Aspen she'd been through this many times with authors and was an expert. "Wasn't it wonderful how many people showed up for you?" she chirped, expertly pulling books from the pile to make a neat stack in front. "If you can sign these copies, we'll put them out on the front table for our readers."

"Of course. Thank you." Aspen began signing, trying not to look over as Kellie loaded the other eighty-nine books on a cart to wheel them away. Despair threatened, but she focused on signing and tried not to think of all her precious babies going to the graveyard after she'd worked so hard. After she'd hoped so deeply. After she'd dreamed so big.

They'd be returned. Every last one. Already, the store realized she wasn't as big of a draw as first believed, so her books would be quietly shipped back instead of being peddled to the patrons. Shelf space was precious and limited. She'd just missed the #booktok surge and hadn't been able to go big with the younger crowd yet. Only her first book sold well, and still managed to keep a certain amount of promotion.

There was just no space for her last two books.

Aspen packed up her stuff, thanked the staff, and trudged to her car. The thought circled her mind like Clorox in the toilet, and all the hopes she'd pinned on her release got flushed.

It was official.

She was a one-hit wonder.

The phone rang as if on cue. Aspen winced and stared at her agent's number. Answer now or later? Rip the Band-Aid off quickly or by tiny quarter inches? Slumped in her car, soul battered, she decided to get it over with.

"Hey, Nic. How are you?"

The familiar, husky voice poured over the phone. "Shitty. How'd the signing go? How many showed? How many bought?"

An image of her savvy, sharklike agent flickered in her mind. When they first met, Nicolette had scared the living hell out of her. She was well known in the industry for being protective of her clients and extremely picky about who she took on. Aspen had landed in the slush pile—the graveyard for manuscripts by unknown authors struggling to get seen. It was a true Cinderella story from start to finish, ending with Nicolette representing her and signing a multi-million-dollar, three-book contract at auction.

They'd gone through a lot together, and Aspen had learned Nicolette was like a fierce mama bear with her clients, trying to shield them from the worst of the industry. When Aspen's second book tanked, Nicolette told her to shake it off and move forward. But this was her third book, and her last chance to gain a new contract. Nicolette was definitely concerned.

Aspen cleared her throat. Humiliation wriggled inside her, but she couldn't lie. Not to Nicolette. "There was a huge crowd."

"Wonderful."

"Fans were excited. Happy to meet me. The bookstore staff said they'd never seen such enthusiasm or a long line on a Sunday afternoon."

"Fantastic."

"I sold one book."

"Fuck."

Aspen twisted the opal ring around her index finger to calm her nerves. "But a ton of people said they'd buy it later. They just weren't prepared to do it today."

A snort came over the line. "How many did the store have you sign?"

She twisted the ring faster. "Ten, maybe?"

"Rotten bastards. They promised fifty in the emails with the publisher."

She thought of the piles being sent back and fought nausea. Her publisher would freak. A soft warning had already been issued about Target limiting buy-in because the last one didn't sell, and if they couldn't get the indie bookstores on board, they were done. The first few weeks of release were supposed to be the gold mine. After a month, the title was considered backlist, and she'd never be able to regain traction.

"What about the book clubs? Did *Cosmo* pick it up?"

"Nope, they went with a Reese pick."

"Okay, but I still have that radio spot, and sales spiked pretty high with that DJ."

"They canceled. Pushed you out for Rob Thomas, who has a new song out. They said book spots aren't doing well anymore, so they're limiting them."

Dammit. She loved Rob Thomas, and now she resented him. Would she ever be able to enjoy his music again?

Why was this so hard? Weren't writers supposed to create, take naps, and fight with their muse? Why was she burned-out, stressed-out, and heartsick? Why was social media a cauldron of hell, and how on earth could she go viral to help her sales?

The silence that hummed over the line was a precursor. Nicolette cleared her throat and began speaking calmly like she was trying to tame a wild horse. "Darling, we have a problem. Sales aren't picking up, and we're done with the book tour. I spoke with Bella. We need to get her a proposal with three chapters to approach a new contract. But there's a certain…element she wants from you."

"More sex?"

"No. More emotion. Specifically, angst. It sells best, and *Fifty Ways to Leave Your Lover* was brimming with that type of drama. To be frank, your past two books were good. Well written. Solid. But they lacked the intense, raw emotion of the first book. That's what connects readers, darling. You know that. If you can wrangle that type of writing into your next proposal and truly wow them, they'll consider pubbing another book."

Chills skated down her spine. "And if not?"

"Well, they'll pass. We can pitch to some other places, but with your last book numbers, we have a challenge. Many won't want to take a chance, and if so, the pay would be lower than you're used to."

"I see. So, even though I'm a Goodreads Choice Award winner, a number-one pick on Amazon, a #1 *New York Times* bestseller, and broke records for the Book of the Month Club in sales, I'm now officially washed up."

"You're not washed up! You're in a bit of a funk. You need a good pivot, darling. I think the past four years have been a whirlwind. You went from a year of touring to writing two more books back-to-back. You're in burnout. Maybe you need to take some time and figure out how to get back to the magic that was *Fifty Ways.* A change of scenery may do wonders. Inspire you. Give us something different but familiar."

Aspen wanted to bang her head against the steering wheel and weep. She despised book-talk language. Everyone wanted a fresh hook. A twist on an old type. Something different but familiar. What were they talking about? Did they even know?

Nicolette continued. "The good news is *Fifty Ways to Leave Your Lover* is still selling well, and Hulu reached out. I'll bring you in on the conversation as soon as I nail down some specifics. Isn't that exciting? It can lead to a whole new surge for the book."

"Yep, that's great. Listen, I'd better get going. Can we talk later?"

"Absolutely. It will all be fine, darling. Keep your chin up and think about what I said. Get inspired!"

Her agent clicked off.

Aspen stared at the phone for a while, then glumly dropped it back into her purse. She drove home, parked her car in the garage, and walked inside.

After the book went viral, she'd replaced her cramped, one-bedroom studio with a renovated townhouse in the West Village. With gorgeous windows, hardwood flooring, and open, airy space, she was always grateful each time she walked through the door.

Grateful she no longer had to scrimp and save to pay her bills and eat pasta most nights.

Grateful her book had been plucked from the slush pile to make her a household name.

Grateful she had her health, sanity, creativity, and her sister.

But today, it was hard living in pure gratitude. Because the truth not only hurt. It seared and burned and plundered her heart and soul.

She had written one great book, and the world was done with her. No matter how hard she studied craft, read, and worked long hours to compose the best story she could, her fans couldn't resonate with her new stuff.

She knew why. It was her deepest, darkest secret. One she hadn't told even her agent.

Aspen had only been able to write her breakout book because it was entirely autobiographical.

Nibbling on her bottom lip, she dropped her coat and bag onto the supple cream-leather couch and made her way into the kitchen. The wraparound white marble counters, high red stools, and red appliances added the perfect pop of color. Her bare feet padded over the ebony plank floors. With mechanical motions, she brewed herself a cappuccino, added cinnamon, and sat in her favorite red plush chair facing the window.

She sipped the hot brew and pondered her dilemma.

Readers only cared about her first book because it had burst from her essence, caused by her broken heart. The character Josh was based on Ryan. Ryan, the great love of her life. Ryan, her college English professor, who taught her poetry, living with passion, and diving into her heart when she dared to try and create. Ryan, who asked her to marry him on bended knee in the snow, in front of a horse and carriage, in the middle of Central Park.

Ryan, who left her at the altar to run off to California with her supposed friend and fellow classmate.

Ryan, who inspired *Fifty Ways to Leave Your Lover* and made her famous.

Yet he'd ended up stealing something more precious than her heart.

He'd taken her creativity.

Aspen groaned and squeezed her eyes shut at the thought. The book had literally dripped grief, rage, and passion from its pages. Many critics tried to rip apart the craft, calling her prose wordy and shallow, citing her inept abilities to mimic Nicholas Sparks, but none of it mattered. The masses kept buying it, pushing it into multiple print runs and inspiring endless knockoffs and licenses, from games to art to talks with Hulu.

No one knew she'd written that book in a drafty room late into the night, working mornings and weekends around her full-time job as an office manager at a local college. No one knew the words poured from her like a demon releasing its rage, spinning her story into an epic revenge tale where she thrived and blossomed under the challenge.

There was nothing to make up because it was real. Her last two books had been spurred from her imagination. She'd thought the books were better written, with full character arcs and exotic settings readers would flock to. Her publisher had seemed to love the second. The third gave them some hesitation, but she'd worked hard on edits and felt it was a book to be proud of.

She'd been wrong. The stories sucked. They were intelligent but flat. Everything seemed to work on the surface, but readers couldn't be fooled.

She hadn't identified with any of the characters like she had with her first book. No raw passion bled into her prose.

She was a fraud, and everyone knew it.

The house was silent. No pets, no lovers, no clutter. Somehow, she'd managed to slowly cultivate an emotionless life. She worked on her book, made appearances, saw a few friends, and Zoomed with her sister. The few dates she'd been on had been uninspiring and not worth it. No wonder her writing had flattened like a bottle of soda left open.

She had nothing to write about anymore.

Aspen finished her coffee and washed her cup, then looked around her perfect house, with her perfect existence, far away from the brokenhearted, broke girl she was four years ago.

And she cried.

Chapter Two

"I'm coming for a visit."

Her sister squealed. Aspen hoped it was delight because she'd run out of ideas, and getting out of town was the only thing left to try. "How long?"

"The summer. I'm going through some…stuff. I need a place to think."

Sierra was three years older, divorced, bossy, and fabulous. She'd followed her husband to North Carolina, where he shocked her by falling in love with his boss.

Her sister had handled the whole thing with her usual class, quickly divorcing him, heading back to school to kick-start her career, and sending him and his new husband Christmas cards each year. She worked at a local retail store and got fired for trying to tell the owner how to run it successfully. When the store closed, Sierra took out a loan, bought it herself, and now ran a thriving clothing boutique. She was a true badass and owned a legendary shoe collection that reminded Aspen of the character from Jennifer Weiner's book, *In Her Shoes.*

Except Aspen was a size ten and couldn't fit into her sister's clothes or shoes. Not that she'd ever try. When she was ten years old, Sierra had beaten Aspen up for stealing her new jean jacket. Aspen had lied to her parents about getting jumped on the playground, suffered through a meeting with the principal where she lied to protect her sister, and gained Sierra's respect forever.

Hey, blood was blood.

"I'm so happy. I desperately need some company. When will you be here?"

"Two days. I'm packing now."

"Is it man or book trouble?"

"Book."

"Good. We can solve that easier. I'll have the wine open. Text me with updates."

Sierra clicked off. Aspen smiled. Her sister was direct and despised small talk. Maybe it was being around demanding customers who made a big deal out of a mismarked price or threw a fit when their size didn't fit, which made Sierra avoid any encounters that wasted her time outside of work.

After a sleepless night, Aspen decided to take her agent's advice and leave town. There was nothing she hated more than a self-pity party, and after yesterday, she was done. She needed to figure out a plan to make sure her next book hit all the marks. It had to be fresh, new, and burn with emotion. It had to *dazzle.*

But first, she needed to refill the well and let herself people watch. Hear new stories, see new things. She was positive North Carolina would help. Plus, she missed Sierra. It had been a few months since they'd managed to squeeze in a visit.

Leaving New York in the dust felt damn good.

About thirteen hours later, Aspen pulled onto the single-lane road always stuffed with summer traffic. Passing through the charming town of Duck, she stared greedily at Duck Donuts—her favorite place on Earth—but kept her focus on the goal. There'd be plenty of time for eating, cocktails, and shopping. She and Sierra excelled at those things.

The traffic eventually disappeared, and the roads opened through to Corolla. The small town was less crowded than some of the other hot spots on the Outer Banks, a bit less touristy except for the jewel in the crown for tourism.

The wild horses.

She finally pulled up to the house, sighing with relief. Stretching and groaning, she got out and looked up at the beach house that sang of everything the island was about. Sun, sand, and surf. Relaxation and carefree fun. The salty air teased her nostrils, and her skin prickled in the heat. Already, her body sighed with anticipation.

The two-story, lemon-yellow home boasted a wraparound porch, lush landscaping, and white shutters. The roof sloped at an angle, and a tiny deck popped out from the primary bedroom. A hammock was strung between two weeping willow trees.

Aspen walked up the stairs, knocked on the screen door in warning, and let herself in. "I'm here!" she yelled, taking a quick sip from her water bottle. She was severely dehydrated, not allowing herself to drink anything to cut down on stops.

Her sister popped out of the kitchen with a big grin. "The bitch is back," she teased, giving Aspen a quick, warm hug. "Dayum, someone needs a shower."

Aspen stuck out her tongue. "I need a bathroom and a drink."

"Go, you know where it is. I'll get the sweet tea."

She bolted for the bathroom, decorated in a coastal theme of sand and blue colors, seashell towels, and a beach-scented candle. For her sister's no-nonsense personality, she enjoyed fashion and home décor, taking pride in all her spaces to make them feel authentic yet beautiful. Aspen had hired a decorator and called it a day. As for fashion? She loved it, but her daily clothes consisted of sweats, T-shirts, and bare feet. Other than signing tours, she rarely left her haven.

When Aspen left the restroom, Sierra was perched on a kitchen chair, swinging her sandal-clad foot. She pushed a pink glass across the table, and Aspen drank greedily. The cool, sweet liquid coated her dry throat, and she groaned with pleasure. "I missed your tea."

"You can make it at home."

"I don't cook."

Sierra grunted. "It's a drink. There's no cooking."

"Says you. How are things?"

Her sister shrugged. Aspen studied her older sibling. No one ever guessed they were related, completely different in both looks and lifestyle. Sierra loved the beach for vacation and the vibe of small towns. Aspen craved concrete under her feet and the rushed chaos of everything New York had to offer. Her sister's appearance favored their mother, with pin-straight, caramel-colored hair, hazel eyes, and curves that made men drool. Aspen got all their father's Italian genes. Her dark hair was wild and curly as if it lived in a separate state, her olive skin tanned easily, and her eyes were mud-brown. She'd also gotten the height in the family, and her legs reminded her of a coltish racehorse not fully bloomed into a thoroughbred. Basically, Aspen had always been a klutz rather than graceful. Her body was almost boyish, and when she was young, she used to drool over her sister's clothes, praying she'd wake up in the morning with breasts.

Yeah, that never happened.

The worst, though? She'd gotten her father's nose—a little too big for her face—which she hated, but she was too afraid to go under the knife for a nose job. At least her brows were nice. Full and curved and looked like they were microbladed. Who would've thought eyebrows would become such a hot new trend? She got more compliments on her brows than anything else—which was a bit sad—but Aspen was realistic. She wasn't ugly, just not drop-dead gorgeous like the heroines she wrote about in her books. But she'd made peace with her face and body over the years and didn't dwell on what she didn't have. Just used what she did to her advantage.

"Everything's good," her sister said. "I'm just in a rut."

Aspen propped her elbows on the table. "How so?"

"I miss being with someone. I'm almost thirty. I eventually want kids." She rolled her eyes. "I've tried, but there's no one new to date."

"Makes sense. You've gone through the pool of eligible men here. How about tourists?"

Sierra shook her head. "God, no. This is my home, and I don't want a long-distance relationship. Or a weekly affair. I've done those."

"You can always come back to the city with me. Plenty of men to choose from."

"No, thanks. I'm a country mouse, remember?"

"As a city mouse, I don't get it. Other than summer, there's nothing to do here."

Sierra wrinkled the cute, pert nose Aspen was jealous of. "Yet you plan to shack up with me for two months, looking for inspiration."

"That's different. I need to write a new book, but it has to be different. More like the first one."

"You can never duplicate a first-time success. The public won't let you."

Aspen glared. "They will if I do it right. I just need to shake things up, and that's where you come in. Starting tomorrow night. I want to go out to the most social club you have. Check out the town and the vibe this summer."

Sierra let out a long sigh. "In Corolla? Honestly, if you want action, you should've stayed in the city."

"I need different." She didn't say out loud what she knew. She needed something to pique her emotional state. Or some*one.* Anything to rev up her hormones or throw her into drama. A feeling she could translate onto the pages of a new book to thrill and excite the reader. She didn't want to tell Sierra that her career was at stake.

Especially since she had no idea what would propel her into bestselling territory. This stupid career made no sense. She was a better writer now, yet she couldn't wow her readers like that damn first book. Why were they so stubborn? Why did they always want basically the same thing, yet the publishers pushed her to write fresh and new?

Trying to make sense of it all made her head hurt.

Her sister studied her with a familiar laser gaze that told Aspen she was about to be analyzed. Even though they were only three years apart, Sierra had tried to assume a maternal role after they lost their parents. But Aspen refused to allow her sister the extra responsibility, pushing back on her advice to prove Aspen could run her whole life. They'd had some epic fights in the past, but as they grew older, Sierra eased off except for the occasional heart-to-heart. Guess this would be one of them.

"I'm worried about you. You're completely isolated in the city, alone with your imaginary characters. And even though I'm thrilled you came to visit; the only reason is to write another book. Are you ever going to take a break?"

Aspen smothered a deep sigh and tried to be patient. "I love my work. If I was the CEO of a billion-dollar company, would you question me the same?"

"Yes."

She grinned. "I guess you would. Though I bet you work just as much."

The slight glare told Aspen she was right. "It's different. I'm surrounded by the community here. I'm not locked up in my house for weeks without seeing anyone. Your deepest relationships are with your Uber Eats drivers."

"And look, we're still happily together."

Her sister shook her head with obvious frustration. "I'm worried you're hiding from life. I'm worried you were so heartbroken because of Ryan, you don't want to risk another relationship. I'm worried no one's looking out for you, and I'm too far away to help."

"That's a lot of worries."

"Aspen. I'm serious."

"Okay, I get it." She reached over to pat Sierra's arm. "I'm okay. I swear. I love my life and my writing, and I rarely think about Ryan anymore. But you are right about one thing. I need to get out and have some adventures. Particularly with an interesting man who can light up my summer. And to do that...I need you to go out with me."

Sierra rolled her eyes, making even that gesture look classic and Grace-Kelly elegant. "Fine. We'll go clubbing and look for hot men like we did in our early twenties."

Aspen lifted her hand in enthusiasm. Sierra half-slapped her hand back grudgingly.

"Almost left me hanging, sis. I'm gonna unpack and take a nap." She flashed a grin and headed to the car. She had a good feeling about the next few weeks and how they'd shake out. She would find her muse, enthrall her agent, and get back on the must-read list with her readers.

She just knew it.

"This is our big night out?" Aspen hissed, wriggling in the wooden chair for a better position. "Beer and nachos?"

Sierra regarded her with a haughty gaze. "You can have wine and potato chips."

Aspen glared with frustration. The Beer Garden had a great outside vibe, but it wasn't exactly the crowd she was looking to mingle with. Hidden from the main road and tucked in a backyard, the bar and tables were spread out on a patch of green lawn. Everything was done in faded driftwood. Groups of people clustered about, waiting for tables to open. The heat pushed into her lungs and sweat prickled her skin. She'd never craved air-conditioning as much as she did now.

"It's really hot," she said, pulling at her cute, white lace top that had looked fresh and clean an hour ago. Her denim shorts were damp and clung to her ass in not a great way. She thought to wear her hair down to look sexy and inviting, but the curls had expanded to mega lengths, creating an Aqua Net eighties vibe. "Stop laughing at my hair. Why didn't you tell me we'd be outside and in Hadestown? Plus, you haven't introduced me to one person yet. How am I supposed to have new experiences when I'm not meeting anyone?"

Sierra didn't seem to care about her complaints. "You said you wanted a lively place with music. This place is packed with people I don't know. Locals like to stick to less touristy places during the summer, like the simple bars with good food. And I'm not laughing at your hair. I'm more concerned it's a deadly weapon."

"Very funny. When does the music start?"

"Ten. I'm usually in bed. Did you know you can grab half-priced drinks at five?"

Aspen snorted and sipped her beer. "No wonder you're not meeting new men! It's only nine. Come on, we need to push some boundaries. Grab us another round and let's mingle." She held out a twenty-dollar bill and pushed it into her sister's hand.

Sierra blinked. "You're not done with *that* drink."

"I want to be ready. Do they have an inside to this place?" She slapped at a mosquito. "I'm not really an outdoorsy person."

"Yeah. I know." Sierra shook her head but grabbed the bill and headed to the bar. Aspen took her time studying the crowd and surveying possibilities. Shadows darkened the area with the dying sun, but lights were strung around, offering a party atmosphere. The musicians were setting up, and a crowd was already forming. Good. Maybe she'd dance and bump into a sexy guy. A man with broad shoulders that filled a doorway, a jaw to cut glass, and thick, blond hair like Hemsworth. He'd look into her eyes with purpose, shivers would race down her spine, and she'd know he wanted her.

Maybe she'd even have sex.

One could dream.

She turned with a sigh, and her gaze caught on a guy standing by the bar. It was his towering height that first caught her attention—then stayed because of his ridiculous sexiness.

He was huge, easily six-foot-three, with well-developed muscles. But not overbuilt. Big hands were propped on the table, feet braced a few inches apart, looking like he was ready for battle. His dark hair was a bit long, slightly messy, and had some curl. Even from this distance, the strands hinted at a glossy sheen, which made her a little jealous. His features were classic: Roman nose, square jaw, slashed cheekbones, and, dear God, was that a cleft in his chin or her imagination? His brows were full and fierce. He wore ragged jeans and a simple T-shirt that stretched over his broad shoulders. In a crowd of well-dressed, socially animated people, he stuck out immediately, like he didn't give a flying fig what anyone thought.

A petite blonde hung on his arm. Literally. She was pretty much gripping his biceps and staring up at him with such adoration that Aspen winced.

The worst part? The guy didn't seem interested. She appeared to be chattering away, looking desperate for his attention, and he nodded, a slight frown creasing his brow, his focus firmly on the TV mounted behind the bartender.

Talk about cringeworthy.

Sure, he was gorgeous, but no woman should put up with such behavior. Aspen frowned, wanting to walk over and talk some sense into the blonde. If he was ignoring her on a date, it didn't bode well for future ones or a relationship.

Sierra appeared, plunking her drink down. "What are you staring at?"

Aspen jerked her head. "Who. That guy over there. He's a lousy date."

Her sister squinted, then shook her head with a laugh. "Oh, that's just Brick."

She blinked. "Who?"

"Brick. He's a local. Runs a tour place. He's the heartbreaker of Corolla."

"You did not just tell me his name is Brick. From—"

"*Cat on a Hot Tin Roof*. Yep, I'm not kidding."

"God, I love that movie," she murmured, shivering at just the memory of a young Newman and his bad-boy ways. Even if he hadn't been as hot for Elizabeth Taylor as his friend.

Sierra frowned and sucked at her straw with a touch of violence. "Yeah, 'cause Mom set us up for failure. Showing us all those ridiculous classic movies and making us believe men could be like that. I'll never forgive her."

Aspen took in her sister's bitterness with sympathy. Mom had loved movie night, introducing them to the revolving cycle of gorgeous, charming men and the women they fell for in true Hollywood style. Mom was a romantic who'd married Dad three months after they met and never fell out of love. They'd lived an idyllic life until their single-engine hopper plane crashed while headed to an island on vacation. In Aspen's mind, her parents had died the way they'd lived. Together, hopelessly in love, in their own tragic ending that was film-worthy. Devastating but fitting.

Sierra disagreed. She'd called them batshit crazy to take some half-assed plane with a pilot they paid under the table to save a few bucks.

Her sister's divorce had done a number on her, and it was easier to blame Mom. But Aspen had to stand up for her idol. "She loved the fairy tale. Dad was her lobster. Her one and only. She believed we could have that, too."

"Yeah, how's that working out for you?"

Aspen wrinkled her overlarge nose. "Not good, but we still have time to find the dream."

"There's no dream in marriage. Instead of crap like *An Affair to Remember* or *Casablanca*, we should've been shown *Knocked Up*. Those are the types of men out there. All we have waiting for us is porn, lies, and ugliness."

Now, Aspen was getting depressed. Her sister really needed some therapy or a man to give her hope again. Where Aspen had grieved deeply after losing their parents, Sierra had turned to rage and action, throwing herself into the tasks necessary for survival after being orphaned. Thank God they'd both been of legal age and left with enough life insurance for security. But emotionally?

Aspen wondered if either of them would ever get over such a traumatic loss.

"She showed us *The Way We Were*," Aspen pointed out. "That was tragic. No happily ever after. Just broken tears."

"That's what you'd get with Brick. I'd suggest a hard pass."

Her attention got pulled back to the man by the bar. The blonde gave him a pretty pout and pushed her generous breasts into his side. He spared her a glance, nodded again, and lifted his beer in obvious disinterest. "Why? He doesn't look the charming type."

Sierra grinned. "Oh, trust me, he is. The man has a reputation that precedes him. Best to stay away and keep your heart safe."

Aspen regarded her sister in fascination. "Are you messing with me? Because you sound ridiculous."

"Nope, it could be straight from one of your books. Every woman who's gotten involved with him has experienced heartbreak. And I don't mean a bruise or a few tears. I'm talking weeks of sobbing and gaining at least five pounds. The man should come with a warning."

"He sounds horrible," Aspen said, half-thrillingly.

They watched the couple in silence. The blonde was now sipping her wine and gazing at him with a look of helpless grief, as if she realized she wouldn't be able to break through his barrier.

"Do you know he smells like cookies and spice? It's like an aphrodisiac," Sierra said.

"Did you ever try to date him?"

Sierra paused. "Well…"

"You didn't!"

Her sister groaned. "It was winter, and I was lonely. He likes to frequent Sundogs so I saw him there, and we had a drink together. Let's just say he was very upfront about his noninterest."

"Bastard. How could anyone reject you? You're a catch."

Sierra gave her a grateful pat on the shoulder. "Thanks. It was for the best. To be honest, I knew we weren't good for each other. I appreciate him in a physical capacity, but there was no real spark or connection."

"Good. I just don't get it. Sure, he's good-looking, but he's got a dud personality. How can any woman fall for him?"

"Don't know. But I also heard—never mind."

Aspen jabbed her finger in the air. "Oh, hell no. You'd better finish that sentence."

"I heard he's amazing in bed." Sierra lowered her voice. "Like, so good he makes you cry."

Horror washed over her. "From pain or pleasure?"

Her sister shrugged. "Maybe both. Who knows?"

Aspen wondered what it would take to make her cry during sex. Even with Ryan, she'd moaned a lot, but it was more the heart connection than the physical. She was so in love with him, her body followed her emotions. She'd never experienced wild, messy, nasty sex just for the sake of release.

Maybe she was missing out.

Perhaps if she experienced that type of freedom, she'd be able to write a great book.

The thought pinged in her brain as the band began playing to an energized crowd. Finally, Brick took pity on his date and paid the bartender. Aspen respected the blonde's ability to walk since her entire body was plastered to his in what was probably a last-ditch effort to get him to fall in line. He politely clasped her elbow and guided her through the crowd, but Aspen bet there'd be no crying in his bed tonight.

Brick looked like it was the end of the date.

Sierra shook her head. "Poor thing."

"Okay, I didn't come here to get depressed for my hurting sisters. Let's dance."

She grabbed Sierra and pulled her into the mass of moving, sweaty bodies, trying to focus on surrendering to the music. She chatted up some men, but nothing got further than some surface conversation and offers of a drink. By the end of the night, she dragged herself into bed and fell asleep, wondering if she'd ever be able to write an extraordinary book if she couldn't find anything extraordinary to write about.

Chapter Three

Brick Babel needed a miracle.

Too bad he didn't believe in them anymore.

He stared moodily at the empty waiting room and swished the stale coffee around in his mug like fine wine. No one was here on a bright, sunny summer afternoon. Sure, it was Wednesday, but Maleficent's Wild Tours! had been fully booked. Maleficent had given him a triumphant grin as she drove by, pretending to wave but really sticking up her middle finger to him.

Like her namesake, she really did have some witch-like blood. Brick had literally caught her laying some weird twigs tied in a bunch on his doorstep. When he tried to ditch it, the awful scent had drifted up, and he'd smelled like a skunk for a week.

That hadn't helped the bottom line of his business either.

Tamping down a groan, he checked the clock and trudged to the back. He had no signups for the three o'clock afternoon tour, but he still had a Hail Mary for the six. Dumping the mug in the sink, he considered his limited options.

The business was going under.

It was time to get real and begin making a plan. When Grandpa Ziggy willed Brick his beloved tour company in the Outer Banks, Brick had been taken aback. Sure, he remembered the wonderful times he and his mom had while vacationing in Corolla . Remembered riding next to his grandpa in the open-air Jeep, bumping over sand dunes in pursuit of the ghostlike presence of a wild mustang. There was so much about his grandfather that he held dear: the scent of his cherrywood pipe, his gnarled, strong hands when he gripped Brick's shoulders and talked about legacy, family, and preserving the wild. And most of all, the way Brick felt around him. Not only loved but also seen. He'd been able to talk to Grandpa Ziggy about everything without feeling stupid. He'd been Brick's only male mentor and father figure after his dad left them for greener pastures at his birth.

But Brick had not expected to inherit a crumbling, bankrupt tour company in a far-away beach town. He'd had bigger fish to fry and a city to conquer. But then his grandfather died, and the lawyer announced the good news.

Seemed he was the only one left that his grandfather could give it to.

Too bad he also got stuck with the mountain of debt currently killing him. He'd struggled to keep afloat for a year now. Soon, he'd be pushed to declare bankruptcy unless he found a bunch of new tourists, a new vehicle, an additional tour guide, and a few grand to stop the building from crumbling around him.

Brick was screwed.

He'd managed to betray his grandfather's trust. That stung more than being broke and eventually homeless.

You gonna whine like a toddler or fix the problem? You got free will. Are you choosing self-pity or working your ass off to find a way?

Grandpa Ziggy's voice rang in his ears. Usually, it inspired him. But he was all out of piss and vinegar today. He'd been working endless days and nights this past year to create a financially viable business out of nothing.

Maybe I wouldn't want to cry like a baby if you'd done anything decent here to make a profit, he shot back. *You stuck me with the problem and offered no solution.*

The gruff laughter took him by surprise. *Ran out of time. Gonna blame me for that, too?*

Brick turned around to make sure no ghosts were actually responding to his inner thoughts, but other than the creaky pipes and loud chatter from the nearby souvenir shop, he was alone.

Doubt assaulted him. Easy to blame his grandfather, but Brick was the one who hadn't been able to save it. Had he actually imagined the town's residents would surround him with love and support, helping him rebuild Ziggy's Tours just because he'd come for a few sporadic visits during his childhood? Had he believed he was living in one of those Hallmark movies?

He had no history. No trust. And no experience with island tours or wild horses.

And, of course, after Anastasia, his reputation preceded him.

Not in a good way.

He pushed the thought away, refusing to go there. He needed to focus on the future of his grandfather's legacy and find a way to save it. His home was already mortgaged to the hilt, but with his business skills, Brick had been confident he'd secure funding. He composed spreadsheets, financials, and an ambitious marketing plan, each item broken down with cost analysis. He secured contractors for decent prices and figured he'd squeeze out enough collateral to push through.

But the banks hadn't even been polite. It was almost like a hell-to-the-no answer when he tried for business loans. And this past spring, the parking lot had cost him a ton to pave since his only fellow tenant was the beach store, consisting of a young trio who really liked to smoke weed and host parties for their friends amid the T-shirt racks.

The bell rang merrily, and his heart leapt with hope.

Instead, as if his thoughts had conjured him, Marco strode in with his usual laid-back pace and big grin. The young man wore a bright yellow tank with a sea turtle, ragged shorts, and flip-flops. His mustache reminded Brick of a seventies porn flick. Sunglasses hung from a cord around his neck. His brown skin glowed with health, and for one awful, flickering moment, Brick was jealous.

Not of Marco's appearance but the lack of stress or care in the man's expression.

"Hey, man," Marco greeted, sandals flapping against the floor. "How's it going?"

"Good. You?"

"Fantastic. Did you see the crowd that came in this morning? Sold out of my clearance sweatshirts. Did they book any tours?"

"No, they were on their way home, so I missed out."

Marco shook his head, shaggy brown hair slapping against his cheeks. "Sucks. Hey, can I borrow a plunger? Got a flood in the back."

"Sure. Need any help?"

"Nah, I'll call my buddy if I need it snaked. When's your next tour?"

Brick tried not to wince. "Probably six. Was a slow afternoon."

"Sure. If you got time, come on over and hang. Got some extra sandwiches from Del's. Burger and Patsy are there. You can partake of some of our stash if you'd like." Marco winked. "Ziggy used to join us on Wednesdays. Said hump days were made for a reset if you know what I mean."

Holy crap. His grandfather had smoked with this oddball crew?

"Appreciate it, but I've got to catch up on some paperwork."

The lie almost blistered his tongue, but Marco just nodded. "All good, man. Invite is always open."

Brick retrieved the plunger and handed it over. Marco lifted a hand. "Thanks, I'll return it."

"Keep it. I have a spare."

"Awesome, man!"

He sauntered away, swinging the plunger. Brick shook his head. He wondered how Marco managed to make rent or any type of profit, but maybe it was a hidden drug ring. Since weed was pretty much legal, did that even bring in a decent profit anymore? But Marco didn't strike Brick as a dealer. More of an indulger. He said he'd bought in with a few friends two years ago after coming to the Outer Banks on vacation. They'd decided they wanted out of the rat race, pooled their money, and rented the space.

What twenty-two-year-old was tired of the rat race?

Brick had once dreamed of everything Marco ran from. But his life had been one missed opportunity after another until he finally accepted that he wasn't meant for what he'd imagined. Each time he had a chance for something big, life cockblocked him. Better to suck it up and do his best to succeed with the tools he'd been given.

Brick rubbed his head and tried to refocus. He needed to get the six o'clock trip booked and had three hours to do it. He had increased his ad spend to hit the incoming summer crowd and scattered coupons in all the local businesses.

Settling in front of the computer, he brought up Facebook and Instagram, doing a quick post on a special for the sunset tour. At the last minute, he threw in a complimentary champagne toast. The hell with it. He'd go to the liquor store, grab a cheap bottle of Prosecco and some plastic glasses, and do a pretend toast to the sunset.

Hours later, the bottle of sparkling wine and glasses lay unused on the counter.

Brick packed up, flipped the sign to *Closed*, and went out to get drunk.

The next morning, Aspen sat at the makeshift desk she'd created with one of her sister's folding tables. She'd spent the last hour getting her workspace perfect so there were no excuses, even though she knew that when the writing was going well, it could be done successfully in a moving car. But when the writing was going badly, not even a mansion on the beach could inspire.

The bright-yellow tablecloth stitched with colorful butterflies would keep her energy up. She'd picked some fragrant blooms and stuck them in a baby-blue jar on the corner of her desk. The beach chair had been outfitted with a lumbar pillow, and she'd brought her favorite water bottle that said *Art Harder, Motherfucker*—a nice fan piece from Chuck Wendig's merch store. Her laptop was open with her notes for the next book.

If only she could write something.

Huffing out a breath, Aspen tapped her fingers mercilessly against the butterfly surface. While she waited for a big inspiration, she figured she'd play with some brainstorming ideas based on her new location. Her idea was solid: a television/movie star comes to a small beach town to film and falls in love with the grumpy B&B owner. He's a single dad of a two-year-old boy, trying to provide a stable family home for them and make ends meet. The B&B is falling apart and needs renovations, but he can't afford it. Filled with local color—she'd get that from her summer here—they dislike each other at first. The heroine finds him gruff and rude. He finds her a rich and entitled brat. Hello, enemies-to-lovers, grumpy/sunshine, single-dad, and fish-out-of-water tropes.

Something pushes them together—Aspen wasn't sure what yet—and they begin to fall for each other. But the heroine is called back to Hollywood for a huge role, and he has to stay back with his son. They try a long-distance relationship, but things break down between them along the way, and they end it, realizing they're from different worlds. Three years later, her career has exploded, and she's engaged, but she never forgot him.

On her wedding day, the heroine realizes she can't go through with it because she's still in love with the hero. She leaves her fiancé at the altar and takes off to find the B&B owner, risking everything on love. Aspen knew it was a solid story, but it lacked something. Last night, tossing and turning with disappointment, she'd finally gotten her light-bulb moment.

The entire book would go viral because of the ending.

Because the reader would never learn the heroine's choice.

Aspen had a foggy picture of the final scene showing the heroine running out of the church in her wedding dress, taking off in some car—

an Uber? Cab? She'd figure it out later—and heading to the airport. She'd board the plane in her gown, and the next scene would be her walking to the hero's door, ready to confess her love and see if he still cares about her and wants another shot.

The end.

It was diabolical. Brilliant. And risky.

Readers would wonder if the hero took her back or if her risk was for nothing. The specific ending would make her book worthy of a club pick. It would put her back on the map.

All she needed to do now was write it.

Aspen read over the outline again and tightened some ideas. Would Nic love it? Or was it too out there to be categorized as romance or women's fiction? She played with some various hook lines and a kick-ass blurb, trying to ignore her pounding heart. This pitch had to work, or she'd be out of a contract. She'd have nothing new left for her readers. She'd be a washed-up has-been. She'd be known forever and ever as the one-book wonder.

She'd die.

Her finger paused on the *send* button, but then she chickened out and closed the document. It needed more finesse. Maybe she'd write a chapter or two. Her publisher had never asked for an outline or sample chapters before, but given she wasn't selling, she'd be treated like a new writer now. She'd have to sell this on a detailed outline, with actual written pages rather than the one paragraph that used to work before.

Nerves tumbled in her belly. Sweat dampened her skin. She couldn't deal with this right now. Her brain froze at the idea of writing that first page—which had to be perfect. It needed intrigue, emotion, and to set the stage for a chapter that would suck a reader in and keep them flipping pages. It had to be as good as—or better than—*Fifty Ways to Leave Your Lover.*

The more she thought about all she needed to accomplish, the more panicked she became.

Aspen immediately pulled out the unmarked notebook with the bright, purple-paisley cover. Her fingers moved over the page, sketching the familiar figures that helped her relax. The only sound was her breathing and the scratch of the pen. Rough forms emerged before her as if insisting she pay attention to them instead of the book she should be working on.

A grumpy pig wearing glasses and holding pies. A purple bunny with a mischievous, conniving face. A snake with road rage that wore a necktie.

The characters began their usual interplay, and soon, her body relaxed, and a chuckle escaped her lips. The dialogue was sharp and witty, and the banter between them had her shaking her head in amusement. Aspen wasn't sure how much time had passed before she heard her phone ringing. It was as if she emerged from a sharp, colorful, imaginary world back into dull reality.

She glanced at the phone and winced. Guess she didn't have to go to the mountain. The mountain had come to her. Aspen tapped to accept the call.

"Are you somewhere fabulous? Are you creating something fresh and exciting for me to pitch?"

Nicolette's upbeat tone immediately had Aspen's guard up. "I'm at my sister's house. In the Outer Banks."

"Wonderful! The beach is pure inspiration for writers. Any ideas yet?"

Aspen bit her lip, hesitating. "Well, yes. I'm working on a pitch for you now."

"Excellent. When will I have it? I'll read it immediately. Do you have chapters?"

"Not yet. But the concept is solid, and readers will definitely remember it. The ending will sell the book."

A delicate pause. "Endings are crucial but harder to sell. Can you tell me the hook for the beginning *and* the end? Give me a hint."

"Opposites attract. Grumpy single father. Small, quirky beach town. Glamorous Hollywood actress meets hot, struggling farm boy."

A pause. Aspen held her breath. "Can you squeeze in some fake dating and one bed? I know it's not technically a romance, but those situations sell tons on Booktok."

"Um, sure." She'd make it work. Even though she was seriously straddling romance and women's fiction. At this point, if it sold better, she'd do it.

"Yes. To all of it. But you know there's a glut right now. Promise you won't bore me with another beachfront B&B that needs renovation."

Fuck.

She cleared her throat. "No, of course not. I mean, there are no renovations in this. Think quirky town feel interspersed with eccentric secondary characters. I just need to work out some kinks before I send it."

"Then I won't keep you on the phone. Get to it. They want a minimum of three full chapters this time. Write me a bestseller, darling, I know you will."

Her agent clicked off, and Aspen realized that, as much as she loved the woman who'd taken a chance on her, she sometimes really hated her, too. She stared glumly at her notes and hit the delete key. What was she thinking? She knew better than to reach for the same old plot type at this point, but why did it seem that every other author on the planet was doing everything better?

At first, she'd wanted to blame her publisher for the poor book sales of books two and three. Everyone knew traditional marketing wasn't the best—more like throwing spaghetti at the wall and seeing what stuck. But as her team poured endless advertising dollars into social media, a multi-city book tour, a billboard in New York City, radio spots, and even a few talk shows, Aspen realized something even more horrible.

She couldn't blame the flop on anything but her book.

And most everyone knew it. She'd already fielded a bunch of emails from authors who were gleefully checking in after she didn't hit the *New York Times*. A few were genuine and sympathetic, but it was the outliers that made her squirm at night, sleepless. She didn't do happily ever afters, so they couldn't technically be romances. Life was too brutal for her to feel comfortable writing them. But the bulk of her stories hit popular enemies-to-lovers, grumpy/sunshine, and friends-to-lovers tropes. Aspen was also proud of the witty banter between her heroes and heroines. But she didn't really belong in the romance world since her books weren't classified as romance—as they shouldn't be.

If only she could end her book with a happy for now. Maybe then she could cross over. Sometimes, her isolation depressed her. Straddling categories made it harder to lean in like other authors. But right now, nothing mattered except writing a great book, no matter how she got there.

She shook her head hard and refocused. Time to get deep. Forget the B&B idea. What did she want to write? What was she passionate about?

Music. She loved music. Maybe she'd write a love story in Nashville. A singer who exploded to stardom and left the woman he loved behind but returned later because he realized life was nothing without her. Like…*A Star is Born* but with no drugs. Unless she wrote him with a substance use disorder.

But she didn't really like country music.

After a few moments of hard thinking, she decided to peek. One. Little. Peek.

She brought up Amazon on her browser and stared at the home

page. It was better not to look—it was worse than reading reviews on Goodreads, where writers went to die—but she couldn't help herself. She clicked on the Top 100 and began scanning the most iconic two pages of worthy people. By the time she reached the eighties, her heart was beating out of her chest.

Please, please, please…

She got to the end. Her new book wasn't there. It had hit briefly, then dropped like a stone. Trying to be brave, she typed out the title and held her breath.

12605.

Oh, this was bad. Opening a portal to hell, she fell into checking her stats on all the booksellers and felt the doom settle over her. The book was practically extinct, and it was only a month old. She'd even fallen off the Top 100 at Barnes & Noble. All that PR and work, and she hadn't made a blip on the radar.

By the time she was done poking around, her energy was in the toilet. Still, Aspen tried to rally, reminding herself she was only as good as her newest book, and it had to get written. She stared at the blank page and called on her bitchy muse. She put her headphones on and tried to get inspired by music. She drank coffee.

And came up with nothing.

Growling, she got up from her seat and headed out. A walk on the beach would clear her mind.

Aspen grabbed her sun hat, flip-flops, and phone, then made her way down the sand-dusted path to the ocean. The wind was hot, tugging at her hat, and she studied the block of houses lined up with wraparound porches and brightly painted shutters, most of them summer rentals. She smiled at a group of kids returning from the beach, sunburned and fatigued but with that satisfied spark in the eye that said it had been a good day. With every step, her tight muscles loosened, and her frantically working mind eased.

She forgot what it felt like to be out in nature—or even outside. Even though New York was a walking city and offered beautiful parks, she never made use of them. Aspen had fallen into being a happy hermit, with DoorDash her best friend. She spent most summers running from one air-conditioned place to another. She'd been right to come here and give herself a break. Her muse did not do well with too much pressure. She preferred to pop in and out before deciding whether or not to stay. Plus, if she smelled fear, she disappeared into witness protection.

Concrete gave way to a worn boardwalk leading past the dunes.

Climbing up the steep stairs, she reached the top and looked at the view.

The tide was in, so the sand strip was a bit narrow today, but the water churned and spit out decent-sized waves. Children's screams drifted in the air. Colorful blankets, chairs, and umbrellas dotted the shoreline. The smell of salty brine filled her nostrils.

She climbed down, slipping off her sandals and curling her toes in the sand. Took in a deep breath and watched the gulls screech and dive and glide. A toddler screamed and ran from a prying beak trying to steal his sandwich. The sky was pale blue with a few wispy clouds. The ocean seemed to go on forever, stretching to the end of the world, reminding her she was so much smaller than she believed.

Aspen made her way to the water, where the sand was firm and damp. Crabs popped up and scurried for cover. She began walking and let her mind wander, allowing random ideas to play out so she could sift through some good ones for her book.

Unfortunately, her mind kept getting stuck on one topic.

Brick.

She wondered if the blonde had tried to seduce him and if he'd let her. She wondered what made him want to go through women like tissues. Had something happened in his past? Or was he simply a player who liked to take advantage of his good looks? Sometimes, there was no reason for certain behavior, but many women loved to tame a bad boy. Who wouldn't get off on the magical vagina theory? It was a bestselling trope for a reason. Feeling like the woman who finally turned a player into a committed male was a heady thing.

Aspen had experienced that with Ryan. She'd known many students had a crush on him, but Aspen was the one who'd finally caught his eye and kept it. At least, she'd thought. That type of feminine power was like a drug and could easily blind anyone to the truth. God knew that's what'd happened with her.

The fallout was awful, and though she had no desire to repeat the actions that'd brought such devastating heartbreak and betrayal, Aspen held on to one secret.

She missed being in love. She missed the seduction and the closeness. She missed a man's smell and the look in his eyes when he wanted her. It had been too long, and Aspen was beginning to understand that her writing had suffered after cutting herself off from relationships. A writer couldn't bring angst and love to the page when they were living in a safe bubble. If she didn't do something bold to mix things up, she was destined to be a one-hit wonder and never publish again.

A summer affair could fix everything.

The thought skipped like a pebble over water, then lingered. She could ask her sister to help her man hunt for an appropriate candidate. Someone who was available, interested, and attracted her. She needed to rediscover all those giddy, nervous emotions when around a man she wanted.

That's what her stories were truly missing. She was writing about them but in a more cerebral way. She'd lost the talent of creating a connection and belief with her readers, dragging them into the heroine's heart and mind. Writing *Fifty Ways to Leave Your Lover* had been a catharsis; she'd bled on the page. With her second and third books, it had been all craft and careful thought. She'd lost the guts.

Aspen needed to experience a blistering love affair that broke her into pieces.

Then, she'd write another book of the month.

With her focus suddenly clear, she brainstormed ways to make it happen as she walked the beach.

Chapter Four

Aspen sat at the bar, sipping wine with her sister and two girlfriends. The Sunfish Raw Grill was laid back, with a casual bar and vibe that catered to a relaxed crowd. Aspen thought a girls' night would be a perfect opportunity to get the lay of the land, meet some people, and make new acquaintances. She rarely had a chance to hang with her sister's inner crowd. Her visits usually focused on one-on-one time that was always cut short by work or other responsibilities. This time, she could really immerse herself in Sierra's world and hopefully bring new material to the page and her cranky muse.

Brooklyn worked as the general manager at Sierra's store. She was warm and had a bubbly personality that Aspen immediately felt comfortable with. She was married with kids, but her silvery blond hair and big, blue eyes drew looks from all the men in the bar. Aspen loved that she'd married her high school sweetheart and spoke of him in glowing tones. It gave her hope.

Inez was the opposite. She had wicked curves with a booty that made men drool, coal-black hair braided to her waist, sooty, dark eyes, and an edgy manner. With her heavy makeup, tats, and piercings, Aspen had been a bit wary. After a glass of wine and some light chatter, she wanted to be Inez's bestie. The woman had a cutting sense of humor that almost made Aspen spit out her drink, and she was just plain fun.

"I can't believe we finally get to hang out," Brooklyn gushed. "I'm kind of fangirling. I love your books so much."

"Thanks, I really appreciate it."

"I haven't read them," Inez offered. "But I only read horror. No offense."

Aspen grinned. "None taken. I'm a horror fan, too. I mean, hello, Paul Tremblay and Stephen Graham Jones."

"Right? Intellectual yet fresh."

They fell into a dialogue, comparing their favorites until Sierra groaned. "Enough with the books. Can we talk about something worthwhile, please?"

"Like the latest *Bachelor* episode, oh, woke one?" Aspen teased.

Sierra actually blushed. "I only watch it when nothing else is on," she muttered. The girls laughed and called her out on it the way only girlfriends could. Gently. "Fine, I f—ng love it, okay? Along with *Love is Blind* and *Married at First Sight*. Pull my feminist card and call it a day."

"I'll toast to that," Inez declared. They clinked glasses. "So, if you're staying for a while, do we need to hook you up with some hot men?"

"Yes," she said in unison with her sister.

Brooklyn let out a delighted squeal. "I love playing matchmaker! I'll ask Jorell if he has any single guys you can try out. Sierra has been one big disappointment, so I need another crack at it."

Sierra shrugged. "They were super nice, just not my type. Maybe Aspen will have better luck."

"That's because you 're looking for Mr. Perfect, and he doesn't exist," Inez said without sting.

Aspen noted a flare of pain in her sister's eyes and wanted to give her a hug. Sierra had never really gotten over the divorce when she found her dickhead husband cheating on her. Trust was a barrier impossible to cross without making peace with the past. Aspen had mentioned counseling, but Sierra had immediately shut the suggestion down. Another trait Sierra held dear: stubborn pride.

Sierra shrugged again. "If I'm going to take a shot at being vulnerable with someone again, I need to feel some kind of connection. Get it?"

Everyone nodded in agreement. Aspen sighed. "If only people could match on paper and not have to deal with mysterious elements such as chemistry. We'd all be better off."

"Yeah, but we'd be bored. Plus, you wouldn't be able to write your books and be a megastar," Brooklyn pointed out.

"True." She kept her writing doubts to herself. No need to burden the group with her book failures and how desperately she needed success. Aspen sipped her wine and did a quick survey of the crowd. Many were in groups like hers: friends out after work, a few guys hanging in flip-flops and bathing suits, a scattering of couples eating oysters and drinking beers. No one compelled her to approach and strike up a conversation.

Maybe she'd have to be more creative and not focus on restaurant/bar hangouts, but—

Him.

Her gaze snagged on the lone man at the end of the bar. Perched on the stool, he was doctoring up a raw clam with sauce and lemon, attention once again on the television. Denim stretched across his tight ass. Lean biceps shone with a deep tan and flexed as he reached out to grab a napkin, his simple white T-shirt straining to accommodate. Thick waves of hair gleamed blue-black in the dim light, curling around his neck and ears.

"Uh-oh, I know that look," Sierra said with a laugh. "Who'd you find?"

Before Aspen could speak, everyone turned to look at once. Her sister gasped. "No! I told you about him, dammit."

Brooklyn's eyes widened. "Oh, wow. I have to agree with Sierra on this one. Brick is well known around here for his…exploits."

Intrigue dug deeper as Aspen stared at the man. His jawline could cut glass. Even from here, a crackle of sensual energy seemed to emanate from his aura, and her female parts tingled.

Inez gave a low whistle. "You know how to pick them, love. At least, you'll be guaranteed the time of your life. It will just be short." She waggled her brows dramatically. "The relationship, not the sex."

Aspen refocused on the group. "Wait. You know him, too?"

Brooklyn and Inez shared a look, then burst into laughter. "Brick's reputation is legendary. Everyone knows someone he's dated and dumped. And what happened with *her*, of course."

"Who?" Aspen asked.

"Anastasia," Sierra said gravely. "His fiancée."

The women paused as if honoring her name. Aspen leaned in. "Don't stop now. Tell me the whole story."

Brooklyn jumped in. "Brick moved to town after his grandfather passed to run the business. Every female in town was desperate to go out with him, but then Anastasia showed up and began telling everyone they were engaged, but he left New York without her. Just dumped her and said he was moving to OBX to start a new life."

Inez took up the story. "She was heartbroken. Anastasia said she left her job and followed him so they could stay together. But when she arrived, Brick ignored her. Said they were done and refused to see her. It was so hard to watch."

"That's terrible," Aspen said with a gasp.

All three nodded.

Sierra shook her head. "Brick actually started dating other women right in front of her. He tried telling everyone they'd broken up in New York, but no woman chases a man to a different state if they're not together. Anastasia would cry in the bar and beg him to take her back, but he was so cold. Eventually, she left town, and no one heard from her again."

"Why would anyone want to date him after that?"

Inez sighed. "He got even more famous after that. Women chased him constantly, and then the stories began. I had a client in my tattoo shop who wanted Brick's initials within a black rose. Said she needed a daily reminder to never pick men who crush her again."

Aspen stared at them in disbelief. "Okay, I'm all for a good story, but don't you think this is a bit ridiculous? No man holds that kind of power. I mean, yes, he's very hot."

Pity gleamed in her sister's eyes. "You're already tempted, aren't you? You'll be like a lamb in a slaughterhouse."

She shifted in her seat, feeling her ears grow hot. "I'm hardly an inexperienced virgin here. What exactly does he do to these women?"

"He has this magnetic pull. Yes, it's his looks, but also his voice and the way he stares at you like you're the only one who will ever understand him." Brooklyn snapped her fingers. "Oh! Kind of like Christian Grey from *Fifty Shades*."

Aspen leaned forward. "Does he do kink?"

Inez shook her head. "Doesn't need it. I heard his missionary position can give multiple orgasms."

A delicious shudder shook her. "Okay, so he's gorgeous, good in bed, and listens. Anything else?"

"He gets you hooked, then disappears."

Aspen blinked. "Stops calling?"

Sierra jumped in. "Stops calling, texting, all of it. Total ghosting. When the poor things reach out, confused and upset, he gives them *the speech*."

"What's the speech?"

"That he told them upfront he doesn't do love. That he warned them it was temporary and was afraid things were getting too serious. That it's best if he cuts the cord early rather than hurt them deeper down the line."

Aspen sucked in a breath. "That's awful. Almost…diabolical!"

"Told ya," Sierra said. "He gives the speech to everyone before the very first date."

"And what woman can resist the speech?" Inez asked. "It's like a gauntlet being thrown down. Everyone wants to be the one to tame him and make him love them."

Aspen pondered the warnings. "I truly doubt any man can make you love him in that short of a time. It's not possible. It's just lust."

Brooklyn shook her head sadly. "Lust doesn't cause women to get tattoos, move away, or lock themselves in their houses, crying for days on end. Lust stings. He gets them to love him. Anastasia should have been a warning, but it only made him a bigger temptation."

Silence fell over the group and, as one, they all turned to stare at Brick.

As if he sensed the weight of their judgment, his head slowly cranked around and he met their gazes.

Warmth settled low in Aspen's gut as those piercing ocean-blue eyes met hers. Pinned to her seat, unable to move, she stared back with a helpless fascination she didn't even try to hide. After a moment, he inclined his head in a polite greeting, then turned away.

The breath whooshed out of her lungs.

"Yep, she's a goner," Inez declared.

"Is he dating anyone now?" Aspen asked.

"No, he's stayed out of the game for about two months. I think he's sticking to tourists and one-night stands now."

"Maybe he ran out of victims," Aspen suggested.

The girls laughed. "God, no. Someone is always trying, and the gossip makes him even more demand-worthy," Inez said.

Brooklyn smirked. "He's the ultimate bad boy."

"Does he go for a specific type?"

Inez grinned. "Yeah. Female. He's an equal opportunity heart-breaker."

"You don't need that stress in your life," Sierra said urgently. "You had one rocky relationship that almost destroyed you. Don't even look his way, babe. Let it go and focus on your book."

Yes, the book was the most important. The only good thing that'd come out of her heartbreak with Ryan was her bestseller. It had almost been worth the annihilation of her emotions. Too bad she couldn't open that portal again, just enough to write a worthy story, then quickly close it. Wouldn't that be perfect?

Her brain suddenly exploded as the thought caused a trail of mini light-bulb explosions.

What if she could?

Aspen stared at the man across the room. He brought the clamshell to his sensual lips, opened wide, and sucked the meat into his mouth. The muscles in his throat worked as he swallowed, and his tongue licked the leftover moisture from his bottom lip.

This was a man who could force her to feel things she hadn't in years.

This was a man who could shatter, wound, and damage her emotions.

This was a man who could storm into her life and cause complete wreckage.

Dear God, he was perfect.

A slow smile curved her lips.

Brick was the answer to all her problems. She'd get him to date her and break her heart. And then she could finally create the next book of the month.

Aspen hopped off the stool. "I'm going over to say hello," she announced.

Her sister and friends gasped in unison. "What?" Sierra practically shrieked. "We all told you what would happen."

"Exactly."

She headed to the bar.

Chapter Five

"Hi."

The beer was lifted halfway to his mouth. His brow furrowed with a frown, but he didn't greet her back. Just took his time sipping his beer while regarding her with wariness rather than welcome. He placed the glass down. "Hi."

She waited for some dazzling conversation to woo her, but he just swerved his attention back to the television. Maybe she had to do all the wooing since he was such a hot commodity. "I'm Aspen."

He nodded in acknowledgment but didn't respond. The man was even sexier up close. It was like his features had been arranged as a gift to women. Just a hint of stubble framed his full lips. His brows were dark and fierce, blending with the thick strands of hair falling messily over his forehead. Long lashes made his eyes even more intense. God, he even smelled good, like fresh-cut grass and clean cotton sheets from the dryer. Sierra had said he smelled like cookies, but Aspen found this scent much sexier. She had an awful impulse to lean in and sniff to see if it was his clothes or skin but managed to control herself just in time.

Aspen wasn't used to pursuing men, but if this was to work, she'd have to push past her discomfort and commit. "What's your name?"

"Brick."

"From *Cat on a Hot Tin Roof*?"

That got her another look, longer than the first. Was that a touch of boredom? "Yep."

"I think parents should sign a contract before they name their kids." She paused, waiting to see if he seemed interested in her finishing. His brow quirked, so she went on. "It would say once their kid reaches twelve years old, they get to change it without needing parental permission."

A beat passed. Another. "Why twelve?"

"It's old enough to know if the name suits and young enough that they wouldn't have to revise a long paperwork trail. Plus, kids aren't possessions. They should get a say in their name."

"Would you have changed yours?"

"No, I like it. Even though I hate skiing. Would you change yours?"

"No."

She hoped for an explanation, but he seemed done. Pushing his plate away, he reached for his wallet and threw his credit card onto the counter. The bartender scooped it up, shooting her a sympathetic glance. Aspen winced. Ouch. Trying to pick up a hot guy in a bar was hard work. She suddenly sympathized with all the men who'd taken shots and gotten cut down.

"I'm visiting my sister, Sierra, for the summer. Do you live here?"

"Yep."

She swung her high-heeled foot back and forth. He didn't seem very charming so far. Perhaps she'd caught him at a bad time. "That's nice. Maybe you can recommend some places to check out while I'm here. Any must-dos?"

The bartender placed the bill in front of him. Brick took the pen, added a tip, scrawled his name on the bottom, then pocketed his card. "The beach."

He didn't even smile when he said it. This guy was kind of a jerk. Frustration nipped at her. Was she just not his type? It should've been easy if he was a serial dater. Plus, she was a tourist, which fit into his parameters. But he was getting ready to leave, and she was desperate.

Aspen leaned forward with her most enchanting smile. She knew she looked good tonight. Her hair had been ruthlessly tamed by endless products and Sierra's heavy-duty straightening iron. The air-conditioner kept the strands crisp and in place. Her outfit was cute, and her shoes gave her extra height to show off her legs. Her makeup accented her assets and minimized the length of her nose. Even Sierra had said she was a smoke show tonight. Her voice dropped to a throaty invitation. "Maybe you can help me out? I'd love a tour of the area. I mean, when you have some time available."

He stopped and suddenly gave her his full attention. Carved features reflected a hard mask. Full lips pressed together in a straight line. Those baby blues held little emotion.

"Aspen, I hope you have a great summer with your sister. But trust me, I'm the last man you'd want a tour with."

Tipping his head, he strolled past her. She reacted without thought, reaching out to stop him.

The quick motion made her lurch forward. Her heel caught on the metal bar of the stool base, and she tumbled off in slow motion.

Brick threw his arms out to catch her, and she fell against him.

A sizzle of electricity shot through her system, catching her off guard. Aspen jerked back, which made his arms tighten to keep her balanced. A slight gasp fell from her lips at the intense connection of his bare skin brushing hers. Within seconds, her entire body lit up as if recognizing something it desperately needed, and her fingers encircled his sinewy wrist, hanging on for dear life.

Her gaze shot to his. Those eyes narrowed, delving deeper, straight to all the secret parts of her soul.

Lips parted in surprise, body curving softly against his hard muscles, she waited for his mouth to lower to hers in a blistering kiss.

Brick stepped back and removed his hands.

Then walked out of the bar without a backward glance.

WTF?

Wait. Had that encounter just happened, or was she caught in the middle of a book scene and had made the whole thing up?

Her head spun from the rejection. Humiliation skittered through her. She'd so obviously wanted to kiss him—a complete stranger—and he'd coldly dissed her. While her body had exploded like a firework, his had remained unaffected.

The bartender stopped in front of her, her voice dripping with sympathy. "Need a drink?"

"Umm, no thanks." Feeling her face redden, Aspen slowly walked back to her group, who watched with horror and respect. "What'd he say?" Sierra whispered frantically, grabbing her arm as if to reassure herself that Aspen was still in one piece.

She blinked. "He rejected me."

The women all stared. "Tell us every single word," Inez demanded.

Aspen repeated the entire encounter, caught between feminine hurt and fascination at his parting words. It seemed so much more than him not being interested in her or that she wasn't attractive to him. It was almost as if…

Her mind seized on the answer at the same time Sierra practically shrieked out the words.

"He was trying to save you!"

Brooklyn nodded. "She's right. That was an obvious warning. He threw out the lifeboat and practically demanded you grab it. He knows he's a dickhead and doesn't want to hurt you."

Inez jabbed her finger in the air. "Yes, agreed. That was too weird of a sentence. Maybe he finally realizes he's poisonous. Maybe he's getting therapy."

"Or maybe because you're my sister, he knows he'd be watched." Sierra let out a breath. "At least, that's over. Got to give the man some credit for admitting his assholery and trying to protect you. Now, you can get on with your summer and leave Brick behind you."

The women seemed to happily agree, launching into a dissection of his past exploits and what must've brought him to his truth. Aspen heard it all from a distance. Her ears roared, her heart beat fast, and something bigger than disappointment, frustration, or hurt grew to monstrous proportions inside her, demanding to be front stage.

Sheer determination.

He would not safely walk away and try to save her from heartbreak.

Aspen needed it. She needed him to dazzle her, make her fall in love, and then destroy her. She needed every shred of painful emotion so she could translate it to the pages of her new book.

He didn't get to be a martyr. Aspen would do anything required to grab his attention, seduce him, and fall into a blistering affair that would eventually blow up her world.

She had no choice.

And neither did Brick.

Brick let himself into his grandfather's house and heard the eager click of nails on the floor. Locking the door behind him, he turned to greet Dug, who wiggled his fat butt in greeting. Brick smiled, shaking his head at the ugly dog before him. Dug was always thrilled with his company, though Brick was normally grumpy. Grandpa Ziggy had a wicked sense of humor. Besides inheriting a bankrupt business, Brick also got Dug—the dumbest dog he'd ever had the pleasure of meeting.

Brick patted his head, inciting a happy grunt. "I'm going to be mad if you pooped in the kitchen again."

Dug grinned, dripping a generous trickle of saliva. Yeah, he'd done it. No matter how often Brick put him out, the dog didn't seem to realize potty had to be done outdoors. And it wasn't like he'd learn it soon since he was already ten.

"You know what I dreamed of for years?" Brick said to the dog. "A lab. Well trained, intelligent, and energetic. A dog that's a symbol for America. But I got you instead."

Dug's strange, stubby tail wagged.

Brick grinned. Anyone who first looked at Dug wondered if he was crossbred with a rodent. He still wasn't sure what his breed was. Part poodle, part Chihuahua, and part beast, Dug had been found walking the streets, happily trying to introduce himself to any stranger he came across. Ziggy said he wasn't scared, even though he looked like he'd dropped from a horror movie and was a dirty bag of bones. His grandfather had taken him home, given him a bath, fattened him up, and kept him. He loved the Disney movie *Up* and named him after the lovable, not-so-intelligent Dug in the film, yet this one looked nothing like his namesake.

This Dug had poodle-like hair in spotted black and gray, a tiny, stubby tail that moved only an inch or two, and a long, anteater-like snout. His ears stuck straight up from his head, and one flopped to the side. His overbite was shudder-worthy, and his tongue stuck out, doling out trickles of drool. The vet said something had damaged his leg, and it healed wrong, so he walked with a shuffle like a country two-step that just confused onlookers. He was terrible at commands, and even when Brick tried to firmly discipline him, Dug just happily drooled and took his punishment with sheer ignorance.

Brick had given up after a few weeks of trying to smooth out his rough edges. Once, he'd taken the dog to work, but any interested tourists that stopped in quickly left. Maybe it was Dug's deep breathing, which sounded like beastly snorts because of his teeth. But over the months, a bond had developed between them, and he liked that Dug was a link to Grandpa Ziggy. It was nice to be with another soul who'd loved Ziggy. There was no one else left to remember his legacy.

Walking into the run-down, shabby house, Brick clicked on the television for background chatter and let Dug out into the backyard. He grabbed some paper towels and Clorox wipes to clean up the small log left on the floor, then freshened up the water bowl. Settling in for the rest of the evening, Dug pressed tightly to his side, Brick's thoughts shifted to the woman from the bar.

Aspen.

He'd immediately felt the weight of her girlfriends' stares and hoped to shut her down politely and quickly. He was no longer interested in being the subject of female gossip or bets. Constant come-ons by giggly women hoping for a quick roll in the hay so they could run back to their friends with a scorecard left him stone-cold. He'd sensed their shocked whispers while he was finishing his beer and knew the game well. It was his punishment for being locked in a small town after a touch of infamy. Now, he was an expert at turning women down, preferring his own company to the eventual drama of another breakup.

What surprised him was the flicker of regret he felt as he sent her away.

She'd been…interesting. Nothing jumped out at him that made her extraordinary. She was attractive, with pretty, doe-like eyes and shiny, brown hair. Her face was heart-shaped with a pointy chin. Her lips weren't bee-stung, and her lashes weren't extravagant. She didn't have Caribbean-blue eyes or sculpted cheekbones. Her body wasn't full of drop-dead curves, though her figure was trim and her legs long. Separately, Aspen shouldn't have been able to hold his attention for longer than a conversation. She wasn't his usual type—he had a weakness for blondes. But he kept replaying their discussion.

She was witty. Direct. She reflected a no-nonsense manner in her attempt at a pickup, and he admired it. Brick had a feeling she didn't take bullshit nor needed to be treated like blown glass. He'd gotten used to being with women who were too easily hurt, and they'd begun to affect him.

It had been a while since he'd had sex, which was ridiculous since his so-called exploits were still going strong. Apparently, women also lied about getting laid. Instead of being home with Dug on Memorial Day weekend, he'd heard he'd been breaking in Mia Hawthorne, the local vet, then dropping her after forty-eight hours of orgasms.

Good for him.

Brick groaned at the entire situation, settling in to watch the baseball game. Dug's awful snoring competed with the announcer, so he raised the volume and pushed Aspen out of his head.

He probably wouldn't even see her again.

Which was for the best.

Chapter Six

"Hi. Can I get a tour?"

Brick stared at the woman across the desk and blinked. She wore a sunny yellow tank top with polka dots and cuffed denim shorts. Her hair was caught in a high ponytail and swung with sauciness as she cocked her head, regarding him over her tortoiseshell sunglasses.

"You want a tour?" he repeated.

"Yes. To see the wild horses. You have one going at two, right?"

He narrowed his gaze and tried to figure out what her plan was. He didn't know if he was glad to see her again to get her out of his system or concerned about stalker tendencies. Her eyes were wide with innocence, but he'd seen this game before. Many times. He kept his tone patient. "Yes, we do. Unfortunately, there aren't enough people signed up. We need a minimum of five."

Aspen shrugged. The scent of citrus rose to his nostrils, fresh and bright. "That's okay. I'll pay extra."

He clenched his jaw. "You'll pay for five tickets instead of one?" he asked suspiciously.

"Sure. I'm here, and it will be like a private tour."

Exactly what he was afraid of. She'd listened to gossip and wanted a sexy hookup to brag to her friends about. Disgust rose amid a strange yearning to be what she thought he was. He opened his mouth to tell her no, then realized he could use the money.

Badly.

Choking back his reservations, Brick handed her the registration paper. "Please fill out the form and sign at the bottom. That will be two hundred and fifty dollars."

She plucked a pen from the cup and slid her credit card across the counter. He rang her up and gave her the receipt, being careful not to touch her. When he stopped her from falling off the stool at the bar, a strange shock had hit him, making him uneasy. Probably a scientific explanation, but he didn't feel like doing another experiment. All Brick knew was that his body had rippled with arousal, which was completely inconvenient.

"Thanks."

"Grab a bottle of water from the cooler. I'll get the Jeep ready."

He exited the shop, cursing under his breath as he crossed the lot. Fine. She wanted to play this game; he'd play. He'd be polite, informative, and the perfect distant tour guide. By the time they were done, she'd know he wasn't interested in what she wanted to propose.

Besides, he didn't care about the tip. He'd gotten a full booking, which would pay the electric bill.

Last night, he'd stopped for Mexican food and ended up chatting with a bunch of guys on vacay who'd said they wanted to book a tour. He'd given out his cards and reserved the ten o'clock morning slot, ridiculously excited. While waiting outside for his guests, he spotted Maleficent's pink Hummer driving past. She'd beeped and waved merrily while Brick watched the same men he'd booked laughing behind her.

It wasn't the first time she'd played dirty and stolen his customers.

But now, he needed this tour, and if Aspen was going to pay, he'd do it.

Brick took his time checking the supplies on the Jeep and prepping it for the ride. The sun was high in the sky and burned relentlessly. Most people preferred early mornings or sunset, but he couldn't afford to cut out the afternoon shifts, which was great for large groups who liked to combine lunch with an outing for the afternoon.

He grabbed his hat from the driver's seat and went back inside.

"Jeep's ready. Did you use sunscreen?"

"Yeah, thanks for checking." A smile curved her lips. "I've never gotten around to seeing the horses. Have you worked here long?"

He ignored the question. "Follow me."

Brick figured she'd sit behind him amid all the empty rows, but the woman didn't miss a beat as she settled herself in the passenger seat right next to him. He must've given her some type of look because she offered him another dazzling smile. "Since it's a private tour, I can see best up front."

Brick tried not to grind his teeth in irritation. Oh, yeah, she had an agenda. But all he needed to do was focus on the tour and not touch her. Easy enough.

He started the engine and pulled onto the road, making the familiar drive to the dunes. He passed Maleficent in her bright-pink Hummer, packed with tourists, nodding politely at her jaunty wave. Her tour ran at one in the afternoon, so she was on her way back. Brick noticed she stared at Aspen curiously. Probably trying to figure out why the woman had booked a solo tour with the less popular company.

The thought of her puzzlement cheered him up.

Brick fell into his lecture.

"We'll be taking an adventurous trip to the dunes to spot the wild horses. These horses are descendants of Spanish mustangs and have been traced back to the island from the 1500s. They were originally brought over by the Spanish on ships and are now the only remaining kind left in the world. Please note we are not allowed to leave the Jeep. Please do not try to touch any of the horses, yell to get their attention, or engage in any behavior that may scare them. They were here before us and deserve respect. I'll be happy to answer any of your questions as we go through the tour and will be pointing out historical information and fun facts for your enjoyment."

"What if I get excited and clap?"

He blinked. Then caught the amused twitch of her lips. Oh, yeah, she was a smart-ass. "We turn around, and you forfeit the fee for not adhering to the rules."

"Guess I booked the serious tour instead of the fun one."

He refused to allow her to tease him or soften his demeanor. Brick sensed this woman was dangerous, and the faster he got this damn tour over with, the better. "I guess so. Still, no refunds."

He entered the beach and began easing the Jeep over the sand. Then returned to his lecture. "We'll be taking a twenty-five-mile tour on the back roads of the beach and dunes and will see a variety of other animals along the way, such as dolphins, who enjoy playing in the surf beside the tour vehicles. In the grassy dunes, you may spot some white-tailed deer and the occasional fox. Some have been lucky enough to spot a wild boar."

Her doe-brown eyes widened. "I hope I'm not lucky today."

"They would be more afraid of you."

"That's what they said about the giraffes on the zoo safari, but one ended up eating my hair."

He barely caught his laugh at her droll humor but kept his focus. "The herds consist of dominant stallions, mares, and their offspring. Right now, there are only one hundred wild horses left in Corolla. No one is allowed to get within fifty feet of them or feed them since it can be dangerous."

"No apples or carrots?" she asked.

"The horses subsist on a natural diet of sea oats, grass, acorns, and other vegetation. Anything outside of that, like apples or carrots, can cause them painful colic or even death."

She shuddered slightly. "That's awful. I promise you won't have to worry about me. I once tried to feed a horse at a fair and ended up getting half my arm swallowed and chomped on. It was a terrifying experience."

His lips twitched. Was she trying to make him laugh? He glanced over to study her face and caught the mischievous gleam in her eyes. Hell, no. If he gave any indication that he thought she was funny, she'd take it as an invitation. He knew how these stakeouts worked.

"I'm glad that won't be a problem because, once again, we'd turn around, and there would be no refund."

"You're extremely focused on that no-refund policy, huh?"

"I like to be clear and concise on my tours."

"I respect that. No worries, I'm having an absolute blast. Why would I want to break the rules and end this kick-ass tour?"

He hadn't bantered in a while, especially with a side of snark. Brick was actually having a little fun. They drove down the beach as he continued sharing facts about the horses.

"What if one is hurt? Will they allow people to get close to help?" she asked.

He nodded. "Yes, there are employees from the Corolla Wild Horse Fund who work to solely preserve and care for the horses. Guides are also trained to spot issues and can call them in. The horses have become much more domesticated since the explosion of homes in the past years. They're no longer afraid of people like they were in the past."

"Isn't there a limit on sold property where people can build, though? A protection order? Because with more people, there may be more assholes who would ignore the rules and feed them."

He was surprised by her questions, which were both sympathetic and intelligent. "Unfortunately, there's no restriction on property sales. The organization has a land acquisition fund to try to keep as much property around the horses open for conservation purposes. For now, everyone seems to be focused on protecting the mustangs, but with no solid rules in place, there are no guarantees."

Aspen cocked her head and studied him. He felt watched in a completely different way than other women assessed him. Like she was digging under his skin instead of just enjoying his looks. "How long have you been working here?"

"About a year and a half now." Eighteen months and twelve days, to be precise. Grandpa Ziggy's funeral would always be seared into his brain as the turning point of his life.

"And you do this tour almost every day?" she probed. The wind whipped up from the ocean and brought her fresh, lively scent to his nostrils. Orange blossoms. It was like she knew a fresh peeled orange was one of his favorite smells.

"Yep. Except Mondays. Coming up on the right, you'll see a protected section marked for the loggerhead sea turtles. Rescuers camp out to save the baby turtles trying to make it into the ocean. Many don't survive, so the local volunteers and community have strict rules set for protection."

"How beautiful to donate your most precious commodity to helping animals," she murmured.

He asked the question automatically. "What commodity?"

"Time. Don't you agree?"

She turned her head and, somehow, their gazes met and locked. This close, he fell into the sooty depths and had the oddest craving to know everything about this woman. Her secrets, successes, and heartbreaks. He hadn't felt the tug from his gut since…

Anastasia.

Even the memory of his ex's name caused a chill to skate down his spine. He tamped down his emotion and returned his focus to the trail ahead. She didn't ask him again when he refused to answer. He continued speaking, pointing out different parts of the herd and sharing facts as they went deeper into the dunes. Maybe she'd stop asking personal questions if he peppered her with information.

But his respite was short-lived.

"Do you get sick of doing the same tour day in and day out? Don't the horses get boring?"

Surprise cut through him. No one had ever asked him that. Tourists didn't even seem to see the guides as real people—just someone who knew a lot about a subject and could pass on interesting information and entertainment for a few hours. They tipped, then left without a second thought.

Brick was okay with that. He liked the polite distance in the relationship—a simple commodity exchange without emotion. But he'd never really thought of his job as something to like or dislike. He'd stepped into his responsibility because he loved his grandfather and had made a promise. Not because he always wanted to be a tour guide in a small beach town.

Why would Aspen care to ask? Or was it part of her seduction game?

"No."

The Jeep bumped up and down the dunes. He followed the familiar paths, snaking around gorgeous million-dollar beach houses perched on stilts, white-washed colors withstanding the ocean elements, and a common area for the horses to linger. Slowing down, his expert gaze flicked into the hidden spaces.

"Why not?"

He let out an annoyed breath. "I thought you were paying me to show you the horses, not answer personal questions."

"How about the combo special for a bigger tip?"

Brick refused to laugh at her cheeky comment. "I'm not an easy sellout."

"Pity."

His body immediately lit at the husky, feminine drawl. He was used to women being aggressive in the hunt to get him into bed but had constructed a solid wall of distance to protect himself. It was rare that he responded physically to some light flirting or even a bold comment.

Yet some undercurrent in her tone was like a laser slamming into his dick and bringing that part of his anatomy to life. Brick shifted in his seat, cursing under his breath. This was ridiculous. He'd been able to deflect moves from a variety of women—many stunningly beautiful and practiced in getting what they wanted. He could handle Aspen easily.

He decided to answer her question. "Repetition is part of life. We're all gonna get bored. I've learned to pay attention to the surprises."

She cocked her head. Wild curls danced around her shoulders and refused to settle. "Explain."

He yanked the steering wheel left and bumped over the dunes leading into the maze of high-priced mansions, all trying to outdo each other. "It's about focus. If we're looking for something, we usually find it, right?" He pointed out a small brown mustang hiding behind a whitewashed pillar under a garage. The breathless gasp from her lips filled him with satisfaction, but he refused to delve further into why. "This is Duncan's favorite spot in the afternoon. He's a bit of a loner and likes to go off on his own. But every time I see him, he gives me a different reaction. Sometimes, he's a brat and likes to spit like an alpaca. Sometimes, he ignores me or tosses his mane in disgust. I've gotten mooned on a few occasions. And once, he gifted me with an actual smile and made a little girl on the tour giggle. I never know what Duncan's gonna give me each day."

They watched Duncan in silence for a while. He shook his head to clear away some pesky flying bugs, then swiveled his neck around to level a steady gaze at both of them. Brick met those deep, dark-brown eyes that held years of wisdom and mystery. Then was presented with his wide ass and flicking tail as he crapped right in front of them.

Brick sighed. "Well, that wasn't very pleasant."

Her laughter hit him. The sound was bold and unapologetic, almost rough in its purity. He was used to lyrical half laughs, like tinkling bells, light and delicate. He liked how Aspen didn't try to dampen the volume to something tamer. "Guess he doesn't like me," she said.

"It's me, not you."

She shot him an amused look. "Says every man I dated in the past."

Brick wanted to probe but refused. Mucking around with Sierra's little sister would be disastrous, even if he was beginning to enjoy her company. He drove away and pointed out the various homes, filling in some history while expertly finding most of the horses scattered in their favorite hiding places.

Aspen quieted and seemed mostly content to soak in the atmosphere and study the mustangs. As he began to head back, the Jeep climbed to the top of a dune, and he stopped short, staring at the scene before him.

"Look," he whispered, directing her attention to the open beach ahead.

A herd of mustangs pressed tightly together raced down the edge of the surf. Hooves flashing in a blur of speed, bodies moving as one, manes flying in the wind, Brick watched and witnessed the glory of freedom and joy in the wild animals he'd grown to love and ached to protect. The sun hung brightly in the sky, throwing sparks of light off the rolling waves, and he suddenly wanted to reach over and take Aspen's hand to share the moment with her.

Instead, he tightened his fist and enjoyed her reaction. The joyous smile and wonder on her face gave him a bolt of satisfaction. She, too, understood nature had gifted them with a rare sight.

"That was incredible," she whispered. "Do you see that often?"

He shook his head and began the journey back. "No. Only in coffee-table books. Guess this was your lucky day."

Her gaze lasered in on him. "Guess I was with my lucky guide."

He grunted in response. The scent of her caught on the wind and filled his nostrils. Why was he analyzing her laugh and scent like a drunk poet? This was unlike him, and he needed to wrap the tour up quickly and get her the hell out of his Jeep before…

Before he did something he'd regret.

He fell back into tour-guide mode for the rest of the trip until he was back on the roadway. "I like what you said." He shot her a questioning glance. "About repetition and paying attention."

"Good. Add it to the tip."

She grinned. "Thought you weren't a sellout."

He thought of his almost bankrupt tour company and grandfather. The words popped out of his mouth. "Guess we all have our price."

She pursed her lips, a thoughtful expression flickering over her face. "Duly noted."

His brain screamed, "*danger,*" while his body yelled, "*game on.*" It had been too damn long since he'd indulged in any invitation, and Aspen's was a killer. But all roads led to disaster, and he'd been clearly shown that one night of pleasure wasn't worth the price. He'd learned that lesson too well.

He parked the Jeep in its designated spot, ignoring the awful groaning sound from underneath. The mechanic had told him the rotors were grinding, and if he didn't get new brakes, he'd ruin the vehicle—which was starting to need more Band-Aids to keep running. More money to spend and not much left. He was on borrowed time and needed a damn miracle.

Brick pushed the dark thoughts away and faced his paying guest. "This concludes our tour. I hope you enjoyed yourself and visit the Wild Horse Museum to support all the work they do to protect the land and the horses. Would you like a water for the road?"

She gave him a sunny smile as if knowing he was trying to get rid of her. "I'll go in with you. I need to use the restroom."

Brick grunted. He almost told her it was broken—but that would be too rude, even for him. Instead, he trudged inside and pointed to the door. "You may have to jiggle the handle."

"Thanks."

The door closed. He checked his messages and looked outside at the empty parking lot. No one had booked for the sunset tour, but he'd pretend to have another group coming in so he could get rid of her quickly. Aspen threw him off balance, and he couldn't figure out why.

The faster she left, the better.

Aspen stared into the mirror at her reflection. No wonder he seemed hesitant to flirt back. Her hair had exploded around her head in an attempt to fight the humidity, and her makeup had melted off her face. Sweat dampened her tank top so the cloth stuck to her. Not sexy cling like Sierra, where she'd have a man drooling. Nope, this was just wet and nasty enough to have a man not want to touch her. Thank God her sunglasses were oversized to cover half her flushed face.

This was not going the way she'd planned.

Oh, the tour was cool, and they'd actually managed to have a conversation amid his grunts, manly silence, and stick-to-the-script lecture. So far, she couldn't figure out why he attracted so many women. He was hot, but not charming. Even his refusal to speak held aggressive tones of innate grumpiness. Did others find that attractive? Maybe she was the rare female who sought out a man with an easy personality and a sense of humor rather than looks.

But she was positive such rave reviews wouldn't disappoint. Verbal and emotional intelligence was probably overrated.

Aspen worried he hadn't found her worthy of his attention, but she'd caught him staring at her in the way a woman innately recognized. It was all she needed to confirm that he'd be on board with a sexy one-nighter. Or two. She needed enough to get attached and then broken for the whole thing to work, but she didn't have to tell him that.

Unfortunately, Brick was stubborn. She'd need to find a way to get to his house and be invited in, and Aspen had no idea how to manage such a feat. It was nice that he was trying to save her from his deadly sex skills, but she really had no time to waste on these ridiculous meetups. She'd thrown out plenty of open-ended banter, and he refused to play each time.

Fine. She could be stubborn, too.

Aspen did her best to smooth her curls with water, then fished in her bag for a hair clip to put the mess into a bun. She patted herself down with damp paper towels and stood under the weak vents of the air-conditioner until she was finally dry enough to reemerge.

She exited and found him hunched over the desk, seemingly involved with typing busily onto the computer. Irritation skittered across her nerves. Really? He was pretending he was slammed with work when this tour company obviously had zero tourists?

"Thanks again for the tour." She propped her elbows on the desk. "I learned a lot."

"Welcome. Enjoy the rest of your day."

She tried not to wince at his dismissal. "Oh, here's your tip." Aspen laid a twenty down, which forced him to actually look at her. She smiled slowly, like she'd seen Sierra do when she flirted.

A frown creased his brow as he pushed the bill back. "No, thanks. You paid in full, and I'm the owner. Don't need a tip."

How did he become more attractive when he looked annoyed? A wayward strand of hair fell across his eye, and he raked his fingers through the thick mess, making her itch to do it for him. His shoulders bunched beneath the cotton of his T-shirt, broad enough to fill a doorway like a hero in a romance novel. She bet he was a work of art bare chested.

Aspen slid the twenty farther toward him. "You deserve it. Gave me more than I bargained for."

His lips pressed into a thin line. Too bad they looked sulky and kissable. She wondered briefly what he tasted like and hoped she'd find out soon. They needed to get this affair going. She was on a deadline.

"I said, no thank you."

The bill reversed course and, for some reason, it ticked Aspen off. "I insist. You worked hard."

The twenty practically flew off the counter with her shove.

He blinked and treated her to a blistering stare. Unfortunately, his temper only made those baby blues deepen into a Caribbean ocean of temptation. He snapped the money up and slammed it in front of her. "I don't want it. The tour wasn't that good. Now, I have work to do, so can you please take your tip and go?" Her jaw unhinged at his rudeness, and he seemed to realize he wasn't being customer friendly. "Again, thank you for visiting Ziggy's Tours, and have a good day."

She stared back in shock. "You are really bad at this. Do you have anyone coming in for the next tour?"

She noticed a tiny twitch in his right brow. An easy tell for a lie. "Of course. We're fully booked. I'm very busy."

A snort emitted from her throat. Sierra always said, instead of sexy, she sounded like an amused piglet. She leaned in with pure invitation. Hopefully, her shirt gaped enough. She'd deliberately worn a push-up bra for this moment. "Want to grab a drink afterward? I'd love to hear more about the, um, horses."

Seconds ticked by. His jaw clenched, but she noticed his gaze dropping very quickly to her cleavage before skittering back to her face. "No, thank you. The museum will have plenty of books you can purchase, and the proceeds go straight to help fund the organization."

God, this was embarrassing. Dammit, she knew there was some type of spark between them. If she truly felt he wasn't interested, she'd drop the whole plan. But she refused to surrender because he was pretending. "I'm a slow reader. It would be so nice to grab a little more one-on-one information. You're such a great…guide."

One golden brow arched. ""Too bad I'm swamped. They have picture books."

She almost wanted to laugh at his stubbornness and polite insults. If she wasn't desperate, Aspen would've run away crying. "Right. Because of the full tour for six o'clock."

"Yep. Thanks for the invite, though."

She caught the twitch but didn't say anything. He waited her out and crossed his arms in front of his chest. Why didn't he want to go out with her? Was he trying to save her from his big, bad moves in bed, afraid she'd fall in love with him?

God, she hoped she did. That would be epic for the book.

Aspen decided to back off. She needed to be smart about her approach, and if she pushed too hard, he'd label her a stalker and desperate, and that wouldn't help her plan of seduction at all. "Okay, I understand. Thanks again." She pocketed her twenty and headed to the door.

The bell tinkled, and a tall, lanky guy came in carrying a plunger. "Yo, man, I'm returning your plunger. Burger surprised me with a new one!" His shaggy brown hair hit his shoulders, and his mustache was seventies-worthy. The scent of weed floated around him, but he gave her a big smile it was impossible not to return. "Oh, hi. Did you book a tour with Brick? He's the best. No one shows you the horses like he does."

Brick's voice snapped out. "Thanks, Marco, she was just leaving."

Marco's puppy-dog-brown eyes saddened. "You didn't want a tour?"

Aspen laughed. "Just got back from one. It was great."

His face lit. "Awesome! Maybe you can tell all your friends how great it was. Get my man here a bit more business. Ever since his grandpa—Ziggy—died, he's been struggling. Can't seem to fill up his tours."

She practically felt Brick emanating annoyance from across the room.

This was too good of an opportunity to pass up. "Well, good news. Brick said his six o'clock tour is completely full."

"Really? That's the first time in months. That's awesome! Was it that new TikTok I did that helped?"

She pressed her lips together to keep from laughing. Brick's voice grated, rough to her ears. "Yeah, that must be it. Marco, I'm sure you're needed next door. You can keep the plunger if you need a backup."

"Oh, cool, thanks. May be a good idea. You haven't seen what Patsy can do in there after he eats Mexican. Hey, wanna stop in and look at our T-shirts? I can give you a great discount for booking a tour with Brick."

Aspen grinned. "I'd love a T-shirt."

"Hey, Brick, come with us. Wanted to show you these new Boogie Boards that came in and get some advice on what to price them. You think three dollars over what I paid is good?"

"No! For God's sake, you need to do the math, not just stick a price on it that you dream up."

"Riiiight. I forgot." He turned toward her and leaned in. "This guy is a genius when it comes to business. I just can't understand why his is going bankrupt. Tell your friends if they book any tour here, I'll give them a free T-shirt. Sound good?"

A blistered curse was spit from across the room, then came a choking sound. "Do not give away anything free and stop spreading rumors that I'm bankrupt. We're fine. We're thriving."

Oh, this was fun. It seemed Brick's next-door neighbor pressed his buttons, but Aspen thought he was a sweetheart. Marco seemed like a wealth of information, and the more she gathered, the better. "I'd love to see your shop," she said. "And I will definitely spread the word. Anything to help out Ziggy's Tours."

Marco winked at Brick and then took her elbow in a friendly gesture. "Then follow me…"

"Aspen."

"Wicked cool name."

"Thanks."

She strolled out, imagining Brick's furious face, and tried not to laugh.

Chapter Seven

Brick stepped through the door and right into a pool of pee.

"Dug! What the hell? Bad dog!"

Dug bounded around him in sheer delight, his tongue hanging out of his mouth while his body danced in some disjointed attempt to show off. Brick glowered at the animal in frustration. He'd deliberately had the dog walker come in to try to get Dug on a schedule and break the bad habits Grandpa Ziggy had allowed, but nothing worked. Brick could let him out every half hour, and Dug would still happily potty anywhere he felt like, grinning like it was a gift.

"I'm mad at you. I've had a shit day, and you ruined my shoe."

The dog's eyes rolled back, and he began to hump Brick's leg.

"No! Oh, for God's sake, I'm living a nightmare. What did I ever do to deserve this? Who did I piss off in a previous life?"

Dug humped harder.

Shaking the dog off his leg, Brick kicked off his expensive, wrecked sneakers and headed to the kitchen for the cleaning stuff. The satisfaction of paying the electric bill with Aspen's money melted away under her invitation for more. Though she wasn't his usual type, he'd been tempted. But his reputation preceded him, and he knew Aspen was curious. It had nothing to do with him as a man. He'd unwillingly become a legend of heartbreak, where stories were traded in hushed whispers, and females crowded his once-private space in a competition he wanted no part of. Aspen was just the newest one in town. He'd hoped Sierra would have warned her away, but maybe her sister telling her he was dangerous only made him more appealing.

He cleaned up the pee and mulled over the disastrous past hours. Aspen had trotted off with Marco and spent over an hour in the store like she had nothing better to do. Then they'd all returned with Patsy and Burger—where the hell did they get those nicknames?—to ask about the fully booked tour he'd lied about.

She knew it, too. Her dancing brown eyes told him she was reveling in his discomfort, but he refused to concede defeat. He'd pretended to prep the Jeep, refill the cooler with water, and finally managed to get rid of her. Then, he told Marco and the gang that the group had canceled due to a family emergency, locked up, and got the hell out.

Too bad he was still thinking about her. Even though he tried to rush the tour, he'd enjoyed their conversation. It'd left him wanting to ask questions. He wondered what her job was, what had brought her here for the summer, and why she was so damn determined to chase him when she knew about his reputation.

Brick pushed the gnarled thoughts aside and let Dug out even though he'd already done his business. He was just about to tackle dinner when his phone buzzed.

He shook his head and answered. "About time you surfaced," he muttered into the speaker. "Where've you been, man?"

A low laugh rumbled through the phone. "Literally in jail. But I'm sprung, and I need your address."

Brick took a moment to sift through the words. "Are you kidding me?"

"Nope. I'm in town. Be there soon."

He recited his address, and the phone clicked.

Fifteen minutes later, Kane Masterson was at his door. Brick stared at his friend, who'd been MIA for the past year. The man could still turn a woman's head with his russet hair and tall, lean build, though he looked a bit worn around the edges. Fatigue was stamped into the lines of his rugged features. Those shocking green eyes held a touch of bitterness that hadn't been there the last time. But his grin was the same—bold, big, and full of mischief.

"Prison looks good on you."

His friend let out a bark of laughter. "Thanks. I have two bags and a car that almost broke down an hour ago. Can I bunk with you?"

Brick cocked his head, pretending to assess the situation. "You didn't even bring a bundt cake, dude."

Kane sighed. "Still an asshole, huh?"

"Some things never change. Come on in."

Kane trudged past and dropped two battered duffel bags on the floor. He looked around, taking in the house, and scratched his head. "Nice place. Grandpa Ziggy had good taste."

"To you, maybe." Hearing the sounds of a new visitor, Dug madly scratched at the back door, so Brick let him in. "Check out the dog I inherited."

Kane stared at the creature with the same expression most newcomers had when faced with a dog resembling a Frankenstein project. He knelt to pet Dug, who wriggled and was so happy that Brick wouldn't be surprised if he peed again. "What the hell is this thing?" Kane asked.

"Just a dog. Meet Dug."

Kane grinned. "Definitely not a chick magnet. Bet you haven't gotten laid. A woman would run after seeing your buddy here."

Brick laughed. There was something about being around Kane that made everyone happier. He was a smart-ass and trouble, but damn if he didn't bring a spark of life to a room just with his presence. Brick realized how much he'd missed him now that he was back. "Wanna tell me what the hell's been going on with you?"

Kane straightened and considered the question. "Ziggy got any good whiskey, or did you drink it all?"

"His stash is still untouched. I'm saving it for a shit day that nothing can save."

His friend waved his hand in the air. "Then bring it out, man. Because the only way I can tell this story is drunk as a skunk, and it might as well be the good stuff."

Brick grinned. "I missed you."

"Back atcha. Now, let's get smashed."

Aspen stared at the page with her furiously scrawled notes and new working outline for the book. After the tour, she'd realized Brick Babel was the perfect hero for her story. He was like his namesake—hard and cold as a brick that refused to break. When he was talking to her, she'd caught a glimpse of what he could be like if he dropped his guard, like he'd forgotten she was a woman intent on seducing him. Aspen had almost caught her breath at the beauty of his reflective expression: the deep ocean-blue of his eyes and firm jaw as he looked at her, sharing the story of Duncan, the wild horse that had captured his heart.

That was the man she needed. A guy like that could break her open and make her hurt with want. Her body had lit up and exploded to life like a Fourth of July spectacular. She hadn't felt such lust since…

Ryan.

Aspen waited to see if the memory of his name still hurt, but too much time and energy had finally passed. Now, the thought of her first love only inspired a tiny wince. God, she'd been so young. Falling for her professor was such a cliché, but it was the winding, twisted road of emotion he'd led her down that had made *Fifty Ways to Leave Your Lover* such a hit.

Aspen needed to open her heart to Brick to make this new book work. She couldn't play it safe, or the emotion would be flat. She was hopeful all the raw elements were already there for a spectacular affair. If only his personality was a bit better. Because right now, grunts and veiled dislike wouldn't get the job done. She may need to gather more recon on the man for her next approach because she couldn't keep booking tours to force her presence on him.

She was definitely in a pickle.

Her phone flashed, and she picked it up. "Hi, Nicolette. I have a fresh proposal for you. It's a bit unformed, but I think you'll agree it will be perfect once I write it."

The silence on the other end made her stomach clench. "Aspen. I just got off the phone with Bella. I planned on getting ahead of the pitch, shaking her a bit to see if she liked your new idea, but I have bad news."

Her heart pounded in dread. "What?"

"They want you to write the book first before they present an offer."

The breath whooshed out of her lungs. Disappointment crushed her spirit, but the shame was the worst. The feeling of failure. The idea that the world would gleefully shred her and call her a one-hit wonder. "I don't understand. Why now?"

Nic's sigh was dramatic. "Money, of course. Everyone is tightening their belt in New York, and *budget-conscious* is the new *it* word. Bella felt terrible and begged me to tell you she believes in you and will fight to the death. She suggested a sequel again."

Aspen closed her eyes in despair. "I don't want to write a sequel, Nic. I already gave my character a hopeful ending. Trying to extend that story might ruin the first one."

"I know, darling, I know. It's just that readers are so attached, and they want to see what happened to Mallory after she dumped that monster. Think of the global phenomena of *Fifty Shades*—three books, plus Christian's POV. It's a gold mine of opportunity. Bella said if you agree to the sequel, we're okay with a proposal, and you can get started immediately. Seven figures guaranteed, and I know I can sweeten the deal. But if it's something new? You have to write the book."

Aspen let the silence lengthen. She'd been fighting the push to write a sequel for the past few books because she had no desire to return to that part of her life. She wanted to leave that broken, young part of herself behind forever. She was different now. Returning to that world was like stepping back into the past, and Aspen only wanted to focus on her future.

But she knew how the publishing business worked. She knew how badly readers wanted to sink back into their favorite world. She was no George R.R. Martin, who told the world to screw off and that he'd finish *Game of Thrones* when and if he wanted.

The time may have officially expired on her stubbornness.

"What about other publishers?" she questioned. "Can we take a new proposal on the road?"

"Absolutely. We need to give Bella first right of refusal, but we can go wide once she passes. I'm sure others will want it, but I have to warn you, it may not be as good of a deal. They'll want hard numbers, and that may hurt us a bit."

Another stab of pain hit Aspen. Why did she feel like she was failing Nicolette, too, by refusing to write what everyone begged for? Was she being selfish? Could she manage to find a way to write a sequel?

"I need to think about it, Nic," she said.

"Absolutely. Think and call me if you want to brainstorm. Oh! I also got a request from The Island Bookstore for you to do a signing out there. Saturday evening at the Corolla location. Donna ordered a nice supply, and you'd be the only featured author, of course."

She almost groaned. God, she didn't want to do a signing out here and reconnect with her imposter syndrome. But there was no way she would decline an opportunity to sell more books. Especially when she needed another contract. "Sure. Sounds great!"

"Fabulous, darling. I want you to stew on this new idea and text me anything at any time. Whatever you decide, we will make it work. No worries."

"Thanks, Nic."

She hung up the phone and stared at her proposal. All the excitement from her new idea sputtered out and left her empty. Maybe this was it.

Maybe she wouldn't write anything else again. Maybe she'd retire, make readers everywhere wonder where she'd gone, and then open a tiny used bookstore and refuse to sell even a single copy of *Fifty Ways to Leave Your Lover*. She'd take up knitting, get a cat, and only read cozy mysteries.

Right now, that sounded lovely.

Aspen closed the document and shut her laptop. Staring moodily out the window, she automatically picked up her notebook and sketch pad. Her pen began moving, and soon, her favorite characters were on the page and keeping her company. Allowing her muse to play and be free, she created a bakery filled with pies and watched as Piggy—her grumpy sidekick—convinced Purple Bunny to sell the baked goods to get rich and then giggled helplessly as Piggy ate their entire supply that night and tried to pin it on his arch nemesis, Coral Snake.

When she looked back up, over an hour had passed, and she felt calmer. Her fingers lovingly stroked the paper where her secret characters had sprung to life, and then she closed the notebook with regret. If only she could live in the world of *Zany Zoo*. It seemed to be the only time she was truly happy writing lately.

Holding back a sigh, she headed into the kitchen, where her sister was putting the final touches on dinner. Hair tied back, dressed in leggings and an oversized blue sweater with *BEACH GIRL* stitched on the front, Sierra floated around her domain with a relaxed confidence that made Aspen smile.

"What are we having?" she asked, taking a seat at the counter.

Sierra pushed over a cutting board of onions. "Shrimp stir-fry. Cut those."

Aspen pulled a face. "I hate crying."

"It'll be good for you. You need the detox."

Aspen grinned and began chopping. The silence stretched comfortably as they both fell into their roles. A pang of love hit her. She had always been the loner, comfortable with her own company and living amid the imaginary worlds she created. Sierra craved connection—as long as it was on her terms—building a strong foundation of friends and a career around people. But when they were together, it was as if they were two halves of a whole, finally complete. Sierra was one of the best parts of Aspen and knew all her weird habits and how her brain worked.

On cue, her sister came over to collect the onions and threw them into the skillet with a dash of seasoning. "You going to tell me how your stalking went?"

She choked out a laugh and wiped her teary eyes with the back of her hand. "Not so good. He lied about having another tour so he could get rid of me."

"Harsh." The sound of sizzling oil hit her ears, and the heavenly scent of garlic filled her nose. "Would be nice if you finally shared why you're chasing after him. I know it's more than a few orgasms or because you're bored."

Aspen sighed. She'd kept the truth from her sister before, but it only lasted a short time. Eventually, she always toppled. She hated lying anyway; it messed with her calm. "It'll sound far-fetched, but I need you to support me on it. Okay?"

"Okay."

"My career is in the toilet, and I need some romantic drama and heartbreak to write another bestseller."

The wooden spoon dropped to the floor with a clatter. Sierra stared at her with a focused, narrowed gaze. "I'll get the wine. Tell me everything."

She did. She spilled all her awful insecurities and her plan to ignite her muse by using her own heart. Sierra stayed silent as they both quickly drank their first glass of rosé. Finally, dinner was on the table, and Aspen felt lighter after sharing her secrets. "This is really good," she said, forking up a tender shrimp and blistered tomato. "I wish I liked to cook."

"It's good you don't like it 'cause you suck. Remember the time you heated up the French bread pizza the wrong way? The cheese dripped to the bottom, and you set the toaster oven on fire."

Aspen rolled her eyes. "I thought the bread got crispier if it was facing up."

"And that time you tried to make hard-boiled eggs in a frying pan instead of water? The eggs exploded everywhere."

"Okay, can we not go on a Food Network memory trip?"

"Fine. Your problem is trifold. You lost your writing mojo because you don't believe in yourself anymore. Ryan's probably still screwing with your head."

Aspen's jaw dropped. "Wait. What? Ryan is in the past. I proved my point by making a multi-million dollars on my book. He has no power over me."

Her sister's eyes held a flare of sympathy. She refilled both their glasses. "Babe, he spent over a year whispering in your ear that you weren't talented enough to make it. He got deep in your head when you were vulnerable. Add the element that you actually loved the asshole, and you've got some deep insecurities. Your heartbreak didn't make it a great book. Your ability to write with emotional depth did."

She blinked. "That's the nicest thing you've ever said to me. Kind of."

"Second, the publishing business is shit. I mean, the fashion industry sucks, too, but at least it's not my personal product they're saying they hate. I'm lucky enough to sell other designers' stuff. But the bottom line is they want a sequel because they think it will guarantee success. Nothing is wrong with your books or writing, but the market wants what it wants."

"I know," Aspen said glumly, chewing on a crisp sweet pepper. "I'm screwed."

"What if your sequel is the same book you were going to propose?"

She opened her mouth to ask her sister to explain, then shut it. Immediately, her mind fired up with all the possible ways the current story could be dropped into a book. At the end of *Fifty Ways to Leave Your Lover*, the heroine, Mallory, wrote a bestseller and left her past behind in a wave of glory. It was an F-you to her ex-lover and the doubts he'd seeded. It was full of female empowerment and walking into the sunset alone and proud.

But what if that same writer, years later, ventured to a beach town for the summer for some R&R and became enmeshed in another heartbreak?

"I see my work here is done. Your eyes just rolled to the back of your head."

Aspen breathed out in awe and dropped her fork. "Sierra, you're a genius. I'll pick up the sequel years later. Mallory will be struggling with her identity as an author and fall hard for the local guide who ends up breaking her heart again. All I need to do is get Brick to want to have an affair with me so I can write about it."

"This is a really twisted setup, but I actually get where you're going with it."

She took a few sips of wine. "Should I try harder to seduce him?"

"No, he gets that all the time. You need to find a different hook."

They were silent as they thought hard. "Can you give me more background on him? Maybe I can find an angle."

Sierra rotated her glass to swish the pink liquid around. "He's not a talker, so most of what I've heard is gossip from the women he's dumped. But word is out that his grandfather Ziggy's tour company is going bankrupt. Not sure how long he'll be able to keep it afloat. And he's been pretty private these past months. Women have tried, but no one has broken through yet."

"Hmm, Marco also mentioned that the business is going under.

Think he's trying to change and be a better man?"

Sierra rolled her eyes. "Doubt it. I think he'd indulge given the right opportunity. I mean, the man is a sex machine, from what I've heard. Maybe you need to be clear that you're leaving in August to return to New York and rarely come back so he feels safe."

She nodded. "Good idea. Too bad I need to jump through all these hoops to make him interested. Would be easier if I could just pay him."

They both laughed. "Madame Aspen and her hot new client. Yum," her sister quipped.

"Right? That way, I wouldn't have to play games, and we'd both be clear on our goals."

"Money for orgasms?"

"No. Money for a romantic drama that will help me write the most authentic story I can. Get your mind out of the gutter."

Sierra's eyes held a familiar drunken sheen that said she was on her way to tipsy. Aspen wasn't feeling any pain either. Her sister spoke loudly. "Orgasms will be a side benefit, though. Can't fall in love without mind-blowing sex."

"Sure, you can. Haven't you ever seen *Love is Blind*?"

"Of course. But when they have no physical spark, they usually break up."

"Sex won't be off the table, but he needs to be comfortable with it," Aspen said primly.

"You can draw up a contract. How fun!" Sierra poured the rest of the bottle into their glasses. "What clauses can we put in?"

Aspen tapped her lip as she pondered, then realized it felt a bit numb. "He'd need to spend a certain amount of time with me so we'd bond. And he has to be a good listener. It will be hard to fall for him if he's all about himself."

"Definitely. The last few dates I went on were miserable. It was the *him* show. When I told them I owned a clothing shop, they literally said it was cute and loved how passionate I was about my hobby."

Her eyes widened. "Oh, that's bad. What'd you do?"

"Ordered everything expensive on the menu, including champagne, then ditched them when I was done."

Sympathy flickered. They were both having some hard luck out in the dating world. But at least Aspen had her imaginary friends to keep her company. Her sister didn't even own a pet. "That's my girl."

"Back to the contract. What other terms would you implement?"

Aspen scrunched her brow and thought about the possibilities.

"Maybe do something that could bond us. Like skydiving. Something scary pumps up the endorphins, and within a shared experience, the feelings resemble love and lust."

"Brilliant. I read that in an article once."

"I got it from *The Bachelor*. That's why they do those ridiculous stunts like bungee jumping."

"There needs to be kissing. Lots of it."

Her stomach dipped to her toes at the image of Brick's gorgeous, sulky lips. "Definitely. A good make-out session can be just as powerful as sex."

They finished the wine and brainstormed all the potential ways Aspen could fall for Brick. By the time they finished eating and cleaned up, Sierra had a steady hiccup. "I gotta go to bed. We're doing inventory for the fall season, and I have to get up early."

She blew her sister a kiss. "Drink water. You've always been a lightweight."

Sierra stuck out her tongue and sashayed to her room, stumbling slightly toward the end of her elegant exit. Aspen grinned, heading out onto the front porch.

She sat in the rocker and stared into the darkness. The crickets chirped, the fireflies ignited, and the distant sounds of the ocean drifted on the warm breeze. She sank into the familiar comforts of being with her sister in a beach town where everyone knew each other at the local bar. It was a nice change from getting lost in Manhattan or having no one to talk to after hours of writing.

She almost laughed as she replayed their conversation about Brick. If only life could be like a rom-com. The local heartbreaker would immediately fall for her, seeking her out amid all the beautiful women because he saw something no one else did. Her imagination went into overdrive, creating a lush fantasy that included Brick sweeping her off her feet and getting her to fall for him as they spent an idyllic summer together. The tearful goodbye at the end would tear them apart, where he'd insist they could never work permanently, but that he'd never forget her. She'd always be the one who got away. She'd be his greatest regret.

Shivers raced down her spine. Aspen sighed with bliss and gently rocked back and forth. If only…

Suddenly, she jerked up, the idea crystalizing into reality, brimming with endless possibilities.

What if the whole thing could actually work?

What if they could give each other what they needed without game playing and wasting valuable time?

What if a business transaction could really turn into something real? Hell, fiction was based on truth all the time. If they set up certain parameters, it may be possible to create love from nothing but effort and focus. And if it worked, she'd have a bestseller everyone clamored for, and he'd have his grandfather's legacy. It was a win-win.

Aspen slowly smiled in the dark and made her decision.

Chapter Eight

Brick stared at his bank account balance with a sickening, nagging feeling in his gut. He'd been living off credit cards and pulling funds from various sources for a while now, but his time was officially up.

The rent was three months late. His creditors were leaving messages. The Jeep needed maintenance, and his insurance increased again. No matter how he tried to pivot or believe a pot of money would magically present itself, he was out of time.

Ziggy's Tours was going under. And this time, there was nothing he could do to stop it.

A sense of foreboding slumped his shoulders. He'd failed his grandfather. And though he'd been roped into taking over the company, Brick felt as if he'd betrayed his mother and *his* childhood. This had been his safe place—a magical escape where wild horses roamed free and beach time was the only schedule that mattered. He may have wanted to be in the city, but the Outer Banks ran in his blood. The love for simplicity soothed his very soul.

Somehow, over the past year of fighting his destiny, he realized he'd had it all along.

And now, he'd lost it.

He stared morosely at the screen and tried to come to terms with his new reality. All the things he wanted to do to turn Ziggy's Tours into a success revolved around money. The banks had all turned him down. The only thing that could possibly save him was a big influx of cash so he could finally compete with Maleficent and bring his vision to life.

Too bad Kane was just as broke as he was. He knew his friend would've given him the money without hesitation, but Kane's story was even worse, and Brick could only offer him a place to stay while he got back on his feet.

He shook his head at the irony. They'd once been two big, bad bachelors about to rule New York City. Now?

They were two financially ruined, single has-beens.

The bell over the door tinkled, and he looked up. Yeah, his day was taking a crash dive into the ocean, and there was no damn life raft.

Maleficent prowled over like a female panther bent on playing with her food. Her inky black-and-blue hair spilled down to her waist, and she was dressed in a black denim jumper with platform heels. Endless beaded bracelets were stacked on both wrists, glittering with shiny, colored crystals that hurt his vision. Her dark-red lips parted in a sharklike smile. "Brick. Just came over for a friendly check-in. How are things?"

He tamped down a groan and grinned back, trying not to gnash his teeth. "Great. Heard you were expanding to Mondays now. Seven days a week, huh? Going to hire some extra help?"

Her gaze gobbled up the small room, noting the water damage he hadn't fixed from the last storm, the ancient coffeepot he hadn't replaced with a Keurig, and the empty waiting area with chairs that held a light film of dust from lack of use. "No need. I have a feeling we'll need a tour company open daily, and I don't mind the work. How's your new sunset champagne tour doing?"

His jaw hurt from his fake-ass smile. "Great. I'm thinking of adding another one for Thursday nights."

Maleficent looked fake-surprised. "Really? I'm impressed. I haven't seen your Jeep out in a while, so I figured you weren't getting the groups you needed. I used to tell Ziggy you could only go so far on name alone. Eventually, you have to upgrade and update to keep up with the times. But you know how stubborn he was. Glad you don't share his vision."

Oh, yeah, she was definitely playing with him. She'd been a thorn in his side from day one, gleefully tearing the place down day by day after Ziggy passed. Besides poaching his clients, she'd stolen his precious ad space with the local papers. He'd tried reaching out to some big southern influencers, but when the group came by to book, Maleficent had met them on the outskirts of town, and Brick had never heard from them again. When he created interesting videos, she copied them and extended them to full-blown movie trailer ads. Each time he had an idea, she stole it and made it bigger. He simply couldn't keep up without the budget.

"Ziggy's vision for this place will always have my respect. He led the way for you."

She threw her hands up in defense. "Sure, I'd never say anything bad about Zig. But just because he made a career out of touring doesn't mean you need to. Truth to truth? You never seemed like you really fit here, Brick. Small town. Not much going on. Don't you want more for yourself?"

He refused to show weakness or doubts because wasn't that what he'd been thinking since the day he heard the will? "Got everything I could ever want right here," he drawled lazily. "We're both living the dream."

He caught a spark of disappointment in those witchy, dark eyes, making the whole dialogue worth it. "Sure. That's us. Well, I'd better get back. I figured I'd be a good neighbor and check in on you. Let me know if you need anything."

He tipped his head and watched her retreat. But she'd be back. Maleficent sensed blood in the water. He wouldn't be surprised if she bribed the rental agency to send her copies of his bills, so she knew the moment his business went under.

Muttering a curse, he rubbed his eyes and tried to think of a way out.

He couldn't sell the house to save the business—it had been just as important to Ziggy. Maybe he'd ransack the basement for antiques to sell. A fundraiser was too embarrassing. Empty the tiny balance of his 401K and take the tax hit?

Maybe Dug was a rare breed of dog he could sell for profit.

He was making a cup of bad coffee when the bell tinkled again. At that moment, he manifested a giant group piling in for his next tour, but when he turned, Aspen Lourde was framed in the doorway.

"Hi."

His gaze roamed over her bare legs, tiny red shorts, and the T-shirt she'd obviously bought next door under duress. It had a giant surfboard on it that said *Catch the Wave*, and the sleeves were stitched a bit crookedly. Was it weird that a tiny pang of respect hit him that she was nice enough to not only buy but wear Marco's cheap T-shirt? Her out-of-control hair had been ruthlessly pinned into a bun, but curls were poking out in random places already. She was completely average in every way, yet her face had been the last thing he'd seen before he fell asleep last night.

Guard up, he stared at her with suspicion. "Hi."

She shifted her weight and pushed her sunglasses to the top of her head. Big, brown eyes regarded him with a mix of emotions he couldn't decipher. "Can we talk?"

"Sure."

He waited, but she looked around a bit nervously. "Maybe somewhere private?"

A humorless laugh escaped his lips. "This is as private as it comes. I have no bookings for this afternoon and Marco's at lunch, which will be about two hours."

She nodded and began pacing. Curious, he watched her and wondered what her deal was. What did she really want from him? He'd had women stalk him before, but this felt different. He took pity on her as he splashed some coffee into his mug. "Want something to drink while you find your words?"

Irritation must've edged out her discomfort because she cranked her head around to glare. "Are you always this ornery?"

His brow shot up. "Ornery? I've been called a dick and an asshole, but *ornery* is a little harsh, don't you think?"

Frustration hovered around her like a cloud. "You lack important social skills for such a hot commodity in this town. I'm simply wondering if you're hiding a sparkling personality beneath all that grumpiness."

He almost laughed but stopped himself just in time. She didn't need further encouragement but damned if he didn't enjoy her sharp jabs. He must have a bit of sadomasochism in him that he didn't know about. "May I point out you're the one stalking me? If you don't like my company, nothing's stopping you from ignoring me."

She pressed her lips together and fumed. "This is more difficult than I thought it'd be," she muttered. "But I'm out of time, and I think you may be, too."

"Cryptic. Why don't you get right to the point, Aspen? Tell me what you really want."

Her name slid over his tongue like whiskey: smooth, rich, and with a hint of sting. He resisted the urge to say it again. She fidgeted under his stare, and he caught the flush of red on her cheeks, making him more intrigued.

"Fine. I'm here to offer you a deal that will benefit us both."

He cocked his head and waited.

"Can I have some water?"

He grabbed a bottle from the small fridge, opened the cap, and handed it to her. She drank greedily, and he watched her pink lips purse around the nozzle and suck hard. Then, with a satisfied sigh, she licked her lips.

He hardened immediately, imagining that mouth wrapped around other things. Smothering a curse, he ripped his gaze away and turned. His voice came out a bit rough when he finally spoke. "What type of deal are you talking about?"

"I'm willing to give you money to save your business."

Shock vibrated from every cell as her words registered. Brick faced her again, squinting hard. "What did you say?"

"Ziggy's Tours. I know your business is on the brink of failure, and you need funds to reinvigorate it. I can give you the money you need to pay your bills and renovate the place."

Disappointment crashed through him. Dammit, she had a screw loose. No wonder he was attracted to her. "Sure. Thanks for the offer, Aspen, but I'm good."

Her teeth snapped together, and she took a step forward. "You're not listening. I will give you whatever amount you need—and it's not a loan. You get to keep the money. I just need a simple favor in return."

He began to laugh because he'd obviously stepped into an alternate universe, and he wasn't even high. "You're willing to give me a large sum of money—a literal stranger—in exchange for a favor? Excuse me if I'm not jumping up and down at this offer, which makes no sense. What could I possibly have that you'd need?"

This time, the flush overtook her face, and he spotted a gleam of sweat on her brow. "You."

He blinked. Waited for more, but she seemed to be finished explaining. "Me?"

Now beet-red, she threw her head back and faced him in pure challenge. "I will save your business if you have an affair with me."

His gaze swept over her body as he tried to figure out when his brain cells had collapsed. A dozen answers swirled in his mind, but only one question popped out. "You want to pay me for sex?"

She half-closed her eyes and let out a tortured groan. "No! It's not like that, even though it sounds weird. You see, I'm a writer. And I have terrible writer's block. My next book needs to be written quickly and turned over to my editor."

"Sex with me is research?"

"Stop saying the word sex." She paced furiously, energy crackling around her as she grappled with her words. "My first book was a huge hit because I used my personal experiences to write it. I suffered a bad heartbreak, but I poured it into my story, which really touched my readers. I haven't been able to tap into that type of emotion again, and my books are tanking. There's only one way to guarantee I break out of this rut and write a hit again. I need to fall hard for someone and get my heart broken. I think that man might be you."

It took him a bit to process. His first conclusion was the confirmation that Aspen Lourde was not a normal person. Then again, he'd heard writers scored high on schizophrenia tests, so maybe they were created like that. Second, he was slightly irritated that he'd once again been slammed with his reputation for destroying women when it simply wasn't true. And finally, he couldn't seem to stop the word *sex* from repeating in a loop in his caveman's brain that thought it was a great idea. After all, it was a win-win. Pleasure for money. Orgasms for saving his business.

He'd be able to satisfy his curiosity about her and figure out why she fascinated him.

But, of course, he couldn't say yes to this ridiculous arrangement.

Right?

The next question had to be answered. "You pay me, and I break your heart. But what about sex?"

She glared, which made her look a bit adorable. "Why do you have to focus on that one thing after my big speech?"

Brick scratched his head. "It's a big thing."

"Sex isn't required," she said carefully. "I don't want you to feel pressured to go to bed with me because you're getting paid." He took in her obvious embarrassment with a flare of sympathy. He had to give her credit. She was pretty damn brave to approach him with such a bold offer. "Especially if, well, if the attraction isn't there. I'm looking more for an emotional connection. I need to feel like you're interested in me. I want to do things together. Have deep conversations. Create a relationship where I can experience attachment and put it into the story I'm working on. Any type of physical…um…touch will only be um—"

"A bonus?"

Another groan. It looked like her stomach hurt. "Yes."

He went a bit deeper into this fascinating tunnel of possibility. "What about kissing?"

Aspen shook her head in defeat. "Kissing would be good for bonding. If that's okay with you."

"I like kissing. But I'm concerned about some of the other requirements. How do you know you'll be able to fall for me? Won't it feel forced?"

He studied every emotion flickering across her face. Not that he was going to do this. But it was a good idea to delve into every aspect of her offer so he could point out the problems. "I don't think so," she said. "Not if we follow a precise outline to help speed up the intimacy. How do you usually get women to fall so hard for you?"

He jerked back as she hit a sore spot. His reputation was all smoke and mirrors. Most of the dramatic stories revolving around his prowess were fake. In truth, he'd politely turned down many attractive women because he didn't want to see them get hurt. After Anastasia, he'd hooked up with a few locals, but it never went anywhere, and Brick knew he'd just been desperate for something—or someone—to stop the pain. He hadn't realized the gossip about Anastasia had already spread through Corolla and Duck, whispered in hushed horror and sympathy, growing his reputation into something he'd never intended.

Before long, he was approached consistently every time he went to the bar. Women booked tours just to flirt and ask him out. Once, he'd prolonged a date to overnight, and every detail was relayed and chugged through the gossip machines by lunch. His friends were jealous and asked him to share the wealth, but Brick didn't like living with such public scrutiny. If he even had a drink with a woman, it turned into an imaginary sexual encounter, ending with the female residents glaring and the men high-fiving. He'd pretty much stopped dating over the past year. Much easier to just stay home with Dug and focus on salvaging his grandfather's business. Things had finally died down, but his past exploits were vivid enough to keep his reputation alive.

He wasn't about to share that truth with Aspen.

Brick cleared his throat. "Well, I think it's what you said. We spent quality time together, and had chemistry. But it wasn't like we were trying to force anything. It just happened."

She nodded. "You seem to work fast. I heard you don't spend much time with your women before you dump them."

His jaw clenched. "It's usually mutual."

Her gaze poked and tried to shred his layers. He maintained his stone-faced expression. "Not really. I heard you like to break hearts. Get women to fall for you and then cut them loose. Is it true?"

Unease settled in his gut, but he ignored it. If that's what she wanted to believe after hearing the gossip, he wasn't about to defend himself. Brick shrugged. "If that's what everyone says."

Curiosity gleamed in those brown eyes. "Do you know why? Do you get bored being with the same woman? Do you get restless? Or are you scared of falling in love and taking the next step?"

Whoa. No way was he answering those questions like he was on a couch, spilling his innermost demons. "Why do you need to hire someone to have a relationship with you?" he challenged. "I'm sure plenty of other men could give you a good experience to write about."

She winced. "Not really. I spend a lot of time alone while writing. And when I'm out, I have trouble picking up random guys at the bar—I'm not comfortable in that scene. Plus, I'm running out of time. The book needs to be written this summer. You're good with women and have a knack for getting them to fall for you. You're perfect for the job. I won't be around to bother you when it's over, so it will be an easy disconnect. I leave in August."

Brick wondered if she'd put some kind of spell on him because he was beginning to consider the deal. Yes, it was absurd and far-fetched, but it was as if the universe had walked in, handed him a stack of cash, and waited to see if he was stupid enough not to take it.

"Okay, let me quickly summarize here. You want to hire me to date you for the summer while you write your book. In the end, I break it off, you move back to New York, and we never see each other again."

"Pretty much."

"What if you don't fall for me?"

"I have faith that if you give our relationship complete focus, you can do it."

His lips twitched. "And if I don't? Do I have to give back the money?"

She shook her head, her expression serious. "No. But you have to give this an honest try. If we're having a conversation and you're only interested in the baseball game, there's no way I'll like you."

He frowned. "When did I do that?"

"At the Sunfish bar. That poor blonde was desperately hanging all over you, and you didn't give her the time of day. It was painful."

Ah. She was talking about Victoria, the new teller at his bank. She'd been overly flirtatious and much too young for him but managed to discover where he hung out after work and joined him there. He'd figured being rude was the fastest way to discourage her, but Brick hadn't known they had an audience. Victoria had followed him to his car, plastering her body against his until he pleaded a migraine and escaped. Brick didn't relay that information, though. Better to keep Aspen off balance. "She was boring." He regarded her thoughtfully. "Are you boring?"

She practically bristled with outrage. "No. But your looks can only take you so far. I need you to also seduce my mind. Can you do that?"

His pants tightened, and he suddenly wanted to close the distance between them and show her what real seduction could be like. He liked that she found him attractive. A primitive rush of satisfaction shot through him. Brick wondered if she would melt and moan in his arms if he kissed her or dig her nails into his shoulders and bite. Did she purr like a kitten during sex or prefer using her claws?

Both options were tantalizing.

He wrestled his focus back to the conversation. "I can try. Anything else I need to do?"

"I made a list of suggestions to keep us moving toward the goal."

Oh, this was good. She may be a writer, but she was also practical. "You mean ways I can seduce you?" he asked.

A tiny frown creased her brow. "Ways we can become close," she corrected. "A sample of activities to do together. Spending time with shared interests is key."

"Like watching a movie?"

Why was it so much fun to tease her? He watched as she evidently struggled with his answer. "Sure, but I was also thinking about taking a walk on the beach or doing an art class together. Maybe you can take me by the dunes so I can learn more about your work. Quality time. Stuff like that."

That didn't sound so terrible. "What will you tell your sister?"

"She already knows."

His eyes widened. "Wait. She knows about this plan and is okay with it?"

"Yeah, but we're the only three who will know. I think it's best if we keep the terms secret. You can say you found a bank that gave you a loan, and I'll say I took your tour, and we fell for each other immediately."

"You've thought out all the details."

"Pretty much."

"The only question you haven't answered is the one we began with."

She tilted her head. "You mean if you're interested enough to take my offer?"

He crossed his arms in front of his chest and slowly grinned. "No. What about sex?"

Oh. My. God.

She'd totally underestimated him.

Aspen stared at the gorgeous, built male a few feet from her and tried not to drool. He seemed to suck up all the air in the room with his presence, and she was having a hard time making intelligent, reasonable points so he'd accept her offer.

But the word *sex* was really throwing her off.

His white teeth flashed as he grinned, and the soft cotton of his T-shirt stretched tightly across his broad chest. The scent of coffee and cinnamon drifted in the air, along with his unique, spicy scent that seemed to fog her brain. Why was his voice as seductive as his body? All rich and deep, with a lazy drawl that sent shivers sparking along her nerve endings.

He was way out of her league.

Even with Ryan, he'd owned the nerdy intelligence that'd caught her up in his spell, but it had begun with his brain. Besides some banter, she had no idea who Brick was as a man, but his physical presence was a constant reminder that her body was begging him to touch her. His reputation made complete sense to her now. No wonder he could be grumpy or rude, and women didn't care. He was a walking, breathing, talking temptation, fogging any brain with a drop of estrogen.

But would he be able to dig under her skin to elicit genuine emotions? Or would it just be a lustful infatuation that didn't translate to the page of a real love story?

Guess she was willing to find out.

Aspen cleared her throat and tried to appear calm, like they were negotiating a business deal. "I'm not opposed to sex, as long as we're both interested and neither feels pressured."

His eyes practically smoldered with a blue fire that made her breath seize in her lungs. Goodness, he was intense. Underneath that I-don't-care attitude, she suspected he may care about some things a lot.

Like…sex.

Again, his heated gaze raked over her body as if he could see through her clothes and couldn't wait to get started. "Okay, sex is on the table. Public affection okay, or no?"

She frowned. "I don't know. I've never tested that out before."

His brow lifted. "You've never made out or held a guy's hand on a date?"

Unease slithered through her. "No. My last relationship was kind of a secret, and then my other dates were too casual."

Curiosity flickered over his features, but he moved on. "We'll see how it goes. Any fears or triggers I should know about?"

Why was she suddenly thinking of a safe word? And why was that so hot? "I hate sports."

His lip quirked. Her hands curled into fists. The need to touch his mouth and see if his lips were as soft as she imagined was almost painful. "I can work with that." They silently stared at each other, and Aspen realized this was really happening. "I can send you a detailed expense report on what I'll need. It will have to be done fast so I can launch a reopening."

Aspen waved a hand in the air. "It's fine. Just tell me what you need, and I'll pay it."

His gaze narrowed. "Your books do good, huh?"

A smile stole her lips. "I do okay."

"We'll need to structure it as a loan. I don't feel comfortable taking your money without repayment."

"It's not a problem. We can—"

"I'm paying you back, Aspen." His voice got low and growly, and her spit dried up. "Your money will serve as a bank loan and receive interest. I already have renovation, marketing, and vehicle costs in a spreadsheet. I'll make sure the costs are updated since they're last year's prices and get all the paperwork over to you."

Oh, wow. He was much more professional than she'd believed. Respect flared. Most men would take the money and run. He insisted on a loan with interest and real spreadsheets. She nodded. "Okay. If you feel more comfortable that way, I agree."

"Then I guess we have a deal."

Startled, she watched as he held out his hand, and Aspen realized she'd won.

But will your victory be your downfall? that sneaky inner voice whispered. Was it her bitchy muse or wise Mom who wanted to keep her from making a mistake?

She ignored both voices, stepped forward, and grasped his hand.

Butterflies exploded in her belly at the warm, rough hand enclosed within hers. Just like the first time she'd accidentally fallen against him, heat crackled between them like an electrical charge. Their gazes met and locked, and damned if he didn't look a bit surprised, too—unless he was rethinking his agreement but realized it was too late.

Slowly, their hands fell apart, but the spark lingered, making her palm sensitive. Would she implode if he touched her naked skin? Would she whimper and beg like a harlot once he kissed her?

And why, oh why, was she using the word *harlot* in her head? She must have heard it somewhere—it was ridiculously antiquated, and she refused to allow it to emerge in one of her stories. Unless—

"Where did you go?"

She blinked and was brought back to the scene. "Sorry. I fade away sometimes." He cocked his head with concern. "Don't worry, I always come back."

"Inspiration stuff?"

She laughed. "I wish. More like my random, disorganized brain grabbing onto a thought and spiraling. That inspiration thing is overdone to make writers look cool. Most of the time, it's just cranking out words in dirty pajamas and unwashed hair while weeping at the suckiness coming out like vomit."

Oh, my. He looked regretful again. But if he was going to date her, he'd have to get used to it, especially if she was on deadline. "Huh. You hear voices, too?"

"Yep."

"Good to know. I'd better get back to work. I'll get you those expenses in detail. See you tonight."

She blinked in confusion. "Huh?"

He smiled like she was dim-witted. "I need to start on this renovation, and then I'll pick you up for dinner."

Her mind tried to shift to keep up. "We're having dinner?"

He flashed that wicked grin that did very bad things to her erogenous zones. "Oh, yes. Best to begin this relationship ASAP and get to know each other better." His eyes warmed, making her nipples tighten, and her throat close up. "In all ways."

"R-r-right."

"Be there at six."

She must've given another nod and left because Aspen found herself in her car, staring dumbly through the windshield. Guess they were both doing this. She'd have her book, and he'd have his business. Hopefully, they'd be able to connect so she could get to a point where writing about a broken heart scored her the next book of the month. Everything was in place for it to be a success.

Beginning with dinner.

Aspen drove back to her sister's place and wondered what to wear.

Chapter Nine

"We going out?" Kane asked, watching him exit his bedroom. Brick had swapped out his usual T-shirt and jeans for a deep-blue button-down with snug khakis he used for special occasions. He'd abandoned his sneakers for a pair of soft Italian leather shoes he wore with no socks. His aftershave was clean with a hint of sea salt to mimic a beach day. He figured Aspen deserved a nice first impression in public. It would also show the gossipers he cared, which would both fuel and tame the fire. He didn't care about his reputation but he didn't want Aspen to be looked upon as a chaser or hanger-on, even though her sister could probably protect her.

For the deal to work, things needed to even out, and Brick intended to do his part.

"Nope. Got a date. Can you feed Dug and make sure he goes out?"

His friend regarded him with interest. "Can I come with you?"

Brick laughed. "No."

"Ah, it's one of those dates. Shall I remove myself tonight so she doesn't think you need a roommate to make rent?"

"Nope. Not gonna have sex tonight. This is a getting-to-know-you session."

"Fascinating. You said you haven't dated anyone since Anastasia. This woman must be special."

It was hard to keep the truth from his friend, but he wanted to adhere to the rules. The fewer people who knew, the better. "She's a writer, here for the summer. Took one of my tours, and I asked her out."

"I'm glad, man. God knows one of us needs to have a ray of sunshine."

Brick tried not to wince as he said the next words. "Yeah, more good news. One of the very last banks I applied with came through. I got the loan, so I'll be renovating Ziggy's Tours."

"That's great!" Kane beamed, making a flicker of guilt cut through Brick. "I'm happy to help in any way you need. Free labor right here for the free rent."

"You don't owe me shit. You're my friend and would do the same for me."

Gratitude gleamed in Kane's green eyes. "Thanks. But I need the distraction."

Brick nodded in understanding. The story Kane had shared last night had been hard to hear. Once the wealthy business owner of a property investment firm, he was now bankrupt and just released from jail after they dropped the case. He'd trusted the wrong people and got screwed. But Brick knew it wasn't only his wallet that was hurting—it was also his heart. And he'd do anything to help his friend navigate the loss. "Then your ass is mine. I have a crew coming Monday at eight."

Kane grinned while Dug raced over and crashed into his leg. "Ouch. Are you sure his vision is good? He bumps into things a lot."

"Nah, he's just enthusiastic. Vet recently checked him out."

As if the word were a command, Dug began enthusiastically humping Kane's leg. "Great. Don't come home too early. Might as well give Dug some action since I'm not getting any."

Brick spit out a laugh. "Have fun."

He headed out, making the short drive to Sierra's house. The pretty yellow colonial with the wraparound porch was picture-perfect, wedged into a neighborhood of brochure-worthy snapshots as families walked to the nearby beach and kids played basketball in the driveways. Brick took a moment to settle himself before going to the door. It had been a while since he'd tried to make a woman like him. If Aspen had just wanted to have sex, it would be easier. This intimacy thing was too real—she was literally hiring him so she could fall in love. Or come close. That meant he needed to bring his A-game and actually…

Open up.

Because women loved emotion more than anything.

Cursing at his suddenly nervous heartbeat, he blew out a breath and left the car. The moment his shoes hit the front step, the door flew open, and Aspen raced out. "I'm ready," she said in a high voice, glancing back as if chased by a threat.

On cue, Sierra came bounding out, letting the screen door slam behind her. "Brick. I thought we could have a chat before you head out."

Ah, crap.

He remembered her approaching him once and his dismissal. She was a classic beauty, well-liked in town, and owned a local business. Hurting Sierra was not on his bucket list, so he'd rejected her as gently as handling an explosive. Entangling himself would have been his death warrant. Game over. Thanks for playing. Time to move.

Aspen groaned and shot her sister a pissed-off look that Sierra ignored. He forced a polite smile and figured he'd get it over with. They may be seeing each other a lot this summer. "Sure."

"Want some sweet tea?"

"You are not Dad grilling my new date," Aspen hissed. "This is weird."

"No, what's weird is our drunken, joking dialogue that you took seriously. I need to know Brick realizes what he's getting into."

He cleared his throat. "Sweet tea sounds good. Thanks."

He gave Aspen a supportive glance and stepped inside. The space was airy, light, and decorated in a classic beach theme. The scents of peonies and baked goods drifted in the air, immediately relaxing him. This was the home he wished for at Grandpa Ziggy's, Unfortunately, it felt more like a temporary rental than a safe retreat.

Sierra handed him a frosty glass, and he sighed with pleasure as the sweet, cool liquid trickled down his throat. When he paused, he noticed both sisters staring at him with a strange look. "What?"

Sierra sighed. "You should come with a warning label. Dangerous to any persons with estrogen resulting in side effects such as brain fog, butterflies, and a desire to throw yourself off a cliff."

"Sierra!" Aspen yelped. "Oh, my God."

Damned if his cheeks didn't heat at her backhanded compliment on his looks. "Um, thanks?"

"Look, I just want you to know I was joking with Aspen when we came up with this half-assed plan. I had no idea you'd actually agree to do this."

He shrugged. "I need to save my grandfather's business. It was a clear yes for me."

Frustration flickered over her features. "That's what I was afraid of. But I need you to tread carefully. I've seen a ton of broken-up women from your actions, and I don't want Aspen to be the next one."

He blinked. "But that's the job she hired me to do."

Aspen stepped between them. "You need to stop. It will be worth it, and you have to trust me. I'm going into this with my eyes wide open, and your interference will mess it up. Okay?"

Sierra glanced back and forth between them, then finally shook her head. "Not okay. This is a ridiculous plan, and I refuse to politely step aside and watch this disaster unfold."

Now, he noticed Aspen growing hot with anger. The whole awkward conversation reminded him of that time he and Kane experimented with magic mushrooms and thought they'd solved the world's problems regarding plastic. Aspen lowered her voice to a hiss. "Not now. We will discuss this later. I think you're forgetting that I don't need permission to date anyone."

"Around here, you do. I can make things uncomfortable."

Brick winced. Sisters could be vicious and scary. Aspen jabbed a finger in the air. "Don't you dare threaten us. I'm capable of handling my own life."

"Apparently, not."

Brick cleared his throat. "Um—"

Aspen grabbed his hand and dragged him toward the door. "We'll talk tonight when you're more rational. Right now, we're late for dinner."

"You'd better not touch my sister," Sierra threatened. "Or I know where to find you."

Holy shit.

"Thanks for the tea," he managed to say before the door shut behind him. Aspen raced to the car and jumped into the passenger seat in true getaway fashion. He got in and turned toward her. "I guess I flunked the family test."

She chewed worriedly on her lower lip. "I'm so sorry. That was embarrassing. Sierra worries a lot. Just ignore her."

He pressed the button for the ignition and pulled away. "Don't know if I can. Is it wrong to admit she scared me?"

Aspen groaned. "After Mom and Dad died, she tried to step in, so she's bossy. I think she feels guilty that she left me to get married and then all the crap with my ex happened. I promise I'll talk to her later and get her to understand."

He thought about how difficult it must have been for them, losing their parents so young. He had a lot more in common with Aspen than he thought. They'd both been pushed to grow up and make something of themselves faster than most. "Makes sense. Families are complicated." He glanced at her curiously. "I had no idea I was suddenly the big, bad wolf. Did you both really come up with this plan while drinking?"

Aspen winced. "I guess? I remembered it all, but Sierra's always been a lightweight. Where are we going?"

He took her obvious change of subject in stride. "Paper Canoe. Good seafood on the water. Sound good?"

"Sure."

Silence fell between them, but it had a hum of awkwardness. This was new territory, so Brick figured it was probably normal for them to be confused about their role. But he was the one getting paid. He took that shit seriously. It was time to earn his worth.

"You look really pretty." She wore a simple sundress in bright white with little yellow roses. Her hair had been ruthlessly straightened and held a glossy, rich shine as it spilled down her shoulders. Lips painted a rich cocoa brown, her makeup was simple, and her jewelry was understated. The bright scent of floral and citrus danced in the air. She'd made an effort for him, which gave him a pleasant buzz.

She jerked back and then shot him an assessing look. "You don't need to give me compliments as part of the deal."

A half laugh burst from him. "Sorry, I didn't see that in the rules. Are you drawing up a contract that goes over what I can and can't do?"

Her lips pressed together. "No contract. I don't want a paperwork trail. This needs to feel as real as possible."

"You're trusting me enough to keep my side of the bargain, even while you shovel money my way?"

One shoulder lifted in a half shrug. "Yeah."

"Why? What if I was some charlatan who stole your money and didn't try hard with this relationship?" he asked curiously.

"I don't know," she said after a slight pause. "It's a gut thing. You loved your grandfather enough to rebuild the family business. You love the horses. You may suck with women, but you have a sense of honor, so I guess I'm trusting you."

A ripple of satisfaction cut through him, even as he wanted to warn her it was a stupid move. Not many people gave him a chance to prove himself. Aspen had, and it made him feel a bit funny in his gut. He decided to change the subject. "Since there are no stipulations, compliments aren't off the table. I happen to like giving my lovers verbal appreciation."

She shifted in her seat and refused to look at him. "Even if it's a lie?"

"I won't lie, Aspen. I promise. I won't say anything that's not true."

Her head swiveled back around. He felt her heavy gaze on his profile. "What if you need to say it to get me to connect better? In a way, I'm forcing you to lie."

A smile touched his lips. He liked how she thought over things and told him straight out. Aspen didn't seem to do well with game playing, which was funny since she was the one who'd set up the rules for this one. But she didn't give off any vibes of trying to mess with his head. "I'll make you one promise, okay? If I kiss you, it's because I want to. If I put my hands on you, it's because I want to." He swerved into an empty parking space with one quick movement. Then turned toward her so his gaze crashed into hers. The air tightened with tension he was interested in exploring, and suddenly, whether he was getting paid or not, Brick was happy he had time to linger and dive into this strange connection. "And when I say you look pretty, it's because you do."

He smiled, enjoying her surprised reaction and the dilation of her pupils. "We're here. Let's go eat."

This time, he made sure to open her car door and escort her out. He believed in being a gentleman and enjoyed treating his dates with the respect and care they deserved. Usually, he was trying to run off his companions, so it'd been a long time since he'd been able to indulge in some old-fashioned dating protocol. He guided her by the elbow, registering her slight shiver. She was the perfect height for him, even without heels. Brick imagined tucking her into the crook of his shoulder or how their bodies would fit while dancing.

The Paper Canoe was well known for its talented chef, trained staff, and comfortable yet elegant atmosphere. Situated overlooking the water, their table was positioned for a perfect view. Low, romantic music drifted through the speakers. The recited specials were lengthy and varied. He noted that Aspen ordered a lemon drop martini and preferred sparkling water.

She sat back in her chair and gave him a small smile. "Wow. You're trying to impress me."

"It's our first date. First of anything is important."

"Guess so. It's nice, though. Most of my first dates are coffee get-togethers, where we meet in a busy café and see if it's even worth ordering a second cup."

"You live in New York City, though, right? Plenty of opportunities to meet men and date."

She began laughing as if he'd told a great joke. "Trust me, it's brutal out there. A shark fest of happy hours and overcrowded bars or clubs filled with Tinder-seeking hookups. Plus, working from home alone keeps me a bit isolated. I've been known to not change out of my pj's on a good writing week."

The waiter came over, and they ordered fresh oysters and cups of lobster bisque. Aspen went with the grilled mahi mahi, and he settled on the filet mignon. A basket of warm bread with caponata, butter, and extra-virgin olive oil was set between them. She sniffed with appreciation and immediately smothered a slice in butter.

Brick copied the movement. "I've never known a writer before. Tell me about it. Were you always creative?"

She nodded. "I remember always wanting to be a writer. I'd sit in my room for hours with a stack of books and feel transported to another dimension. It became my safe place—the world of imagination all writers offered. I never thought about being anything else, but as I grew up, all I heard were endless people telling me it wasn't a real job and I'd end up broke and regretful."

Brick remembered seeing men in expensive suits rushing to work, disappearing into important skyscrapers with a sense of purpose. He only knew he wanted that feeling. To be important in life. To have money to make a difference or do whatever the hell he craved. When he confessed his secret desire to work at a top *Fortune* company and make his name well known, his circle happily informed him of all the ways it wouldn't work. "Everyone has an opinion, and everyone wants to share it."

She sipped her cocktail and slicked her tongue across her lower lip to catch the sugar crystals. A sudden urge to lean across the table and taste how the sweetness mixed with her taste punched him in the gut. Knowing he had the right—she was his for the summer—only made the primitive part of him grunt in satisfaction.

"Right. If everyone concentrated on their own dreams and stopped trying to crush others', we'd be a happier society."

He grinned. "Agreed. So, you ignored the advice and pushed through the naysayers to create a successful career?"

She wrinkled her nose. "Not quite. I got day jobs and wrote on the side, but by then, the negative voices had overtaken my brain. I didn't think I had the talent. I enrolled in college focused on writing and literature, thinking I'd have real credentials when I graduated and be able to get a job or get published." Aspen paused, and a shadow flickered over her face, dimming her light. "Some stuff happened. Years passed. But finally, I was able to write a book that a publisher loved. They gave me a big advance, put a lot of marketing into the release, and it hit big. The rest is history."

Yeah, she'd skipped the most important stuff. Namely, what she'd tried to explain in his office about needing to get her heart stomped on again to put it on the page. Dozens of questions skittered through his brain, but he doubted she was ready to crack herself open and share her secrets. Not on the first date. "That's a lot of years of writing and believing in yourself. Not many people have such patience and perseverance."

Her golden-brown eyes flashed with pleasure. "Thank you," she said quietly. "It was tough sometimes to keep believing in myself. Most people see the success and think it was an overnight thing. Like I showed up, got lucky, and should be endlessly grateful that I was picked from oblivion." She rolled her eyes. "Especially from some of the smaller literary circles. God, the *Times* gave me a terrible review, and I cried for days."

He'd never thought how awful it would be to deal with critics. "Why didn't they like it?"

"Too much melodrama. Which, yeah, it had some of that, but readers were able to connect with the emotion. My next two books didn't do the job of the original. That's the main reason I hired you."

"Because your first book was basically autobiographical?"

She took another sip. Licked her lips. "Yeah, a lot of it came from personal experience, but I wrapped it in fiction, so the truth was blurred."

"Do writers mostly write from experience?"

"I think so. In order to write well, we need to pull pieces of ourselves out and examine them. Twist the ugliness into a story and try to make sense of it. It's a big, broken, emotional process, but in the end, I always hope I've left the world a bit better. By sharing. By being honest."

Emotion tightened his chest at the rawness of her words. He wondered what it would be like to consistently face your demons and use them in a story. To lift the blanket hiding the monsters and allow them onto a blank page, knowing the world would read it and judge you, even if you swore it was fiction. Would he be able to do it?

Probably not.

The waiter interrupted them, dropping off appetizers, and they happily feasted on the oysters and soup, falling into silence. He was used to women filling the air with endless chatter and had never minded. But right now, Brick appreciated her comfort with just being in the moment. She hadn't reached for her phone once to record a TikTok or show off the scenery or the beautifully plated food.

"Do you read?" she finally asked.

"Not really. Only nonfiction. I was one of those difficult teens who skipped English class and made fun of Shakespeare."

She grinned. "I always say you just never got the right book in your hand. Most dislike the so-called classics. When I read my first romance, I thought I'd reached nirvana. I finally understood the value of an entertainment read and the power of a story focused on female empowerment and pleasure. For others, it's a comic book, anime, or fan fiction. I hate when people are snooty about what they read."

"Agreed." They chatted about books and their experiences in school until the main courses arrived. "Do you ever think about moving here to be with your sister?"

"Sometimes. But I've been in New York my whole life. Sierra followed her asshat ex-husband here and never left. This is her home. I'm afraid I'd never make the Outer Banks mine like I have in the city. I've gotten dependent on food delivery and Task Rabbit and having a store five minutes away, so I don't have to go out much."

He laughed. "You really don't like the outside world, do you?"

She laughed with him. The sound made him want to make her do it again. Like her words, it was loud, bold, and unapologetic. "Not really. I'm a hermit—always have been. Sierra was the one who got the social skills and fashion sense."

"I think you're doing okay for yourself here," he said. "Maybe this summer is exactly what you need to see what you've been missing."

Their gazes met and locked. The air simmered with electricity—a delicious tension Brick hadn't experienced in a long time. Who would've thought Aspen Lourde had the power to surprise him? She wasn't his usual type. She was paying him to be with her. Yet, he was intrigued.

Maybe this job would be much more pleasurable than he imagined.

She was either having a very early pre-menopausal hot flash, or her body was reacting to that lazy, sexy grin by urging her to rip off her clothes to cool off.

So far, this night had been unexpected. She'd figured she would need to work at being interested in conversation with him. After all, her previous attempts had been filled with grunts, rude comments, and stubborn silence. But when Brick Babel put his mind to it, he could charm the literal pants off a woman.

No wonder he was lethal. In just a few short hours, she was buzzing from interesting dialogue, fabulous food, and unwavering attention. She couldn't remember the last time a man had listened like he cared, with full focus. The fact made her a bit sad because…were most women starved for this type of attention? Is that why it was easy to fall for him? Because he knew the secret cravings of women?

Being wanted?

Being *seen*?

Aspen tried to remind herself that he was doing it because she was paying him, but it seemed genuine enough and not fake. By the time the check came, and he took care of it with a subtlety that didn't call attention to the gesture, she was a bit buzzy. And it had nothing to do with the alcohol.

It was the first date she'd been on that she actually enjoyed.

God, she was in so much trouble.

But trouble was good. She was on the path to getting invested and then getting hurt. Exactly what she needed.

He escorted her from the table and suggested a walk. They took their time meandering down the boardwalk that twisted around the water. Shops buzzed with customers, and tourists enjoyed ice cream cones, homemade fudge, and lemonade as they flitted about. A little girl with blond pigtails skipped past them, singing a childhood rhyme while her parents tried to keep up. There was a sense of community, even around strangers, that she never got in New York. Aspen was sure he'd walked this route thousands of times and was bored of the same quaint town center, but he seemed content when she snuck a glance at his profile. "Are you happy here?" she suddenly asked.

He shot her an amused look. "You ask a lot of questions."

"I'm nosy. Career trait, I guess."

He took his time answering. The heat settled heavily on her skin and curled her ruthlessly straight hair with wicked glee. They paused under a gnarled oak tree for a bit of shade and stared at the water, rippling under the dying rays of the sun. "I don't know."

She cocked her head. "Explain."

Aspen liked the way his lip quirked and how the skin around his eyes creased when he seemed deep in thought. "I never planned to move here. I grew up in New York and had a different vision for myself. In college, I dreamed of making my way to the executive offices in finance. I'm good with numbers. I liked the drive, the fast pace, and the lure of money."

"You don't seem that type at all," she said.

"I was. Not that I got a chance to try."

His tone was accepting, but Aspen sensed other emotions boiled under the surface. "Sierra said you were from New York, but I never asked what part?"

"Beacon. It's in the Hudson Valley, about an hour and a half from Manhattan."

"Yes. I was there once on tour. It's such a pretty place by the mountains."

He nodded. "Grew up there. Went to NYU for business. Then returned for a while to help my mother." Shadows jumped in his eyes. "Being a single mom isn't the easiest thing."

Her voice softened. "What happened to your dad?"

"Left when I was born." His shrug held no bitterness. "Can't miss what you never had."

She wanted to dive in with more questions, to pick apart his past and childhood, but Aspen knew it was too soon. She was lucky he'd given her as much as he had when she'd only received half sentences before. "I bet your mom was amazing."

His face cleared, and those blue eyes brightened. "She was. A real firecracker, like Grandpa Ziggy. But she'd made a life in New York and had always wanted to get out of OBX. We visited, though, and I have great memories. Just never expected to inherit Grandpa's tour place."

She mulled over what he'd shared. "You think you'll like it once your grandfather's business is what you envisioned?"

"I'm gonna give it a try." He dragged in a breath and turned. She took her cue that he was done with his part of the getting-acquainted portion of the date. "Want some ice cream?"

She did, but she was a mess when she ate it and wasn't ready to expose that part. "No, thanks. I'm full."

"Then I'll take you home."

She refused to accept the flare of disappointment, so Aspen gave him a big smile and nodded. "I have all the estimates and cost analysis ready to send you," he said, back to business. "The crew is scheduled to come Monday to begin work."

"What are you going to have done?"

"A complete inside renovation. New signage. One new Jeep and repairs on the old one. New computer system. And a healthy marketing budget to do some new techniques I've wanted to try."

She caught an edge of excitement in his words, which made her happy the money would be well spent. "Sounds great. I had no idea tour companies could be so competitive. I see Maleficent's ads everywhere. Is she your main problem?"

He gave a half snort. "Hell, that woman is a menace. She has connections with some of the locals and bought up all the ad space so I couldn't get in. She poaches my customers, too. It took me a while to figure out why I was struggling, but then I found out she was Grandpa Ziggy's nemesis. Some affair gone wrong, I guess."

Suddenly, he stared at her with pure suspicion. "What?" she asked.

"If I break your heart successfully, are you going to change your mind and try to sue me?"

"God, no! You do your job, and I'll be back on top. We don't even have a contract, remember?"

His shoulders relaxed, and he opened the car door for her, then got in. "So, is it specifically the money that drives you to write a bestseller? Or something else?" He pulled out of the lot and onto the congested main road.

Aspen sighed. "I wish it was the money. It seems so much easier to get than this awful, invisible need for attention. To be read. To have your books recommended and shared and buzzed about. To be asked questions by book clubs and receive emails from readers about what it meant for them." Just talking about all the things that filled her up about having a breakout book made her ache with longing. "I could find money anywhere. What I crave is so much bigger."

Startled, she realized she'd leaked out a piece of her inner truth and darkness better kept under lock and key. It wasn't nice to reveal those types of wants. It made her feel needy, selfish, and jealous. But underneath, it was a simple burning desire that she'd been born with.

To be read. To make a difference. Stories changed lives, and being a part of it was etched into her very DNA.

Aspen waited for him to say something derogatory or make fun of her, but he didn't seem to think her words were strange. He just nodded and kept his attention on the road. "Must be nice to feel so much about something."

His remark made her curious. Was there anything in particular he felt passionate about? Did he wish there was? Were intense affairs with women his personal craving? Or was everyone overthinking the reasons, and it was simply a physical need for him? She wanted to ask so many questions, but Aspen was sure she'd reached her limit. Shadows stole the light as he pulled up to Sierra's house. He cut the engine, and they sat together in a growing, tense silence that suddenly crept in and stole all the fun and ease of the evening.

Her fingers curled in her lap. Nerves jumped in her belly. The air seemed to crackle with a growing awkwardness mixed with sensuality, creating an odd energy like oil and water. Aspen cleared her throat. Ugh, she hated ending a date. That looming first kiss always freaked her out. Again, she wished she had Sierra's ability to play it cool and smooth. "Well, that was good. Thanks for dinner." She inched away from him and grabbed at the handle.

"Come by tomorrow. I'll show you the plans and get you the printed files."

She pushed the door open. "Oh. I have a book signing in the afternoon."

"Stop by beforehand."

His casual invite made her realize they were really doing this. They were going to seriously date. Maybe sleep together. And she was paying him to do it because she was so thirsty for a bestseller that she'd sell her own soul to get one.

It was too much. She needed to get out of here. "Sure." She dove out of the car, stumbled on the concrete, and headed toward the porch.

He was beside her in seconds, frowning. "I'll walk you up."

Why was he suddenly so polite? Aspen almost missed his grumpiness and wished he'd just peeled out from the curb and left her alone. Her heart pounded madly in her chest. She felt like she was sixteen again and hoping Tommy Carter would finally French kiss her, but sick that if he did, she'd be terrible, and he'd laugh at her. Thank God Brick couldn't see the rush of heat flooding her cheeks. She muttered an "okay" and flew up the steps, desperate to disappear inside.

He caught her around the waist in one swift move and gracefully spun her around. Her back pressed lightly against the doorframe. Her front was inches from his muscled chest, but he held her loosely as if trying to reassure her he was safe.

Yeah, right.

No woman was safe in Brick Babel's orbit, let alone inches away, where she could smell his clean ocean scent and gaze into lazily amused ocean-blue eyes. "You're nervous," he stated. His husky voice touched all the secret places that had been ignored for way too long.

She blinked and tried to fight through the sensual brain fog. The pheromones drifting from his male aura were off the charts. Already, her skin tingled, and her female bits were warm and…moist.

God, she hated that word, but it was the one that popped into her head.

"No. I just thought the date was over."

That lip quirked again, and in horror, she barely stopped herself from reaching out to touch his mouth, glide her finger across the plump softness. Aspen froze like a fawn staring up at a lion, wondering if she'd be devoured fast or slow. Would he tease her first or sink his tongue into her mouth and just take her all at once?

"I thought we were just getting started," he murmured, reaching up to grasp a lock of hair, twisting the strands around his index finger. His thumb stroked up and down, forcing her full attention to the intimacy of his hand in her hair, the slight tug at her scalp, and the brush of his knuckle barely grazing her cheek. It was the most sensual gesture she'd ever experienced, that first playful touch, his gaze fastened on her face as if watching for every tiny reaction to see if it pleased her…or not.

Her throat worked, but words barely spit out. "What are you doing?"

"Nothing you don't want. But we're on a fast track here, Aspen. There's a lot to accomplish before the end of the summer, and you can't be wary of me. You need to be relaxed, or this will never work."

"Good luck with that."

His low laugh seemed to surprise both of them. A gleam of satisfaction shone from his eyes. "Why? Do I make you uncomfortable when I'm too close?"

"Another loaded question." He leaned an inch closer, his breath a warm caress against her trembling mouth. Holy hell, her body was on fire, aching for anything he wanted to give her. Her nipples hardened and begged for the pressure of that hard chest dragging against them, thighs trembling to experience his foot kicking them apart to step between them, to glide his fingers over her throbbing center. "Are you trying to make sure I get my money's worth?"

Those fierce brows creased in a frown. "I'm making another rule. We don't talk about the money between us again. This is just us now. What we're feeling. What we do." His eyes darkened. "What we want."

His words spiraled in her mind like the *Guardians of the Galaxy* Disney ride, making her dizzy. She fought for dominance in a shifting world where he held all the control. "I need to know you're not putting on a show. Which is ridiculous since I'm paying you to—"

His fingers gently pressed over her lips while he touched his forehead to hers. "Shhh," he whispered. "The rules, remember?"

Sparks shot around them. A tiny moan tugged from her chest, up her throat, to spill from her lips. His thumb was there to catch it, rubbing with light strokes. He kept talking, spinning a delicate web of sensuality around them. "I want you to get used to my touch because my hands are going to be all over you. I want you to get used to my mouth on yours because once I taste you, I won't be able to stop."

Did she squeak? Did her knees collapse? Heat washed over her, through her, between her legs in an achy trembling need that stripped away all civility and reduced her to a primitive female desperate to be touched.

"I need your permission before I kiss you, Aspen." His gaze pierced hers. "Before I do, know one thing. I don't do fake. I'll kiss you when I want to, and this will be the first and last time I ask for permission."

In complete shock at his raw, sexual words, she stared back helplessly as he stepped in, and the hard bulge of his erection pressed against her thigh. Jaw tight, eyes blazing, he waited, and Aspen had never wanted anything as badly as she wanted Brick Babel in this moment.

The word was a shaky breath. "Yes—"

His mouth captured hers before the sound faded; the warm, firm strokes of his lips an erotic assault that she not only welcomed but begged for. Aspen had been kissed before. Some were good, some were bad, and some were fantastic. But she'd never had a man overtake her with such raw physical energy; an addictive combination of brazenness and care, arrogance and humbleness, all mixed up to tear down any barriers because of a desperate need for more.

His tongue teased the seam of her lips, then sank deep to tangle and play with hers. He tasted of whiskey and sin, making a low hum of pleasure that vibrated through her whole body. Aspen reached up to thrust her fingers into his hair, moaning as his teeth lightly nipped, only to dive back in until her head fell back, her toes curled, and she was ready to rip off her clothes and have sex with him right then on her sister's front porch.

He eased away with obvious regret, murmuring her name as he cupped her jaw, indulging in one last taste until a few inches of space separated them. She gazed at him, half drunk, barely noticing the lust in his eyes and the tight clench of his jaw. The air sizzled, slowed, settled. Her tongue unconsciously reached out to capture the lingering taste of him on her bottom lip. His breathing was ragged as he stared.

Silence ticked.

"Wow."

Another quirk of his lip. This time, she knew how his mouth felt and tasted and would never be safe again. Damn him and his seductive mastery. Damn him for being irresistible to any female with a pulse. "A big word for a writer."

She blinked. "I'm saving them for my book."

This time, he laughed, and she had an impulse to stroke his hair back from his brow, caress his rough cheek, or smile back with stupid giddiness because he was so beautiful, and she'd made him laugh. "At least, you're not nervous anymore."

Aspen shook her head and tried to regain her composure. "Mission accomplished. I can't complain about the methods."

A gentle smile curved his lips. "Good night, Aspen."

Then he left.

She stumbled through the door with one thought.

It was already happening after only one night. She was smitten with Brick Babel.

And Aspen couldn't wait to read what happened next.

Chapter Ten

"I thought we were going to talk last night."

Aspen winced as she poured coffee and slid onto the stool. Her sister looked beautiful in a floral summer dress, white strappy sandals, and a fashionable straw hat. Another big difference between them—Aspen despised mornings and could barely form words. Also, she looked like a grumpy, messy teen with her crazy-ass hair, sweat shorts, and oversized T-shirt. "Sorry, I thought you were asleep."

Sierra grunted. "How was your date?"

Aspen sipped the hot brew. "Great. He gave me four orgasms last night. Now, he's waiting for you to beat the hell out of him as promised."

Her sister gave her a hard glare over her coffee mug. "Hysterical. You're really fun in the morning. As usual."

Aspen threw her head back and met her stare head-on. "Sorry, but you pissed me off. I'm clear about what I want with him, and you embarrassed me. This thing with Brick will be a game changer for my book."

Sierra slammed the mug onto the counter. Liquid sloshed over and dribbled onto the floor. "I don't care about the stupid book, Aspen. Do you know how it felt watching you go through that crap with Ryan? There were times I was terrified you were falling apart, alone and locked in that apartment for a year while you wrote. I cannot go through that again. I will not let Brick destroy you for fun because you're chasing a bestseller."

Anger morphed into frustration. She understood her sister's concern, but she had to pursue this alone. "You can't protect me from everything," she said. "I wasn't able to save you from a nasty divorce or from being cheated on. I worry about you, too. That you keep thinking you're not enough because of your stupid ex."

Surprise flickered across Sierra's features, but her voice still held a stubborn tone. "That was different. I can demand that Brick stay away from you, and he will. With a few well-placed words, I'd make sure the whole town knew about this deal and stop you both."

Aspen jumped from the stool. "I need this!" she yelled. "I don't need someone to protect me anymore. All I want is for you to support my choice so I can finally *feel* something. God, it's been too long since my real life was more exciting than my imaginary one." Her shoulders slumped as the fight went out of her. "Just be my sister, okay? Trust me to navigate this on my own."

A few moments ticked by in silence. Finally, Sierra let out a string of colorful and impressive curses. She crossed her arms in front of her chest, looking pissed. "Fine. I hate this whole thing, but I don't want to ruin our summer. I just hope you know what you're getting into."

It was the closest she'd get to an approval, and Aspen was grateful. She crossed the room and hugged Sierra, which started off stiff but then softened. "Thanks. I hate fighting."

"Me, too."

"You still coming to my book signing?"

"Of course. It'll be great." She paused. "Will Brick be there?"

"No, but I'm heading to the tour place later. Are you going to be nice to him next time?"

Sierra gave her a half laugh. "I'll try."

"Good enough."

"I'd better get to work. I'll get there early for a seat."

Aspen tried not to show her nerves. The idea of doing a book signing with her sister in the audience was a big deal. She wanted Sierra to be proud but had a bad feeling that no one would show up. Or if they did, everyone would only want to talk about *Fifty Ways to Leave Your Lover*. She kept her tone light. "Oh, not many people will be at this."

"Are you kidding? You're a big star. I'm sure it will be packed. See you later."

Aspen watched her sister leave and tried to remind herself that, no matter who showed up to support her, it was a win—even if no one bought the new book.

She grabbed another cup of coffee and tried not to think about it.

Brick glanced at his watch and noted Aspen should arrive soon.

The thought of their kiss last night hit him right in the solar plexus with a sucker punch. He hadn't expected such a primitive reaction. Yes, she intrigued him. Yes, their conversation had both amused and challenged him. The woman was attractive, good company, and a straight shooter. They had chemistry.

But he hadn't been prepared for a literal explosion of raw hunger. A base need to conquer and possess once his hands touched her skin, once he tasted her sweetness—still lingering on his tongue. He'd only felt that once before, and not so strongly.

With Anastasia.

The memory usually ripped him with pain, but the wound only throbbed now. He tried to reassure himself that it was just a coincidence. Besides, Aspen was a summer fling with strict rules and boundaries. No way to get hurt again. Sure, there was a connection, but he was glad. It would make getting her to fall for him easier. He'd been on his best behavior last night but had sensed her uneasiness when he took her home.

Was it wrong that her obvious awkwardness charmed him? She liked to blurt out her thoughts without a filter—another trait he admired. Brick figured the best way to get things moving was to wield his sexual charm like the asset it was. There was no ego involved; women had been easy to seduce and win over since he was young, paving a path that made life easier until he fell hard and got the shit beat out of him.

Brick rubbed his hands over his face and tried to focus. Okay, the kiss was legendary. And he'd gone straight home, jumped in the shower, and stroked himself off to the image of her sweet, plump mouth opening under his, ready to take his dick in one satisfying thrust.

He'd been on this self-imposed celibacy break for a while. He was happy Aspen would be the one to break it. And all he had to do was keep the charm factor high, tease out some shattering orgasms, and tell her some secrets to build intimacy. Then, something else would hopefully break.

Her heart. By her demand.

The door banged open. "Heading out for the day," Sal called. "Deliveries are set for tomorrow. The whole crew will be here."

"Thanks. Appreciate the work on short notice."

Even though it was Sunday, Sal had shown up early to do his initial measurements, confirm materials, and go over the reno plans. Brick counted himself lucky to have had the foresight to plan ahead, even when all the banks rejected him. Getting contractor work done last minute was almost impossible without damn long waits and delays.

Sal grinned. "Better than doing another damn deck for the summer people. Was hoping you'd call me, especially since you put down that retainer to jump the line when needed. Glad Ziggy's place will be back to its former glory."

Brick laughed and waved, then headed to the back and grabbed a fresh T-shirt. He'd gotten a bit sweaty and figured a quick change would do before he saw Aspen. Stripping off the old one, he threw on some deodorant and turned when he heard someone come in.

He stilled, nostrils flaring as her wide-eyed gaze flicked over his bare chest like a caress. Brick studied the naked desire on her face, and a wave of heat surged between them, driving the breath from his lungs.

Ah, fuck.

He hardened immediately, helpless under the greedy stare that looked upon him like a treat she wanted to devour but was too afraid to ask for. Fists clenched, he remained still until she was done.

Her gaze lifted and clashed with his.

Those brown doe eyes held both lust and fascination, and Brick wondered what expression she'd wear when he thrust deeply inside her that very first time. Would she squeeze him tightly and welcome him in? Would that pretty stare lock on him and hold, then fall apart as he made her come? She gave off a sense of reserve as she seemed to circle around him, still wondering if he was friend or foe, possible lover or enemy. Brick couldn't help the wolfish grin that stretched his mouth at the thought of being both.

Either way, he had full permission to do what it took to gain her affection. And damned if he didn't intend to have fun.

He rubbed his chest and lowered his voice to a purr. "Was just changing for you. Got a bit dirty."

The word made her blush, which he found adorable. Her jaw worked, and she cleared her throat, shifting back an inch. "Oh. S-sorry. I can wait outside."

"No need." He crumpled the old shirt in his fist and blotted his neck, trapping her stare once again. Brick made sure to stretch, calling attention to his abs, which were on full display from the low dip of his jeans. "It's damn hot without the air on."

Her tongue reached out to slick her lower lip. "Yeah."

She seemed to run out of words after that. Brick tried not to grin. "Why don't you come on over here? I want to show you something." His hand deliberately dropped to rub his stomach. Settled suggestively by his crotch. "Something you'll really want to see."

Shock flickered over her face, and she half-turned, cheeks mottled red. "Not now!" she hissed.

He laughed then, unable to help it, and wondered at the need to hug her and playfully tug at her hair. It was a strange reaction to be torn between heat and lighthearted banter. Most of his relationships revolved around sex, not talk. Aspen shook her head in a muted temper, but then she was laughing with him. "You're an asshole," she muttered. "Put on a damn shirt."

"If you're sure."

She rolled her eyes. "Do all women fall for that little show? Do they drop at your feet in hormonal lust at the sight of your half-naked body?"

He gave her a half smile. "Sometimes. I usually prefer dropping to mine." His voice deepened. "For other things."

She arched a brow, but he caught the slight tremble in her body. Still, she fought hard to hide the reaction, speaking cooly. "You're a real expert. The Dom-tone thing is a nice touch. Hinting at being able to pleasure a female is classic seduction material. I can't wait to see what else you've got in your arsenal."

"Aspen?"

"What?"

Brick leaned over the counter, palms flat, casually displayed for her viewing entertainment. He kept his body fit for health and his satisfaction but enjoyed the honest appreciation of Aspen's helpless, sweeping stare. "I'm not hinting."

She made a little sound under her breath. "If I wave the white flag, will you get dressed? I'm already nervous about this stupid book signing and not up to par for verbal foreplay."

Brick frowned and shrugged on his new T-shirt. "You get anxiety over these things? Thought you've done several before."

"I have, but they're never easy. I worry no one's going to show up. Then I worry people will but won't buy my book. Plus, Sierra is coming with some friends, and I'm not used to having people I know well there."

He studied her, dressed the part in white linen pants, a lacy white blouse, and high-heeled sandals. Her hair was smoothed into a tight topknot, and she'd put on makeup—sparkly pink shadow, lipstick, and blush, giving her face a beachy, rosy glow. "No one would ever know. You look like the famous author you are."

"Thanks." She still looked tense, but he wasn't sure how to calm her. "This is my sister's home. I just want it to be successful." She wrinkled her nose. "Also, I hate reading aloud and the Q&As. I'd rather just sign."

Amusement cut through him. "Isn't it a thrill to meet readers, though?"

"Sure. I adore my readers, but I love them more from a distance. Like via email. Face-to-face means pressure, but I'm always grateful. When I was young and writing in my notebooks alone on a Friday night while Sierra dated, I never thought I'd actually have people wanting to leave their house to come see me."

Her confession connected on a soul-deep level. It was nice not to pretend with her. She seemed to own her shit, which was rare in anyone nowadays. "When I took over for Ziggy, I had to deal with the fact that I'd failed him," he admitted. "I was the one to finally run it into the ground, even though I got here late. I assumed I'd step in and be the savior."

She tilted her head. "You will, though. Save it. I can't believe you have people working on this already. Sierra had to wait over a month just to get her patio repaved."

"I've had them on standby for a while. I drew up plans with an architect, got the necessary approvals, and hired a team. Figured the easiest part was getting a loan. I was an idiot."

"What about mortgaging your home? Do you own?"

"It's Grandpa Ziggy's house and mortgaged to the hilt." A humorless laugh escaped. "He had a twisted sense of humor, all right. Leaving me a bankrupt legacy. I spent over a year hoping for a miracle."

She threw her hands in the air. "And here I am."

"Here you are." The air cranked with intensity. She regarded him as if he were a scientific experiment, so he didn't disappoint. "Did you think about our kiss?"

She opened her mouth to answer, then shut it. "Maybe."

Satisfaction surged. "So did I. Especially…later on. When I got home." Brick watched her face, wondering how far he could push. Did she like dirty talk as much as he did? Or did she prefer a more subtle, vanilla-type lover? Of course, it could be too soon, but they were on a short timetable, and he'd rather find out now. "I imagined a lot of things."

"Oh." The implication seemed to hit her all at once. "Oh!" A half groan strangled from her lips, and Brick fought the impulse to close the distance, pick her up, and swallow that sexy sound whole. Embarrassment mixed with curiosity as she tipped her chin up and met his gaze head-on. Her pupils dilated. "You…did stuff while thinking about me?"

Heat blasted through his veins. Oh, this was fun. He propped his chin on his open palm and answered in a slow drawl tightly packed with innuendo. "Oh, yeah. Lots of stuff."

She hesitated. Then forged on. "Like what?"

He couldn't help his smile. Damned if he didn't admire a woman who could give as good as she got. "First, I imagined you laid out on my bed. Naked. Waiting for me." He stretched out the pulsating silence. "I took off my clothes. Got in the shower. And put my hands on myself, pretending it was you."

The pulse in her neck was beating overtime. Her body stiffened, and he bet if he cupped her breast, those sweet nipples would be hard. Were they a light, flushed pink, or dark red under that virginal white? He was dying to find out. "Brick."

His name sounded sweet on her tongue. Even better when she eventually screamed it. "Aspen?"

"You're very good at this, aren't you?"

"I'm good at lots of things."

She shook her head. One random curl escaped the knot and lay against her cheek. His fingers itched to brush it back. Only one blistering kiss and less than twenty-four hours had him fully on board with this summer affair. Plus, he got his business saved as a bonus. God had finally blessed him after being pissed off for a long time. "I appreciate your effort in all ways. But right now, I need to focus on my signing and not you in the shower, naked, doing…stuff."

He laughed, surprised by her challenge. Good. Aspen was no shy virgin, which would make this whole thing much easier. But she was definitely a bit innocent. He doubted she was used to sharing sexual fantasies, given how she blushed and stuttered, but the woman was turned on and willing. He could work with that.

"Duly noted. Just remember, I don't have to always make the first move. Men enjoy female advances now."

Aspen tilted her head and gave him a level stare. "Shall I strip to my bikini underwear and play innocent when I get a reaction?"

"Yes, please."

He enjoyed her half giggle, but they were interrupted when Marco strolled in. "Aspen, you're back! Looking sweet, too. Going to work?"

"Hi, Marco. Kind of. I have to go to a book signing."

"Cool, anyone I know?"

She wrinkled her nose. "Um, me."

Marco's eyes bugged out. "No. Way. You're a real author? That's fire, man. Isn't it, Brick?"

"Definitely fire."

"Hey, I'll come and see you. When is it?"

"About an hour. And no, Marco, don't worry about it. You need to run the store."

"Nah. Burger's there to run it. Brick, you going?"

"Wouldn't miss it."

Alarm blazed in her brown eyes. "No, honestly, you want to skip this one. It's a small store, I'll be talking about women's fiction, and you'll be bored. But thanks anyway."

"Absolutely not," Marco stated. "I love going to the bookstore. And I love reading romance. That stuff is how you figure out women. Biggest selling genre out there, and I know dudes who actually make fun of it."

Brick stared at him with surprise. He read romance? Grudging respect settled within, especially the way he supported Aspen.

Marco continued. "You know, reading saved my life. That's how I found out how to be a business owner. I sucked at school, got bored real quick in the classroom. So, instead of going to college and wasting four years studying stuff I'd never use, I read books. I like audio. Hell, no one needs a degree anymore between books, the internet, and YouTube. Plus, AI, man—it'll be doing everything for us soon."

Aspen wrapped her arms around her middle and squeezed. Why did she suddenly look pale? "I'd really rather you not come. I'm used to doing these things when I don't know anyone in the crowd."

"I'm sure you invite friends to your signings," Brick said. "Co-workers? Family?"

She shook her head. "No. I go alone."

Didn't she have anyone in her life to show up for her? Or was she such a loner that she'd gotten used to facing things by herself? Brick grabbed a bottle of water and walked over. "Breathe, baby. Here, drink this." She grabbed the bottle and took a few sips. "We only want to support you, Aspen. What type of boyfriend would I be if I didn't go to your signing?"

She shot him a glare, but Marco caught the slip. "No way! Dude, you work fast. And I was going to try hooking her up with Burger."

"Thank God I got there first," Brick said with a straight face.

Marco nodded. "Yeah, Burger's an animal. Probably the long hair and beard."

Brick's phone rang. He glanced down. "Sorry, I have to take this. It's one of my suppliers for the renovation."

"Hey, Aspen. Come over to the store for a minute. I wanted to get your opinion on something."

"Sure."

"I'll meet you next door," Brick said. Maybe she needed a distraction. It would be nice to see Aspen in her element, signing books for readers who loved her stories. He hadn't planned to attend, but it may be a good idea. And if he could help soothe her nerves? Even better.

He took the call and watched them head next door.

This was ridiculous.

She stood next to Marco, Burger, and Patsy looking at three identical T-shirts in various colors, stacked in bins. The back room smelled like sweat, salt, and skunk. The guys were too sweet, stumbling over themselves to try and show her the differences in pale yellow, lemon, and citrus gold, asking her opinion when her stomach was roiling with anxiety.

Aspen nodded, sipped her water, and let the low-level argument wash over her as each tried to convince her which color would be best. At this point in her career, she'd made peace with most public appearances. After she scored book of the month, she did television and magazine articles, podcasts, and plenty of signings. In the beginning, she'd been ready to pass out with fear but managed to fight through by sheer willpower. The fan love and approval eased the way until she could perform without major issues.

Until this latest book.

Having Sierra and her friends there should be comforting, but it only added pressure. The idea of sitting and smiling for over an hour while no one bought her new book was humiliating. And Ursula, the bookstore owner, was enthusiastic to hear her talk about her life as a famous writer to keep customers engaged. It was bad enough that she felt silly being scared in a small, quaint beach town bookshop, but now Brick wanted to come?

God, no. He was already haunting her damn dreams. She couldn't stop replaying the kiss in her head—how hot it was, how his tongue thrust slowly and deliberately, tangling with hers, getting her all worked up. The way his fingers threaded through her hair and tugged. The firm grip on her hips to pull her in with just enough force to feel claimed.

He was a physical danger to her libido, fogging her mind and seducing her body on the very first date. He was exactly what his reputation had promised. He was precisely who she wanted him to be, which was messing her up badly.

Seeing him stripped to the waist with a sexy, knowing smile had turned her mute. All those defined muscles naked to her hungry gaze. Eight-pack abs she wanted to touch, taste, and test to see if they were as hard as she imagined. Jeans riding low on his hips, the perfect amount of swirling dark hair covering his chest. Flat, brown nipples peeking out to tease her. Her teeth ached to bite and lick all that toasty golden skin. In seconds, she'd been reduced to a shivering, helpless, needy female who wanted him.

It was a nightmare.

Yet this was what she was paying for.

If only she could write. All those achy feelings after he'd left drove Aspen straight to her laptop, desperate to pour her heart into the new story—the sequel the world was waiting for. It was supposed to be easy. She hadn't felt so alive since writing *Fifty Ways to Leave Your Lover*. She'd finally found the secret sauce, but after writing a few pages, she read it back and realized it was…

Flat. Like cardboard. She couldn't translate her emotions into the story. It sounded like a bunch of telling and no showing—a classic beginner's mistake.

Frustration made her want to scream. She'd spent hours trying, then began some character outlines, hoping to reconnect with her heroine for inspiration. But nothing worked. She ended up sketching her *Zany Zoo* comics in bed, relief pouring from her very soul as the pent-up creative energy finally found a decent outlet.

She fell asleep by dawn, only grabbing a few hours, which made her anxiety today worse.

"Hey, Aspen. You okay?" Marco asked, frowning in concern. "You look stressed out."

Burger and Patsy stopped arguing about the differences between sunshine-yellow and lemonade. She forced a smile, feeling silly. "Nah, I'll be okay. I just get a little nervous before events. It's stupid."

Marco had told them about her book event, and they'd actually discussed closing the shop so they could all attend. Aspen waited for the guys to laugh off her remark, but they all wore serious expressions like she'd confessed a real problem. "That's not stupid," Burger said. He wore a tank that said *Just Love, Man*, ripped jeans, and flip-flops. His hair was long and straight and so much nicer than hers. With his scruffy beard and serious, dark eyes, he reminded her of a modern-day rocker Jesus. Also, how'd he get the strands so shiny?

Patsy shook his head. "When I had to do public speeches in school, I'd vomit." He was the opposite of Burger, his head shaved clean with Coke-bottle-type glasses and a proper collared shirt with pleated khaki shorts. The three of them were so different, but even with their arguing, they had an evident bond. They'd make perfect secondary characters in her book. Aspen would dig a bit deeper and get their backstories later.

Marco snapped his fingers. "Want something to bring you down a level? Just to chill out?"

She hadn't eaten today, which was normal when she had a public appearance. "Sure, you got anything with chocolate?" she joked. Something about the sugar and caffeine in the sweet always gave her a hit of happiness.

The guys shared a delighted look. "Hell, yes! We've got brownies. Want one?" Burger asked.

"Seriously? You have chocolate?"

Marco grinned. "Sure. Best chocolate you can get around here." He laughed, and his friends also laughed. She wasn't sure why brownies were funny, but maybe a square would help settle her stomach.

"I'll have a small piece."

"I knew you'd be into it," Burger said, staring at her with renewed interest. His grin held male appreciation. Uh-oh. Looked like he may be thinking about Marco's suggestion to date her. She'd have to set him straight soon.

Marco came back with a chocolate square and a napkin. "Thanks." She lifted it and took a bite. The texture was dense and rich, so she took another one. They all looked excited that she was eating the dessert, which was weird. She gave them an awkward nod while they watched. An aftertaste hit, and she frowned. "Did one of you make these, or did you buy them?"

"I made them," Marco said proudly. "Can't even taste it, right?"

She blinked. Why wouldn't she want to taste the chocolate? "Um, right." Being polite, she ate some more, but there was definitely a funky flavor that didn't taste right. Aspen wanted to dump the rest but hated to hurt Marco's feelings.

So, she finished it like medicine. Could brownies go bad? Maybe he'd made the batch with old milk.

Pushing the thought away, she offered a smile. "Delicious."

Burger, Marco, and Patsy all did a high five. They were so cute. She took a slug of water to wash away the lingering bitterness. "I like the sunshine-yellow one and the sky-blue shirts. Very OBX."

Patsy whooped, and Marco looked disappointed but took it in stride. "How'd you all decide to open a souvenir shop?" she asked.

"Well, we all met at the Smoke Shop back in Boston and got tight. We had a dream of being our own bosses, living near the beach, and getting out of the city," Marco said.

Burger agreed. "Got tired of everything being about status and money. We wanted to surf the waves and live free in the sun."

Patsy jumped in. "We pooled our money for a while, then hit on an instant lottery card for twenty-five grand. That was it. We quit and headed south to travel. We thought about opening a bar at first, but liquor licensing and liability was a bitch."

"When we found this place, we knew it was meant to be. Especially when this store was up for rent pretty cheap," Marco said.

She pictured the three of them creating their own future, with the passion and ignorance of the very young. God, she remembered those exact feelings in college. On fire to write her stories and change the world. Rebelling against the patriarchy of the so-called classics and craving to create books for women with emotion and messiness without apology.

Until Ryan stole her innocence. Now, she couldn't tap into the joy of just writing any longer. Her work needed to come from pain.

A twinge of sadness threatened. She didn't want to think about what she had lost. Better to revel in what these three young men had created together.

They chatted a bit more about how they'd figured out retail wasn't as easy as they thought, but working together made them happy. Oddly enough, the edge of sadness morphed into a warm, gushy feeling that made her begin to tear up. Her vision blurred, so everything started to take on an edge of softness. Wow. She felt so much better. All the stress and worry had eased away. She needed to come over and hang with Marco more often. Who would've thought he'd have such a calming effect?

Aspen reached out and pat Marco's arm but found she missed by a few inches. "Your story makes me so happy." She sighed. "You're the dynamic trio. The triplet musketeers of retail."

A giggle escaped her at the witty words. She was definitely on her game today. Aspen wasn't even nervous about speaking to a crowd and almost welcomed the opportunity to share her journey as a writer.

"That worked fast," Patsy muttered. "She must be a lightweight."

A bell rang out. Aspen straightened and glanced around in awe. "An angel," she whispered. "Every time a bell rings, an angel gets his wings."

A deep voice rang out from behind. "And pisses off the devil to do more bad deeds."

She spun around, losing her balance and falling against Brick's hard chest. The same one that had been naked a little while ago. Damn, she wished he was still naked. She wanted another peek at that masculine magnificence.

Aspen squinted up at him, pressing her cheek against the soft, washed cotton. She sniffed hard. *Yum*. The fabric held some of his special cologne. "I thought you were like the devil when we first met."

"And now?"

She looked up with a dreamy smile. "Still not an angel. But you're growing on me. Like a plant. Not ivy. That other stuff that's green and clings to a house."

He blinked. "Moss?"

"Yeah, moss. I should put that in my book. Something different. I'm tired of writing about men smelling like spice and musk and sin."

She heard the low laughter around, but it sounded like it came from a distance. Her body was warm and tingly, but she figured it was Brick's closeness. Her hands were stroking his chest, and she couldn't stop. Her fingers seemed disconnected from her brain.

"Hmm, moss doesn't sound as sexy."

"Well, every woman has a special scent that's sexy to them. For instance, one of the women you slept with said you smelled like freshly baked sugar cookies."

Brick gazed down with a bit of puzzlement, a tiny frown creasing his brow. "Are you kidding? Who said that?"

"Um, I don't remember. Sierra mentioned it." She took another large whiff. "But I think you smell like lemons and sunshine. That's my favorite."

Concern flickered across his features. "Aspen, are you okay?"

She tried to pat his cheek, but it moved. Little sparks of light gleamed around his head, making him look like he had a halo. She tried to touch it, but it was like stardust, disappearing the moment one wanted it to be real. "You are like an angel," she whispered. "So. Cool."

His voice lashed like a whip, and Aspen winced. "Marco. What the hell is wrong with her?"

"I had brownies," she managed to say, still trying to touch the halo. A giggle escaped. "Stay still!"

Marco sounded distressed. "She said she was nervous and wanted something to relax so I offered her the brownies I made. I didn't know the weed would affect her so much. It was lightly laced. Just a hint."

"Did she ask for it?" Brick asked in astonishment.

"I thought so. I told her they were special and that it would help her relax. Right, guys? Didn't it seem she knew?"

Burger and Patsy shared a glance and shrugged. "Sure. We assumed we were having the same conversation."

"You don't assume when you're talking about weed!" Brick roared.

"Weed, like moss?" she asked, wondering why Marco's statement seemed important. "Like how Brick is growing on me?"

"Holy shit, she's high as a kite," Brick hissed. She was scared of his tone, but he held her gently, allowing her to keep swiping at the invisible halo no one else could see but her. "Are you kidding me? She has to sign books in half an hour."

"I didn't mean to get her like this." A desperate whine edged Marco's tone. Burger and Patsy jumped into the dialogue, and it looked so lively, Aspen tried to focus on what they were saying, but a bubble of laughter overtook her, especially when she saw how animated they were. Hands flying in gestures, deep frowns, worried faces—it all jumbled together like a giant fun house until she was doubled over and gasping for breath. "Stop making me laugh," she sputtered.

"This is a disaster," Brick said, shaking his head. "How's she supposed to give a talk like this? I have to call the bookstore and cancel."

Oh, no. She heard that, and it wasn't funny anymore. Her head popped up. "Ursula promised lots of people to show up. I am not canceling. I feel good."

Marco began to pace back and forth. "We can help her. Be her…assistants. It hit way too fast, which means it'll fade. She's gotta drink a lot of water."

"I like water."

"Fuck my life. Get me a few bottles now," Brick ordered. "Come on, baby, let's sit down. I need you to drink a lot of water for me, okay?"

This time, she found his cheek and patted it hard. "Aww, I like it when you're nice. And without a shirt. That's nice, too."

He groaned and eased her onto a folding chair. "Good to know for future reference. Here you go, drink as much as you can."

She guzzled the water and swiped the back of her hand over her lips. "Yum."

Marco pressed three more bottles into his hands. "Great job. How about some more?"

"No, I'm full."

"Just try. Please, Aspen? For me?" Brick asked.

A joyous smile curved her lips. It was sunny inside her body, and she wanted to share it with the world. Might as well make Brick happy, too. "Sure."

She managed to drink more, and the men had some type of group discussion she wasn't a part of. "It's time for me to go now!" she shouted.

Brick jerked. Had she yelled in his ear? He looked scared. That made her laugh again, and the cycle began all over.

"At least she's not paranoid," Marco said, taking her other arm and escorting her out of the store. "I'm sure the weed will wear off by the time she needs to talk."

"It'd better. I can't tell anyone she's high," Brick snapped.

"It's legal, man. Not like she's going to prison. I'm sorry, I feel awful." Why did Marco sound hurt when he spoke? She wanted to console him, but they were dragging her outside to the car.

"Being legal has nothing to do with it. What if she can't function? What am I going to tell her sister?"

"Don't yell at Marco," she scolded. "He gave me the nice brownies. He made the nerves go away."

Brick snorted and settled her in the car, then came around to the driver's seat. "Aspen, he gave you brownies with pot in them. Did you realize that?"

The light bulb went on, and everything made sense. That was why she felt like this. Her limbs were loose and free, but she didn't have much control over them. Hopefully, she'd be able to sign her name. At least she wasn't panicked anymore and didn't care about people not buying her book. "No." Aspen wiggled her fingers, trying to focus. "No wonder they tasted yucky."

"I'm sorry, Aspen. I screwed up bad. I thought you knew they were pot brownies, and now I drugged you and feel terrible," Marco said.

His sadness suddenly made her want to cry. "No, pot is good, Marco. You did a good thing, and I'm not mad. Ignore Brick. He's being judgy, and we need to live in a world that's free."

A choked laugh came from her left. She glared at Brick but wasn't sure she was perfecting the anger she wanted. "Oh, you're free all right. Flying high in the clouds. How the hell are you supposed to talk and sign books?"

Marco jumped in. "We can do it, man. We can tell everyone she had a…headache. And that I had some leftover muscle relaxers, and she took one, but it hit her too hard. No one has to know what really happened."

"I ate weed!" Aspen cried out.

Brick swerved a bit and shot her a look that had her cracking up again. Why were things so funny? He cursed, and Marco shoved more water at her and begged her to drink, and then they arrived at the bookstore. Brick unbuckled his seat belt and turned toward her. His eyes were deep and dark and filled with an intensity that made her tummy drop in a beautiful free fall. "Aspen?"

She reached out to touch his chest. This time, her hand worked. Her palm hit a wall of muscle she was dying to explore. "Brick?"

A muscle ticked in his jaw. "You have to try very hard to focus. Readers are coming to hear you talk about your new book, okay? Just answer questions about what you wrote and try not to laugh. Do you think you can do that?"

"Of course."

"And don't say anything about pot or weed or brownies. Okay?"

A giggle almost erupted, but Brick had said not to laugh, so she swallowed it down. It tasted like a popped bubble gum bubble. "Oh. 'Kay."

"We'll be right there to help. I'm going to say I'm your assistant. Marco, too."

"Oh. 'Kay."

A dark expression flickered over his face, and his brows lowered in a frown. "Let's go."

"Brick?"

"Yeah?"

Aspen pressed her lips together with hidden glee. "I'm high."

He sighed and raked his fingers through his hair. "I know. Remember, let's keep it a secret."

She put her finger over her lips. "Shhh. It's a secret."

Then she got out of the car.

Chapter Eleven

"I have a secret," Aspen announced in a loud whisper to her sister. "But Brick doesn't want me to tell."

He almost groaned in defeat, but the event hadn't begun yet, and he had work to do. After meeting with Ursula, he'd convinced her that Aspen had a headache, and though she was willing to answer questions, Brick would be the one to read an excerpt from her new book. Marco would be in the audience as a decoy in case they needed a distraction.

They were at the thirty-minute mark since she'd eaten the brownies, and Marco swore she'd be better at an hour.

He hoped Aspen took a lot of bathroom breaks to slow time.

But now, Sierra shot him a suspicious look at Aspen's confession, and he wasn't sure how to play it. "What secret?" she demanded, squinting hard at her sister's face. "And why do you look so happy?"

"Because she loves book signings," Brick cut in smoothly. "Right? Aspen was just telling me in the car that meeting her readers gives her a high."

"I'm high!" Aspen cried out. A few people glanced over. "Oops." She clapped a palm over her mouth. "That was the secret."

Sierra stared. Brick forced a laugh. "She's been cracking jokes all morning."

He was saved when Ursula motioned them over to start the event. The store was small, so a table had been set up in a cozy corner with a stack of Aspen's books. Sharpies, bookmarks, and postcards were laid alongside the pile. All the folding chairs were taken, and people lined up throughout the aisles, crowded in tight to hear Aspen speak. Many clutched books to their chests. Brick registered the excited hum of energy vibrating around him as she took her seat behind the table and Ursula began introductions.

Brick tucked himself against a corner bookshelf to keep a close eye on Aspen. She tilted her head to the side, hands folded neatly, and listened while Ursula read off a list of achievements, from bestsellers to optioned movies to sales of over a million dollars. He noticed the books displayed were all her newest release—titled *Meet Me at Our Spot.* The cover was colorful, with a couple on a picnic blanket and the Eiffel Tower in the background.

Ursula stepped aside, and applause rang out. Aspen smiled and nodded while Brick held his breath. She was definitely grinning with a bit of glee, and her brown eyes gleamed with moisture. What if she cried? Would her fans like that and feel appreciated? Body stiff with tension, he prayed she could speak without giggling and going off on a strange tangent.

He was going to kill Marco later.

"Thank you. I'm so...touched to see all of you here." Aspen beamed from behind the table, taking in the crowd, misty with emotion. "I always dreamed of being a writer but never thought I'd make it. I thought it was a career you had if you were very smart. I thought I needed to be well-versed in all the literary classics and get As in stuffy classrooms on my essays. I thought everyone knew more than me—the secret that would finally get my stories published and read. I spent so long trying to figure it all out." A tiny frown creased her brow. "This is my third novel, and I think I finally found the answer."

She paused, and everyone waited, sensing a big revelation coming. Brick waited with them, expecting an underdog story of rejections and success like the Rocky of the fiction world. A story filled with inner truths that people could relate to in pursuit of all their dreams. Maybe the pot had helped. She was able to open up, share more, and connect with the audience. Or perhaps the edge was finally wearing off, and he didn't have to worry anymore. It didn't matter as long as she seemed back in control of herself.

Aspen surveyed the crowd, drawing out the anticipation.

"Hi, Sierra!" She began to wave frantically, blowing kisses to her sister, who looked frozen in shock. "My sister's in the audience, guys. Isn't that cool? Oh, and there's Brooklyn and Inez, my new friends."

There were laughs and glances toward the women. Her friends grinned. Sierra nodded politely, smiling back, but Brick saw the moment she realized her sister was not herself. "Okay, I'd better read something, right?"

"What was the answer?" a woman called out.

Aspen blinked. "To what?"

A low murmur swept through the crowd. The woman spoke again. "You said you found the secret to being a writer by your third book. What was it?"

Aspen scrunched up her nose as if trying to remember. Brick held his breath. "Oh. There is no secret. I guess I lied."

Fuck.

The woman looked confused, but Aspen kept talking. "Let's get this show on the road. Um, this is from my new book, which just came out. It's not doing well, so it'd be nice if you bought it." Another round of laughs, this time more strained.

Aspen plucked one of her books from the pile and rifled through it, taking a long time between mutters to decide what segment to read. Ugh, this was stressful. Squaring his shoulders, he walked over and discreetly whispered, "I'll read for you, Aspen. Just give me the page."

"You're being so sweet, Brick," she exclaimed way too loudly. "But I got this. I can read fine."

The weight of multiple gazes burned through him. He nodded and withdrew to his spot. Probably not a good time to push. Hopefully, she'd find the damn page, read it, and refocus. Finally, she stabbed her finger at a page, brightening. "Here it is. Oh, you'll like this part. Um, okay, so the heroine and the hero grew up together at this lake upstate. First, they were friends, and then they got into a fight and hated each other. A decade later, they find themselves in Paris, working on the same project but on different sides." Aspen waved a hand in the air back and forth like she was conducting a symphony. "They had this big argument in public, and they're really mad, but there's this chemistry between them they can't seem to get over—don't you love when that happens?—and the hero, Cal, shoves the heroine, Rachael, into a conference room to continue the argument. Here we go."

She squinted at the page, cleared her throat, and began to read.

"You're still the same sulky, bratty kid I had to deal with ten years ago," Rachael hissed, leaning in with fury. "I don't care if it's the last thing I do, but I'll make sure your proposal never gets passed."

Cal practically growled in her face. "Try it. I'll get the votes to throw you off this board before you blink those pretty little lashes. And you're still the same spoiled, pampered princess who manipulated every guy you came in contact with. Except me.

That's why you hate me. Because I saw right through you from day one."

"Try it," Rachael threw back at him. "A few well-placed calls will yank that generous bank loan. How will you tell your mom you failed again?"

She saw the rage on his face, and somehow, she was pressed against the wall, her hands gripping his shoulders, mouth an inch away. "Sure. The same time you tell your dad you failed again to show any value except buying off others to do the real work. How can anyone respect you when you're afraid to get your hands dirty?"

Rachel gritted her teeth. Her nails sank into the cotton of his dress shirt and hit solid muscle. "I can get as dirty as anyone if it's something I believe in."

His lip lifted in a snarl, and suddenly, all that angry tension took a hard turn and exploded into a furious sexual energy, whipping between them like a hurricane. "Prove it."

His mouth slammed over hers.

Rachel lifted onto her toes and met him head-on. His tongue surged into the dark, wet cave of her mouth, tangling with hers, thrusting in a demand to conquer. But Rachael refused to surrender, pressing her breasts against his chest, hooking her leg around his hips so he stumbled forward, ripping his mouth from hers with a vicious curse. "The ultimate tease," he taunted, lips damp.

"Shut up and do what you do best."

Their mouths fused again, and she ripped at the buttons on his shirt. He slid his big hands under the twisted hem of her blouse, cupping her breasts, unhooking her bra with one deft snap of his thumb. And then he was rubbing and tweaking her hard nipples, swallowing her throaty cries of need as his knee pressed hard against her aching center. Rachael became a wild animal, needy for more, stroking the hard muscles of his chest, dipping down under his slacks to cup his straining erection, her teeth sinking deep into his lip while she teased and punished in her own way.

And she was dragged back to that one fateful night, the hot summer by the lake that changed everything.

Aspen sighed with satisfaction. "Isn't hate sex the best? Okay, does anyone have questions?"

A stunned silence fell over the room.

Ah, fuck.

An hour later, Aspen felt her smile wobble as the event drew to a close. Thankfully, she was back to her regular self, and that amazing, floaty, happy sensation had been replaced by another less positive one.

Dread.

She'd read a sex scene to a nice crowd on a Sunday afternoon. If anyone had brought kids, would she have gotten sued? It was as if she'd been viewing herself through a filter, watching but unable to control anything. Another deeper part of her admitted the awful truth.

She'd liked not giving a crap.

It was fun to just get in front of people and not care what she said. The free-fall giddiness reminded her of when she was deep into writing a scene she loved, and all her senses were completely connected to her mind, body, and soul. Like riding the carousel as a kid, the wind whipping in her hair as she went around and around, up and down, caught in the tinny, magical carnival music and the possibility of her horse detaching and riding off into the world while she clutched its painted mane.

Yeah, maybe she was still high.

"I loved *Fifty Ways to Leave Your Lover*," the woman said, clutching her book like a well-loved child. "I read it a million times. Do you think there will ever be a sequel?"

"I may be working on that right now," she offered, glancing at her sticky note and scribbling Cassandra's name in black Sharpie. "I'm so happy you loved the book. Have you read the other two yet?"

"Not yet. I'm so busy, but I know this one will be wonderful, too."

Aspen held back a sigh, recognizing the familiar excuse. The woman wouldn't read the new book. Once again, she was too obsessed with her original. Half her readers didn't like the other books because they differed from *Fifty Ways.* The other half didn't want to read anything that wasn't the original characters from her first book. Maybe her agent was right. This sequel would drag everyone back to her fictional world, and maybe she'd get another shot at showing her audience that she could write other stories. "Totally understand. Here, take a pen. It was lovely to meet you."

"You, too. Um, one other thing. I didn't realize you were with Brick Babel." A gleam of envy and admiration flickered in her dark eyes. "Are you moving here permanently?"

Here we go. This was the third woman today who'd taken it upon herself to warn Aspen about the wicked Brick Babel. "No. I'm just visiting my sister."

She glanced over at the object of their discussion. He was sucking all the air from the room, leaning against the shelf, head down. Masculine energy swarmed around him and gave off pheromones to any female nearby. Coal-black hair mussed, worn denim cupping his tight ass, biceps braced as he focused on flipping through the pages of a book. Was that hers? Her stomach tightened at the idea of him looking to find the sex scenes now that she'd given him a taste.

Cassandra cleared her throat. "I don't want to seem rude or speak out of turn, but please be careful. He dated my cousin, Michelle, and she hasn't been the same since."

Aspen couldn't help being fascinated. Had Brick dated a different woman each night? It didn't seem that he could get around to so many in such a small coastal town. "I thought he stuck to tourists," she ventured.

"He switched up once enough of us locals began sharing information," Cassandra said. "Eventually, the women he hurt formed a support group."

Aspen blinked. "There's a Brick Babel support group?"

Cassandra nodded. "They try to warn susceptible women who don't know about his reputation. Members meet every other Sunday. It's a safe place. You're welcome to join…afterward."

She didn't know whether to laugh or cry over this new fact, so she just thanked her and finished with the last two readers.

Table clear, room half-emptied, she quickly calculated that she'd sold twelve new books and signed twenty-two reader copies of *Fifty Ways*. She thought wistfully of the whirlwind year when bookstores didn't have enough room for customers and demand for her presence swept the US. Hitting the number-one slot on the *New York Times* was a true fairy tale. The real problem?

Aspen had never considered that the glory would eventually end.

Now, she realized there was no guarantee of repeated success, and here she was chasing the hit years later. Somehow, she'd lost her value of writing a good story and the quiet satisfaction and pride of reaching the end. All of it had morphed into a messy ball of icky emotions from envy and sadness to frustration. Finally writing the sequel could be exactly what she needed to exorcise the demons and reclaim her mojo. God knew she missed the young girl who scribbled for hours in a room alone, chasing the story. Those were the times she was the happiest.

Aspen pushed the disturbing thoughts aside and thanked Ursula. She tried not to apologize for selling such limited quantities and reminded herself that tons of authors were grateful for even one purchase. Beating herself up wouldn't help her muse when she tried to write later today.

Marco came over with her new book clutched in his hand. "Aspen, that was amazing! Can you sign my book?"

"You don't have to buy it, Marco."

He looked offended. "I want to. I loved the scene you read. You're such a badass. Are you feeling…better?"

She laughed. "Yeah, but I wasn't feeling that bad an hour ago, either."

"I'm so sorry, Aspen. I fucked up. I never would've given you the brownie if I thought you didn't know."

She waved a hand in the air. "It's okay, I'm not mad." She took the book and scrawled a short message with her signature. "Thanks for babysitting me."

He glanced over his shoulder. "Brick is pissed. I never saw him so protective over a girl before. He really likes you."

Startled, she lifted her gaze.

And crashed straight into Brick's.

Book lowered, those baby blues were trained intensely on her face as if checking to see if she was okay. A blush threatened when she thought about him listening to her read that sensual scene. His eyes darkened as if catching her thoughts, and his lower lip quirked in amusement. A shiver raced down her spine when she thought of those lips over hers, coaxing, teasing, demanding.

Dragging in a breath, Aspen broke away from the intense stare and returned the book to Marco. "Um, yeah, we're still getting to know each other."

Her sister appeared, arms crossed in front of her chest. She looked like the typical older sibling ready to rip her apart. "What was going on with you today?" Sierra asked. "I swear, it was like you were on something."

Both she and Marco winced. "Was it that noticeable?"

"To me? Yes. You were giggly and unfocused and…oh, my God, that scene you read? I mean, it was hot and well-written, but Brooklyn's grandma was here, and her eyes got so wide I thought they'd pop out of her head."

"Bet she bought a book," Marco said. Sierra gave him a hard stare, and his shoulders dropped. "I'd better go check on Brick."

Sierra watched his retreat with suspicion. "He's involved. He and his crew are always smoking weed at the T-shirt place and—" She broke off, noticing Aspen's guilty look. "You. Did. Not."

"Not on purpose. I ate a brownie and didn't know."

"How could you not know? Did he drug you? Did Brick? Let me know, and I'll go kick their asses so hard—"

"No!" A half laugh escaped at her sister's warrior expression. "I swear, it was just an honest mistake. I bet I'll find the whole thing hysterical tomorrow. Tell me the truth. Besides the reading, did I do anything else bad?"

Some of the tension left her sister's body. "You rambled a little. And at one point, you were looking at the ceiling and trying to catch something, which weirded us out."

She groaned. "I kept seeing these little stars floating above everyone's head."

Sierra grinned. "Damn, you were tripping. I wish I'd videoed it to make fun of you later."

"You have enough blackmail material on me. You don't need any more."

"True. My fave is when you got drunk and vomited all over Slater's shoes when he came to pick you up for junior prom. You always sucked at pre-gaming. Should've known a little brownie would get the best of you."

Aspen sighed. "Why do you always have to bring that up?"

"'Cause it's fun." She jerked her head. "Going home with him or me?"

"Don't know. Did you realize there's a support group for women he's hurt?" Aspen whispered.

"Sure. I'd say be smart enough not to be a member, but I think that's exactly what you want. To write the book well. Right?"

Her sister made perfect sense. She nibbled her lip. "Maybe I can interview them. Get a sense of how Brick works his magic."

"If that's what you need. He was looking out for you today, though. It was a new look for him."

She frowned. "What do you mean?"

Sierra shrugged elegantly. "He hovered. Stared at you the whole time as if trying to anticipate what you'd need. I don't know. It was kind of nice."

She didn't have time to process the statement because Brick was walking over with Marco. "I'll drive you back to grab your car," he said. "Are you ready?"

Her sister raised a brow, but Aspen ignored her. "Sure, let's go." She hugged her sister goodbye, and they headed out. "Buy something?"

Brick held up the bag. "Some new reading material."

"Thought you didn't read much."

"Oh, I want to read this now."

Aspen wanted to squirm with discomfort. Like signings, she preferred not to know the people reading her work. Brick would get a firsthand view of her brain, thoughts, and vulnerabilities. Hopefully, he wouldn't get around to reading it or quit after the first chapter. He may only want the CliffsNotes version of her.

Marco chattered nonstop about the signing and knowing someone famous. They dropped him off at the shop, but when Aspen moved to leave the car, Brick reached out and grasped her wrist. "You need to eat."

She tried to ignore the sizzle of heat running up her arm from his touch. It was so…cliché. "I'm good, I'll eat later."

"Nope. You didn't have any breakfast, and lunch was a pot brownie. I'm taking you to lunch."

"I can stop later."

"Now, Aspen. You look like you're ready to collapse."

She took in his determined expression and realized he was right. She was depleted from the whole day. Usually, with the toll on her energy, she slept hours after an event. Her stomach was a bit nauseous. "Okay. Somewhere quick, though. I need to write."

He nodded and drove to Sundogs. They grabbed a table, ordering two lemonades, a crab cake sandwich, and a burger. Jimmy Buffet sang from the speakers, and the casual beach vibe relaxed her. She sipped the tart liquid and regarded him across the table. "I'm waiting."

Brick cocked his head. "For what?"

"To be yelled at. Or taunted. I know I said some things to embarrass myself. Take your best shot."

He only grinned. "Honestly? You were great at the signing. Made everyone laugh and feel connected. I always thought those things were boring as hell, but you proved me wrong."

They were good at banter, so she'd expected to trade barbs. A warm rush of pleasure flowed through her from the compliment. "Sierra said I giggled, was unfocused, and shocked everyone by reading a sex scene."

Those massive shoulders lifted. "So what? It entertained and got people to buy the book."

Aspen analyzed the statement, poking for any judgment, but none was there. "Is that why you bought it?"

"No. I'm curious to know how you see the world."

The comment threw her off, but their food came, and she dove in with gusto. The remaining fogginess dissipated, and her body clicked back into place. "Did you know there's a support group for women you broke up with?"

He winced. "I was hoping it was just gossip."

"Nope. Cassandra said her cousin was devastated after dating you.

Do you remember her?"

Brick ate a fry, not seemingly concerned. "Meredith?"

"No, Michelle."

"Oh, yeah. Please don't tell me she's in the group."

Aspen had gotten a salad with her sandwich and kept getting distracted by his fries. Sensing her greedy stare, he pushed his plate to the middle, adding more ketchup. Aspen swiped a fry and enjoyed the salty crispness. So much better than a salad. "Cassandra said she is."

Brick shook his head. "You gotta be kidding me. I had one date with her."

"Must've been a multiple-orgasm date."

His brows snapped into a frown, and that mouth firmed with displeasure. He was sexy, even when pissed. "I didn't sleep with her. Took her to dinner, heard about her desire to be married like her sister, and drove her straight home. I didn't even kiss her goodnight."

Aspen paused in the act of stealing another fry. "Oh, wow. It's the magical pussy challenge, I think."

Brick choked on a sip of lemonade and regarded her with wide eyes. "What the hell did you say?"

She grinned. "It's a big trope in romance, but it also exists in the real world. Basically, women fall for a guy who's unavailable and believe they can change him. It's pretty heady stuff."

"What type of term is that? I've never heard it."

"Why would you? We hope that once you have physical contact with us or great sex, you'll suddenly want to change your ways because we're the one. The one who gets to tame you and win you for marriage or love or whatever."

"Because you have a magical pussy."

She grinned smugly. "Exactly."

"Is there such a thing as a magical dick?"

A laugh broke from her. "Not that I know of. It's usually the men who are running."

Suddenly, a shadow flickered over his face. In seconds, Aspen caught a flash of pain in those ocean-blue depths, but it was gone so quickly she wondered if it had been a trick of the light. "Sounds about right."

Aspen wanted to probe but wasn't sure what to ask. His reputation was legendary. No way it was created by innocent women sharing some exaggerated gossip. "You're not going to argue that all the women are lying about being hurt by you, right?"

He wiped his mouth with a napkin and leaned back in the booth. A charged silence settled over the table. "No. I'm saying it became easier to lean into the gossip and make me the villain at some point."

"So, there's truth to some of the stories?"

"Yep."

"Which part?"

A slow, smug grin curved his lips, flashing white teeth. She caught her breath at the bold confidence in his gaze as it swept over her and heated. "Guess."

Her nipples hardened, and her belly dropped. She forced a laugh. "I don't want to know."

Brick regarded her with laser focus. Her skin prickled in response. "But you will. Very soon."

The spit dried up in her mouth at the sensual threat, and all Aspen could think about was being able to kiss and touch him without stopping. Of tumbling into bed with all that naked male glory pressed against her, unchecked, uninhibited, and…wild. Would sex with Brick allow her to tap into the part of herself she'd lost after Ryan? Could she reconnect with the emotional side and breathe new life into her characters? Would being vulnerable and getting her heart broken by this man unlock the key to a bestseller?

She needed to find out. It was too late to back out of her plan. But to get there, she needed to open up to him.

"You're thinking way too hard, Aspen." His tone teased her out of the spiral. "Finish the fries, and I'll take you home. It's been a long day."

She opened her mouth to push back, then realized he was right. She needed to rest her overactive brain and figure some things out. Aspen ate a few more fries. Brick paid the bill and then drove her home.

"Did you talk to Sierra about us? She seemed less intent on destroying me today," he said teasingly as he walked her to the door.

"Yeah, we had a fight, made up, and now she's agreeable."

"I think it was nice that she was trying to protect you," he said. "Always wished I had a sibling to lean on after losing my mom."

She caught the flare of vulnerability in his gaze and ached to touch him. She clenched her fingers into fists to keep from reaching out to comfort him. Brick gave her a quick, gentle kiss on the lips and smiled. "I'll see you tomorrow."

She nodded and went inside. Sierra wasn't home, so she went to her bedroom and powered up her laptop. Dragging it to the bed, Aspen propped up some pillows and began to write. She played with ideas for her heroine, but over and over, she kept cycling back to the hero.

An isolated, slightly grumpy, sexy man who lived alone on the beach, spending his time with the wild horses. A man who crushed hearts too easily until he met the heroine—a free-spirited writer from New York who changed everything. Suddenly, he was the one whose heart got stolen, taken by a woman who never intended to stay. The one who brought a bittersweet sense of karma to a single summer that would heal her and destroy him.

Aspen chewed her lip. And wrote. Fingers on fire, the new story formed in jagged pieces, based on Brick, his past exploits, and the one woman who could change him.

The magical pussy trope struck again. But this time, it was bigger, deeper, a sprawling story of two souls that would change each other in one idyllic summer in the Outer Banks. Fact mingled with fiction. It was a story Aspen was living, but instead of focusing on the heroine, she realized it was the hero's tale. Told mostly from his POV, it would be different from anything else she'd written yet still familiar.

Brick was the key.

She wrote until she collapsed onto the pillows, exhausted. And fell asleep with a smile on her face.

Chapter Twelve

Brick placed the book down on the nightstand. His mind spun as he tried to make sense of the world he'd just left, one Aspen had dreamed up to offer an escape for others to enjoy.

She was a great writer.

His finger tapped the hard edge of the cover. He wasn't a big reader, but she'd cleverly hooked his attention from page one, spinning a romance story within the bittersweet edges of reality. Her voice still rang in his head, and Brick had been able to weave together some pieces of her personality by sifting through the clues.

Aspen was a romantic but didn't like to admit it. Her writing had a sense of dreaminess to it as if she finally allowed herself to be seen because she was safe using fiction as her shield. When she spoke, she was no-nonsense and downplayed her softer self. He wasn't sure why this release wasn't as big a hit as her first, but he intended to read *Fifty Ways to Leave Your Lover* next. He wanted to start with her newest to get a solid comparison.

After all, he was key to her next book.

Rising from his bed, he got ready for the day and drove to his shop. It had been a few days since they'd gotten together. The renovations were in full swing, and he'd spent yesterday shopping for a new Jeep. Aspen had dropped into the writing cave, which was a good thing, so he hadn't wanted to interrupt.

But it was time to move further in this relationship. Even though the deal was ridiculous, Brick wasn't comfortable taking her money and not accomplishing his goal. Reading her book would help him narrow in on what she wanted in a relationship, but he needed more quality time with her.

She'd agreed to join him on his run to check on the horses. Even without a tour, Brick liked to keep the familiarity of his route on a schedule. The horses had become family, and he cared about each one. Judy was also babysitting a new sea turtle nest, so maybe he'd connect with her and see if he could help.

Brick spoke with Sal and the team, who confirmed the reno would be done by next week. Losing two weeks at the height of the summer wasn't ideal, but he'd still have the rest of the season to make up for lost funds. Marketing may be a problem since he'd passed most print deadlines, but he'd come up with an alternate plan.

Aspen pulled into the lot, parked, and walked toward him. She wore denim shorts with a ragged hem, a pink T-shirt, and white sneakers. Her hair was caught in a ponytail, allowing those wild curls to escape randomly. Oversized sunglasses hid her gaze as she stopped in front of him. His body lit to attention. Something about this woman called to him and reading her book had buried her voice in his head.

Brick realized something else at that moment.

He'd missed her.

"Hey," she said. "How're renovations going?"

"Great. Right on schedule, so I can reopen in a week."

"Impressive. And you got the Jeep?" she asked.

"I did. We're breaking it in today. How's the writing?"

"Good." She hesitated, lips pursed, but she didn't say anything else. "I may have pushed through a block."

Amusement cut through him. She seemed half in this world and half in the other. Brick figured there was one way to get her focused on the moment. "Aspen."

"Hmm?"

He slowly reached out, hooked his fingers into her belt loops, dragged her forward, then slid her sunglasses up to rest on top of her head.

Those golden-brown eyes were wide with surprise and a fiery heat that made satisfaction flow through him. "I didn't get my hello kiss."

She blinked. Her pupils dilated. A shaky breath escaped her pink lips. "Oh. Right." Hesitantly, she laid her hands on his chest, tilted her head, and waited.

He stared at her tempting mouth and enjoyed the slight tremble of her body against his. She was adorable, standing still for his kiss like a well-behaved pupil. That wouldn't fly. Aspen needed to be challenged on all fronts if she was to keep falling for him and keeping her engaged in his company was a priority.

Brick stayed silent, studying her now-confused expression.

"Well?" she asked.

His lip quirked. "Figured it'd be nice if you kissed me first."

She actually blushed, which only turned him on more. Drawing in a breath, she pressed her lips to his in a full-mouth, properly sweet kiss. "Hi."

He tamped down a laugh and frowned. "That wasn't very enthusiastic. Why don't you try again? This time, open your mouth so I can taste you."

Irritation stamped her features. "I don't need kissing lessons," she muttered.

"Then show me what you got," he challenged, drawing her up higher so she was on her tiptoes, thigh to thigh, hip to hip. The scent of orange blossoms filled his nostrils. "Would you write about a kiss like that for your readers?"

"No. But you're not one of my readers."

Brick flashed a grin. "I'm research, baby. And the man who'll be in your bed very soon."

Her nails dug into his muscles. "You're so arrogant," she ground out.

"I'm confident. Now kiss me like I've been on your mind for the past few days. Make me believe it."

A beat passed. The tension squeezed between them as their gazes locked. He was hard and aching to taste her, but damned if he'd move before she did. "Like I've been on yours?" The question mocked, but Brick sensed vulnerability underneath. She knew he was contracted to seduce her, after all. He needed to show her that their physical chemistry had nothing to do with their bargain. Then she'd begin to open up.

"You have, Aspen."

He absorbed the slight shudder and the flash of anger in her eyes. And then she reached up, wrapped her arms around his shoulders, and kissed him.

Her soft lips felt like heaven, molded to his. He groaned as her tongue slipped through to touch his, growing more daring as she opened wider and tangled hers with his, allowing him to be pulled deeper into the kiss. He captured her sigh, sliding his hands to cup her denim-clad ass and drag her higher against him. The sun beat down, and he lost himself in her sweetness, enjoying how she clung tightly, surrendering completely to the embrace that held no games, no lies, and no more teasing.

He eased away slowly, nipping her bottom lip and savoring the last essence of her taste. A slow smile curved his lips. "Much better."

She half-snorted. "Didn't realize you were into PDA."

"Depends on my patience. Don't have any issues with people seeing how badly I want you. Ready to roll?"

She nodded, her cheeks hot. He took her hand and led her to the Jeep. The bright yellow was an eye catcher, with comfortable-sized seats and soft leather. "This is beautiful. How did you move so fast?" she asked, running a hand over the sleek hood.

He winced. "Had my eye on this exact model for months. My action plan has been ready to launch, I was just waiting on the funds. Losing two weeks of summer isn't ideal, but I'll be able to salvage the rest and have a cushion. Thanks to you."

"I'm glad we can help each other." He noticed that she seemed uneasy, whereas before, she was almost businesslike in her approach to hiring him. In a way, Brick admitted it was a good thing. Much easier to be distant when you didn't care. There were signs she was softening to him, which would automatically raise her defenses.

Was it wrong to feel regret that he'd promised to bring pain?

He shook off the disturbing thought. It was all worth it to save Grandpa Ziggy's dream. It wasn't as if he was doing anything to Aspen on purpose. He needed to keep his head in the game.

He got the Jeep ready, and she buckled in beside him. "Did you put on sunscreen?"

She smiled. "Yes. Even extra on my large nose."

Brick laughed and tugged on an escaped curl. "I like your nose. It has character."

She wrinkled the part in question. "Now I caught you in a lie. I was always jealous of Sierra's looks over mine. Typical sibling rivalry."

He pulled out onto the road. "I always wondered if women looked at beauty differently than men. Sure, there's a classic type the world recognizes. But mostly, it's about chemistry."

"Like when men say it's all about personality, then hit on the blonde bombshell at the bar?"

Brick grinned. "Yeah, that happens a lot. But most of the guys I hang with admit the real stuff is because of the connection. Take your sister. You would've been the one I'd hit on, not her."

She gave a feminine snort. "Riiight."

"I mean it. Sierra's beautiful, but you have an intensity I was drawn to. When you first approached me at the bar? I liked your directness and the way you looked at me."

"Like you pissed me off?" she teased.

"Like you wanted me."

He heard her sharp intake of breath. Brick remembered when he'd first touched her and how the ripple of awareness had taken him by surprise. The way her golden-brown eyes flashed fire and tempted him to linger, rather than try to save her from him.

"Sierra said she made a move on you, but you refused."

"I knew Sierra wanted a distraction. There was nothing real between us."

She chewed at that lower lip as she sifted through his words. "It's not real with us either."

"Yes, it is." He shot her a look. "Fact with fiction, remember? No way I can kiss you like that without real feelings. Just like you can't write a great book without true emotion."

Her obvious surprise satisfied him. Reading her work had granted him a deeper look into the places she only shared on the page. He wouldn't tell her that, though. He wanted to read *Fifty Ways to Leave Your Lover* before he was ready to probe and lower some of her walls. It was the key to moving forward in their relationship.

They bumped up and over the dunes and the ocean came into view, wild and free under a blue umbrella sky. The salt air filled his lungs and took him down a few levels to an inner peace. This past year, Brick realized that each time he came out, another fragment of him settled. He wondered if those old dreams of making his mark in the business world would finally disintegrate and leave him free, like Grandpa Ziggy. Maybe it wasn't a bad life, after all.

Maybe it was the life he'd always needed.

The Jeep danced over the sand, and they came up to the protected barriers of the sea turtles. Judy was out, crouched over the markers. Brick neared her and called out. "Everything okay?"

The older woman had short, red hair with Irish skin, freckles, and serene green eyes. She was dressed in her usual uniform of a brightly colored T-shirt and cargo shorts. A fanny pack encircled her generous hips. "Hi, Brick. Ran into a snag. Had an issue with some of the eggs so need to watch them overnight. I'm short volunteers today and taking care of my granddaughter. Can't bring her with me since she's under the weather. Got a nasty cold."

He looked down at the sand covering the precious cargo. Judy's group worked tirelessly to keep the babies safe from predators. He scratched his head. "I can do it tonight."

Judy brightened. "Really? You're a lifesaver. Can you bring a partner with you?"

He turned to Aspen. "Wanna pull an all-nighter with me?" he asked in a sexy voice.

She laughed. "I'd love to help. As long as you know what to do."

"Brick knows the drill, but I like to have two at a time out here. Thanks again. Text me if you have any questions." She gave a low whistle. "Sorry, just noticed you're in a fancy new Jeep. Are you finally doing those renovations?"

"Yep. Should be done next week. I'm doing a blitz. Trying to drum up more business."

Sympathy flared in her green eyes. "I hear you. Local businesses can be tough. We're struggling lately with funding and volunteers, even though it's the height of summer."

"I'll put out the word."

"Thanks again, Brick."

He waved and continued down the beach. "I didn't know you helped out with the sea turtles," Aspen commented.

Brick shrugged. "I help out anywhere I'm needed. Locals try to stick together. Judy's been heading her nonprofit for years, but sometimes it's hard. Economy, tourism, what's hot and what's not in today's culture. We all take turns feeling the pinch."

"Must be nice to feel like part of a community who cares about one another."

"Yeah, it is." He'd been resentful since taking over Grandpa Ziggy's place, forced to live a life he hadn't planned. After the Anastasia debacle, he'd sunk deeper into his isolation, which only helped fuel gossip in the small town. But lately, Brick wondered if he'd been so focused on what he didn't get that he'd missed out on opportunities he *could* have. "Do you have a writer's group where you get support?"

She shook her head. "I'm a loner," she admitted. "My agent reads everything first, and I work with publicity teams and editors, but I'm not close with other writers." Shadows flickered over her face. She seemed to pick her next words carefully. "I didn't realize there was support out there if I'd just asked. I got used to pushing through alone."

"Sounds familiar."

Their gazes met and understanding passed between them. Brick longed to probe the secrets she hid. It was the first time he'd wanted to strip a woman emotionally in addition to physically. He wasn't sure how to handle the strange urge, so he broke away and focused on the twisty path leading to the beach houses.

Brick spotted the small band of horses pressed together, chomping sea grass, and pointed them out to Aspen. "Are they related?" she asked.

"No, but they're a makeshift family and just as tight. Some like the herd, and others like to be the lone wolf."

"Like Duncan?"

He grinned. "Absolutely. We'll circle back and find my friend to gauge his mood today."

Brick did the rounds through the dunes and pricey homes to play a game of Where's Waldo. Counting in his head, he made sure everything looked good and noticed the tracks were light today. Maleficent hadn't gone out, so this was the first round of the day. He squinted at the sun, which was high and clear, but weather was expected later.

He gave Aspen some additional background on the various horses as he searched. Duncan wasn't behind his favorite pillar, so he checked his usual haunts. After retracing his route, Brick's gut twinged with a warning. Where was Duncan?

"Has he disappeared before?" Aspen asked.

"Sure, but we've been to all the places he'd be. Unless he's under another garage. I'll circle back to the main dunes by the beach and see if he's taking a swim."

Duncan wasn't there.

"Should we call someone?" she asked hesitantly. "Who's in charge if something goes wrong?"

"I can call it in to the Corolla Wild Horse Fund, but I'd feel like an ass if Duncan just found a new resting spot. Let me do one more round. If you don't mind."

"Of course, not."

The Jeep climbed the dunes, and Brick went farther in, past the main houses and into the more isolated area where Duncan rarely went. His gaze swept expertly, probing all the spots the mustang would love and caught a flash of a brown mane. Slowing the vehicle, he squinted to make out the outline of a horse half hidden behind a column. "There. He's lying down." It was rare for the mustang to lie prone during the prime afternoon hours. Unless he craved deep sleep, Duncan preferred to stand. That same warning bell rose inside. "I'm going to check on him. Stay here."

He climbed out of the Jeep and approached carefully. As he got closer, he saw the horse was flat on his side, eyes open, breathing hard. Brick kept his distance, making sure he wasn't just interrupting dreamtime. "Hey, Duncan. How are you, boy? Everything good?" His voice was low and soothing as he knelt to study the magnificent wild creature. He rarely had an opportunity to be so close since he'd never encountered any trouble on his runs. But something felt different now.

And then he saw it.

Brick sucked in his breath and muttered a vicious curse. The rinds of a watermelon lay a few feet to the side of Duncan, obviously chewed up and ingested.

Fuck.

One of the most important rules drilled into tourists and guides was the danger of feeding the horses. They subsisted on a diet of wild foods, and anything like carrots, apples, or watermelons could seriously damage them.

Slowly, he eased closer to Duncan. The horse was panting but didn't seem to be choking. "It's okay, buddy. I'm gonna get you some help. Hang in there."

He grabbed his phone and dialed the Corolla Wild Horse Fund, explaining the problem. Snapping a few photos of the horse, he described Duncan's condition and forwarded them over. He was given permission to do some basic checks while he waited for the vet. Even trained guides were limited to touching and interacting with the mustangs, and Brick didn't want to make things worse.

He kept his energy calm, speaking to the horse as he completed a few simple first-aid tasks. Not wanting to leave Duncan, he texted Aspen and let her know the vet was coming and told her to stay in the vehicle.

Duncan managed a pissed-off snort. "Don't worry, buddy. I'm going to find the idiot who fed this to you and make sure it doesn't happen again." Their gazes met, and Brick's heart ached at the banked pain in the horse's big, brown eyes. He tamped down his anger, knowing the horse didn't need his negative energy right now, and talked to him until the vet arrived.

The doctor was brusque yet kind as she examined Duncan. "He doesn't have anything stuck in his throat, and that was my main worry. He's probably got some nausea from the food you found. I gave him some meds, but I think the best plan is to watch him carefully and wait it out. If he gets worse, I'll need to take him offsite, and Duncan won't be able to return."

Frustration coursed through him. Brick was always happy when a life was saved, but the horses were already at a limited number, and once they needed to transition for vet care, they couldn't come back home. Wild was wild. If Duncan left, he'd finish his years at a farm but could never be truly free again. "Understood. Can I stay and wait with him?"

The doctor nodded. "He seems comfortable with your presence. If we're lucky, he didn't eat much, and it will pass through him."

Brick prayed luck was on Duncan's side.

He returned to the Jeep and filled Aspen in. "I'll take you back so I can spend the rest of the day with Duncan."

She touched his arm, and his muscles jumped under her touch. "Will you call me as soon as you know?"

"Of course."

He was quiet on the ride to the office but found comfort in her hand over his. When she climbed out, a worried frown creased her brow. "Is there anything I can do to help?"

"No, but I promise to call. I'll confirm with Judy on what time tonight, if you're still up for it."

"Definitely." She stroked the hair from his brow in a gentle gesture. "Duncan's going to be okay. I feel it."

"Thanks."

She walked away, and Brick returned to the beach, hoping she was right.

Aspen walked into her sister's store. Flirt was situated in one of the small strips off the main road in Duck, squashed between a café and a toy store. The main boardwalk and shops that lined the water were across the street, but the location was still prime since many tourists walked the strip and could easily cross to check out the colorful window displays.

Aspen let out a breath as the warm, feminine energy swirled around her, the air scented with a faint hint of lavender. The shop was filled with unique clothing, jewelry, and accessories with a beach vibe. There were no cheap T-shirts or mugs here. Instead, shelves displayed delicate perfume bottles, jewelry boxes, and candles. Artwork by local artists was strategically placed on the walls. Everywhere she looked, something grabbed her eye, whether it was a bold color, a glittery stone, or something with quiet elegance. Each item had a place to serve a shopper's impulsive ways and wandering gaze. Sierra had always been a master at décor, and her store throbbed with her essence of classic beauty, craftmanship, and a dash of fun.

Aspen watched her sister chat with a customer, expertly guiding her to a rack of clothes to present a gorgeous blue beach dress embroidered with delicate lace. Plucking a few other items and putting them together, Sierra set the woman up in a fitting room, then caught sight of her.

"Hey. Thought you were writing today."

Aspen smiled and made her way to the counter. Immediately, a rack of beaded bracelets caught her eye, and she picked up a pale-pink one with a seashell in the center. "I just left Brick's, and I'm kind of freaking out. I wanted to see you before I tried to get in the headspace to write. How much is this?"

"You get a family discount, so ten bucks."

"Nice, put it aside for me."

Sierra dropped the jewelry into a little box. "Uh-oh, what happened? Did you fight? Or have sex?"

Aspen glared. "Neither. We went on a run to see the horses, and he found one that was sick. Duncan. It's his favorite horse."

Sierra looked stricken. "Do you know what was wrong?"

"Someone left a watermelon out for food. He didn't choke, but I guess he had a reaction."

"Tourist bastards," Sierra muttered. "Last year, we lost a foal who choked on an apple. We were in mourning for a while, and Brick took it hard. Those horses are part of our heritage here, and their numbers are decreasing. Did he call the foundation?"

She nodded. "The vet came right out. They don't want to take him away or he can't come back, so Brick's keeping watch to see if Duncan can rally. It's so damn sad."

"And frustrating. Good for Brick. He takes his job seriously. Once, he ran off a group of kids who were hiding apples and trying to get close. He probably saved some horses."

Aspen thought of his face when he came back from Duncan. Yes, there was worry, but it was the actual pain in his eyes that'd riveted her, the obvious love he had for the animals that were part of his job. She'd caught a hidden side to him that touched her. Hearing her sister's story confirmed he also had an assured confidence in handling emergencies. "He said he'd call with an update later. I'm supposed to meet him for a turtle watch tonight."

Sierra cocked her head. "Another Judy recruit, huh? Sometimes, she's a little protective with the eggs and likes to have all shifts covered. Bet you scored the midnight to four watch."

"I don't mind."

Sierra studied her face, then smiled. "Stay here. Take a look at the matching earrings, you may want them, too."

"You have no pride trying to profit from family."

"Correct. You made me buy your last book, and that was plain mean."

"I needed the extra sale." Sierra stalked off to check on her customer while Aspen grabbed the matching earrings and a cool scarf with smudged sunset colors melded together. Why did Brick keep throwing her off? Was this why women fell for him so quickly? The intriguing combination of male sexuality with a hidden, tender heart? And the way he'd gotten her to kiss him this morning? So. Hot. Her belly fluttered when she thought about those teasing blue eyes locked on hers, lips quirked as he waited for her to make the move.

Aspen admitted she was starting to fall. In only two weeks, he'd begun to haunt not only her dreams but also her thoughts. She looked forward to seeing him in a way that went beyond the physical. And writing this new book brought him to the forefront as she tried to gather clues he gave in their interactions to carry back to her story.

Aspen tried to remind herself that Brick was playing for high stakes. She'd literally banked her last book advance with plans for a lavish European trip, so she'd been able to skip a loan and pay for whatever he needed with cash. Brick had forwarded a meticulous spreadsheet with vendors, contacts, schedules, breakdowns of each cost, and final totals. The bulk went to the renovations and new Jeep, along with fixing up and detailing the second Jeep. The final portion was earmarked for marketing purposes, which he was still tweaking. It was straightforward, and though expensive, she respected the transparency and insistence on her knowledge of every step to show where the money was going.

Aspen was blessed to have a viral book. She'd made most of her money on the advances, though her second and third book hadn't earned out. Other than her apartment, health insurance, and retirement, she wasn't a huge spender. Plus, Brick insisted it was a loan, with interest. The deal she'd struck with him was fair. She wanted Ziggy's Tours to succeed.

And Brick.

Sierra popped back out, rang up the customer's purchase, and returned to Aspen. "Was going to invite you out with Brooklyn and Inez. They're dying for an update. How about tomorrow after your all-nighter?"

"Sure, I'd love to see them and hang out."

"So, how serious has it gotten with Brick? There's been kissing. Any under-the-clothes foreplay?"

Aspen groaned. "Not yet, Miss Nosy. Actually, I'm not even sure there's a place for us to have sex. I'm with you, and his friend moved in with him temporarily."

Her brow lifted. "Who's the friend?"

"I forgot his name. Hey, maybe he's cute and single."

"Worth a peek. I have a date Friday night. Some guy who wandered into the store looking for a surfboard. We did some flirting, and he asked me to go out for margaritas and Mexican. He was cute."

"Nice. I could never meet a man, even in a damn bookstore. You can close a deal in seconds anywhere."

"I never closed Brick."

She sighed. "I actually asked him about that. I think he liked and respected you, so he didn't want to muddy the waters with sex."

"A nice rejection, I guess. Usually, I'm good at first impressions but not staying power."

The pain was hidden, but Aspen caught it. She reached out and squeezed her hand. "You're meant to be with someone wonderful. And he'll be worthy of you and all you deserve. Okay?"

"Okay." They smiled at each other. "You know, I have this cute pink T-shirt that would look great with the matching bracelet and earrings."

"Bitch."

They laughed, and Aspen ended up buying the shirt.

A few hours later, she sat at her laptop and tried to write. She'd been making progress on the sequel, using Brick's POV as her main content for her fictional hero. Aspen liked to free write her first draft, not worried about the mess or inconsistencies since she believed in fixing that stuff later. Her plot was loose and allowed for surprises, which was her blueprint for writing. She always tried to counsel new writers not to worry about their process—too many worried about the right way to get to the end. Aspen believed in the no-rules philosophy, as long as you could get there. Knowing aspects of her personality had helped in the past, and she'd taken the Gallup Strengths test and worked with a counselor. Becca Syme was a genius in her field in helping writers understand their strengths and how to focus on them instead of the weaknesses. After *Fifty Ways* hit big, she'd struggled to find who she really was as a writer. Taking Becca's course *Write Better, Write Faster* had been a game changer.

Aspen figured her intellection strength was slowing her down, and she needed more time with Brick to dig deeper before she understood his character enough to write about it. Glancing at the clock, she worried about Duncan and hoped he was okay.

Abandoning her story, she turned to her happy place and took out her notepad. Falling easily into her *Zany Zoo* world, she composed a new story of Piggy and Purple Bunny taking a road trip and all the disasters that befell them. Sketching out the illustrations as she went, Aspen giggled as her pen flew like lightning over the pages. If only writing her book was this fun, she'd be so much more content.

She had over a dozen notebooks filled with stories and drawings she adored. It was like she took refuge in the characters, and the stories brought the joy she'd been missing over the past two books.

Her phone rang, and she snatched it up.

"Duncan's going to be okay."

Relief sagged her shoulders. "Brick, that's wonderful news. What happened?"

He sounded tired but pleased. "We probably got to him in time before he tried to finish the watermelon. Worked its way through his system, and now he's up and moving around again."

"You saved him."

"Nah, I got lucky. Any of the tour guides could have helped. I was just the one to find him first."

His humbleness was part of his nature, which she respected. "Are you still watching the turtles tonight? You must be exhausted."

"I'm good. Going to work with Sal in a bit and maybe grab a quick nap. Make sure you dress in layers and will be comfortable. Pick you up at midnight?"

"See you then."

She clicked off. She wondered when their nightly rendezvous would turn into more. More kissing. More touching. More…everything.

Aspen smiled and went back to work on *Zany Zoo.*

Chapter Thirteen

Aspen walked across the beach under the crescent moon. Beams of light fell and sparkled over the dark, quiet water. Stars streaked the night sky. They held flashlights as their feet crunched over the sand. Brick held her hand, strong fingers entangled with hers in a shocking sort of intimacy. What was it about holding hands that could make you feel more vulnerable than kissing? Maybe because kissing could be termed impulsive, and the other was a conscious choice.

She'd dressed in a hoodie, a T-shirt, and yoga pants. Brick towered over her in a similar outfit, except he wore jeans. They reached the markings for the turtles and did a perimeter check to see if there'd been any disturbances. Two beach chairs had been set out for them.

"We got lucky. Was supposed to rain," Brick commented.

"So, what's the big plan for tonight?"

White teeth flashed in the darkness. Her tummy did a slow roll as his thumb stroked her sensitive palm. Goose bumps broke out on her skin. "This. Us hanging out with the babies, keeping watch." His voice lowered to a sexy growl. "Maybe a make-out session later."

She laughed, but it came out high-pitched. Lord, why did he make her act like a shy virgin? "We gonna share scary stories so I'll jump into your arms and seek shelter from the monsters?" she teased.

"Once I tell you about the headless OBX killer, that might happen."

Aspen rolled her eyes. "I love scary movies, so that won't do. Those creepy crabs crawling over my bare feet may, though."

"Noted. I shall protect you from sea creatures."

"What type of predators are we looking out for?" she asked.

"Raccoons, birds, and those creepy crabs. After Judy's people mark the nests, they watch them for any disturbances. Any holes can harm the babies when they hatch, so we keep the sand smoothed out and shed as little light as possible. The journey to the water is hard to survive, so they need help."

"Oh, my God. What if they hatch tonight? What do we do?"

He grinned. "They're not hatching tonight, or the professionals would be here. They mark the incubation time. These turtles are loggerheads, so they have an estimated sixty days to hatch. It's too early to happen tonight, but late enough that Judy wants all shifts covered. We're at the forty-five-day mark." His face tightened. "And if we have any smart-ass stragglers out there feeding the horses, who knows if they'd disturb a nest for fun?"

"I'll never understand that type of cruelty."

"The sad part is most of them don't think it's cruel. Simple neglect for nature is just as bad as a sin."

Emotion washed over her as he spoke. Aspen was isolated from so much of the natural world, surrounded by concrete and technology, glass and steel. Being here was giving her a different perspective. A deeper connection to nature that brought a sense of wholeness.

She gestured to the tote bag slung over his shoulder. "What did you bring? I think I can go a few hours without snacks."

He snorted and dropped the bag onto the sand. "I can't. No need to suffer, even if we're working the night shift. Wanna see?"

"Sure."

He unzipped the bag. She couldn't help but notice the way the worn denim of his jeans cupped his perfect ass or the muscled lengths of his arms under his sweatshirt. Brick withdrew a plaid flannel blanket, a thermos with two metal cups, and a various assortment of chips and granola bars. "I didn't know what kind of chips you liked, so I brought them all. Sour cream and onion, plain, salt and vinegar, dill pickle, or barbeque." He looked up. "Which is it?"

She pressed her lips together to keep from laughing. This man had won the lottery. He went from sex on a stick to adorable boyish charmer. "Barbeque all the way."

His face lit up. "Me, too."

"What's in the thermos?"

"Hot cocoa with a touch of Kahlua for warmth. Can't let you freeze out here."

"It's like seventy-five degrees."

"I know. Chilly, right?"

She jerked her head. "What's that machine thing?"

"Ah, this is my secret weapon. No scary stories needed." He whipped out an oversized black boombox circa 1980s. But then it got more intense. Brick took out a stack of CDs and placed them on the blanket. "Music is essential during a night watch."

This time, she couldn't help but laugh, especially at his obvious pride in his bag of supplies. "Okay, I'm impressed," Aspen admitted. "You're moving closer to a make-out session."

"Told ya. Now that I know your chip flavor, what's your music taste? Take a look."

She sat on the chair and happily went through the pile, which contained a surprising variety. Foo Fighters, Metallica, Jimmy Buffet, Saint Motel, Matchbox Twenty, The Weeknd, Billy Joel, and many others. She hit pay dirt at the very last one. "You have Taylor Swift."

"Of course. She's a legend."

"This is amazing. Do you have vinyl at home?"

He shook his head. "Nah, I never got into being a true collector. There's just something about an old-school CD and boombox that's fun. You need to be more intentional about choosing what to listen to rather than randomly skipping through a thousand songs. I like the commitment."

She burst into laughter, and he seemed confused at her humor before the realization flickered over his face. Then he laughed with her. "I guess only with my music."

"Guess so." She was touched at how he'd thought out their time together, like it truly mattered. When the doubts crawled in, reminding her this was part of his payment plan, she shoved them to the side. It felt real in this moment, and that was all that mattered. "Music won't bother the nest?"

"No. They probably like it. What are we starting with?"

"We'll save Taylor. Let's go with Foo Fighters."

"Nice choice."

He popped in the CD, and the music streamed from the tinny speakers. They both scouted the area and filled in any holes they found, checking for any killer creatures that may sneak in on their watch. When all was clear, they sat side by side, staring at the ocean.

"You're quite the nature whisperer today," she said. "First Duncan, now the turtles. When you were back in New York, did you miss being out here? Because I feel like I'm in a different world, even in this short amount of time."

He poured the cocoa and handed her a cup. "Your sister's been here a while. Figured you'd feel like this was your second home."

She took a sip. The rich flavor held that delicious hint of Kahlua and made it dessert. "To be honest, I was never close with my brother-in-law, so I didn't visit much. And then, when they got divorced, Sierra came to me for long weekends."

"I'm sorry she went through that. From what I know about your sister, she's a good person."

Aspen nodded but wanted to question if he was also a cheater. The story about Anastasia proved he was just as bad, even cruel. The thought bothered her, but she'd been the one to seek him out. She had no right to judge when he never pretended to be anyone else. "It messed her up. I'm glad she stayed here, though. She built a life with friends and a successful business. A beautiful house. Sierra found her place."

"Is New York your place?"

She pondered the question and took another sip. "I always thought so, but I'm realizing I've never given another place a try. Us New Yorkers are pretty stubborn."

Aspen glimpsed a faint smile. Those powerful legs were stretched out in front of him, ankles crossed. The wind blew coal-black locks into a disarray that only made him look sexier. She had a terrible impulse to touch his hard jaw and smooth her fingers over his skin. It looked like he'd shaved. "Yes, we are. I've been thinking about it lately, especially now that I'm able to do the renovations. I spent a lot of time wishing Grandpa Ziggy hadn't stuck me with his tour company and house. I had my own dreams of staying in the city, wearing a three-piece suit, and chasing the money. It's what I went to college for and envisioned for my future. Each time I got close, I hit a block. But lately?" He shrugged. "I'm wondering if I landed exactly where I was supposed to be."

"Where did you work before this?" she asked curiously.

"Sales." His eyes flashed with the memory. She wished she could dig deeper and glimpse who he'd been back in New York. "I got my degree, got a job, and immediately started on my MBA. But my mom got sick, so I headed back home to take care of her." His face tightened. "It was a hard time, but being with her was worth everything."

"I'm so sorry," she said softly, reaching out to touch his arm.

His smile was fleeting. "Thanks. I miss her every damn day. Afterward, I went back to school and scored an internship at a financial investment firm. Met Kane there. He was already a big player in real estate properties. It was a fast world I thought suited me. I'd only worked there a year and a half before I got the call about Grandpa Ziggy. Now, I finally have an opportunity to save the business he built from scratch."

He recited his story with little emotion as if reading facts from a book. A man who quit school to take care of his sick mother and left everything behind to rebuild his grandfather's business didn't seem like a cheater. But there was too much gossip and shared tales to believe in his innocence.

How many hearts had he demolished before he returned to OBX? Where did Anastasia fit in? He never mentioned his ex-fiancée. Aspen pictured him in a custom suit, hitting bars at happy hour, the world open to his youth, attractiveness, and hunger for more. "Do you think you can make a profit with all these new investments?"

"Failure is not an option. No matter what I need to do, I'll make it a success."

"What do you do in the winter?"

"I have enough put aside from my savings. Last year, I worked as a bartender, which I enjoy. Did that to get myself through college. I run a few popular holiday tours with Santa, and a winter festival."

His gaze swung to hers, probing. Aspen stilled under his scrutiny. She got the impression he was ready to kick the focus back to her. "Tell me about your writing. After you turn in a book, what comes next?"

Aspen snorted. "Too much. I heard back in the good old days that all you had to do was write a book and work with your editor. Today, you immediately become the CEO of your business."

A frown creased his brow. She fought the urge to smooth the line with her fingers. "Doesn't the publisher do all that?"

"God, no. They're responsible for getting it out to distributors—bookstores, Amazon, Apple, Google, etcetera. They also do the audio for me and any foreign translations. They get the cover, do the edits, proofing, and printing. And sure, they definitely try to get media coverage and send the book out for early advanced reading and influencers. But there are millions of books out there and a lot of noise to cut through to grab readers' attention. If I was an indie author, I'd have to do all those tasks *plus* all the publicity. My trade-off is gaining lower royalty rates on each sale and losing my rights. It was worth it because I was lucky to get a hefty advance."

"Your first book hit big. Made you famous, right?"

She couldn't help the surge of pride when she thought about how her life had changed. From a broken heart, a year of total isolation and frantic writing, straight to landing an agent and a multi-million-dollar deal. Aspen had experienced a true Cinderella story. "Yes, it did. What happened to me was like hitting the lottery. Oh, sure, I wrote a great book—that's the foundation. But the stars aligned to create that moment in time for my book to get picked and resonate so deeply with readers. There are so many great books out there that never get the recognition they deserve. So much of it is random—some influencer picks it up, talks about it on social media, and suddenly you're going viral." She wrinkled her nose. "Unfortunately, you're only as good as your last book."

Curiosity lit his eyes. "Was there a book club or influencer that made the difference in it going viral?"

She smiled. "I like to say it was the perfect storm, where every good review or shout-out counted, but there were certain influencers who were next level. For example, @jens_toweringtbr, @2babesandabookshelf, @secretreadinglife, @megsbookclub, and @nurse_bookie created videos that made readers want to click. Jenny cried on camera. Kayleigh named the book her fave of the year. Sandra did these cute Reels, where she asked people if they'd read it, then fake-yelled at them to buy it now. Michelle created swag for readers to win in contests, and Megan started a reader support group because she was already begging for a sequel. Those were so authentic and real, the public responded."

"Amazing. I love how strangers were changed after reading your words." His focus on her face shredded her barriers, probing to see more than she usually showed. "What happened that made your first story so successful?"

Aspen couldn't help wincing, which he seemed to tuck away for future reference. Though it was a while ago, and she'd healed, talking about it was still hard. She decided to keep things simple. "I trusted someone I shouldn't and got my heart broken. A common human experience story."

"Don't." He said the word low, and surprise shot through her. Brick reached out and took her hand as naturally as if they'd been longtime lovers. "Don't pretend it was less just because it happened to others."

Emotion choked her throat. Her insides loosened as if he'd made room for her to share. "I guess you're right."

"Will you tell me about it?"

His question held respect and true intention. How long had it been since a man had looked at her with such care and focus? As if truly interested in the experiences that made her the woman she was today.

Not since Ryan. She wondered if she'd surrounded herself in Bubble

Wrap to ward off the pain that came with opening up again. Aspen had been so involved with her writing and career that it had been easy to ignore her love life. Being with Brick reminded her of other needs.

Both physical and emotional.

She spoke carefully. "I was a freshman in college. Went to a private school that focused on writing and combined a Master of Fine Arts degree. Ryan was my first professor in literature. He also taught in the creative writing program and was a published author. He was quite popular with the students."

"I bet," Brick muttered, obviously pissed.

A smile touched her lips. "I became his favorite student. He said I had talent and took me under his wing. It happened slowly, but I took all his classes, assisted him during office hours, and became completely enmeshed in his world. By junior year, we were having a full-blown affair and were in love. We kept it quiet due to his job and planned to get married after I graduated."

God, she'd been so young. So in love with him and the world he'd unveiled to her. "He began having some trouble getting his new book published, and that was when he started getting tough with me. My stories had more issues. He was more critical. We fought, and I started pulling back with my writing so I could help him. Finally, he announced a new book deal after I graduated, and we got engaged. Set a wedding date."

Brick remained silent, but his hand tightened on hers, offering support.

"I figured it would all magically work out once we got married. We'd both be writers and famous and rule the world as a power couple. I had no idea what was really happening. Or maybe I didn't want to know. He was sleeping with other students. I showed up on my wedding day with a church full of people and got a text that said he was sorry. He couldn't do it. He ran off with another student who he said was his true soulmate. She was also a friend of mine. And I never saw Ryan again."

Aspen didn't mention the space in between. The depression and spiral she fought through. How writing had saved her, and how she'd rediscovered her power through grief. But sitting next to Brick, protecting the baby turtles in the darkness, everything she confessed was safe. Yes, she'd given her story to the masses, but it was done on her terms.

"I'm sorry he took advantage of your trust," Brick said simply. "Did the asshole ever try to reach out after your book was published?"

She shook her head. "Never heard a peep. I didn't look him up online because I have no desire to know. It took me forever to convince

Sierra not to hire a private investigator and a hitman for a double discount."

He laughed, and she relaxed. Aspen was glad he didn't grill her; he just accepted what she decided to give him. "He was a predator, feeding on your talent and innocence in order to make himself feel better. Men like that are empty inside. Makes me sick."

"Agreed. Thanks for trashing him."

He grinned, and the mood lightened. The CD ended, and he got up to change it. The familiar strains of classic Billy Joel rang out, and she couldn't help but belt out a few lines of *Piano Man*. Brick joined her, and they finished their cocoa, trading karaoke lines that were more enthusiastic than talented.

He didn't take her hand again, and she missed the contact.

"Maybe I can help you with some marketing ideas," she offered when the song ended. "I'm always trying to drum up outside-the-box solutions. The whole blue ocean strategy is my bible."

He snapped his fingers. "Read that book in college. Find the blue waters outside the competition and put your marketing efforts there. Stop trying to compete in the red waters, where everyone is fighting for a share."

"Exactly! If Maleficent is your main competition, what niche could you fill that she can't?"

Brick took their empty mugs, dried them with a paper towel, and tucked them in the bag. "Been thinking about it. We have similar schedules: early morning, afternoon, and sunset. Same coupon and referral sales. It may be worth stretching my advertising reach. I stay local, but I was thinking of partnering with some businesses in the city to catch upcoming tourists."

She nodded. "Great idea. Who books tours the most out here?"

"Definitely families. I'm happy to try a sunset champagne run for couples, but it's the minority."

"How can you go after the kids? Anything to offer them?"

Brick rubbed his chin. "I could offer a treasure chest. Pick a prize. Maybe a pirate hunt, where they get something fun if they see a horse."

"Yes! The kids would love being involved."

Those blue eyes lit with a flare of excitement. "I can run some ads with that theme at popular kids' activities: bouncy houses, baseball fields, mini golf."

"Love it."

They nibbled on granola bars and chatted about other possible outlets, discussing how to craft the hooks to grab attention. It was similar to doing things for her books for Facebook and Instagram ads, so she had fun brainstorming back and forth.

The lilting strains of a piano filled the air, along with a husky voice singing about loving a woman just the way she was. Brick got up, dusted sand off his jeans, and reached out his hand. "Dance with me."

She blinked. "Huh?"

That lazy smile touched his lips. "Dance with me, Aspen. I love this song."

She felt her cheeks redden, the usual awkwardness descending on her. God, why wasn't she flirty and smooth like her sister? "Um, I dance like I sing. Not the best."

His voice dropped to a husky growl. "All I want is an opportunity to put my hands on you."

She stared, speechless. "Oh."

He reached down, grasped her hand, and tugged her out of the chair. Still unable to create words, she followed him as he led her a few feet from the turtles' protected area. In one smooth movement, he eased her against him, both hands resting on her lower back. Her heart pounded crazily, but Aspen followed her instinct, reaching up to grasp his shoulders. Brick moved back and forth over the sand, swaying, his gaze almost gentle as he gazed down at her. "Why so surprised?" he teased. "Hasn't a man asked you to dance before?"

"Not on the beach. Most men I know despise dancing and disappear to the bar at every wedding or party."

A shiver raced down her spine as his fingers brushed the top of her buttocks. His body was like a muscled wall, hard and unyielding. "Their loss. Your scent has been driving me crazy all night. I needed more of it."

Her jaw almost unhinged. "Really? I think it's the dryer sheets I used for my sweatshirt. Plus, Sierra baked cookies, and I was in the kitchen awhile. Could be either of those."

Amusement flickered over his features. Oh, God, she was saying the stupidest things. Why didn't she just tell him it was her usual Dior? "No, it's just you." He ducked his head and breathed into the crease of her neck. "Citrus with a hint of spice. Like you taste."

Her stomach dropped to her toes. Her nails dug into his shoulders as his voice rumbled against her ear, low and sexy and full of delicious intentions. "I-I'm glad you like it."

His teeth nibbled on her earlobe, his breath a hot rush. "I do. You're sweet. Been thinking about all the other places I want to taste."

Aspen gasped at his thrilling words, and then the sound was covered by his lips on hers.

She opened herself to the kiss full force, already too far gone to think of resisting. Head falling back, she reveled in the firm, soft movement of his mouth gliding over hers, his hot tongue sliding inside to tease and play. Rich chocolate and cinnamon hit her senses, making her hungry for more, and then she was on her tiptoes, looking for it. Her fingers plunged into the silky strands of his hair and twisted tightly. He muttered her name and demanded more in return, turning forceful in his need as those big, hard hands finally cupped her ass, tilting her closer.

Their mouths devoured each other as heat poured through her body. She sank into every sensation as her core grew wet and needy for his fingers and tongue. As if he knew, he rocked his erection against her, rubbing her aching clit until she was clinging hard, practically grinding against him.

"I want to make you come."

Her head spun. His teeth nipped her lower lip. She moaned, curling her tongue around his, drunk on his taste and the feeling of his muscular body against hers. "Brick."

"Let me touch you. Make you feel good." His whisper was purely carnal, his blue eyes gleaming with need. Her control was slipping away because Aspen wanted nothing more than to beg him to slip those talented fingers into her panties and let her ride them to orgasm.

But they were on a public beach, and she wanted privacy. It had been a long time since she'd had sex, and a quick orgasm wasn't what she needed right now.

Hell, she wanted it. But what she needed was an intimacy much deeper than a release. Even if she was terrified to push herself there, it was the only way she knew how to truly connect.

Shaky, Aspen gathered all her strength to break the contact of that perfect mouth and everything it could do to her. Brick stared into her eyes for a few beats. Then, slowly, he pulled away.

"I'm sorry. I'm just—"

"Don't you dare explain." He lowered her to the sand and buried his fingers in her hair. His forehead pressed against hers. "You deserve more than a hookup in front of a crowd. I'm the one who's sorry."

"What crowd?" she asked, suddenly on high alert.

"The turtles."

Aspen relaxed and gave a half laugh. "We would shock them."

"They may hatch after they see the things I do to you, and then Judy would be mad."

She laughed again. How could he be so erotic yet funny at the same time? It was as if he sensed everything she needed and offered it to her without reservation. He didn't even seem to mind her slight awkwardness. Even now, he pressed a kiss to her jawline, letting her body adjust as she came down from the heights of sizzling lust. "Very true," she managed to say. "God knows how the crabs would react."

He grinned, keeping her wrapped tightly in his arms. "You're a hell of a woman, Aspen Lourde." She took that as her exit to pull away, but he shook his head, holding her. "Not ready to let you go yet. The music's still playing."

"You still want to dance with me?"

He stroked her cheek. Those blue eyes shimmered with an emotion that made her want to look deeper, but some part of her said it was better not to. "Yes, baby. I do."

The endearment made her eyes suddenly sting. She smiled and shook off the strange heaviness in her chest. "Okay."

She settled into his embrace. He held her loosely and guided her across the sand.

The ocean waves danced. The moon hung in a perfect silvery crescent. The turtles slept.

And they danced.

Chapter Fourteen

Brick looked up as Kane walked into the house, carrying a cup of coffee and a box of Duck Donuts. "Was wondering where you were," he commented as his friend opened the lid and snatched up a pastry. "We keep missing each other. Hey, did you have an interview? You're dressed up."

Kane dropped to the chair across from him. His hair was slicked back, and he wore white linen pants, a cream T-shirt, and leather boat shoes. Brick got the impression that he'd just left his yacht.

Dug waddled over, plunking his butt down next to Kane. Head turned up and tongue lolling, he stared with intensity as the man bit into the donut. "Dude, these are sick. They literally have a chocolate coconut one with toasted pieces. And the carrot cake? Are you kidding me?"

Brick laughed. "You're from New York. Aren't you used to some of the best pastries in the world?"

"Not like this. No, Dug, you'll get sick." The dog didn't budge or blink. Brick wondered how long it would take Kane to buckle. It was hard to enjoy anything with Dug focused on a stakeout.

Kane munched on his treat with greed. "As for my outfit? Have I not taught you anything? A man dresses for success at all times." Kane shuddered. "I swore I'd never dress sloppy again once I got out of prison. I was lucky enough to walk away with a decent wardrobe stuffed into those two duffel bags. They took everything else."

Brick's lip twitched. "Thought you said you were in there for only a few days? You got out on bail."

"Long enough for it to rate as the scariest time in my life. They don't like white-collar criminals in lockup. Bad shit happens to them."

Brick knew his friend used his sharp sense of humor to gloss over the details of what had happened, but there were deeper scars. Kane shared only a few details, but the bottom line was brutal. Once a successful property developer with a fat bank account, he'd lost everything. His money, his job, his luxury apartment, and his reputation. He was lucky the criminal charges were dropped. When Brick repeatedly asked why he hadn't told the truth about who really stole the money and forged the documents, Kane refused to answer.

His loyalty had almost made him a convicted criminal. Yet Kane never broke.

Brick figured he'd be perfect in the mafia.

"You gonna tell me how last night went?" Kane asked, breaking off a crumb and giving it to Dug. "I see you didn't sleep at home."

"Thanks for noticing, Mom. I'll check in next time."

Kane grinned, starting on his second donut. "Just an observation. Stay at her place?"

"Nope. We pulled an all-nighter with the sea turtles. Then I drove her home."

His friend raised a brow. "Going slow, huh? You must like her. That's her book you're reading, right?" He pointed to *Fifty Ways to Leave Your Lover* on the coffee table. He was halfway through and a bit obsessed. The book had the type of writing that made him want to stay up all night to finish. But Brick knew it was more than the plot or the skilled prose.

It was about Aspen. The way she'd written the heroine, Mallory, with such raw honesty and vulnerability, allowing the reader to experience not only the ups and downs of first love, but also the brutality of betrayal. With each page, there was a careful buildup as the story took shape, giving Brick a sense of dread, despite him knowing the ending.

Even though Aspen had told him the real story, he felt he understood her in a new way.

Brick took a sip of his coffee. "Yeah. She's a good writer." He'd never tell Kane about their arrangement, but he also didn't want to lie. Better to keep his explanation simple. "I do like her."

It was the truth. He *did* like Aspen, a whole lot more than he'd planned. Last night had been special in ways he still didn't understand. Brick knew his job was to not only seduce her but make her fall emotionally for him. He'd planned to share some intimate dialogue on the beach with a bit of dancing. He'd planned to kiss her again and make her want him.

But it had become so much…more. Brick forgot about his plan and followed his gut. He'd loved talking business with her and brainstorming. He found the strength she held to carve out her success story and follow her dreams inspiring. He'd craved holding her in his arms and being close, which had nothing to do with a thought-out plan. Her slight shyness hinted at an inexperience that satisfied some strange, primitive instinct inside, making him want to be the one to show her how much pleasure he could give. He couldn't wait to finally take her to bed. To make her his.

For a little while.

Kane whistled. "Good for you, man. I promise I'm working on getting out of here. Maybe another week."

"I'm not screwing around, Kane. I want you to stay. The place is big enough. There's no reason for you to go somewhere else. You're like family. I missed you. Okay?"

His friend swiveled around and gazed at him. For a rare moment, Brick saw not only the gratitude but also the new edge of pain in his friend's green eyes. Yeah, Kane had a mess of emotion buried deep. Normally, he evoked an easy charm and confidence that made people happily bend to his will. Cracks had appeared now. The lifestyle he'd once enjoyed was gone, and he needed to rebuild—inside and out.

Brick knew he'd listen if Kane ever wanted to talk, but his friend had never been one to share his feelings. "Thanks. I appreciate that more than you know."

"Then prove it. Save me a damn donut."

Kane snorted. "Think I could buy out the owner? Build a Duck Donut dynasty?"

"You'd get bored. Plus, you'd end up eating too much of your supply and wouldn't fit into those designer clothes you ran away with."

"Asshole. I'll give you the Oreo one. I know you're old-school," Kane said.

Dug's eyes began to water because he refused to blink.

Kane threw up his hands. "Fine. But if you throw up, Uncle Kane is not at fault. You asked for this."

Brick shook his head as his dog snagged another piece. At least there were carrots in it.

"How are renovations going? Sal's a good guy. Smart and competent, which is hard to find nowadays," Kane said.

"Yeah, I lined him and his team up a year ago when I thought I could pull this off. Had them on retainer so they jumped right in when I called.

They're working overtime to get it done in a few days."

"Incredible. Glad you finally got a loan, even at high interest. If you plan to give more tours, I'm happy to jump in. Or work behind the desk. Anything you need for the free rent."

"That could be useful if you're game. Gotta study up on the wild horses and your history, though. You can shadow me a few times if you're really interested. But no pressure."

"Nah, it'd be good for me. I'd like to get out there and meet some of the locals. It's nice here. May stick around."

"Good." Brick finished his coffee and stood. "I'm heading out but come by later. You can ride with me on a run and see what it's like."

Brick cleaned up and got ready. He was at the door when he heard Kane's distraught yell.

"Dug, no! Ah, I told you no donuts!"

Yeah, he'd crapped in Kane's room. Brick quietly snuck out and gently shut the door behind him, laughing all the way to Ziggy's Tours. When he arrived, he noticed a bunch of strange sticks arranged along the curb outside. A few bundles held sprigs of leaves, like herbs, and they were smoking, giving off a strange, heavily perfumed scent that wasn't quite pleasant. Frowning, he moved one with his foot and saw two letters sketched out roughly in black ink.

BB.

Son of a bitch. Maleficent was up to her old tricks again, trying to put some damn spell on him. Even though he didn't believe in that stuff, something about the bundles gave him the creeps. Did she have some type of voodoo doll where she stabbed him with pins?

The other day, he'd gotten a wicked headache that came out of the blue.

And there was that strange pain in his knee that flared now and then.

No. He would not let that woman get into his head.

Brick crushed the bundles with his shoe, stamping out the smoke, then headed inside to grab a towel to pick them up. No way was he touching them with his bare hands.

He greeted the crew, studying the new space with satisfaction. It was looking like he'd once imagined. Instead of a shabby, sad reception area, there was a spacious waiting room, a new desk, and a dedicated coffee/refreshment spot for guests. The disgusting carpet was gone, and new beechwood flooring had been installed. It gave the space a professional, open vibe that immediately made a person want to stay.

"Looks great," Brick said as Sal walked over.

"Not much left. We'll finish up tomorrow, and then my guy will paint. The new door is coming later today."

"Appreciate it. I know getting this done with your workload was a bitch."

Sal flashed him a grin. "Made you a promise and glad to keep it. Ziggy was a legend in these parts. I like knowing I was part of salvaging this place."

Brick shook his hand, grabbed a towel, and went back outside.

He was discarding the stick bundles when Maleficent came roaring into the parking lot in her bright-pink Hummer, which was empty for now. She marched over, hands on her hips. "What are you doing?"

He straightened and glared. "Disposing of your ridiculous attempt to curse my property."

"Dramatic, much? It's just some sage to clear out bad-tempered spirits. I was doing you a favor." She rolled her eyes, heavily accented in black liner. Her dark hair hung freely to her hips in inky black strands threaded with blue. She wore a skimpy black tank top, shorts, and high-heeled boots. The outfit should look ridiculous, but somehow fit her. "And I meant, what are you doing to the place? Why are you renovating? How did you get a new Jeep?"

Satisfaction coursed through him. After all her tricks, he'd finally trumped her. "Got a loan," he drawled. "Fixing the place up."

Fire lit her dark eyes. "Ziggy doesn't deserve a second chance at this place," she spat.

"Lady, you just have to get over whatever my grandfather did to piss you off. This is my business now, and I intend to make it work. Even with your efforts at sabotage."

Her red lips pulled back in a sneer. "You're just like him. Treating women like playthings, discarding them when you want to move on. You don't deserve this place either!"

Brick held on to his temper. "I just want to run my business in peace, okay? Can we try to get along here? Be friendly competitors?"

"No." She narrowed her gaze on him, then spun on her heel. "You can't flick me away like an annoying gnat. I'm the voice for all the women you and your grandfather destroyed. Especially Anastasia. She deserves justice."

With one last furious glance, Maleficent got into her happy pink vehicle and drove away, kicking up a cloud of dust.

Brick closed his eyes and groaned.

Well, that went well.

He'd just have to watch out as he moved forward. Hopefully, she'd tire of her revenge plot, and he could run Ziggy's Tours in peace.

"I have to go away on a buyer's trip for a few days," Sierra said.

Aspen looked up from her notebook, casually shutting it to shield the contents from her sister's natural nosiness. Once again, she'd started out working on the book but was only able to write a page. Even though her brain spun with creative energy from her night with Brick, she ended up doodling and writing another *Zany Zoo* chapter. The beach had inspired her to create an epic vacation story where Coral Snake pops the tires on their car and strands Purple Bunny and Piggy in the middle of a deserted island. The local residents—otter-like creatures—pop out of their hidden caves to help, and a battle ignites. Aspen thought it was her best installment yet and found herself losing time, caught up in her writing.

Which wasn't a good thing when she was on a deadline.

"Where are you going?" she asked, standing up to stretch.

"Myrtle Beach. I need to meet a supplier. It's a female-run local company that donates a percentage to nonprofit women's shelters. I think it'll be a great fit for us."

"That's awesome. I'll take care of everything here."

Her sister arched a brow. "You didn't come home until six this morning."

"I told you. We were babysitting the sea turtles."

Sierra continued to gaze at her. Aspen tried not to squirm, even though she wasn't hiding anything. Her sister should've been a private investigator. "You didn't sleep together yet?"

"Nope."

"He left you chastely at the front door after hours alone on a beach in the middle of the night?"

"Yep."

Sierra gave a sharklike grin. "There was definitely fooling around. I can tell."

Aspen groaned. "Yes, we kissed and…fooled around. We're moving slow. I can't just have sex and get my heart involved. It needs wooing."

Her sister laughed. "As it should, babe. Just want to be sure you're on track for the epic Brick Babel fall and heartbreak. Does he kiss as good as

I imagine?"

Aspen literally shuddered as the memory of last night took hold. They'd danced to Billy Joel's entire CD, kissing, touching, and basically falling over each other like it was senior prom night. After she'd pulled away, Brick had known instinctively how far to push their physical intimacy. Aspen had never made out and fooled around without any worries before. Even with Ryan, she'd always been calculating how to make sure she pleased him or followed his lead. This was the first time she'd been allowed to experience her pleasure on her terms with no endgame.

It was a freeing experience as a woman. And it was sad that she'd never had it before.

Brick had given her that gift in one perfect, romantic night.

"Yep, it's better than I imagined," Sierra commented. "Your face says it all. Just please don't do it on the living room sofa, okay? It's my favorite place to sit, and I don't want to imagine dirty deeds with my sister on the velvet couch."

"Stop!" Aspen couldn't help but laugh. "Though I should get you back for doing it with Terrance Fisher in my bed. Ugh. Gross."

Sierra shrugged. "I knew Mom would be checking my bedsheets for clues. She wouldn't bother with yours."

"You're diabolical."

"And you're a show-off, using big words." Sierra walked away, leaving Aspen shaking her head with humor. She'd forgotten how much fun it was to be with her sister. She liked chatting over dinner, sharing their favorite TV shows, and hanging out with glasses of wine. Over these past few weeks, Aspen had begun to realize that even though she liked her own company, she'd been verging on loneliness.

With a sigh, she refocused on her book. Nicolette had sent over the publishing contract with a deadline date in three months for the first draft. Usually, Aspen took eight months to write the first draft, then dealt with developmental and copy edits. But because her publisher had a huge demand for the sequel, they wanted a quick turnaround and a crash publication date for next spring. Aspen wasn't used to the added pressure of such a tight timeframe to write, but she'd confidently told Nic she could deliver and swore she'd get it done.

Groaning, she read over the last few paragraphs. It sucked. Why wasn't it good? Brick was delivering everything she wanted. She was already a bit addicted to his company, and her body craved his. There were emotions brewing. She'd even tried to craft a scene where the heroine dances on the beach during sunset with the hero, and though it was everything Aspen had felt in real time, the scene fell flat. Panic edged her nerves, but she wrestled it back.

We have to get this done, she told her bitchy muse, who was somewhere in Mexico, drunk on margaritas and not helping.

I don't like this story, she drawled. *I'll come back when you give me something more interesting. We wrote this book already.*

It's the sequel, Aspen hissed. *It's different.*

Yawn. *I have a new idea for* Zany Zoo *if you're interested.*

I'm not. Get back to your paying job, please, or we'll be failures.

Silence.

God, she needed help. Definitely more inspiration. Maybe something to raise the stakes of her emotional attachment to Brick.

Aspen stared at the blinking cursor and came to a brand-new conclusion. One that had her heart pounding, her palms sweating, and her nipples hardening.

It was time to have sex with Brick.

That would jump-start her muse and get her back from vacay.

She was going to have sex with Brick.

Before she could chicken out, Aspen tapped out a text. *Want to come to dinner tomorrow night? Sierra's away on a trip.*

She threw the phone onto the table and chewed her fingernails. He probably wouldn't answer till later. He was doing a million things today, and she was likely the last thing he was thinking about. He was out with the horses, working on marketing, and—

The phone shook.

Yes.

Oh, my God.

She was going to have sex with Brick.

Chapter Fifteen

Aspen checked her appearance one last time and tried not to vomit.

Everything was set. She'd ordered a gorgeous grilled halibut, some roasted Brussels sprouts, mashed potatoes, and a Caesar salad from North Banks Restaurant, then dumped the food into appropriate pans arranged on the stove so it looked like she'd cooked. The table was set with a vase of fresh flowers, a cheerful daisy tablecloth, and real linen napkins. Only one candle was lit, so it wasn't overkill. The French doors were open, and the night breeze drifted in.

She'd dressed in a simple maxi dress with a deep V-neck in a royal blue that looked good with her coloring. She left her feet bare, showing off coral-painted toenails and a silver chain ankle bracelet. Her hair was straightened with ruthless precision. She'd even donned Sierra's magnetic eyelashes, which she'd never used and had taken over an hour to finally get right.

Today's makeup tech was amazing. They actually stuck to the liner, which she'd discovered after reading the instructions and messing up a few times.

She'd skipped a bra because she was small enough to carry off the dress without it. Her underwear was a wispy piece of white lace that barely covered her freshly waxed mound.

And yeah, she'd screamed when the woman ripped off the cloth, leaving her baby-smooth and a bit sore.

But she felt as confident as possible for this night.

The bell rang.

Dragging in a breath, she went to the door to let him in. Immediately, her heart galloped at the sight of him, put together in casual jeans and a pink button-down shirt with the cuffs rolled up, showing off his sinewy, muscular arms. His hair was neatly tamed, and that razor-cut jaw clean-shaven. He smelled of ocean, musk, and temptation. "Come on in," she said with a smile.

"Thanks." He pressed a kiss to her lips, then lifted two bottles of wine. "I didn't know if you liked red or white."

"Both. But we're having fish, so white will be great."

"Perfect. God, that smells good. I haven't eaten all day, and as for a home-cooked meal? Can't even remember the last time I had time to cook."

Aspen hid a wince as she turned and led him into the kitchen. "Figured we could have drinks on the porch, and then I'll serve."

His gaze swept over the kitchen, which looked like it belonged on a magazine cover for cuisine. She'd used Sierra's good china and fancy silverware. The halibut was warming in the oven, and the rest of the meal was in gourmet cookware that Aspen hadn't even known existed. Like the magnetic eyelashes.

She had to get out more.

"This is amazing. I'm so impressed."

She opened the wine—which she did well—and laughed it off. "Wait until you taste it first. I enjoy hosting a nice dinner."

Hosting was the keyword, so it wasn't really a lie.

"Well, I'm a lucky man. How was your writing day?"

A sigh spilled from her as she handed him his glass. "Slow. I'm trying not to get frustrated, but I don't have much time to waste. These are the times I wish I was a plotter, but each time I try, I can't write a word."

"Creative energy is so unique to each person," he commented. He clinked his glass to hers, and the creases deepened around his eyes as he gave her a devastating smile. "Cheers to inspiration. And tonight."

Her belly dipped at the husky timbre of his voice. "Cheers."

She sipped the wine, which was already chilled and had a buttery finish she loved in a chardonnay. "The porch is screened, so the bugs won't bother us," she said as they stepped outside and settled into comfortable, oversized chairs. The crickets sang, and the fireflies glowed around their protected area. He crossed an ankle over his knee and regarded her with full focus. "So, what do you do if the words aren't coming? Do you work better under pressure?"

She wrinkled her nose as she thought about the question. "I don't think I produce diamonds under pressure. I do the usual things to get unstuck. Go for a walk. Take a shower. Do freewriting. Watch a well-written television show. But mostly, I just sit there for hours. Eventually, I write something. One word begets another. I tell myself I can fix it all later."

"I admire your perseverance," he said quietly. "On the other side of a successful book is the events, the press, the readership. A lot of promotion. But what no one sees is the drudgery of showing up day after day. You have great faith."

A prickle of awareness shot through her. She stared at him, touched by his thoughtful observation and how he glimpsed what many couldn't. "I've always believed that," she said softly. "Everyone seems to want the secret sauce. Not everyone wants to do the hard work. A mix of cajoling, dreaming, and waiting. It does take great faith to create something from nothing. And ego."

His brow lifted. "There's nothing wrong with ego. We need to rely on our beliefs when things go sideways—like they normally do. Ego helps smooth the way."

Something shifted inside her at his words. There was a calmness radiating from him, an acceptance of the things she accomplished when no one was looking that he seemed to understand better than anyone.

It made her feel seen.

The voice inside her whispered that Brick Babel was a master at manipulating emotions. That was how he'd managed to break so many hearts. But a truth threaded through his tone that Aspen clung to. Because, at this moment, it was a gift she needed to believe was real.

Especially tonight.

"You're more than a pretty face," she said, needing to lighten the moment.

He laughed, and she reveled in the deep, throaty sound. "That's what my mom used to tell me. Always insisted on high grades, and if I was impolite, she'd smack me in the back of my head."

She laughed with him. "Sounds like your mom was special."

"She was. I miss her every day."

Her heart squeezed with shared pain. "Me, too. I'm glad I have my sister. Do you have any other family you're close to?"

Brick shook his head. "Grandpa Ziggy was the last. My father left when I was young, and I have no desire to find him."

As he stared into the shadows, fingers gripping his glass, Aspen caught an edge of loneliness radiating from him. She longed to reach out and soothe him, bring back the light, but she wasn't ready to cross that line yet. She gave him the words instead. "He's unworthy of being found. It's obvious how deeply you can love. Look at everything you've done to continue your grandfather's legacy, even at the expense of your own dreams."

Startled, his gaze swerved to hers, and she caught her breath at the sudden fire in his ocean-blue eyes. He slowly put his glass down on the table and leaned over, dragging her chair a few precious inches over so their knees were touching. That full lower lip quirked. "Oh, you can't say things like that and not expect to be kissed, Aspen Lourde."

And then he did, cupping the back of her head, his lips moving over hers with a thoroughness that made her sag against him, rendered helpless under his spell. She bloomed under the attention, enjoying the slow, teasing thrust of his tongue against hers, the firm grip of his fingers, and the way he took over and allowed her to sink into the pleasure. His sinful taste lingered when he finally pulled away.

She blinked. "I think we should eat now."

He smiled, pressing his thumb against her damp lips. "I think that's a good idea."

Brick took her glass and hand as they moved into the kitchen. "Can I help serve?"

"No, I've got it. If you can refresh our wine and then sit?"

He nodded. Aspen hurried to transfer it all to beautiful serving pans and laid it out in front of him. "Bon appétit," she said proudly, forgetting that she'd bought the meal instead of cooking it.

The pleasure on his face as he ate made her giddy. She wondered what his expression would look like doing other things he enjoyed, but then she felt her cheeks heat and shoved the thought away. "This is unbelievable," he said, forking up another piece of fish. "Did you use rosemary or parsley? And what's that other ingredient I can't place? A hint of cumin?"

Her stomach clenched. Wait. Why did he sound so authoritative about seasonings? "You…you cook?"

"Yeah, I love to cook. But on my terms, when I have plenty of time to linger and try new recipes. I've just been lazy these past two weeks."

Uh-oh. She focused on her dish. "I didn't know. I guess I figured you'd be more of a DoorDash guy."

"When I'm working long hours. So, which herbs did you go with?"

What had he mentioned? She snatched the first one. "Rosemary."

"I thought so. Did you use butter or cream for the potatoes?"

Shit. "Both," she said weakly. "It's my secret double punch."

"Brilliant." He asked more questions about how she'd prepared each of the dishes until the guilt of her lie squirmed inside her. Aspen must've answered wrong a few times. He looked a little confused when she said she'd used pepperoni in the Brussels sprouts—she'd meant bacon. And what the hell was prosciutto and its purpose? His brow arched when she told him the fish was stuffed with ginger. She should've said garlic.

Desperate, she shoved potatoes into her mouth and tried to change the subject. "When do you plan to reopen?"

"Saturday. My friend Kane said he'd help out until I see if I need another regular driver. I made some calls about offering family coupons at all the mini-golf places, but I can't get ads running until the first week of August."

"Do you have a graphics person?"

"No, I use Canva and try to do them myself."

"I've gotten pretty good with design. Want me to take a look?"

"You're busy writing a book and are already saving my business," he said gently.

"I actually love drawing," she admitted. "It's a nice break for my brain, so I don't mind."

"Then yeah, I'd love a second look."

"How's your social media?"

Brick winced. "Kind of sucky. I have that on the list."

"I'm a genius at those ads, too."

He regarded her over his wineglass. "Is there anything you can't do?"

Aspen sighed and leaned back in her seat, completely stuffed. "Yeah. Write another great book."

"You will, baby."

She thrilled at the endearment, her body perking up at his attention. It didn't sound like a throwaway line but hummed with sincerity. "Hope so." Aspen wrinkled her nose in thought. "I guess I wish I enjoyed it more. It's been a while since I felt the excited buzz of chasing a story. Where everything falls away except for me and my characters."

Her buzz now only came when creating a bunch of cartoons with silly stories.

"Maybe you need a little more inspiration."

She stilled at the sexy growl, slowly raising her gaze.

Brick watched her like a hunter who'd spotted prey he didn't want to startle. Heat bristled around him, and a male awareness flared in his eyes. Sexual chemistry popped in the air, and suddenly, Aspen wanted nothing but for him to touch her.

As if sensing her need, he rose from the table and stood before her. Tugging her from the chair, she tipped her head back and fell into blazing-hot blue eyes. "I can't stop thinking about the night on the beach," he murmured, smoothing his palms over her hair in a calming gesture. "How good you felt against me. How sweet you tasted."

Aspen shuddered and leaned into his strength. Already, her body melted like hot caramel, and she wanted nothing but to let go tonight and be with him. All of him. "Me, too," she whispered.

He lifted her easily, taking her mouth in a deep kiss until her hands wrapped around his neck and clung tightly. Turning, he began walking forward, pausing at the stairway. "Bedroom?" he murmured, nipping at her lower lip, soothing the sting with his tongue.

She fought for breath, but it was a losing battle. It had been too long since a man had put his hands on her with such focused attention. "First one on the right."

Aspen expected him to put her down and walk, but the man just continued kissing her as he moved upstairs without a hitch. It was the sexiest thing ever to be carried, to feel so treasured and delicate under his delving mouth and firm hands. She heard him kick the door open, then shut. By the time her feet slid to the floor, her head spun.

"I can't get enough of you." His eyes blazed. "When I first kissed you, I told you I would no longer ask for permission. But my intention now is to get you naked, put my mouth all over you, and make you come. I'm asking only once."

Her knees almost went out as his words blistered her ears. Her nipples were so hard they ached, and she swayed slightly. It was like her private, dirty fantasies had come true to stand right in front of her. "Permission granted," she choked out.

"Take off your clothes," he growled.

She took a hesitant step back. Goose bumps prickled her skin, and she felt a bit woozy from his demand. Okay, this man was in Jason Momoa and Hemsworth territory. Sexual masculine energy crackled from his very aura, hitting her so hard her lungs ran out of air. Aspen bit her lip. Normally, she was a straight shooter and had no issues being naked or getting her sexy on. But he was a bit overwhelming. And for one terrible, awful moment, she wondered if she'd disappoint him. Her chin tilted up. "I'm shy."

She waited for him to be impatient with her or respond with some smart-ass comment. Maybe she even expected him to just tackle her to the bed to overcome her sudden hesitancy. Instead, he did something unexpected that changed everything.

His ocean-blue eyes softened, along with his expression. He closed the distance between them slowly as if calming a wild horse, and gently cupped her cheek. "Nothing to be shy about, baby," he murmured. "Not when you look like that. Not when all I want to do is get on my knees and worship you the way you deserve."

Her body relaxed, and then he was kissing her, and oh, God, it was like drowning in a deep well of pleasure that she never wanted to surface from. The delicious scent of him rose in her nostrils, and his lips melded to hers, sliding back and forth with teasing motions until she moaned and begged for more. His tongue touched hers, then invaded her mouth with a possessiveness that curled her toes—a sexy invader storming her defenses and ripping them down one hot, slow thrust at a time.

He smoothed his hands over the straps of her dress, slowly tugging them down her arms, exposing her bare breasts. She arched as the cool air hit her, and then hot fingers caressed, tweaking her hard nipples, then cupping both mounds in his palms. "God, you're so pretty," he muttered, lowering his head to taste, flicking his tongue against the peak, and then sucking it fully into his mouth.

Aspen let out a cry, pulling at the buttons of his shirt in a desperate need to feel him against her. But Brick had other plans. The skirt of her dress was crushed in one of his hands as he pulled the fabric up over her waist while his mouth kept up its love play with her sensitive breasts. Aspen felt as if she were drowning in too much sensation, helpless under the sensual onslaught. Her core was wet and needy, and when his fingers slipped under the elastic of her panties, sliding over her clit, she jerked hard, sinking her nails into his shoulder.

"Oh, God."

"Feel so fucking good. You're so wet."

Those talented fingers sank into her channel, rubbing gently back and forth. His thumb brushed her clit. The orgasm exploded through her, curling her toes, and with a loud cry, her body spasmed.

Stunned at the quick, almost violent orgasm, she moaned his name and clung hard as the ground shifted beneath her. His teeth tightened on her nipple as he continued stroking her, letting her ride out the last wave, leaving Aspen panting.

"I-I'm sorry," she whispered, half-embarrassed at how quick she'd come apart. He was still fully dressed!

Her nipple popped from his mouth, and he raised his head. She noticed his pupils had dilated, darkening his eyes to a deep, navy blue, blistering with raw hunger. "Again."

He lifted her and placed her on the bed, then stripped quickly, giving her flashes of a muscled chest with golden hair, a tight eight-pack, and tanned skin. Aspen hoped she could stare at him later, but he seemed to share her pulsing need to satisfy the frantic hunger roaring inside her.

Brick pulled the dress down her hips and divested her of it in one motion. Her panties were damp, and he traced an index finger over the delicate white lace, pressing against her sensitive clit until she writhed in need. "You're so perfect. So responsive. I can't get enough." He pushed her thighs apart and lowered himself, his hot mouth traveling over her stomach to trace the lines of her panties. He pushed his nose against the damp lace and breathed deeply. "I want your scent all over me. I want to taste all this sweetness on my tongue."

Aspen shook helplessly, his dirty words bringing her right back to the edge as she twisted in demand for what he promised. "If-if you keep talking like that, I'm going to do it again too soon."

His laugh was wicked as he tugged her panties down inch by slow inch. "Consider it a warm-up. I intend to fuck you all night long."

And then his mouth lowered, and his tongue swiped at her weeping slit. She shrieked his name at the feeling of his wet heat over her swollen tissues, but he only settled in and began to devour her. Lips, tongue, and teeth explored every inch, teasing her clit with bare brushes that made her wantonly grind herself against his mouth, begging him as he kept her on the razor's edge of release. Her experience with oral sex was limited and mainly focused on her giving the pleasure. She'd never had a man take his time like she was a four-course meal he wanted to leisurely enjoy in his own damn way.

"Brick!"

"I know, baby," he crooned. "Does it hurt?" His teeth skimmed over her throbbing clit as his fingers sank into her wetness with firm, strong strokes.

"Yes," she moaned.

His lips closed around the sensitive knot, his gaze locked on hers as he stared up the naked length of her body, his eyes glittering with hot demand. "Come for me."

Then he sucked hard.

She exploded, letting out a keening wail as she soared so high she doubted she'd ever come down. The orgasm went on and on as he kept working her, and by the time she slumped back onto the mattress, she felt drunk.

"God, I could watch you all day. You're so very sweet, Aspen."

Brick reared up, staring down at her like a satisfied warrior. Since being a kidnapped harem girl was one of her fantasies, his dominance in bed was fulfilling every single silent need she'd so desperately dreamed of.

He reached over, ripped open the packet, and sheathed himself. He was thick and huge, and Aspen experienced a flash of worry for a moment. Would it hurt? Would he even fit? "Um—"

His mouth twitched in a smile. "Don't worry, baby. I'll take care of you."

Poised at her entrance, a tiny moment of panic hit. Where did this awful vulnerability come from? As if once he was inside her, she'd be forever changed. A flash of memories overtook her, bringing her back to the time with Ryan when he'd commanded her trust, taking her virginity and innocence, only to betray her in the end.

"Aspen?"

She blinked, coming back to the present. His gaze burned into hers. His hands were gentle as he cupped her cheeks, pressing his lips to hers.

"Do you want me to stop?"

She relaxed inch by inch, softening under him. Brick wasn't Ryan. And she was the one controlling this relationship, set by *her* terms. "No." Her mouth was greedy over his, kissing him with all the dark and desperate need he'd ignited in her. "Fuck me, Brick. Take it all."

He hissed out a curse, his grip tightening. And then he slowly began to push forward.

Inch by inch, he buried himself deep. Her body fought at first, but he kept a steady pressure, filling her completely. Aspen gasped, feeling overfull and completely overtaken. The sensations washed over her as she squeezed him tightly, her skin prickling, muscles quaking with the need for him to move.

Grasping her wrists, he guided them over her head so she could grip the spindles of the headboard. "Hold on."

He moved.

Head thrown back on the pillow, Aspen let her body go as he took her on a wild ride with each thrust of his hips, shoving her higher and higher until there was nothing left but a desperate, aching hunger. Gaze trained on her face, he devoured every expression as if he owned them, and she tightened her grip on the headboard as she began to spin out.

His fingers bruised her hips. He swiveled and hit a spot that made her insides clench and shiver, and with a low laugh of satisfaction, began hammering at the exact place that did things to her body she'd never experienced.

And then his hands moved from her hips, sliding between them to lightly massage her clit.

Aspen crashed into the orgasm all at once. As she screamed his name, he dipped his head, and she sank her teeth into his shoulder, shuddering helplessly under him. His body stiffened as he followed her over, growling her name. They clung to each other hard as everything shattered around them.

He rolled to the side before he collapsed, tucking her head against his chest. They stayed quiet for a while, breathing heavily, and Brick finally got up to dispose of the condom. When he returned, she was lying like a rag doll, limbs fluid, cheek pressed to the pillow, not even enough energy to cover herself with the sheet.

He pressed a kiss to her shoulder and smoothed back her hair, then lifted the covers and moved her under them with such gentle care her eyes started to sting. "Sleep," he whispered in her ear, stroking her bare back.

Aspen wanted to tell him there was no way she could fall asleep with a naked man in her bed. She'd been on her own for so long, a bed partner made her a tiny bit anxious. Maybe she'd pretend to sleep, then sneak away for some space once he was snoring. Maybe she'd—

She slept.

Chapter Sixteen

Brick watched her sleep and wondered what was happening with him.

He'd almost lost control last night. It was as if a strange, possessive frenzy came over him until he was helpless against the drive to claim Aspen in all ways possible.

It had never been like that before. After Anastasia, there was always a distance inside him, a veiled, invisible wall surrounding his emotions and heart. He'd figured he'd open up again after he healed from the heartbreak, but it had never happened. Brick wondered if it was just how he was built now, where he could enjoy sex and the comfort of physical touch but nothing beyond that. This past year, being so focused on work and saving his grandfather's business, it'd become easier to stay away from any relationships or dating.

But now? Watching Aspen after reaching for her multiple times last night, everything seemed different.

His insides ached with longing, and Brick didn't know what to do about it.

On cue, her eyes flew open.

He watched her face as her brain clicked on and followed the night's events through to now. Her adorable frown and flushed cheeks once again confirmed her innocence. He enjoyed Aspen's slight awkwardness and blushes when things turned intimate, but he hadn't known she was inexperienced when it came to lovemaking.

Was it fucked up that it made him want to howl with masculine satisfaction?

Oh, he loved the way she screamed his name and melted under his touch. But it was the naked wonder on her face and the hunger in her eyes that moved him. With Aspen, she said what she thought and brought that same honesty into the bedroom. When she apologized because the first touch of his fingers inside her brought her to orgasm?

Brick swore to drown her in pure pleasure until she couldn't walk.

He waited for her to come fully awake, blinking in the morning light. She sat up, pressing the sheets against her naked breasts, and stared back at him.

"I figured you'd have left."

He blinked. She always managed to surprise him. "Did you want me to?"

A smile curved her lips, and his breath released from his lungs. "No. That would've sucked."

Brick laughed. Lightness flowed through him at the sight of her. Cocoa-brown strands of hair sprang into wild curls around her face. Her skin showed marks from last night, and her mouth was swollen when she licked her lips. A crease cut across her cheek from the blanket. One foot peeked out from under the covers. The silvery chain clasped around her delicate ankle winked in the sun.

His cock rose to full staff, and Brick wanted nothing more than to climb back into bed and spend the next few hours hearing her moan his name. Instead, he kept his distance and gave her space. "Good, because I didn't want to leave, and I'm glad you're not disappointed. I made coffee. How do you take it?"

"Cream, no sugar."

"I'll bring it in. Relax for a bit."

He made the coffee and carried it back, handing her the mug. She sat up more, back against the headboard, sheet still covering those magnificent breasts. "Thank you. I'm sorry—it must be a mess in the kitchen. I never cleaned up."

"I distracted you, so I took care of it."

She cocked her head in question. "Huh?"

"I cleared the table and did the dishes. I was up earlier than you."

"Oh." Worry danced on her face. She focused on her coffee. "Um, you didn't find anything unusual, did you?"

Brick tamped down his laughter, refusing to let her know he'd discovered her secret. The bags and plastic cartons from North Bank Restaurant had been neatly stacked on the top of the garbage. Of course, he'd known it last night. He was a regular patron there, and the halibut was his favorite dish. But he'd had too much fun hearing her explanations for how she cooked dinner, so he hadn't let on. "Nope. Should I have found something? You didn't spike my wine so you could take advantage of me, did you?"

"No! That was really nice of you. To clean up. I feel bad."

Brick shrugged. "No reason to. If you cooked, I should clean."

"Brick?"

"Yeah?"

Aspen looked up from her coffee with such a miserable expression that his heart squeezed. "I have to tell you something. I lied."

The woman couldn't even handle twenty-four hours of an untruth. "You can tell me anything, Aspen," he said gently. "I don't want either of us to be afraid of saying our truths."

"I didn't cook dinner. I bought it from North Banks and pretended I cooked it."

Brick couldn't stand how adorable she was. He plucked the mug from her hand and placed it on the night table. Then sat on the bed next to her. "I know."

Her jaw dropped. "You knew?"

His lip twitched. "I've ordered the dish before, so I suspected last night. This morning, I found the cartons."

She squeezed her eyes shut. "I am so embarrassed. That was so stupid."

He tipped up her chin, forcing her to meet his amused gaze. "Baby, I don't give a crap that you can't cook. But I have to applaud the effort. It meant you really wanted to do something nice for me."

Aspen groaned. "I did, but I'm terrible. Sierra said I'm a walking disaster in the kitchen. I guess I wanted to impress you for our first dinner together. I'm sorry."

Her sweetness drove right through his walled heart. At a loss for the words to tell her, he kissed her, slow and easy and so thoroughly that when he finally pulled back, her eyes sparked with a lustful hunger. "Don't be sorry, I loved every bite. But I appreciate you telling me."

Suddenly, a very feminine, very mischievous smile curved her full lips. "Brick?"

"Hmm?"

The sheet dropped. The sight of her raspberry-tipped nipples made him suck in a breath. They were hard, likely aching, and begging for his tongue. "I'm very good at other things," she purred.

Her finger trailed down his chest, pausing at the waistband of his briefs. Cupping his erect cock, she squeezed lightly, teasingly, and a groan ripped from his lips. Her nails raked over the soft cotton, and his entire body shuddered. Her laugh was husky as she leaned forward. Suddenly, Brick was under her power completely. "Want me to prove it?"

"Fuck, yes," he gritted out.

She licked her lips. Lowered her head.

And proved it in spectacular fashion until he was the one begging.

Brick guided the Jeep over the sand dunes as he finished up the tour with Kane. They'd been out a few hours while he went over the route, pointed out the horses, and gave him a guidebook lecture of the highlights.

Other than showing up for the tour in a Calvin Klein coral suit and looking like he'd stepped off the pages of *GQ*, Kane was a quick study. Brick knew the man had a photographic memory and an ability to speak smoothly enough to distract if he made any errors. It had served him well in the business industry and made him the shark he was. And it would hopefully help Brick take care of the bump in tourists without trying to bring someone in mid-season.

"I'll do all the tours the first week, and you can watch until you feel comfortable," Brick said, stopping to show him another cluster of mustangs by the shore. "The facts are important, though. Did you look over the guidebook from the Corolla Wild Horse Fund?"

"Read it last night while you were enjoying…dinner." His friend's voice danced with amusement. "How was…dinner?"

"Five stars," he said.

Kane cranked up a brow. "Michelin-rated?"

"Definitely."

His friend whistled. "Good for you, man. Can I meet her?"

Brick snorted. "Sure, Mom. Shall I have her come over tonight?"

"No, I mean it. You look happy. I know I haven't seen you in a while, but last time you were a mess."

"Shit was going down."

Kane stared at him, seeing past the bluster. "I know. I should've been there for you. When all that shit went down."

"I had to leave town, and you were dealing with your own fallout. I know if I'd needed you, you'd have been at my door."

Kane's shoulders relaxed. "Good. But now you're a different person. I like seeing you happy. You were singing when you got home this morning."

"I don't sing, dude."

His friend barked out a laugh. "Oh, you were singing, and your voice isn't the best to share with the world. Sounded like a Disney song, too. And little birdies were hovering around you. Kinda like Cinderella."

"I hope Dug shits in your room again."

Kane threw up his hands. "Nothing to be embarrassed about. I happen to love Disney. *Frozen* was epic."

"I'm not having this conversation with you."

"Fine, but I saw some classics on your Disney Plus account under recently watched. You can't hide crap anymore in this day and age, man."

"You're such an asshole."

Kane laughed so hard, Brick shook his head. He waved to Judy, who was out with a few other volunteers, and she motioned him over. The moment her gaze took in Kane and all his flamingo splendor, the older woman was practically fawning. "Hi, Brick. Oh, my, who is this gentleman with you?"

His friend reached out to take her hand. "Ma'am, I'm Kane. You must be the head of Turtle Haven. I've heard so many wonderful things about you."

Brick almost rolled his eyes, but Judy was smiling with that delighted female expression that was common with Kane. "How nice. It's lovely to meet you."

Brick spoke up. "I'm training Kane to take over a few runs when we reopen."

"If you need any help, let me know. We all try to take care of one another here," Judy said, gaze fastened on Kane.

Brick cleared his throat. "Need anything, Judy?"

"Oh! Yes, I wanted to let you know the babies will be hatching soon. We usually have a long list of people who want to be involved, along with others who just want to watch. Since you and Aspen were so nice to take a night watch, you're welcome to come. I won't know the exact schedule, of course, but I'm happy to text you when it's time and you can meet us out here."

"I think Aspen would love that. Thanks for the invite."

"Kane, you can come, too."

"I'm honored. I can't wait to learn more so I can offer help in the future."

Judy let out a deeply feminine sigh. "What a nice young man you are."

This time, Brick did roll his eyes. "Better get going. Thanks again,

Judy." He took off down the beach toward the exit. "Can you leave the nice older ladies alone, please? My reputation is already shit in this town with women. I don't need any future smear campaigns."

"I love women."

"Yeah, all of them. I mean it, Kane. If you're sticking around, do not screw around with the locals, okay? Do you swear?"

"Sure. I swear. Not interested in women right now, anyway. I have a lot of crap to get together."

Brick let the subject go. When he got back to the office, a truck was pulling up with the new sign delivery. The old one had a letter missing and was so battered it was hard to read. Kane jumped out and helped install the new sign and remove the original. Staring up at the bold black letters with the bright yellow background, Ziggy's Tours announced itself open for business. A wild horse was stamped on the side in the new logo he'd adapted.

Marco strolled out of his shop, shaking hands with Kane and admiring the new sign. "Where's Aspen?" he asked.

"She's writing," Brick answered.

His expression fell, and Brick wondered if the kid had a crush. Not that he blamed him. It was easy to fall for Aspen. "Do you think you can tell her to stop by the next time she's free when you talk to her? She helped a lot with our shirts—the yellow's really selling."

"Sure. Anything I can do?"

"Nope. I need the opinion of a woman with a good business sense."

Brick pressed his lips together to keep from laughing at Marco's suddenly serious speech. "I'll tell her. What do you think of how it's shaping up?"

"Fire, man. Pure fire. Hey, if you're looking for new drivers, I think Patsy can take on some added work. He broke up with his girlfriend last week and has been depressed. May help distract him."

Marco motioned toward the giant picture window displaying a bunch of wares. Patsy stood, looking out, gaze vacant and sad. He swayed back and forth. Brick wondered how many brownies the kid had eaten. There was no way he was letting Patsy around his horses. "Oh, sorry. We're all full, but I'll keep him in mind."

"Great." Marco shook his head soulfully. "Heartbreak is a bitch, man. Glenda said he wasn't going anywhere, so she dumped him. Do you believe it? The guy's a business owner, and she wanted more."

"Awful," Brick said. "He'll find the right person."

"Yeah. At least, you did. Aspen's bitchin. See ya later. I'd better check on Patsy."

"Later."

Marco disappeared, and Kane cocked his head. "Nice kid. They own that place?"

"Yep. Trust me, he's doing better sales than me."

"Not for long." Kane clapped him on the shoulder. "Ziggy would be proud."

Satisfaction curled through him. "I think so."

Funny that a fake relationship with Aspen had brought all this to him. He was right on target with her after the night they'd spent. They'd grown closer, and real emotion was blooming. Brick was sure her writing was on fire today, but eventually, he'd have to take everything they'd built and destroy it on purpose.

For her. For the book. For the bigger picture.

It hadn't bothered him before, but Brick was afraid he was beginning to blur the lines between fact and fiction.

And that left no happy endings for either of them.

Chapter Seventeen

Aspen grabbed her bag and water bottle and headed out the door.

"You're singing."

She yelped and jumped around. Her sister sat on the front porch with her laptop and a glass of sweet tea. Dressed in a cute beach dress from her store, she flipped up her Coach sunglasses and gave Aspen a suspicious look. "You scared me. What are you doing?"

"Going in for the afternoon since I got back late last night. You still haven't told me what happened when I was gone. Must be good if you're singing."

She wouldn't blush. And she refused to go into details of her sex life. They weren't teenagers anymore, sharing exploits. "Sorry, I was writing and didn't hear you this morning. I wasn't singing, just humming. How was your trip?"

"Successful. We're moving forward with the partnership. Did you sleep with him?"

Aspen kept her face neutral. "Yes."

"Tell me everything."

"No." Sierra narrowed her gaze in warning, but Aspen refused to be bullied. "It's my business, okay? I'm not gossiping, and you have to respect it."

Her sister let out a long sigh. "It's worse than I thought. He did what Brick does best—pulled you right into his spell. You were singing Justin Timberlake, and you only do that when you're seriously happy."

Sometimes, Aspen hated having a sibling who knew all her quirks. "Things are going the way they should," she said firmly. "We're enjoying each other's company."

"How's the book?"

She hesitated. That was a tricky answer because she was making progress on the story, but it wasn't flowing like she'd imagined. The night with Brick had been mind-blowing. Their connection had strengthened as if he'd imprinted his touch, taste, and scent on her body. Aspen felt giddy like she was keeping a wonderful secret all to herself.

But each time she tried to write a scene depicting her emotions, it emerged with a distant flatness she didn't understand.

At least she'd filled up a whole new notebook of *Zany Zoo*.

"Still slow," Aspen finally said. "I'm on track to send my agent a partial to look over, though."

"Where are you going?" Sierra asked.

"To help Brick with some marketing stuff. Renovations are almost done, and he needs to hit the ground running to save the summer profit."

"With the money you gave him."

Aspen winced. Yes, it was a business deal, but she didn't like to remind herself that he was forced to be with her. "Loaned," she corrected. "Why are you being bitchy about this?"

"I'm not. I'm worried, okay? I've seen this before with women he's previously dated. The high before the fall is intense. Are you sure you need to do this? Maybe the book can be written if you stop right now, and no one gets hurt."

Aspen briefly considered her sister's plea but knew she had to take it to the end. The book was still a struggle, and she needed to get it to a point where it flowed raw and true, like *Fifty Ways to Leave Your Lover.* "Getting hurt is the only way to make this worth it," she said. "I need you to have my back on this one. Please."

Sierra groaned and pinched her nose. "Fine. I hate it, though."

"Thanks. Gotta go." Aspen zipped away before her sister could launch her second-prong approach to the argument. She drove to Ziggy's Tours with a pounding heart and sweaty palms. Nerves jumped in her belly at the thought of seeing Brick after their night together. They'd spoken on the phone yesterday but both needed to work.

Would it be awkward? What if he was having regrets or doubts about moving forward? Now that he'd secured the money he needed, would he politely end this thing between them while he promised to pay her back?

She parked and got out of her car, noticing the new sign. It was big and bold, and she loved the way it stood out. The front window had a beautiful logo imprinted on it, and when she walked in, her breath caught.

It was a total transformation.

The walls weren't painted yet, and the furniture wasn't in, but Aspen immediately felt drawn to the casual but upscale vibe. The floor was a beechwood mix, and the new counter was high, extra-long, and boasted a sleek blue granite top that gave the place an ocean-type vibe. A cute coffee station offered a variety of hot and cold drinks. New lighting had been installed, giving the space a less garish glare and adding to the natural sun glow. Brick came around to greet her. "Hi. What do you think?"

She shook her head in wonder. "It's beautiful. Anyone who comes in will have a hard time not booking a tour with you. What's the rest of the setup going to look like?"

"The furniture for the waiting area over here will be delivered tomorrow." He pointed to a decent-sized open space to the right. "Brochures and information displays will be by the door, and I'll feature some of Marco's T-shirts there. I have some photographs on canvas getting done, and my grandfather had some beautiful art pieces I'll bring in."

"The sign is epic. Easy to see from the road."

"That's what I wanted." Satisfaction was carved into the features of his face. Aspen's insides squeezed with pleasure at his obvious pride in fulfilling his dream. She must've been staring because he suddenly met her gaze and gave her a slow smile. "Hey, baby."

Her entire body softened, and butterflies tickled her stomach. She felt stuck to the floor, wanting to cross the room and kiss him, but worried it would look too needy. "Hey."

His blue eyes heated, and he took deliberate steps forward. Her mouth dried up as his delicious scent wafted toward her, and she fisted her fingers so she didn't reach out and grab him. Was she staring at him like he was a five-course meal, and she hadn't eaten in days? The sexual energy he gave off fried her brain. "Aspen?"

She opened her mouth, squeaked, then tried again. "Yeah?"

He placed a finger under her chin, tipping her head up. "You know you can touch me, right?" His deep voice slid over her ears like molten honey. "I give you permission for full access to my body."

She blinked. Swayed on her feet. Then brought her hands up to wrap around his rock-hard biceps. "Oh."

His lip quirked with amusement. "Chatty today, huh?"

"Yes?"

He laughed then. His lips lowered to hover an inch from hers. "Take what you want, baby."

Knees saggy from the blistering heat of his body, Aspen surrendered and did exactly what he told her to—what she wanted more than anything.

She leaned in and took his mouth in a hungry kiss.

Digging her nails into his arm, she skipped right over flirty and teasing and went straight to devouring him, her tongue sliding between his lips and touching his in demand. He let out an animalistic groan and accepted her challenge, kissing her deeply and thoroughly, and she opened like a flower to give him full access. Sliding her arms up, she thrust her fingers into his hair and hung on, grinding her mouth against his with all the pent-up arousal she'd banked for the past twenty-four hours since he'd been in her bed.

She had no idea how much time had passed until they finally broke apart. His eyes were slightly wild when he looked at her, and a thrill raced down her spine at being able to make this man want her. "Much better," he murmured, swiping his thumb over her damp lower lip. "Dangerous, but better."

She laughed, knowing her cheeks were flushed. He made her feel like a flustered teen, desperate for both his attention and affection. The only thing that soothed her was the obvious erection visible in his jeans, confirming his desire. Aspen playfully swatted him away. "I'm here for business marketing, remember?"

"Got it. Work first, then we'll break in the new counter." At her confused look, he shot her a wicked grin. "Figured I'd strip you naked, lay you out on this new granite, and take my time feasting on your sweet pussy."

Fire lit up her veins. She was immediately wet and aching. The image of such a decadent fantasy flashed and imprinted on her brain. "We-we can't. There are no shades on the windows."

His laughter burst out in the room, so deep and loud she couldn't help but smile with him. God, she loved that sound. She wished she could make this man laugh all day. "Trust me. After that expression I just caught, my first task tomorrow is installing blinds."

"You're terrible," she said, frowning. "Stop teasing me."

Suddenly, the door opened, and Kane marched in. "Hey, I'm taking off to—oh, hello, beautiful."

Aspen stared at one of the most handsome men she'd ever seen. "Um. Hi."

She heard Brick's sigh behind her. "Aspen, this is Kane. The friend who's staying with me."

"I've been dying to meet you," Kane said smoothly, stepping over to politely kiss each of her cheeks in greeting. "Now I know why Brick has been keeping you from me. He always wants to keep the best women for himself."

She blinked at the male vision in front of her. Wavy, russet hair with strands of gold. Sea-green eyes filled with intelligence and a hint of mischief. A face caught between timeless elegance and beauty with cut cheekbones and arching brows. A short beard hugged his firm lips, keeping him from looking too pretty. He wore a crisp, button-down lavender shirt, perfectly tailored pants, and soft leather shoes that looked Italian-designed. Like Brick, he owned the room, stealing the air and attention from everything around him.

Aspen couldn't help it. She started to laugh.

Kane gave her a curious look.

"I'm sorry. This is just too much. The two of you are actually friends? Do you bring oxygen with you when you enter a bar?"

Kane shot her another curious look, grinning. "I don't understand."

"She's insulting us, Kane. Calling us pretty boys," Brick drawled, shaking his head.

Aspen laughed harder. "Seriously, it's like Thor and Iron Man hanging out together. You don't give a woman even a slim chance at survival. It's not fair."

Delight danced in Kane's eyes. "I like you," he stated. "Now I know why Brick has been singing."

Her head swung around. "You were singing?"

Brick glared at his friend. "Fuck, no. I don't sing."

Kane grinned but didn't push. "Will you join me one night for dinner, Aspen? I'd love to get to know you better."

She bit her lip hesitantly. "Um, Brick will be there, too, right?"

Kane chuckled. "Unfortunately, yes. It's his house."

"Then I'd be happy to have dinner with you."

Brick practically roared with grumpiness. "Out! You are not inviting her on a date at my house. She's mine."

Kane's face fell. "Fine. I knew you were afraid of competition. But I'm a gentleman, so I'll back off. Pleasure meeting you, Aspen."

With a wink, he disappeared. The room seemed to shrink without his large presence. Aspen turned to Brick. "Did you burn New York to the ground as the dynamic duo?"

"I knew you'd be a smart-ass about this."

"It's difficult not to be when confronted with such male beauty."

Brick gave her a warning stare. "I mean it, Aspen. Or we'll find out if spanking is a thing you'd like to explore."

Her mouth fell open like a guppy, and Brick grinned slowly. "There we go. There's definite interest."

"Stop!" She threw her shoulders back and tried to keep her blush contained. "We have work to do."

"Truce." Still grinning, he took her hand and pulled her around the talked-about counter, where he had his laptop set up. "I made a spreadsheet of hook lines for the ads, possible graphics, and media outlets. Figured you could look it over and let me know your thoughts. Want to sit?"

"No, been sitting all day. Standing feels great."

They dove into analytics, and Aspen took out her iPad, where she'd brought up some possible designs in Canva. "You want to hit a niche but not lock yourself into just one. Families will be the number-one priority, but I think you can do something fun for couples, too. What's Maleficent's main client base?"

"Partyers. Younger guys. She's great at grabbing all the rented beach house crowds, friend groups, etcetera. She gives off that fun, flashy persona that does well there."

"Makes sense. Bet she also picks up a lot of impulse buys. I think we go with the pirate treasure chest for kids, and the planners who like to set up their vacay the moment they arrive."

Brick nodded thoughtfully. "Never considered that. I like it."

They spent the next few hours picking apart his media plan and budget and setting up a bunch of new ads. "You need to do videos, Brick."

"Ah, hell, no. I'm not chasing after social media likes or looking stupid live."

She put her hands on her hips. "Listen, you can be very authentic and just be you. But it's a bigger organic reach when you're talking to the camera, directly to your prospective customers. I hated it, too, but I found a way to do it so I was comfortable."

"What do you do?"

She ticked off the stuff on her fingers. "I read excerpts from my books. I talk about what inspired certain scenes or a setting. I talk about being a writer in NY and joke about my isolation. I show my working area. I give shoutouts to other writers. Things that aren't staged."

Brick groaned. "I'm not sure I can offer anything but my ugly mug staring back at people."

She snorted. "One look at you online, and your tours will be booked by every available female, young and old."

"My tour company is not a dating app," he said grumpily. Aspen took in his reddened cheeks with delight. Was the mighty Brick Babel blushing at being a sex symbol? "I hate that shit."

"Look, let's film one right now. I'll show you how easy it is." Ignoring his anxious expression, she grabbed her phone. "I can do it on mine, but it'd be better on yours."

He offered his phone. "I already have an account but haven't posted much. Don't have that many followers."

Aspen tilted her head. "Are you sure you want me looking at your phone?" She knew that was a big privacy thing. He probably didn't want her to see how many other women texted or messaged him daily. Lord knew, she didn't want to see it.

"Sure. Got nothing to hide." He recited his passcode, and she quickly surveyed his account. She snapped a few pics of him and then the logo. "You need to use more hashtags."

"Yeah, I know. Just haven't wanted to."

"You may have the best tour company, but people need to know about it."

He flashed her a grin. "Business 101—discoverability. You're right. I know better."

Aspen liked that she didn't have to battle his ego. Too many men liked to mansplain crap and refused to listen to advice. He seemed to have no issue admitting his weaknesses. "Okay, I'll film you. Why don't you just do an invite to check out the new place? Say you're running specials."

He dragged in a breath and nodded. "Let's do this."

Aspen gave him the signal countdown and pressed record. Brick launched into a quick intro of his place, giving that lopsided grin that was kryptonite to women. He was to the point, funny, and kept it short. When she was done, he looked miserable. "I suck at this."

"Brick, that was amazing. You need to do a few of these. We can set them up to post daily and figure out what hashtags and times work best."

When they were done, a nice inventory of videos, graphics, and ads was ready to go. "You're a miracle worker," he said. "Thanks for helping on this."

"Of course." They smiled at each other. "I want to stop in and talk to Marco. He had a few questions for me, and I said I'd be here today."

Brick tugged on a wayward curl. "He likes you."

"Marco? He's a kid. He likes everyone."

"No. You're easy to like, Aspen Lourde."

"Why do you like to use my first and last name?"

"Not sure. I just like saying your full name. It feels good on my tongue." His eyes darkened. "Like other parts of you."

She put out a hand. "Don't. When you talk like that, I get distracted. And I feel weird."

His brow shot up. "Yeah? Like how?"

She bit her lip, and he laughed. "Off-kilter."

"Know how I feel when I'm near you?"

It was a setup, but she couldn't help asking, "How?"

He pressed his mouth against her ear. "Hard. Needy." His teeth nipped at her lobe. "And happy."

Aspen blinked, shock filtering through her. Before she could process the words, he pressed a kiss to her lips, patted her ass, and pushed her gently toward the door. "Go see Marco before I decide to break in this counter, after all. Then I'll take you to dinner."

She opened her mouth. Shut it. And flew out the door, his laughter echoing in the air.

Brick took his time wrapping up. He made a few more calls to coordinate for tomorrow and responded to some hopeful emails. Many of the restaurants, mini-golf vendors, and museums agreed to let him distribute coupons for tours, mentioning they were glad to see Ziggy's Tours back to advertising.

He'd enjoyed working with Aspen today. She was both creative and practical, which balanced him well, and they'd been able to share ideas that grew organically. He discovered a new part of her he liked every day. Brick hadn't fed her a line when he admitted that she made him happy. It was a simple fact, and it had just popped out of his mouth without thought.

He locked up and headed next door. The T-shirt shop had a few customers browsing, and he nodded to Patsy and Burger who worked the cash register. He looked around for Aspen but couldn't find her, so he spent a little time poking around the inventory. Brick had to admit the store wasn't too bad. When they first opened, supplies had been stark and catered to surfers, but now, there was a bigger clothing selection, children's toys, and even a jewelry counter offering fun items.

Guess they were both finally getting their shit together.

He wandered toward the back and heard low voices. Brick stopped at the door and peeked in.

Aspen was tapping the screen, and Marco was peering over her shoulder with an excited expression. "You think it can work?" he asked.

"Why not? People like to think they're getting something for nothing. You literally have boxes of these tanks that are just sitting here. Buy a tee, get a tank is a great promotion. All you need is foot traffic, and you can upsell them. You have them in all sizes, right?"

"Yeah, I told the guy to cancel, but I missed the deadline. Now I'm stuck with them."

"Look at this heading with this photo."

"That's fire! Hey, what if me and the guys stand outside and take our pic with the promotion on a big banner?"

"Love it. Do some reels, too, and boost them. Make it for a limited time. That's key."

They chattered away, and as Brick stared at Aspen, a funny ache crawled into his chest, buried itself deep, and stayed. Her wild curls bounced around her shoulders, and her cocoa-brown eyes sparkled. Marco must've given her one of those free tanks because she sported a hot-pink Barbie-colored Beach Bum one that she'd tied at the waist since it was obviously big on her. This was a bestselling author who owed nothing to Marco or his souvenir shop, yet here she was, using her precious time to help. She was sweet and shy, witty and sharp. She made him laugh and want. Aspen was not only beautiful, but she also had a kind heart.

And he was starting to fall for her.

Emotion broke over him as he tried to pull himself together. What was happening to him? How had she crawled under his skin so quickly when this whole thing was a carefully contrived setup? How had she snuck under his usually unscalable walls?

"Brick, there you are," she said with a smile. "Marco and I came up with a great idea to get rid of all these tanks he got stuck with."

Marco straightened and shot Aspen an adoring look. "Well, she did. And it's gonna be epic." He launched into their plan, and Burger and Patsy wandered in to hear. All were full of enthusiasm, and then they suggested taking pictures and creating a banner from some old posterboards.

"I think Aspen and I are getting something to eat," he said. Brick wanted some time alone with her. He wanted to share a meal, drink a cocktail, and have a quiet conversation. He wanted to hold her hand and hear her laugh. He wanted to figure out why she was beginning to haunt him.

"We can take a few pics," Aspen said, cutting Brick an apologetic look. "Right?"

Brick sighed, but the guys looked hopeful, so he agreed.

They finally finished up after an hour-long photoshoot and a homemade craft session with markers. The guys all high-fived. Brick finally took control. "We'd better head out to dinner."

Marco lit up. "I'm starving. Can we come?"

Brick opened his mouth to say, "*Hell, no,*" but Aspen responded first. "Of course. You can all join us."

"Awesome, we need a few beers after such a hard day," Marco said.

Patsy scratched his head. "Yeah, man, we were here like at noon, and I must've run up a dozen sales. I'm exhausted."

Burger nodded. "I had no idea work could be this intense," he said seriously, dressed in a yellow bathing suit, flip-flops, and one of the giveaway tanks in turquoise blue.

Brick stared at them in growing frustration. "I don't think—"

Aspen cut in. "Let's go, sweetheart. Marco can follow us there."

Aspen dragged him out of the store before he could protest.

He wanted to say more, but Brick kept thinking how good it felt when she called him *sweetheart.*

Chapter Eighteen

A week later, Brick reopened Ziggy's Tours.

He'd worked around the clock to push his new marketing and ads, papering local businesses with flyers and coupons. Judy had given him a bunch of stuffed sea turtles to give to kids for the grand opening. He'd created some brand-new tours with extra time slots so he could compete with Maleficent's schedule, including a family-friendly morning and afternoon excursion, along with a sunset champagne tour. Kane had done a deep dive into his studies and could not only rattle off endless facts but also do it in a way that made Brick believe he was a local.

Brick sent out invites for opening day and spent hours welcoming people and taking them out for tours. The first day was jam-packed, but the ones that followed were game changers.

People kept showing up.

He tracked multiple clients to his new marketing efforts, and his pirate treasure chest became a hit. Brick had never thought of himself as a kid-friendly person, but he began to enjoy the innocent joy of a child seeing the horses for the first time, bumping along the sand and marveling at the ocean and sky, screeching with excitement when he drove up close to the magnificent animals that deserved to be admired but not controlled.

He settled into his new role with his usual determination to make it a success and felt his grandfather's presence like a kindly pat on the shoulder. As the first week morphed into the second and the end of July rolled around, Brick knew it was time to focus on his newest problem.

Aspen Lourde.

He'd just finished the last sunset tour and was locking up for the night. Kane had gone to New York for a few nights to settle some business, so Brick invited Aspen over. They planned to watch a movie and eat takeout, both craving a quiet night in. He couldn't wait to get his hands all over her. She was beginning to become the most important part of his days, and Brick didn't know how it had happened so fast.

He pulled the file he'd been carefully updating with all his expenses, along with a loan contract he'd drawn up with a local attorney. Each time he tried to mention the statistics of their deal, Aspen waved him off, but it was important to Brick that she knew he intended to pay her back in full. With legal papers and a full expense report, it was time to present it for her signature.

He jumped into his car, picked up some Chinese, and drove back to his house. It was the first time she'd be over, so Brick had made sure to clean the place, do laundry, and ensure the kitchen was spotless. Dug bounced around excitedly, which was good with Kane being away. The dog thrived on company, and he missed his new summer friend.

"Hey, buddy, were you good today?" he asked, checking quickly for any accidents. All clear. He praised Dug, who drooled horribly and stuck out his crooked tooth in glee. He let Dug out to pee, put the food onto plates, and opened a bottle of wine. A gentle knock sounded on the door. "Come in," he yelled.

Aspen stepped in. Dug began barking furiously, then raced over to her full force, sliding the last few feet and bumping into her legs. "Who do we have here? Oh, my goodness. It's a...dog?"

Brick tamped down a grin at her high, half-shrieky tone. Poor Dug usually instilled fear, doubt, or anxiety since he looked like a monster dog from a Tim Burton cartoon. A few women Brick had hosted demanded that Dug be locked up, but he'd ended up choosing his dog instead. He called Dug the ultimate cockblocker.

"I know he looks weird, but he won't hurt you," he soothed. "I hope you're not allergic or anything—" Brick turned and stilled.

Aspen was on the floor, pulling Dug onto her lap, grinning wildly as she allowed him to squirm with delight and lick her face. "What a beautiful puppy you are!" she crooned. She petted his bumpy head and didn't flinch at his drool or crooked tooth. "So handsome! Are you named for my favorite character from *Up*? Daddy was so smart to pick the perfect name, wasn't he?"

His fingers gripped the wine, and his heart beat rapidly in his chest. His skin pinched tightly over his muscles, and it was hard to breathe.

Possessiveness shook him. What was going on? Why did seeing Aspen with his dog make him want to join them, pull them safely against him, and protect them from the crappy world outside that could hurt them?

Aspen giggled and gave Dug all the affection he dreamed of. When she finally got up, Brick noticed Dug's tail standing a little taller and his head thrown back with a bit of pride. Like he knew he was special because Aspen had declared it. "Sorry, I love dogs. And he's a cutie. Oh, wine, yay. I had a crappy day."

She walked over with a beautiful smile, smelling like wildflowers, and Brick did the only thing he could in that moment.

He grabbed her around the waist, lifted her high, and kissed her.

His lips moved hungrily over hers, and with a soft moan, she clung to him, kissing him back. Their tongues danced and played while she buried her fingers in his hair. Brick drank her essence like she was the sweetest nectar he'd ever tasted.

He released her slowly, his gaze pinned to hers. She blinked, then touched her lips. He caught a flash of vulnerability in her cocoa-brown eyes, but it was gone so quickly he wondered if it had been his imagination. She stared at him as if afraid to say anything to break the spell.

"Hey, baby."

Then she smiled, and the odd tension eased. "Hey. I missed you."

"Me, too. I think you recruited another admirer." He motioned to Dug, who sat near her, gazing up with sheer adoration and love as he stood guard.

"Just Dug?" she said, reaching for her wine.

Brick snorted. "And Kane. And Marco. And Patsy and Burger."

She waved a hand in the air. "They're all your friends—who are kind to me."

He reached out and touched her cheek. "You're easy to be kind to," he said quietly.

The air thickened with awareness. She lowered her gaze as if trying to hide something, so he allowed her the secrecy. God knew he needed to hide his own emotions. "Thanks. I like your place. This was your grandfather's?" she asked.

Aspen sipped her wine and wandered the house, Dug trailing her. "Yes. It's run-down and has a basement and cellar filled with junk, but I'm trying to go through it slowly. It's hard to make it mine. I don't want to get rid of anything he may have loved."

Her expression softened. "Yeah, that makes sense. I'm sure it feels like a burden, but for your grandfather, I bet he meant it as a gift."

Brick chuckled. "I'm sure he was also messing with me. He had a wicked sense of humor and liked a good practical joke. Probably figured he'd get away with not fixing anything since he planned to give it all to me."

"Like Dug?" she teased.

"Exactly. He scares the hell out of everyone except you."

"I've been trained to look beyond the cover."

Her words hit home. Brick thought about her book that lay on his bedside table, completed. Half of him wished he'd never read *Fifty Ways to Leave Your Lover.* It had ruined him.

He understood why readers couldn't let the book go without begging for a sequel. Her new book was technically better. The plot was tight, the writing was strong, and all the elements were there for a great read. Brick had enjoyed it. But her first book offered something rare and different.

Too much of it was burned into his brain, not only the way she looked at the world but also her inner vulnerability and bravery. Reading about the asshole who'd betrayed her, using her innocence for his gain, made Brick sick.

He understood what Aspen was looking for in this relationship now. He could see what she needed to write another book like *Fifty Ways.*

He only hoped he could still give it to her.

"Brick?"

He refocused. "Sorry. What is it, baby?"

Aspen stared at him, searching his gaze for something he hoped she found. Her fingers trembled around the glass, and he sucked in his breath as sexual awareness zinged between them, the familiar connection crackling to life. "Remember when you said your body was mine to touch with your full permission?"

His muscles tightened in a deadlock. His cock rose to full staff, demanding freedom. His nostrils flared as he caught her scent and the arousal in her pretty brown eyes. The biggest turn-on was that she was being brave and fighting her natural shyness. He wanted to groan. Drop to his knees and give her anything she asked. "I remember." His voice dipped. "Tell me what you want, and I'll give it to you."

"You. I-I want you. Right now. I want you so much I can barely breathe."

He spit out a vicious curse, crossed the room, and yanked her into his arms.

He couldn't be gentle, not with this ferocious, burning need to imprint himself on her body and take everything she wanted to give. His mouth was brutal as it took hers, his tongue thrusting into her mouth to taste and drink and claim. He tried desperately to slow down, his shaking fingers coasting over her sweet, trim body, tugging off her clothes, but Aspen was just as desperate with her demands.

She ripped at his shirt, and his lip, went wild under his hot hands until he slung her over his shoulder and took her to the bedroom. Hands on her plump ass, he rubbed, dipping between her legs to find her wet and ready. A moan erupted from her lips, and she writhed in his arms, driving him half-insane to bury himself deep inside her.

Brick grabbed a condom and lay on the bed, lowering her onto his chest. She sprawled over him, her hair brushing his bare skin, her hands greedily gripping his cock, kissing him everywhere in a mad fury.

Fuck, he wasn't going to make it. Right on the edge, he panted for control, grabbing her wrists. Her plump mouth was wet, and he remembered the sweet suction on his cock, the way she'd given him pleasure without holding back. It would be a short ride for him tonight, and there was no way he wouldn't wring a few orgasms from her beforehand.

"Brick?"

Her pupils dilated, nipples hard, she stared at him, slightly dazed.

"Not yet. I need something first."

"What?"

He gave her a slow, wolfish grin. "Bring that sweet body up here and get on my face."

Aspen blinked as she tried to process his words. Every inch of her was sensitized and on fire, desperate for the release he could give. She wanted to watch him explode under her, but it seemed he had other plans.

"Get—get on your face?"

His hands cupped her breasts, and he rubbed her tight nipples in slow circles. "Yes. Climb up so I can taste you."

She bit her lip, the dirty request so delicious it felt wrong. She'd never done anything like that, but with Brick, he kept breaking down her barriers, allowing her to feel physically free and powerful. "I don't…know how."

Satisfaction purred in his tone. "Good. I'll show you." His white teeth flashed. "I'll do all the work."

Her pussy clenched with excitement, and she slowly crawled up his body, thighs bracketing his shoulders. Aspen knew her skin was flushed with embarrassment, but she wanted to do it more than she was afraid. He whispered his pleasure, calling her a good girl, and his strong hands reached under her thighs and lifted her, positioning her core right over his mouth.

She stared down in fascination at his hungry stare and the way he licked his lips in anticipation. "So pretty," he crooned. "Hold on to the headboard, and just let me make you feel good."

Aspen obeyed, half-shutting her eyes, legs shaking.

And then his mouth closed over her throbbing, aching center.

"Oh, God!"

His tongue played and teased, licked at her swollen tissues, sucked at her clit as he took his time. A low humming sound emerged that made her gasp and press wantonly against him. The orgasm roared at her, shoving her over the edge in a violent burst of fireworks. She sobbed as he kept going, helping her ride out the convulsions until she was about to collapse. Then he slid her back down his body and positioned her over his erection.

"Condom," he said, ocean-blue eyes blazing with demand.

She opened it and rolled it on.

"Now ride me." He paused. "Hard."

Aspen wriggled into position, lifted, and impaled herself on his cock.

The sensation of him inside her was too much, so she threw back her head and let her body take over. He whispered dirty commands and praised her as she rode him, throwing her into another orgasm, ready to collapse.

Brick grasped her hips and took over, slamming into her with a brutal intensity that broke through all civilities and dragged them both into a primitive world where only pleasure ruled.

Her name was ripped from his lips as he went over.

As Aspen collapsed on his chest, she didn't realize she was crying until he brushed the dampness away with his thumbs and whispered her name. She snuggled against him, feeling both broken and whole, confused and clear, happy and sad…all at the same time.

It was too much to handle.

She pressed her face into his neck and closed her eyes. As if sensing what she needed, he stroked her back and kept silent as night crept in.

Aspen blinked into the darkness. She was wrapped in the warm cocoon of Brick's arms, a perfect counter to the chill of the air-conditioning. The jagged emotional roller coaster seemed to have ended its ride inside her, and she was calm. Her stomach growled loudly.

He chuckled against her ear. "We never ate our food. Ready for a midnight snack?"

"Yes, I'm starving." She sat on the edge of the bed. "Can I borrow a shirt to put on?"

He shot her a wicked grin. "You don't want to eat Chinese food naked?"

Aspen wrinkled her nose. "No. I think we've already pushed my boundaries tonight, don't you?"

He gave one of those deep belly laughs she loved and handed her one of his T-shirts. She slipped it on, loving the feel of the worn cotton and his smell wrapped around her. They headed to the kitchen, where they reheated their food and sat at the counter. Dug sat by her foot, eyes wide, maintaining an intense stare that made her admire his grit and perseverance.

"Dug is so smart," she said, nibbling on an egg roll. "He knows whining is annoying, but if he stays still and maintains eye contact, humans can't handle it. He's mastered the art of begging."

Brick shook his head. "Trust me, he's not the sharpest tool in the shed. He still has accidents in the house, even when he's just been outside."

"I bet he's an emotional dog," she suggested. "He expresses certain feelings depending on where and when he potties. Probably doesn't like being alone. And I bet if he gets insulted, he gains justice in his own way."

"Spoken like a true writer," he said. "You're a master at character."

"Yeah, how would you know?" she teased, breaking off a piece and feeding it to a grateful Dug.

He shrugged. "Just do."

"Where did Kane go?" she asked.

"He had some things to take care of in New York. He'll be back Monday to help me with the tours. Speaking of which, I have some papers for you."

She stiffened. "Okay. You can put it by my purse."

"It needs to be signed." When she looked up in question, he looked uncomfortable. "I told you it was a loan, Aspen. I had a lawyer draw up the contract so I can pay you back monthly. There's a detailed expense form with interest included. You can have a lawyer look it over and get back to me."

"I said I didn't need anyone else involved. This is a deal between us."

His jaw clenched. "I'm not taking your money. And this is just to protect you—so you have it in writing and are clear on the repayment terms. That's it."

Aspen knew it was wrong to want to pretend they had no deal, and this was all real. Paperwork only reminded her the entire thing was fake.

But the orgasms weren't.

The happiness she experienced around him wasn't.

The way he was beginning to be important to her wasn't.

What had she expected? There were bound to be complications when the plan was working so well. She was being ridiculous and irresponsible. Brick was right.

She forced a smile. "No problem. I'll look it over, sign, and get it back to you."

"Good."

They refocused the conversation on lighter things and finished their meal. Aspen ran her tongue over the little strings from the egg roll stuck in her teeth. They drove her crazy. "I'll be right back, gonna use the bathroom. Need to floss." She popped up from the stool and shivered. Her feet were always cold, especially on hardwood floors. "Do you think I can borrow some socks, too?"

"Of course. First drawer on the right. Help yourself. Dug and I will be here."

"Thanks."

She bounded upstairs, grabbing a cozy pair that came up to her knees, and immediately felt better. She used toothpaste and flossed, then tried to smooth out her messy hair but gave up. It didn't matter. Brick had told her many times that he loved her curls, and she was tired of fighting them. With a smile, she left the bathroom, her gaze snagging on something on his bedside table.

Her book.

Her heart stopped. Slowly, she walked over and picked it up, flipping through the pages and finding numerous page marks from him folding the corners. He was one of the criminals in the book world who didn't use bookmarks.

It also meant he'd read her book.

Her fingers stroked the glossy cover as her brain scrambled. Yes, she'd told him the basics of her heartbreak, but she hadn't gone into deep detail. Knowing her truth, Brick had read this book and gained deeper insights into her past. Suddenly, Aspen felt more naked and vulnerable than she had when he was deep inside her. Because now, Brick had been in her brain, had experienced her pain, shared her struggle.

She'd always been okay knowing strangers were reading it because the book felt separate from her, like she'd released it to the world and gained safe distance.

But Brick was different. He was starting to take over all aspects of her life.

Even worse?

Had he judged the silly, young girl who'd slept with her professor, stayed helplessly under his control, and believed in a love that throbbed with falsehoods?

"Aspen?"

Her name sounded from the doorway, soft and firm. She turned and met his gaze. Those ocean-blue eyes brimmed with a calm resoluteness that told her more than words. "You read my book."

It wasn't a question, but he nodded. "I did."

She carefully laid it back on his nightstand. "You didn't want it signed?"

A smile touched his lips. "No."

"Why?"

"Because I didn't know what to ask you to write to me."

The words hit like a sucker punch. He was right. Aspen had no idea what she'd have said. Silence settled as she struggled with the new truth.

"Are you upset I read it?" he asked.

She shook her head slowly. "No. I'm sure you were curious. I just feel...weird."

Brick walked over and sat on the edge of the bed, his gaze intent on hers. "Explain weird, baby."

The soft endearment made her skin prickle. Ryan had never called her anything like that. Maybe because they'd spent the bulk of their relationship sneaking around—the latter half while he lied. Aspen struggled to explain, wanting to be honest. "I'm exposed. You know, all the stuff that most people hide or brush neatly under the rug or stow away in the closet. Sure, I made up a lot of the story, but the emotions I experienced writing it were real." She dragged in a breath and refused to break his stare. It was time to own all of herself—even the broken parts. "I learned most things about love from Ryan. The rest was from books. To say I'm not only inexperienced but not good at relationships is an understatement. I'm not like you, Brick. I haven't figured anything out."

She was stunned when those ocean-blue eyes lit with anger. Face tight, he seemed to be fighting to keep his voice calm. "Are you questioning if I read that book and found you lacking in any way?"

She gave a half shrug. "Yeah."

"Fuck that."

Aspen jerked. "What?"

He clenched his teeth, and masculine temper heated the air. "I'm glad you're not like me. Hell, I've never had the balls to put myself out there for the world to judge and pick apart my decisions. To criticize me for choosing the wrong person to love. You did that, Aspen. You have this great big wild heart you freely gave away, so why is that your fault? It's his. Because he was such an asshole, he couldn't see it was an amazing gift he never deserved."

He stretched to his feet and cupped her cheek. Intensity beat from his aura, and she was fascinated by this suddenly hard, angry man who seemed to want to fight her battles. "You know what I thought when I read that book? That I'd never be worthy of the type of love you can give once you decide who to give it to."

He pressed his forehead to hers while her heart shattered in her chest. The protective way he touched and spoke to her changed everything. And once again, Aspen wondered if she'd committed the ultimate sin by falling in love with a man she'd hired to break her heart.

"I may not be the one, baby. But I'm the lucky bastard here with you right now, and I'm not letting you go."

He kissed her so sweetly, a total contradiction to his blistering, passionate words, and Aspen lost herself in the tenderness. When he pulled away, her world had shifted, and there was no going back.

Overwhelmed by him, Aspen said the only thing she could. "Thank you."

He smiled, then tugged on a curl. "Want to go downstairs and watch a movie with Dug?"

She smiled back. "I'd love that."

They watched Netflix and cuddled on the couch under a blanket, Dug snoring loudly between them.

Aspen gave herself over to the moment and tried not to think about tomorrow.

Chapter Nineteen

One week later, Aspen was returning from a walk on the beach when her agent rang.

She took a deep breath and answered. "Hi, Nic. How are you?"

"Good, darling. How's the beach? Are you still there basking in the sunshine?"

"Yes, and it's wonderful. I forgot what it was like to get out of my apartment and the city."

"I knew it would work—I'm glad I had such a brilliant idea." Aspen pressed her lips together to stop from laughing. She adored her agent, but Nic often forgot that most of Aspen's ideas weren't hers. "I wanted to get back to you on these pages you sent me."

Nic hesitated just enough to make Aspen's stomach drop. "Okay, I'm ready," she said, even though she wasn't. She despised hearing feedback unless it was to stroke her muse's ego and say everything she wrote was perfect and needed nothing. Aspen was sure most writers felt the same.

Nic began. "I think your fans will love it. As usual, the writing is tight and well-constructed. And I'm definitely invested in the story. I want to see what happens next." Her agent always started off with the positive because, under her sharklike mannerisms, she had a good heart. "But it seems...distant."

She closed her eyes. Exactly what she'd feared. "Can you explain?"

"In your first book, I was Mallory, falling in love, experiencing the suffering, all of it. But with this one, it's as if you're telling it from behind a safe wall, watching. I think you need to switch to first-person POV to get deeper."

Aspen already sensed it but found she was fighting the instinct. Third person felt better telling this story. She could gain some space and not become the same character again, watching her life. As much as she loved Mallory, she also had no desire to be her again. She'd moved on, but her readers hadn't. And each time she sat and tried to write, it was a struggle.

Aspen wasn't happy writing this book.

But she had no choice.

"I understand," she said. "I may need a bit of time to sort things out. I have to get the story straight and then go back to layer."

"Of course. You know your process, and I know it will be wonderful. I'm thrilled with these chapters, Aspen. Just keep going. You know how tight our deadline is."

"I know. Thanks, Nic, we'll talk later."

She disconnected the call and stared down at the sandy path. Frustrated tears burned her eyes. The story wasn't working for some reason, and her muse knew it. Aspen had been taking these growing feelings for Brick and trying to translate them into words on the page. She'd skipped ahead to write one of the sex scenes, which came out blistering hot and made her extremely uncomfortable in her seat, but the other pieces fell apart. The plan sounded perfect in her head. Fall hard for Brick, get hurt, write a bestseller. It was the formula for *Fifty Ways.*

She was now falling hard for Brick. How could she not? Besides showering her body with endless pleasure, he was sweet and supportive. The things he'd told her after reading *Fifty Ways to Leave Your Lover* haunted her. She kept imagining what it would be like for a man like Brick Babel to fall in love with her. He called himself unworthy, and though she'd normally suspect it was part of his pattern to charm women, his voice rang with truth.

Somehow, she believed him, which made this so much worse.

He made her laugh. He made her feel good about herself. She craved his company all the time. And when she was with him?

Aspen felt…complete. She'd been comfortable at his house, spending time with Dug, cuddling up to Brick in bed. They'd spent the next day and night together, and since Kane had returned, they were falling into a routine. Depending on his tours and her work schedule, they met for lunch or dinner. She spoke at the local library and another bookstore, which he and Marco attended, and she was glad it went okay, even when she wasn't high.

Sometimes, he'd take her out in the Jeep to see the horses. In the evenings, they'd walk on the beach or sip cocktails on his front porch.

Sometimes, Kane or Marco's crew would join them for a meal.

Being with him was easy. Her normal isolation was such a deep part of who she was, Aspen never questioned it. Never even wanted to change it.

Until now.

Aspen resumed walking, thinking about what she had to do. She was fighting her feelings because she already knew the end. It made sense, but she needed to write a good book.. She had to lean in to the fear, open up, and let go. She needed to fall into another great heartbreak.

There was only one month left.

She may need that support group.

On cue, her phone lit again, and it was Brick. "Hi."

"You up for another all-nighter?"

Excitement bubbled inside. "Are the turtles ready to hatch?"

"Yep. Judy called. She has a group of volunteers but invited us to stay with them. There are no guarantees—they could hatch in the next few days, but I'm up for it if you are."

"I'd love to. I have two podcasts to do, so I'll need to skip dinner."

"No problem, I'll bring snacks. Pick you up later."

She clicked off with a smile. When she got back to the house, Sierra was there. "I'm going to see the turtles tonight!" Aspen burst out. "Have you ever done that?"

"No. I'm not a volunteer, though, and I know Brick is. Also, Judy loves him—big surprise."

Aspen laughed. "You're dressed up. Do you have a meeting?"

Sierra's face dropped. "No. A date."

"That's great! Why do you look so depressed?"

"Because I despise blind dates. Brooklyn's cousin's single friend just moved out here a few towns over. We're meeting for drinks."

Aspen tamped down her laughter. "Well, you look sexy as hell, but I'd advise you to smile and act like you want to be there."

"Ugh. I don't know why I keep trying."

"Because there's a man somewhere out there worthy of your greatness."

A smile twitched on her sister's lips. "Oh, yeah. Thanks for the reminder."

"I need to introduce you to Brick's friend, Kane. It's weird you still haven't met. You didn't see him at the opening?"

"No, he was out with a group when I came by. Why? He's cool?"

Aspen whistled. "Babe, he's a smoke show. Plus, he seems nice. I know he's from New York and living here now."

"I'll keep it in mind, but every single female in town will be clamoring for his attention. How are things going with Brick? You haven't talked about it lately."

"Progressing nicely."

Sierra sifted through her response. "What about the book?"

"A bit of a struggle."

"Hmm."

Aspen cocked her head. "What does that mean?"

"My gut says this whole thing is going to blow up on you."

"I don't want to hear that. You're supposed to be supportive!"

Sierra rolled her eyes. "I'm your sister. I'm here for the truth. I can get you all giddy and sappy when I mention his name. And I know you're having a million orgasms because you won't stop singing."

Caught between horror and laughter, she threw up her hands. "Just stop, okay? I don't need any more voices in my head, other than my damn muse so I can write this book. I'll see you tomorrow. Have fun on your date, but don't be a dirty slut."

Sierra cracked up, making Aspen giggle.

Then she got back to work.

Aspen was amazed by the number of people surrounding the nest when she arrived at the beach. Judy came up to greet them, introducing her to the various volunteers. "I'm sure Brick told you we're not sure about tonight, but it'll be this week."

"What if they hatch during the day?" Aspen asked.

"Sea turtles only hatch at night. It's their best chance to survive, but even with all the help we give them, only a small percentage will make it." Judy's face was creased with concern, but her eyes held a steady light that told Aspen she'd been through the highs and lows many times. "We put in a lot of work this summer and are hopeful with this nest."

Aspen studied the marked-off area where babies would emerge and try to survive. Worry flared. This was nature at its most beautiful and cruel. "So, we just watch? Anything we can do?"

Judy shook her head with a smile. "We've got it under control. Please step away if any activity happens and let us take care of it. Brick's always ready to step in and take the off-shifts, so he deserves a seat to witness."

Another facet of his kindness. Brick never spoke about the things he did in town to help. But just like when he interceded with the wild horse Duncan, he always seemed ready to take responsibility. He was a man who knew how to take care of his own, whether it be his business, family, or community.

"I'm grateful to be here," Aspen said to both of them.

They chatted with the volunteers, who shared their stories and information on the loggerhead sea turtles. They spoke in quiet voices in the darkness, gazes trained on the nest as an excited, nervous energy surged through the air. Brick fed her snacks, and they drank water, keeping watch for hours, bonding with the group, and waiting for the big moment.

Finally, the sun crept up, streaking the sky with vivid orange, yellow, and a hint of pink. The light caught the tips of the waves and danced with glee. The volunteers stretched, groaning, and began packing up.

"Guess we get a do-over," Judy said cheerfully. "You're welcome to come back again later tonight."

Aspen glanced at Brick and smiled. "We'll be here."

Judy tipped her chin, glancing back and forth between them with a curious gaze. Aspen wondered if the older woman was questioning Brick's new love interest or if she was surprised that Aspen was still around. The thought reminded her of Brick's notorious past and how badly she wanted to know the whole story. Especially the bit about Anastasia. But it was none of her business. Even though she'd shared her struggles, Aspen was positive he didn't want to open that Pandora's box. Probably afraid she'd turn in disgust once she knew all the gory details.

But the need to know more danced inside her, waiting for an opening to question him.

Brick interrupted her thoughts and took her hand. "Ready for another workday?"

She snorted. "I'm so tired. I like my sleep."

His eyes danced with amusement. "I heard writers really like naps."

"Cute."

He swung her arm back and forth as they walked down the beach. "I'm good with five hours, so I can push through. But I have a better idea."

"Breakfast?"

"Sure. We'll stop at Duck Donuts, grab a box, and go back to my house. Catch a little more sleep before our days start. I don't have a tour until eleven, and I'm sure you can't string two words together after being up all night."

Her tummy dropped, and her body blazed to life. His gaze seemed to register her sudden excitement, and those blue eyes darkened. "Sleep, huh?" she asked suspiciously.

"Yep. Sound good?"

His face looked so innocent, Aspen couldn't help the laugh that bubbled from her lips. "Liar. You and me in bed hasn't equaled much sleep."

"I'll be a total gentleman. Won't touch you or do anything you don't ask for."

The idea of snuggling with him for a few hours was too tempting to decline. "Okay. But we're just sleeping."

"Absolutely."

Hours later, Aspen had to admit he'd kept his promise.

She was the one who'd asked. Begged. Screamed.

Loudly.

Chapter Twenty

The turtles hatched on the third evening of their watch.

Aspen watched the gorgeous creatures break from the sand and head for the ocean. Volunteers worked with a graceful expertise that was like poetry in motion, ready to block crabs or scavengers poised to interrupt the important journey, checking for hidden holes and smoothing the path ahead, keeping vigil with prayers and hope, even as they knew the odds were against them.

Many didn't make it. Others got to the surf and were taken by the water.

Each loss was felt and grieved. Every success was exhilarating and brought gratitude that balanced the sadness.

By the time the sun rose, the turtles were gone, and Aspen knew the entire experience had changed her.

As she stood with the laughing, sometimes crying volunteers, she was part of a special group she'd never known existed. These people looked beyond their lives to be a piece of something greater, and she was inspired to find a way to give more of herself. To be more than just a lonely writer, happily existing from book to book.

Brick's face lit with a quiet joy that grabbed at her heart. Sunlight falling on his inky dark hair and tan skin on display in his mustard-colored tank, the man was a beach god Aspen couldn't help staring at. He touched her cheek and caught a stray tear that had dropped without her knowing.

"You okay?" he asked quietly.

"Yeah. More than okay." Aspen dragged in a breath full of saltwater and sunshine. "I'll never forget today. It was a miracle I never even knew about. Thank you."

"I'm glad you were here. Do you know this is the first time I've witnessed a live hatching?"

"Really? I thought you'd done it before the way Judy talked."

He shook his head. "Too busy. Sure, I'd watch the nests when I could, help out here and there if Judy needed me, but I've never taken the time to sit all night and wait for a birth. So, thank you."

She blinked. "For what?"

"Inspiring me. Being by my side to bear witness."

His smile was dazzling, flashing white teeth and crinkling the sides of his eyes. The world turned, flipped, and then righted itself. His simple words touched her deeply. The raw emotions inside her swirled together and melded into a light-bulb realization that had her practically gaping at him.

She was falling in love with Brick Babel.

It had happened. She'd done it. He'd done it.

Aspen took a frantic step back to run away.

Her ankle turned, and she fell on her ass.

Brick's reflexes were quick. He reached down and got her upright, gripping her shoulders. "Aspen, what happened? You have a strange look on your face, like you—"

His voice cut out. She stared at him helplessly, wanting to hide but unable to turn away. His gaze pierced deep, holding her frozen in place, unable to speak. Her heart rate sped up, her skin prickled, and she felt as if she was about to pass out.

The breath rushed out of him as he seemed to find his answer.

He couldn't know, though. Right? They were both on three days of little sleep and were probably hallucinating. They were punch-drunk on adrenaline. They'd begin to laugh, sweeping away this moment, and maybe Aspen could pretend later that she'd made up the emotions because of exhaustion.

"I understand," he murmured.

Her cheeks heated. No way was she doing this here, right now, with people behind her, still high on watching the sea turtles find freedom. No way would she accept Brick's pity or regret or pain because she'd finally legitimately fallen for him regardless of their agreement.

"Aspen—"

"I'm very tired," she said firmly, rallying everything inside her to remain calm and controlled. "It's been a lot today, and I just want to go home and rest. I don't know what I'm doing right now."

Her shoulders steeled with resolution. She stared him down, rallying her defenses to fight this one important battle. One she had to win because she wasn't ready for it. Not in this moment.

Brick's gaze shredded her surface defenses, but she refused to back down. Slowly, his expression changed to a polite mask, allowing her retreat. "I'll take you home. It's been a long night."

"Thank you."

He didn't take her hand.

He drove her home in silence and didn't kiss her when she scrambled out of the car, running like the demons of hell were nipping at her heels.

But Aspen knew it was temporary because the man had already caught her.

Brick stared at his phone, willing the three dots to appear with an incoming return text, but it remained blank.

"Fuck."

Two days. Since their incredible moment with the sea turtles, Aspen had gone dark on him for forty-eight hours. And he was terrified that she was ready to shut down and walk away from whatever was going on with them.

He threw the phone onto the counter and wondered what to do next.

The ridiculous plan had actually worked. He was legitimately catching strong feelings for Aspen Lourde. And she'd paid him to finish the job by breaking her heart.

His memory roared back to that perfect moment on the beach. The sun on her skin, the wind in her hair, the curve of her smile. Then the flash of cocoa-brown eyes as she stared at him, completely open and vulnerable. No wonder she'd fallen on her ass. Because when his gaze had met hers, he'd seen the truth.

It had happened for her, too.

And now she was hiding from him and their connection. Could he blame her? Brick wondered if allowing her to disappear was the right thing to do. Take the money and let her move on. She'd gotten spooked. Maybe she'd leave town to return to New York, and this would just be a chapter in her bestselling book.

The painful punch to his chest told him he couldn't let that happen.

Day by day, she'd woven herself more intricately into his life. She was unlike any other woman he'd met. No one had ever made him laugh and ache at the same time or look forward to their next encounter. And yeah, Kane was right.

He was singing.

They'd come this far. Brick needed to find out what waited at the end of this journey with Aspen. But by taking the money, he'd sealed his fate. How could they fight for something real when she'd bought him to do a particular job? Yeah, she'd fallen for him. But the second part of the agreement?

He had to try and destroy her by the end of the summer. Because she still believed it was the only way she could write her book.

Frustration beat in waves inside him. He wanted to roar at the Fates for sending him a woman he was falling hard for, one who could never truly be his. They were on borrowed time. Hell, if he had the damn money, he'd just pay her back and beg for a true shot to see what they could be together. But he didn't. He had his new renovations and a business that was finally working, and he was miserable because Aspen was the sacrifice.

Mood dark, he stepped outside for some air and to wait for a family of four who'd set up reservations. His next tour was full, but he'd agreed to do this run for a smaller group since he had the time. Kane had been great about filling in for additional tours to take advantage of the crowds, and with new ads hitting next week, Brick hoped the rest of the summer would be packed.

If only his love life was as successful.

Marco exited the store and strolled over. "Hey, Brick. You okay? You look pissed."

"Nah, I'm fine."

He felt Marco's stare and gave him a deep frown to mosey him along. Instead, the kid leaned against the window beside him, settling in. The faint smell of weed drifted from him. "Aspen, huh? I wondered why she hadn't come into the store to see me. A fight?"

His brow climbed. What the hell? Was he high and still this dialed in? "No fight. Just a communication issue. We'll smooth things over."

Marco nodded. "Hope so, because she's really into you, dude. And I'm not sure you know, but you've been happier since you started dating. You don't look as grumpy."

He smothered a laugh. Somehow, he figured Marco was right. It had been a long time since he'd felt happy. It was easy to say getting the money for Ziggy's Tours was the reason, but if he was being honest? Aspen was the key. "Maybe. I think she got spooked," he admitted.

Marco scratched his head and nodded. "Feelings are scary. Probably got freaked out and wanted space."

"I'll back off. Wait for her to come to me."

"Bad idea, man. When women have too much time to think, shit goes down you don't wanna deal with. I'd go talk to her. Make her feel not so scared, you know?"

Curiosity sparked. The more time Brick spent with Marco, the more he realized the kid had some serious emotional intelligence, especially for someone who sold T-shirts and was stoned most of the time. "You think? Don't want to come on too strong."

"She needs you to step in and lead. Women are exhausted. They've got too much going on all the time."

Brick barked out a laugh. "Thanks for the advice. You ever been in love, Marco?"

The kid's face turned dreamy. "Hell, yeah. Patricia was my world. We were going to travel together in my van and be free, but the van broke down, and she decided money was more important than love, so she left me. I didn't lead, man. I didn't lead."

Brick slapped him on the shoulder. "She wasn't meant for you."

Marco looked serious. "You should go now. Seize the moment while you're feeling inspired."

"Waiting on my people for this next tour. They're late, but I have to—"

Suddenly, there was a loud beeping. The pink Hummer slowed in front of them, and Maleficent waved to him, along with four people in the back—the family he figured was supposed to have arrived at Ziggy's for their tour. Maleficent hooted with happiness, probably telling the customers they were great friends while she committed betrayal. Brick bet there was an expression of smug satisfaction on her face he couldn't see from the distance.

Son of a bitch. She'd done it again and stolen his clients. How had she managed it this time?

Marco shook his head. "Those were yours, huh?"

"Yep."

Marco turned to face him. "There's your sign. Your tour is canceled. Go get your woman." He pushed away from the window with a lazy smile and headed back to his store.

Brick stared at the kid, slightly shocked.

Yeah, Marco was right. He needed to see Aspen and figure this out.

Brick locked up and drove to Sierra's house. Her sister's car wasn't in the driveway, which was good. They'd be alone. He rang the bell and waited, but no one came out. He knocked. Still nothing. Cracking open the screen door, he listened and heard the tapping of keys. He didn't like interrupting her work, but she was avoiding him, and they needed to talk.

"Aspen, it's Brick. Can I come in?"

The tapping continued. Maybe she couldn't hear him. He eased inside and followed the noise to a back room off the kitchen. Aspen was at the desk, bent over her laptop, with headphones over her ears. Poised in the doorway, he watched her work for a moment, admiring the intense energy she exuded as she chased the words.

He opened his mouth to alert her to his presence, but she suddenly ripped off the headphones, tossed them onto the desk, held her head and yelled, "Fuck my life! This sucks."

A laugh burst from him unchecked, and she screamed, twisting around. Cocoa-brown eyes widened with shock. He threw up his hands. "I'm sorry. I tried knocking and rang the bell, but you didn't hear."

"You scared the hell out of me!" she shouted at him. "I could've died of a heart attack!"

It was the first time he'd seen her in a temper or work mode. She looked adorable with her hair springing wildly around her shoulders, black glasses perched on the bridge of her nose, dressed in yoga pants and an oversized T-shirt that allowed him a generous view of her cleavage. Irritation swarmed around her figure, and a fierce frown furrowed her brows. Brick wanted to pluck her out of the chair and kiss her senseless until she was soft and sweet and clinging to him.

"I'm sorry," he said again. "I didn't want to wait any longer to talk, and you're not returning my calls. Or texts."

Those teeth reached for her lower lip and nibbled. He almost groaned, imagining what her perfect mouth had done for him a few nights ago. "I needed some time."

"I know. But I took Marco's advice and figured I shouldn't wait too long."

Her lips twitched. "Marco, huh?"

"He's wise beyond his years." Her half smile encouraged him to walk farther into the room. "He also misses you."

He heard the tiny catch in her breath. "Marco misses me?" she asked.

"I do, too."

He offered the words in a quiet voice, waiting. In seconds, her face lost its resolve, and she looked lost. "I miss you, too. It's the most awful thing that's happened this summer."

Direct hit. Amusement rose. "Missing me?"

She nodded with misery. "I didn't think it would happen. That I'd become attached so quickly. I thought it'd just be about the sex but it's not."

God, this woman would be the death of him. She was so refreshingly open and honest, even though she was shy and so beautifully innocent. The mixture intoxicated him. "Baby, are you saying the sex isn't good?"

That earned him a full laugh, and he wondered if they were still fighting or if she'd come to a conclusion she'd share. "Please. Your ego does not need any further evidence of your bedroom prowess."

Her cheeks turned a hint of pink, and he reached out to grab her hand, pulling her from the chair. He kissed the top of her head and rubbed her neck where she was probably sore from hours of sitting. Her scent wrapped around him, she leaned in, and he was a goner. "Pulling out the writerly words, huh?" She muttered something against his chest, but her body began to slowly loosen as he worked her muscles. "Is that what happened on the beach that morning? Things got too real?"

Her voice was muffled. "Maybe."

Brick certainly wouldn't push her to confess her feelings. It was enough to see the truth in her eyes and hear her admit she was confused. He needed her to remain open to what they were building and see it to the end of the summer. It was the only way they'd both know what was fact and what was fiction.

"It's not just you, Aspen. I'm feeling the same way. And yeah, it's confusing, even though this was the goal. But I don't want to stop or back off. Not now. Not when this is getting…important."

She sucked in a breath and lifted her head, eyes troubled. "I need to write and deliver this book. The deal has to stand."

Brick nodded. "Then it stands. But we both have to commit to opening up to each other and not holding back. Neither of us deserves to have regrets at the end. Don't you agree?"

His heart beat madly in his chest as he waited. The stakes were higher than either of them had first believed. Sure, they'd agreed to do this, but Brick doubted she'd thought it would work. He had figured they'd have great sex, a good summer, and he'd say goodbye with his family business saved. He hadn't counted on emotion getting in the way.

"You want to continue as is? Keep up a fake relationship for the deal?"

He tipped her chin up with his finger. "No. I want us to continue getting to know each other. This is no longer fake, and we both know it. I'm willing to go all the way because I'm not ready to lose you. We have a month left to be together. Do you want that, too?"

She swallowed. Seconds ticked by. "Yes."

Relief coursed through him, and damn if his knees didn't almost sag. She had more power over him than he imagined. "Good." He kissed her, enjoying the full softness of her mouth, his tongue gathering the taste of coffee, mint, and Aspen's unique flavor that made his head spin. Knowing he'd have her naked and on the bed in minutes, he kept his hands to himself and slowly eased away.

"I'm guessing the writing isn't going well?"

She blinked, obviously trying to refocus on the conversation. His fists clenched to keep from taking what he wanted, but Brick didn't want to interrupt her workday, and he had to get back for the next tour. A sigh escaped her. "Not really. I'm not sure what the block is, but I keep chipping away at it. How about you? Still fully booked?"

"Yes, except Maleficent is up to her old tricks. I booked a family, and she rode past with them in her Hummer. Kidnapped them somehow and wanted me to know it."

"What a bitch." Shadows darkened her face. "I think I may need to go and have a talk with her."

He chuckled. "I appreciate you wanting to fight my battles, but it's okay. With the new computer software, I can track where they found me and see how she intercepted. Much easier now to plug the holes."

"Good. But I still want to have a woman-to-woman chat about business ethics." A knock on the door had her jumping. "Oh, wait here, that's Sierra's delivery. I need to sign for it."

She disappeared, and he glanced around the room, which was obviously a spare for Sierra. There was a big closet and a clothes rack stuck on the far side containing a bunch of dresses. A sewing machine was set up beside the desk. He knew her bedroom was upstairs, so he figured Aspen liked to work in a separate room, maybe to keep work and sleep separate. He studied her desk, grazing over the half-written page of her book, then fell to an open pad with pictures and handwriting.

Curious, he picked it up and casually flipped through it.

It seemed like it was some sort of graphic comic book, but with more story than pictures. The characters were a pig, a bunny, and a snake, reminding him of a teen boy crew being silly and outrageous, sometimes snarky. The drawings were awesome, giving him the exact type of personality traits that seemed to match their narrative. It was done with bite-sized scenes that were complete stories. He'd never seen anything like it before, and as he read more, he couldn't help grinning and shaking his head.

Where had this come from?

"What are you doing?"

Her sharp voice interrupted him. "Aspen, did you write this?" She gave him a wary look, seemingly hesitant to answer. Because she wasn't claiming the story as hers, he offered a bit more. "Whoever did has some mad talent. That stuff is hysterical. Makes me laugh."

Aspen cocked her head. "Really? It's just a hobby. I love to draw and came up with this concept for fun. It's a stress release when I'm writing."

"Damn, you can write adult fiction plus humor? And draw? I'm impressed."

Her face lit up. "Thanks. It felt like a silly thing, so I've never shared it. I'm glad you like it."

"Do you have any more of these stories?"

She laughed. "Sure. I have a lot of stress to work out," she joked. "Probably a dozen notebooks filled with that stuff."

His finger tapped the pad, and he placed it back on the desk. "Well, I'd love to read more if you'll let me. Tell you what, if I got to read stuff like that back in the day, I'd be a bigger reader now."

Aspen smiled. "Thanks for the ego boost. I brought a few notebooks with me if you really want to see."

"Good. For now, I'd better leave so you can get back to work. Dinner? My place?"

Suddenly shy again, she ducked her head. "Sure."

Brick grabbed her, kissed her hard, and stepped back. "Bring an overnight bag. Kane won't be home tonight."

He loved the slight widening of her eyes and the hit of arousal that made him feel like a king.

Brick swaggered as he walked out.

Chapter Twenty-One

The hot, lazy days of August rolled by.

Aspen fell into a pattern and stopped being aware of time. She worked on her book during the day and fought for every word. She mourned the joy her writing had previously brought and grabbed her happiness with her comfort characters from *Zany Zoo.*

After bringing Brick another notebook to peek at, she was stunned to find how hard he laughed when he read her stories. She began to bring her new work to him to share and enjoyed his enthusiastic reaction. It was a needed break from the seriousness of crafting the sequel amid pressure from her agent and editor.

She went to the beach every day for a walk and sometimes sat with Sierra to watch the sunset if she was home from the shop. They grew closer as they shared the mundane parts of their days, and Aspen admitted that she'd missed the connection. Sure, they saw each other regularly, but visits didn't allow for the deeper relationship she was beginning to find with Sierra.

They went out with Brooklyn and Inez a few times. When asked about Brick, Aspen just said they were having fun and enjoying the summer, ignoring Sierra's worried, disapproving look.

Ziggy's Tours began to grow steadily even amid Maleficent's attempts at sabotage. The pirate chest and targeted marketing paid off, and Brick began booking more families, which filled up the vehicles and extra time slots. Aspen liked to visit during quiet times, checking in on Marco and the gang and helping them with their sales schemes. She even did a video with them and posted it on her socials, giving them a shoutout that led to more foot traffic.

Marco also said he got a few DMs sliding in from the publicity and scored a date.

Aspen tried to push off her worries for the end of the summer, refusing to think about how it could end. All she knew was that every time she was with Brick, there were no empty spaces inside her. He filled her up. He pushed boundaries and gave her endless pleasure in bed. He made her laugh and was an amazing conversationalist when he wasn't grumpy, diving into subjects with deft experience and actually listening to her without the goal of changing her mind or swaying her opinion.

She panicked each time she thought about the contract. They'd agreed to the ending, but the process of falling for Brick Babel was changing her every day.

Depending on their roommates' plans, they bounced back and forth between Sierra's place and his. Aspen still felt awkward regarding other people in the house. She was used to her isolation and privacy and preferred them to have the place to themselves.

Also, Brick said she was a screamer. Oh, he uttered it with pure wicked satisfaction, but she'd almost died of embarrassment. No way did she want anyone to hear her.

Sierra was out with her girlfriends and crashing at Inez's house, so they had dinner at the Oceanfront Grill as the evening stretched ahead of them. She giggled as Brick squeezed her knee under the table, knowing it was her ticklish spot. Relaxed from the wine, amazing sole francese, and the heated look in Brick's eyes, they hurriedly asked for the bill. The waitress dropped it off, and Aspen swatted Brick's hand away, shaking her head.

"Excuse me?"

Aspen looked up. A woman with bright-red hair, a pretty, freckled face, and lush curves wrapped in an apple-green maxi dress paused beside their table. Her gaze flicked back and forth between them. Cold judgment beamed from her amber eyes.

"Yes?" Aspen asked.

"I'm Riley. I've heard about you in town, visiting your sister. I don't mean to be rude, but it's important to speak up and do what's right, even though it would be easier to watch another woman make the same mistake."

Brick remained silent, his face tightening. Her heart pounded crazily as she braced herself for what was coming. Her tongue stuck to the roof of her mouth, but she managed to push through. "What is it?"

Ignoring Brick, Riley leaned over and whispered in an urgent tone. "Leave him before it's too late. He's a liar and a manipulator. What he did to Anastasia was tragic."

Brick's voice flicked like a whiplash. "Really, Riley? You're going to do this now, on my date?"

Her head whipped around. "Yes, because you've hurt too many of us. She should know the truth."

"What's the truth? That we never dated? That you know nothing about me?"

The woman made a low noise of distress in her throat. "You think it's a game, but one day, you'll realize what you did. We all know this act now. Pretending to care while you play games with good women who trusted you. It's disgusting."

Brick's jaw tightened, but he remained silent. Aspen stared at him in shock as a wall slammed down around him, closing him off. It was as if he'd retreated emotionally and was no longer there. In fact, he reminded Aspen of the man she'd first met at the bar at the beginning of summer.

Riley straightened and smoothed her dress. "You deserve better. We all do."

With a quick turn on her heel, she disappeared farther into the restaurant.

Aspen looked at Brick questioningly, but he ignored her. "We'd better go." He got up and walked out. There hadn't been a time when he didn't pull out her chair and escort her out, so she grabbed her card and receipt, popped up, and hurried to follow him.

His moody expression and stubborn silence stopped her from asking about Riley or Anastasia. Brick drove with jerky movements, obviously bothered by the whole encounter. Aspen took her time gathering her thoughts as they pulled into her driveway.

Usually, she'd have waved off the exchange as another of his famous heartbreaks that weren't her business, but things had changed between them. Worry niggled at her. She'd heard the story, and yes, it sounded terrible. Leaving his fiancée without a word and ignoring her while he dated other women was simply cruel. Also, very unlike the Brick she knew. But what if there was more she hadn't been told?

Had he gotten her pregnant and abandoned her? Lost his temper and hurt her? She couldn't see the man she'd gotten to know doing any of those things, but it was time to find out.

She finally needed answers, whether he wanted to share or not.

They walked into the house, and he went straight to the kitchen, pulling out a bottle of whiskey. Pouring two fingers into a glass, he raised it to his lips and shot it back.

Aspen winced. Yeah. This would be bad.

"Can I get you something?" he asked.

"Just seltzer, please. I think I've had enough wine for now."

He nodded, filling the cup and handing it to her. The air between them hummed with the growing tension. Aspen took a few sips, then crossed her arms in front of her chest to ward off the ache. "Brick?"

"What?"

"Will you tell me what happened with Anastasia?" she asked softly.

His jaw clenched. Those ocean-blue eyes turned cold and distant, and a shiver ran down her spine. "Do you really want to know the truth?" he asked in a clipped voice. "Don't you think it's easier with this relationship to believe what you want?"

She flinched and tried to ignore the hurtful remark. "Don't *you* think we've come too far to lie to each other now?" she challenged.

He spit out a curse and shook his head, pacing. Frustration clung to him, seeping from his pores, but Aspen couldn't tell if it was because he didn't want to confess his sins, or if he was ashamed of what he'd done. "What Riley told you at the restaurant? Do you believe it? Believe I've lived my life bedding and dropping women to deliberately hurt them?"

Aspen waited to answer, letting the silence stretch as she gave his question some deep thought. "No. But all the signs show she's telling the truth. There's an actual support group your exes attend. The entire town talks about you, Brick. And my sister told me you abandoned your fiancée and humiliated her in public by dating other women in front of her while she begged for closure or explanation. My sister, her friends, and random strangers warned me you would do the same to me."

"Which is exactly what you paid me for, isn't it?"

The pain crawled inside her and buried itself deep. He was right, but she hated it. Because Aspen knew it had become so much more than a deal for this fake relationship. That she was falling in love with him for real, and time was running out. Aspen lifted her chin, refusing to back down. "Yes, it is."

"Then it's best to let it go. Believe what everyone says, and we'll move forward. You set those rules, Aspen, and I agreed."

Aspen realized the right thing to do would be to honor his request. Back off and give Brick his privacy, knowing she'd be gone in a few weeks, and this thing they were doing would end.

But her heart wouldn't let her. Aspen wanted the true ending, not a fake. She wanted Brick's words, even though she may hate hearing how he'd hurt someone so brutally. It was time to rip down the last of the barriers and face each other, knowing there was no holding back.

"I can't." The words dropped from her lips like stones. "I need to know what happened. I'm asking, Brick."

He spun away, raking his fingers through his hair. A sense of desperation clung to him as if he knew nothing would ever be the same once he told her.

"Don't be a coward."

His shoulders bunched. He turned slowly, his gaze locked on hers. Ocean-blue eyes glittered with a shocking array of pain, regret, and fury. "I've never broken anyone's heart, Aspen." A bitter laugh ripped from his lips. "Anastasia Wallace destroyed my reputation, my home, and my soul while the town watched."

Her head spun, and the ground shifted beneath her feet. Aspen stared at him, recognizing that the story he was about to share had never been told before. And once she heard it, she'd never be able to view him the same.

So, she kept quiet. Gave an encouraging nod. And listened.

"We dated in New York. Got serious. I was crazy about her. She worked for a corporate recruiter and was ambitious. She was a fireball, wanting to go to all the parties, stay out all night, and network with the powerful to create connections. Everyone adored her. Anastasia was larger than life and wicked smart. After six months together, I decided to ask her to marry me, and we got engaged."

Shock barreled through Aspen. They'd moved fast. He must've been madly in love. The knowledge caused a heavy weight to sink into her gut, but she remained still and refused to interrupt.

"I was so fucking happy. I thought I had the world at my feet. I'd have the fat job, the perfect girl, and the wedding of our dreams." He shook his head, and she noticed his fingers trembling around the empty glass. "But I was stupid. One day, I came home from the office early because I'd spilled coffee on my suit. It was going to be a quick change since her place was close. I walked in and found her fucking her boss, wearing my ring."

Aspen closed her eyes in shared pain. God, she knew that feeling well. Nothing prepared someone for their life to be suddenly ripped to shreds along with their dreams. A lump stuck in her throat. "I'm so sorry, Brick."

He refilled his glass and slowly sipped. "I used to wonder over and over what would have happened if I hadn't spilled that coffee. Would we have been happily married? Would she have kept cheating right under my nose? Would I have eventually found out? I was sick to my stomach. I confronted them right there and left. She came after me, begged for my forgiveness, saying it was a mistake and would never happen again. But it was too late for me. I couldn't go back and forgive that type of betrayal."

He dragged in a breath. "A week later, I found out my grandfather passed. I left my job and moved out here. I was still in shock and wanted to focus on rebuilding the business. But one day, she suddenly appeared at my door. Told me she was intent on making it up to me. Said she'd settle in OBX so we could be together and start a new life."

Aspen's jaw almost dropped as his words hit home. She'd shown up after cheating on her fiancé? Brick must've seen her face because his humorless laugh echoed in the air. "Yeah, do you believe it? When I freaked out and sent her away, she had a total breakdown. Said she'd given up everything to come after me and wouldn't leave until we were back together. At first, I thought it'd blow over, and she'd leave once she knew I was serious. I was focused on Ziggy's Tours, moving into the house, and settling into the community. I hadn't been here for years."

Her voice trembled. "What happened, Brick?"

He rubbed his head, obviously fighting the memory. Weariness threaded his tone. "I found out Anastasia had rented a place here. She was going all over town, talking to everyone she could, saying she'd moved because we were engaged and she wanted to support me. Said I'd kicked her out of the house because I changed my mind and dumped her. She spun so many lies about our relationship. I have no fucking clue. I was in my head and had no idea my reputation was being created and destroyed by her. She told people I'd cheated on her back in New York, but she loved me and always took me back. She showed up at my house and the business, stalking me. After trying to reason with Anastasia didn't work, I began ignoring her. Unfortunately, that made things worse. So, I did something I should never have done."

"What?"

"I began casually dating. Started going out to bars on dates so Anastasia would see I was moving on without her."

"It didn't go well, I assume."

"She started having meltdowns in public. Crying and begging me not to hurt her. Saying she loved me and couldn't take the way I was treating her. Soon, those casual dates I'd had began talking about how I'd led them on. Before I knew it, things had gotten out of control. Riley became close with Anastasia and started spreading more rumors about how I was sleeping around, and then I became a local legend both in and out of the bedroom."

Horror washed over Aspen. This was a story out of a television movie, absolutely ridiculous but completely believable. "Did you sleep with any of the women?"

"One. I told her about Anastasia and that I wasn't interested in any type of relationship. She said she didn't care and spent the night. The next day, I heard she was weeping about falling hard for me and being rejected. I stopped then and just pulled back, but it was too late."

"What happened with Anastasia?"

"She stayed for four months and finally moved back to New York. But it was too late. Everyone believed her story."

"No one listened to your side?"

"I had no one to tell the truth to. My grandfather was gone. Kane was back in New York. I had no friends or other relatives here. So, for the next year, I leaned into my reputation. I became what they expected and let the stories grow. I dated here and there, but even if I didn't sleep with anyone, I heard about my exploits later."

"I can't believe they lied." She breathed out. "It's like playing the game of telephone. It's easier to keep adding and embellishing than work hard to get to a truth that's not as dramatic or gossip-worthy."

"Maybe. All I know is Anastasia will always haunt me. Riley started that support group in a show of solidarity and won't let anyone forget. It's tiring, but I've learned to live with it."

He emptied his glass and lifted his head to face her. His face was expressionless, but those piercing blue eyes shone with echoes of a deep pain. "Now, you know my side. I gave you what you wanted. But the bigger question is the one that really matters."

"Which is?"

Brick stiffened as if preparing himself for her answer. "Do you believe me? Saying it out loud makes the story sound far-fetched to me." His lips curved into a humorless grin. "Hell, I wouldn't blame you for having doubts. I guess it's up to you what happens next."

The man before her stood tall, hips braced, chin up. She expected rebellion, pride, or even anger. Instead, Aspen only connected to an inner hurt he'd never been able to truly heal from because no one knew. Writing her book had helped her work through the agony. Telling her sister and crying on her shoulder helped her heal. But Brick had been trapped by the lies, forced not to just accept them but build a life based on a man who never existed.

He never had a chance.

Aspen watched him and sensed the wall between them. He'd given her power no one had had: the power to know the truth and hurt him. It was what he expected. It was what he knew.

The trembling started deep inside her, moving throughout her body until her entire being was filled with an empty ache.

"I think there's only one thing left to do," she managed to choke out.

He was carved stone, unyielding, unfeeling, alone. "You want me to leave?"

"No, Brick. I want to take you to bed and show you all night how much you mean to me."

He jerked back, his gaze narrowed in suspicion. Aspen crossed the room to him, reaching out to curl her arms around his shoulders, raising her chin to look him in the eye. "You believe me?" he gritted out.

"Of course, I believe you. What happened wasn't fair or right, but it doesn't matter anymore. You're stronger. You carved out a life you love here, on your terms, and you know who you really are." She paused, dragging his head down so she could rest her forehead against his. "*I* know who you really are, Brick Babel."

His breath broke her lips, and then he was kissing her, hands thrusting into her hair to hold her still for the sweet thrusts of his tongue. She opened and gave him what he asked for, refusing to hold back. The kiss deepened, his animalistic groan vibrating from his chest and sending a thrill down her spine. The taste of whiskey and spice swarmed her senses. In moments, their hands became frantic, desperate for naked skin and the intimate connection Aspen found in his arms.

Clothes spilled to the floor in a tumble. They fell onto the couch, his hands cupping her breasts, her mouth on his chest, writhing beneath him with a desperate hunger that blurred all civil lines. His tongue licked her taut nipple, sucking hard, moving her easily until she was on top of him, straddling his naked thighs.

"Fuck. Need a condom."

Those talented fingers thrust between her legs, finding her wetness and rubbing. She let out a keening wail, clenching around him. "I'm on the pill for my period," she gasped.

"I've been tested. I'm good."

"Thank God."

Heat seethed under her skin, exploding outward as he worked her, watching her fall apart as the orgasm hovered right before her. "Not yet," he growled. He pulled away, grasped her hips, and slammed her down on his cock.

Aspen hissed out a breath as pleasure cascaded inside her. He filled all the empty space within her, and she clung to him with greed, surrendering to his slow, deep thrusts, allowing her eyes to open halfway so their gazes locked in the most vulnerable moment. She whispered his name as he took her higher, a possessiveness that thrilled her carving out the hard lines of his face.

The tension cranked to an almost painful need, and she writhed above him, desperately trying to go over. "Brick, I need—"

"I know what you need, baby. God, you're on fire for me."

She squeezed him tight, and he groaned, pumping in and out in a steady rhythm. Then he reared up, scraping against her clit at the same time he hit that spot deep inside.

Every muscle locked as Aspen screamed, convulsing with tiny shudders as the release rolled through her in endless waves. She gripped him tightly, tearing at his hair while she heard his shout as he followed her over.

It was a while before she slumped over him, boneless, still twitching from aftershocks. He kissed her with a sweetness that broke her heart and then mended it. "I'm taking you to bed."

"I can't move."

"Good. I'll carry you." With easy strength, he lifted her, grabbed a bottle of water from the refrigerator, then started up the stairs. When she made a sound of distress, he paused. "Are you okay?"

"My sister's going to kill me. I promised her I'd leave the couch alone."

And then they began to laugh.

Brick stared into the shadows, listening to Aspen's steady breathing.

She'd believed him.

That fact kept turning over in his head as he made an effort to understand. He'd never thought a woman would accept his story without fact-checking, questioning, and holding major doubt. He'd gotten used to living with the lies the past year, ignoring the heated glares and the line of women who liked to flirt with danger and seek him out to become part of the gossip. No one ever wanted to know who he really was, and that was okay.

Until Aspen shattered his world to pieces.

Even now, she sought him in sleep, her soft body cuddled against his, her elegant hands reaching out to lay on his chest. A mix of raw emotions beat inside him, fighting for release. It was both a familiar and a new experience. With Anastasia, it had been all fire and hunger, like trying to catch a tornado he'd never be able to tame. He'd believed in them, though, until her cheating and lying ripped away any hope that remained. Brick found it easier not to care. Over the past year, he'd gotten good at shutting things down inside him and building a wall no one could cross. He'd believed he was happy enough.

Aspen had changed everything.

But he was on borrowed time.

He touched her springy hair, a smile curving his lips at her beautiful face relaxed in sleep. This was a woman who not only fought hard for her dreams but also for anyone she loved. The way she listened and not only supported but understood the grief he'd gone through allowed him space to finally breathe. Freely.

The realization crashed through him just like Aspen had come into his life.

He loved her.

Ah, fuck.

Brick closed his eyes and fought a groan. He loved her. All of her. He wanted her to belong to him and stay. He wanted her in his life and his home. He wanted her body, her heart, and her soul.

How could a feeling be both awful and awe-inspiring? How could he experience terrible fear and ferocious hope at the same time? It was as if everything inside had shattered and allowed room for new. For her.

Like all the pain he'd experienced was worth it because it had brought her right here. To OBX. To him.

But…

Aspen still planned on writing her book and returning to New York. She expected him to hold up his end of this devil's bargain and break her heart.

That was the missing piece. If he told her his feelings were real, would she stay? Could she write her book anyway, or had this deal secured him to an action he couldn't complete? Was there a way they could both win instead of lose?

His gut lurched. He hadn't allowed himself to open up since

Anastasia, but damned if he would act like a coward. He'd fight for Aspen and battle his instinct to pull back and protect himself.

Aspen had pushed him tonight because she wanted the truth. She wouldn't have done that if this was still a brief affair. Brick was sure she felt more for him but was afraid to admit it.

Just like him.

Which left them at an impasse.

Two more weeks. He'd need to use them well and show Aspen they didn't have to be a temporary summer or a book. They could be more.

He had two weeks to convince her to not only fall completely in love with him but also get her to stay.

Chapter Twenty-Two

"Come out with us tonight," Aspen urged her sister. "You can finally meet Kane."

Sierra had been busy with meetings and covering shifts for her employees who wanted their own summer vacay. Aspen had filled in and had a blast, even though she was a terrible saleswoman and screwed up the cash register a million times. They'd had a lot of laughs, at least.

"I don't know, babe, I've been exhausted."

"Just one cocktail, and you can go home. I want to hang out as much as possible before I have to leave."

Her sister stopped packing her tote and gave her a serious stare. "Yeah, about that. What are you going to do now that the first half of the master plan worked? You still running back to New York?"

She nibbled her lip with unease. Things were…complicated. Since the night with Brick where he'd admitted the truth, the last of the barriers had dropped between them. At night, their bodies faded into each other like they were one. During the day, they talked and laughed and shared without hesitation. She craved him like an addiction, but instead of the fierce ups and downs, it was as if they floated together at the same peaceful pace.

The idea of leaving Brick Babel tore her apart.

"Yep. Just what I thought," her sister said. "I warned you. He has a deadly power over women, and now you're caught in his net."

Her brows snapped down. "Don't say that about him. I heard the real truth, and it's not what you think. Brick has been getting a bad rap for a long time, and I'm sick of it."

Sierra's eyes widened. "Are you kidding me? What did he tell you?"

She hesitated, not wanting to share something so personal. "Let's just say the stuff with Anastasia has been distorted. He shared some things in confidence that I don't feel comfortable telling you right now."

"And you believe him?"

Aspen held her sister's gaze and spoke from her heart. "Yes. He told me the truth. And now I'm asking you to believe me and know I'm not caught up in some spell of his creation."

Sierra took a few minutes to answer. The doubt slowly morphed into acceptance. She nodded. "Okay. I trust you. You're the one who can figure out people faster than anyone and see their true souls. I suck at it."

"Well, I screwed it up with Ryan."

"No, you didn't." Aspen jerked in surprise. "I clearly remember you telling me your gut said something was wrong. You didn't trust him, but you were moving forward anyway."

"I said that?"

"Yeah. I told you it was never too late to change your mind about canceling the wedding, but it was as if you'd committed and refused to back down. But you knew, Aspen. You always know. You just didn't want to listen."

The words lodged inside her for further contemplation. "Maybe. I used to wonder what Mom would have said to me," she admitted.

The pain on her sister's face almost made her regret the words, but then Sierra reached out and snagged her hand. "Me, too. Being an orphan really sucks."

Aspen let out a weak laugh. "You should've been the writer. I get jealous of people who have parents to go to. Sometimes, I feel like Mom is screaming at me to get it right but won't tell me what to do."

"So do I. When my marriage ended, I kept going over what Mom and Dad would have said. I kept thinking I could've taken all the money from the divorce and splurged on a world cruise while I had glamorous affairs in every country."

Aspen nodded. "Yep, they would've definitely advised something outrageous. But you opened your own store and took a risk, and now you're this badass businesswoman. Mom and Dad are super proud."

Sierra shot her a grateful look. "Thanks. Same with you being a famous writer."

"It's the relationship stuff we seem to screw up with," Aspen said. "Weird, right? That was Mom and Dad's strength."

Sierra sighed. "I got married too young because it was comfortable. I felt lost after the accident. And with you? Ryan took advantage of his power and age to control you. That wasn't a healthy, real relationship. You know that, right?"

She blinked. "Not healthy, but it was real. I bled all over the page for that one."

Her sister shook her head. "I'm no expert, but it seemed you gave, and he took. He created the rules without you even knowing. You and Brick are more real, even though you agreed it's fake. I've never seen you this happy without the usual anxiety. You're not judging every action to see if it's right or wrong. You're just…you."

The words hit hard, and she shuddered with aftershocks. Aspen thought over her interactions with Brick and realized her sister was right. Unfortunately, her feelings weren't helping her write the book. Her muse dragged her feet, kicking and screaming as if she knew it wasn't her choice. Too bad the contract was signed, and she'd committed to delivery.

Her sister's next question was a second hit that battered her heart. "How do you really feel about Brick?"

Admitting the words made it real. But this was her sister, and the only person she could talk to and trust. Heart pounding, palms sweaty, she said aloud what had been beating inside her for too long. "I'm in love with him."

Sierra sucked in a breath, and sympathy flickered in her eyes. "That's awful."

"I know."

"God, you're so screwed."

"I know."

"What are you going to do?"

Aspen groaned. "I don't know. I need to think. The end of summer is almost here, and there's not much time left. I decided to follow it through and see where we are next week."

"Are you still struggling to write the book?"

She nodded. "It's the weirdest thing. I'm finally experiencing all these deep, wild feelings but when I try to put it on the page, it's not working. It's so different from when I wrote *Fifty Ways*. It was as if I was pouring out my pain. So, I'm afraid…" She trailed off, hating to say it.

"You're afraid you need the breakup in order to write the book," her sister finished.

A lump settled in her throat. "Yeah."

Sierra shook her head. "You need to figure this shit out, Aspen. Love isn't something you just walk away from because you weren't expecting it.

If Brick is the person you believe, maybe he's in love with you, too." Her sister paused. "Is the book worth giving that up for?"

Oh, God, she didn't know. All she'd wanted was to stick to the plan. But the way he looked at her with tenderness, kissed her with passion, and shared his heart told her they were on the same page. Even though no one was talking.

What a mess.

"I can't deal with all these questions right now. My brain will break."

Sierra nodded. "Okay. I'm here whenever you want to talk."

"Thanks. Will you come tonight?" Aspen asked. "Please?"

"Fine, but just one drink. And to finally see this famous Kane, who's already raising a ruckus around here."

Aspen clapped her hands. "Thanks. I'm heading to Ziggy's. I'll see you later."

She waved and got into her car, driving to Brick's. He had an hour's downtime, so she'd bring him lunch and check on Marco. Her conversation with Sierra kept replaying in her mind, but there were no solutions. Only more questions and what-ifs.

When she pulled up with a bag of sandwiches, Brick came outside to meet her. His face was carved with satisfaction. She gave him a quick kiss and studied him. "You look like the cat who ate the canary," she teased. "What's up?"

"Isn't that a cliché?"

"Nothing wrong with the tried and true. What are you, a critic?"

He laughed. "Kidding. I'm just relishing one small win over my competitor."

"Maleficent? What happened?"

He gave her a smug grin. "Went into town to check on my coupons and flyers in the golf place. Seems Maleficent has been sniffing around there, trying to gather clients, and I ended up meeting a family of six who'd scheduled an afternoon tour with her. I gave him my coupon, told him about the pirate chest for the kids, and he ended up booking with me instead."

Aspen grinned back. "Uh-oh. We have a war."

"I'm not about stealing clients, but it just fell into my lap. Kind of nice to turn the tables on her."

"Cliché, but I understand."

He leaned over and kissed her, nipping at her lower lip. "You're cute. And you look pretty."

She practically beamed with joy. Her breezy, sunshine-yellow mini dress was paired with cute, comfy sneakers. She'd braided her hair to keep it tamed and donned some gold hoop earrings. She was finally getting used to his compliments and actually believed him now. Her confidence had bloomed, and it felt good. "Thanks."

"Let's go eat, and I'll tell you more."

Aspen went to follow him in when a pink Hummer roared into the parking lot like it was pissed off. She turned and saw a woman with long, black-and-blue hair jump out and stalk over. She wore black shorts with a ragged hem and a snug black T-shirt with *Maleficent's Wild Tours!* scrolled on the front in silver glitter. Black boots completed the outfit, giving her a wild, witch-like aura that was completely fascinating.

"Okay, Babel, you've crossed the line. If you think you can steal my clients, you have another thing coming."

Brick pushed Aspen behind her in protective mode and walked over. "You're kidding me, right? You've been stealing my clients for the past year. I just happened to come across them, had a chat, and they booked. I didn't do it deliberately like you."

The woman practically fumed with temper. "I'm only keeping things fair for my business. Ziggy was the one who started it! Poaching my clients behind my back until I caught on and started fighting back. And I'm not going to let you step in and think you're better than me like he did."

Brick looked like he was about to lose his temper, so Aspen stepped between them. Her statement about Ziggy made bells ring in her head. There seemed to be a story behind this business game she was playing. "Okay, we all need to calm down. Maleficent, I'm—"

"Aspen Lourde?"

The woman's face turned from anger to shock, then worship. "Oh, my God! You wrote *Fifty Ways to Leave Your Lover*. That's my favorite book. What are you doing here?"

She smiled, humbled by the compliment. "I'm so glad you enjoyed it. I'm staying with my sister for the summer, working on a new book."

"Set in the Outer Banks? That's amazing. I can't believe it. That book changed me. It was so real and raw." A frown settled on her face as she glanced back and forth. "But what are you doing with Brick?"

She felt Brick stiffen beside her. Aspen reached out and took his hand. "We're together. And he's been upset about the things you're doing to try and ruin his business. Can you both agree to play fair and let the past go?"

A rush of emotions flickered over Maleficent's face, but it was the echo of pain that hit deeply. "You think I deserved to be Ziggy's left-overs? I loved that man. I didn't care if we were competitors, because if he won, we both won. But then he dumped me and began playing games with my clients." A furious glare didn't hide the humiliation; she obviously hadn't let go of what had happened and was continuing to lash out at Brick.

Empathy poured through Aspen. She couldn't imagine having to continuously be around a man she loved who'd moved on, then tried to hurt her business.

"Did my grandfather really do that?" Brick asked in a low voice.

"He sure as hell did. And I decided to fight hard while I had the chance, and your business was finally failing. It was my time, and I took it."

Aspen stepped closer and met her gaze. "I'm so sorry you were treated like that," she said. "I don't think Brick knew the real background. He was involved in his own fight to try and save a family business."

The woman's lips tightened, but some of the anger dissolved. "Well, no one bothered to ask me," she muttered. "You roared into town like you were here to take over with all your big plans. But my business was finally the hot one in town. I wasn't about to let you take that away from me. Not after Ziggy."

"I don't blame you for feeling like that," Aspen answered. "But this can't keep happening. It hurts both of you. Most tourist towns have tons of competitors, and they all manage to get plenty of business. Plus, you each have niches you fill. Don't you think a truce is finally in order?"

Maleficent stared at her, then Brick. "I don't know."

"You can't be truly free until you let go," she said gently. "Ziggy's still haunting you every time you steal a client or do something to hurt Brick. Do you really want to keep living in the past?"

The woman's dark eyes turned glassy. Female to female, she understood her heartbreak, so on impulse, she reached out and grabbed her hand, squeezing tightly. Maleficent dragged in a breath and let it out slowly.

"Maybe you're right."

Her head swiveled to Brick. "You won't be an asshole?"

He grinned and shook his head. "No. I admire what you've built here, Maleficent. Don't want to fuck with it. I just want to be able to run my grandfather's place in the way I envision. Okay?"

Aspen held her breath.

"Okay," Maleficent said grudgingly. "Can I get a signed book?"

Aspen laughed. "How about I bring it to your office tomorrow? I'd like to see it. I'm crazy about the pink."

"Right? Sure, come over tomorrow. Just no spilling secrets to the enemy," she warned. But there was a softer edge of humor to her voice that made them both smile. The woman took off and left them alone.

Brick stared at her. "I can't believe you just did that."

Aspen shrugged. "Sometimes, people just want someone to listen and truly hear them. She must've really loved Ziggy. I bet she'll lay off now that she got to tell her side."

"No one ever took the time to do that," he said quietly. "Only you."

"It's the writer in me, I think. Always delving into people for my characters. I also took this Gallup Strengths test, and I scored number two in empathy. A pain in the ass sometimes, but it has its benefits."

She smiled, but it faded when she caught the look in Brick's eyes.

Passion. Admiration. Tenderness.

Love.

Everything inside her stilled as he allowed her full access, not trying to hide or turn away. Slowly, he reached out and ran an index finger down her cheek, his lips curved in a smile that was almost sad, as if he already knew how things would end. "You're an incredible woman, Aspen Lourde."

Her lip trembled, and a longing to step in and give him her words washed over her.

I love you. I'm not sure how it happened or what I'm going to do, but I don't care. I love you, and I'm yours.

A terrible ache spread through her as she remained silent, frozen in place and terrified of opening her mouth.

His finger dropped. "I guess we should eat."

Aspen managed to find her voice. "I guess we should."

They went inside the office, and both pretended nothing had happened.

Chapter Twenty-Three

Aspen and Sierra had saved a table at Sunfish, which was already packed. Brick came in and squeezed next to her, giving her a quick kiss. "They giving away free oysters or something?" he asked. "This place is crazy."

"Band tonight," Sierra said. "Inez and Brooklyn are joining us."

"Great. Marco and the guys said they'd stop by. Kane should be on his way soon, too."

Aspen smiled as he kissed her again, and Sierra made appropriate gagging noises. Brick lifted his brow. "Is this what I was missing when I didn't get a sibling?"

Aspen rolled her eyes. "Oh, and so much more."

"I found out about the couch," Sierra said sternly. "To say I was disappointed is an understatement. I was promised."

"Oh, my God, stop!" Aspen cried out.

Brick began laughing, especially after he caught her red cheeks. She had no idea how Sierra had figured it out, but Aspen was a crappy liar, so her denial sucked. "Your sister's a wild one," he said with a straight face, earning a smack and a tortured groan.

Thank God Sierra's girlfriends came then. Brick took their drink orders and headed to the crowded bar. "You two are adorbs," Brooklyn announced. "Things are still going well?"

"Yeah, we're happy."

"What are you going to do when you have to go back home?" Inez asked. "Is it serious?"

Aspen kept her smile as her mind flashed back to that afternoon. They'd managed to move past the moment, but it was like the cliché elephant standing between them. Eventually, they'd need to address their feelings, even though the ending had been agreed to. For these next few days, it would be easier to pretend, as cowardly as that was. "Not sure. We'll see."

She shifted the conversation, and they fell into casual chatter, pinging to different subjects as Brick returned with their drinks. Marco, Patsy, and Burger came in, crowding into the group, and soon, everyone was laughing, talking, and drinking.

Sierra left for the restroom, and Kane showed up. He introduced himself to Brooklyn and Inez and high-fived Marco and the guys. "I'll get the next round," he said with a grin that made the girls trade interested looks. Yeah, Kane was a hot commodity. Women were already sneaking glances at his pressed khaki pants, crisp white shirt, and expensive shoes. He gave off an aura of masculine elegance, reminding her of old-school James Bond as a ginger, with that undercurrent of sexuality that gave him the perfect edge.

He went back to the bar with Brick, and Sierra returned. "Kane's here," Aspen said, raising her voice above the music.

Her sister chuckled. "If I finally meet him, will you promise to stop talking about how great he is?" she teased. "You're being a meddling matchmaker."

Aspen threw up her hands. "Just looking out for you, sis. Inez may fight you for him, though."

"Hos over bros, babe."

Aspen cracked up. She didn't know how much time had passed when the guys returned with all the drinks, and Kane got caught up in a dialogue with Marco. Strangers pressed in, and it got harder to keep the group together.

She pulled at Brick's arm. "*Let's introduce them*," she mouthed, jerking her head over.

He nodded, motioning to Kane. "I want you to meet Aspen's sister," Brick said.

Kane took a few steps, and Aspen eased her sister in front of her. "Kane, this is Sierra. Sierra, this is Brick's friend, Kane. He's visiting from New York and helps Brick out with some of the tours."

She glanced at them, excitement dancing inside as she waited for them to make googly eyes at each other or share a heated, knowing stare.

Instead, Sierra's eyes widened, and she jerked back. Her drink fell, shattering to the floor while applause broke out in favor of things getting broken. "You okay?" Aspen asked, checking that her sister hadn't gotten any glass on her.

Sierra didn't answer. Concerned, Aspen noticed her sister's gaze was still pinned to Kane, so she glanced over.

He also stood still, staring at her sister as if he'd seen a ghost. An array of emotions flickered over his face. His voice was barely heard in the noisy bar. "Sierra?"

Her sister jumped like she'd been shocked. "Um, hi. Nice to meet you, Kane." She pressed a fisted hand to her trembling mouth. "Aspen, so sorry, I gotta go. I've got an…awful headache. Tell the girls I'll see them later this week."

"Wait, I'll go home with you."

"No!" Sierra blinked and seemed to be forcing a smile. "No, stay. I want you to stay. I just really need some sleep and alone time. Bye, Brick. Talk to you guys later."

She stumbled out of the bar and disappeared.

Brick frowned. "Poor thing. She didn't look well."

"I know. Kane, I'm sorry, my sister's usually social. She's been tired this week."

Kane's lips tightened into a thin line. Sweat beaded his brow, which was strange because she'd never seen him buckle under even the most intense heat. "No problem. You know, I'm feeling a little off myself. Think I'll head back if that's okay?"

"You, too? Hope something's not going around," Brick said.

He said goodbye to everybody at the table and left.

"Was it something we said?" Aspen teased, leaning against Brick.

"Hope not."

They spent the next few hours hanging out before everyone began to disappear.

"That was fun," she said, climbing into his car. "I never go out like that."

"How come?"

A tiny bit buzzed, she searched for the answer. "I guess I didn't make many friends I wanted to go hang out with. I'm alone a lot and never craved being social. But I'm starting to like it."

"Even in college? Or were those your partying days?"

"They should have been. Got a little wild freshman year, but then my world began to revolve around Ryan. Since he was a secret, it was easier to stop making friends who'd ask too many questions. Easier to be alone."

"Asshole. I'm sorry, baby."

His simple apology soothed the old wound. She'd begun to change again, into her best self. Would she ever be able to return to her isolated existence? Would she fall back into her old routine or crave something new? Her connections in OBX had become special to her. She'd grown and figured out new things about herself.

"I think balance is a good thing," Brick said, pulling away from the curb. "Most people have trouble with their own company. I like that you're comfortable with yourself but have a great instinct about people. I never would've spoken to Maleficent in that way to get her to open up. Same thing with Marco and helping him with the store. Everyone who meets you says you're special."

"That's a really nice thing to say," she said, touched by his compliment.

"Just the truth." He cut her a glance, then took a side road. Bumping down a dark path, she looked out at the abandoned road that seemed to lead nowhere.

"Do I need to be worried? This looks like a serial killer's haunt."

He flashed her a wicked grin. Turning off the engine, he dimmed the lights. "I realized Sierra is at her house, and Kane is at mine. And you're still not comfortable having someone else there, right?"

"I'm sorry. I know it's silly, but I feel weird about it."

"Don't be sorry. I respect you for being truthful. So, I guess we're having car sex."

He pushed the side button, and the seat moved back, then reclined. Aspen was caught between a gasp and a laugh. "Car sex? Are you serious?"

"Yes, because not getting my hands on you tonight is a deal-breaker." His voice dropped to a sexy growl, and he tugged her over. Masking a giggle, she climbed on top of him and propped her hands on either side of his head. In this position, her breasts pushed against his chest, and she straddled his hard, muscular thighs. His erection notched into the V of her legs, making the familiar sweet, hot ache seep through her. "See? It's a classic for a reason."

She wriggled a bit, and her back bumped the steering wheel. "A bit constrictive."

"It will force me to get creative."

He took her mouth in a deep kiss, and soon, her surroundings faded away under the sting of the need to touch and taste him, to feel him pulse inside her and fill her up. Limbs bumped and tangled as she managed to lower his zipper and hike her dress up around her waist. Those talented fingers slipped under her panties to stroke and tease, and she groaned and bit his lip as she moved over him, chasing her pleasure.

"That's right, baby, take what you want," he commanded, tearing the fragile lace to the side and thrusting up to enter her. He slid in easily, and she rode him, her lips fused to his, squeezing tightly and speeding up the pace as release crept closer. His hands cupped her breasts, thumbs tweaking her tight nipples as she began moaning and twisting with her growing need.

Aspen arched hard, desperate, and he shoved one hand between them to find her throbbing clit. He stroked and rubbed and petted her, whispering hot, dirty demands in her ear. And then everything went bright and hot as she exploded.

"Yeah, just like that. Fuck, you feel so damn good," he growled against her neck as he bit hard and caused mini convulsions to quake through her core. Grasping her ass, he jerked his hips and followed, and she watched his face as he experienced his own orgasm, falling apart inside her, gaze locked with hers.

She collapsed against him, burying her face in the crook of his neck. A half laugh escaped. "That was intense."

"Best car sex ever," he murmured, stroking her back and kissing her cheek. Insects and crickets chattered. The night closed around them like a cocoon. The air in the vehicle smelled like sex and cologne. Warm and safe, cuddled against him, Aspen was completely fulfilled.

Her voice was barely a whisper. "Let's stay here a little while. I just want you to hold me."

His arms tightened around her. "I'm not going anywhere, baby."

With a satisfied sigh, she let herself go and surrendered to the moment.

Two days later, Aspen stopped at the store to see her sister.

She poked around as Sierra finished with a client, then walked to the counter. "Hey. Have you been avoiding me? I keep missing you and feel like I'm playing a role in *Weekend at Bernie's.*"

Sierra rolled her eyes. "Always so dramatic. I've just been busy."

She stared at her sister with suspicion, noting something was off. "Do you still have a headache? I felt bad about letting you leave alone that night."

Sierra turned away and began polishing the counter. "Don't be silly. I wanted you to stay."

"What did you think of Kane? Isn't he cute?"

A long pause. "Seemed okay. Didn't get to talk to him."

Aspen frowned. "Is something else going on that you're not telling me about? I'm getting a weird vibe here."

"No. It's nothing. Well, just that Riley came into the shop today. Told me she'd seen you out with Brick and gave me a lecture like I had to save you."

"Are you kidding me?"

"No, for real. I thought over what you said about Brick and started to get pissed off. I mean, she was lecturing me like Brick was some kind of criminal. I told her she didn't know the whole story and to back off, and then we got into it a bit."

She blinked. "You got in a fight?"

"Kind of? I told her she was being a hothead and feeding the flames of the past and to just let Brick get on with his life and leave you alone."

"You said that?"

"Yep. She didn't like it much and stormed out. I'm starting to wonder if you're right. All this talk about him never leads anywhere. He hasn't dated anyone for a long time—until he began seeing you. And since you two have been dating, I have to admit…"

Aspen cocked her head. "What?"

Sierra sighed. "Well, he's sweet. He's really sweet to you, Aspen."

Her insides softened and got melty. At the same time, a strange dread kept pulsing in her stomach. As if she knew time was running out and there was only one real ending. "He is. But I keep waiting for the drama and heartbreak to come," she joked.

Her sister gave her a lengthy stare. "It's not supposed to be like that, you know. You were strong after the breakup with Ryan, but I worry you think it's the norm."

Aspen tilted her head in question.

Her sister continued. "The pain. The heartbreak you're paying Brick to give you. Sure, there are many ups and downs and good and bad in a relationship, but the real stuff is sometimes more boring than you think. It's what I miss the most about my marriage."

It was rare that Sierra shared such vulnerability. "You always said your divorce was a gift because it showed you the truth."

"It did. But the quiet, intimate moments were real. God, I have to believe that. Sharing a laugh over a private moment. Knowing what the other will order at a restaurant—or what they won't. Arguing over the remote and then agreeing to watch a show together. Singing to a song on the radio while you drive. It's special. You know what my favorite time was?"

Aspen waited, knowing her sister didn't need prodding.

"Falling asleep next to someone who cares about you. You're shrouded in quiet and darkness while you listen to their breathing, and for a little while, everything is calm. Safe. You're just in the moment and happy. That part was really, really nice."

Aspen watched her sister's face tighten, then smooth out. Her heart panged. Had she ever felt that with Ryan? No. It had been fierce angst and anxiety wrapped around fragments of pleasure and feeling worthy.

But she'd felt it with Brick, and in such a short time—the sense of quiet intimacy and knowing.

"I just don't want you to close doors with Brick unless you're sure," Sierra said.

"Got it." She'd never really thought about the dynamics of her relationship with Ryan. She always focused on the betrayal and pain, not the actual day-to-day. Maybe Sierra was right. She had no idea what was normal.

Sierra sighed. "I feel bad for Brick getting trashed all over town. Especially since he didn't do anything."

"Agreed. I think it's time I did something about it." Sierra waited while her thoughts spun, then formed a plan. "Where is that support group? Isn't it tonight?" Aspen asked.

Sierra nodded. "I think so. They meet at the wine bar at seven. Have their own separate room set up so they can trash-talk and drink."

"I think I'm going to pay them a visit tonight."

Her sister gave a slow, evil smile. "I think that's a great idea. I'll come with you."

"You will?"

Sierra harrumphed. "Think I'm letting my little sister go into the shark tank alone? Hell, no. I got your back."

It was time for her to go to that support group.

It was time for her to track down the real truth.

"Ladies, we have two new members tonight. Sierra and Aspen have decided to join our support group."

Aspen kept her expression neutral as she looked around the room. Five women were gathered around the table. The room was cute, with a lantern chandelier, a carved table resembling cork, and dark-wood furnishings that reminded her of a cozy library. The bartender—Neal—knew them all by name and brought in a bottle of red and another of white, with a platter of cheese and crackers.

Besides Riley, Aspen had met the waitress Kate when she was out with Sierra. The other three were strangers. All were attractive and around Aspen's age. They greeted her with warmth, and then Riley began a quick introduction.

"This is a safe place where we can talk about our experiences with Brick Babel and try to heal. Many of us have PTSD from his treatment or can't seem to move on due to a hold he still has over us. We all vow to honor everyone's privacy and keep our stories in the sacred circle."

Aspen refused to look at her sister; she'd crack up if she did. This was the strangest thing she'd ever seen, but until she knew why these women were here, Aspen didn't want to judge.

Riley continued. "Before we begin, is there anything you'd like advice on from the group?"

A lovely brunette with olive-toned skin and large, dark eyes raised her hand. "I have a date this weekend with a guy I met on this app, and I was wondering if I should wear a dress or go more casual. Like maybe jeans and a sexy blouse? Because if I show up overdressed, he may get the impression I expect some five-star restaurant for dinner or think I'm uptight."

Lacey—a petite blonde who looked a bit like Pamela Anderson—leaned in. "Jeans, a sexy tank, and a cute blazer. With heels. It's always my first-date outfit and never fails."

The brunette chuckled. "Thanks, but I think you can show up in a bag and score a second date."

Kate chimed in. "No, I second Lacey. Just make sure you meet him there and text one of us the info so you're safe. I don't trust anyone from Myrtle Beach."

The brunette looked upset. "He's a golfer. Hot pic. Said he just moved there."

Lacey sighed. "They're all golfers now. Most flunk out of college and come down south to start a new life. Who starts a new life at twenty-three? I need an adult, not a child."

Riley cut in. "Brick fit the qualities you wanted, right, Lace?"

Lacey shrugged. "Sure. I guess. Hey, I need some advice about work. I'm thinking of moving to the Grill Room instead of Sunfish because the tips are supposed to be better, but the guys are definitely cuter where I am now. Plus, it's more casual and fun. What do you think?"

Aspen watched in fascination as the women drank wine and fell into dialogue filled with all the usual topics. They traded stories about their week, complained good-naturedly, and acted like this was a normal get-together of friends who wanted to connect.

Why was this called a support group?

Sierra seemed to wonder the same thing because her brow rose like asking, "*WTF?*"

Riley seemed to be the only one irritated with the direction the evening took. She raised her voice to a high shriek. "Ladies, I'd like to remind everyone this is now the time to share your stories about how Brick hurt you. Would anyone like to jump in first?"

Silence.

Riley shifted in her seat. "Bethanny, what about you? How did it feel when Brick took you to that fancy dinner, and then you had drinks at his place? You said you got scared, right?"

Aspen leaned in, holding her breath.

Bethanny was a tall, willowy woman with pale skin and straw-colored hair, who liked to bite her nails. Worry spilled from her, and when she spoke, her voice was so faint that Aspen had to strain to hear. "Yes. That dog. I've never seen a dog so strange. I was nervous to be around him."

"Dug?" Aspen asked.

Bethanny gave a small nod. "I think that was his name. He looked like a monster or an overlarge rat. Tried to chase after me, and I got upset. And then Brick told me I should go home because if I didn't like his dog, it wasn't worth us spending time together."

"And that devastated you, correct?" Riley prodded.

"I guess."

Aspen bit back a groan. This was ridiculous. She didn't have all night to spend trying to find the truth, so she did what she did best. She got straight to the point.

"Excuse me, everyone, but I wanted to ask a few questions. About Brick."

The ladies stared at her. Riley tightened her lips. "Aspen has been dating Brick this summer," she explained. "I warned her about him and referred her to this group if she needed help. It seems she's finally seen the light. We're here for you, Aspen. Tell us your story."

Sierra let out a strangled laugh. Riley glared.

"Well, I'm here to learn the truth. I started dating Brick at the beginning of the summer, and we've had a wonderful time. I'd like to ask each of you to tell me what horrible thing Brick did to you. It would help me so much."

"We can do that," Riley said with encouragement. "Lace, you first."

"Okay. Brick and I met at a bar. We talked, and he bought me a drink, then asked me out. I told him I was playing in a volleyball tournament the next day and asked if he wanted to come by and have a beach day. He agreed and showed up to watch. After the game, we ate lunch together."

Aspen waited.

"I was really into him, but he never called again. When I saw him at the bar after that, he was polite, but I could tell he didn't want to see me again, and I felt hurt and rejected."

Silence fell. Aspen cocked her head. "That's it?"

"Yes."

Riley shook her head. "Lace is sensitive to rejection. It was a hard time for her."

Sierra squeaked. A glance confirmed she had mashed her hand over her mouth to keep herself from busting out laughing.

"Okay. Thanks for sharing. Who's next?"

They all took turns telling stories about how Brick Babel had stopped calling, politely refused to continue dating, or told them straight-up he wasn't ready for a relationship. Kate said she'd gone to Brick's house for a sleepover, but her ex-boyfriend called, and she decided she wanted him back, so she left.

"You never slept with him?" Aspen asked.

"With Brick? No. I slept with Max that night, though. Bastard. He used me and cheated again. I should've stayed with Brick, but he didn't want to give me another chance."

Aspen's head was going to explode.

She rubbed her temples, caught between frustration and humor at the so-called *devastating* things Brick had done to them. Finally, she couldn't take it anymore. "Did anyone at this table sleep with him?" she yelled.

The women all looked at each other. Then shook their heads.

"Do you know any of your friends who slept with Brick? Or have you just heard stories about him sleeping around?"

Each of them admitted they didn't know anyone personally but had heard multiple stories.

Sierra uncovered her mouth. "So, the truth is, you just like to get together to drink wine and shoot the shit, and Brick Babel is an excuse to meet. Right?"

Lacey shrugged. "Yeah."

Riley sputtered. "I know what he did to Anastasia—my best friend. No matter how you want to defend him, he's done damage here. People were hurt."

Aspen stood, her temper rising. "All I know is Brick has been taking this shit for far too long. He's done nothing that hundreds of other men in this town haven't also done. And you can believe what you want about your so-called *friend*, but if you dig into the real truth there, you'll find Anastasia was the one who damaged the relationship—not Brick." She jabbed her finger in the air at Riley. "But I guarantee you'd rather believe the gossip than dig for the truth."

She threw her chair back, and Sierra stood up beside her. "From now on, leave him alone. Get on with your lives and rename this the Thursday Wine Club or the Badass Bitches. Anything without Brick's name in it, okay? Because if you don't, I'm going to have to kick a little ass since he's the man I love."

She tipped her head at the ladies' shocked stares. "It was nice meeting all of you."

Aspen stormed out without a backward glance.

Lacey's voice echoed down the hallway.

"I really like the Badass Bitches name."

Chapter Twenty-Four

They'd officially run out of time.

Brick finished locking up for the night as his mind spun endless possibilities. August was almost gone, and Labor Day was the official close of summer. Aspen had said she needed to deliver the book soon, but she'd been struggling. Too many unspoken things hung heavily between them, which blocked them from moving forward.

Tonight, he had to face them.

"Another busy day, huh?" Marco said as he strolled out. "You've been killing it."

Brick nodded. "With a lot of help. I've finally dialed into my niche, and the place is attracting new customers. I've got an ambitious marketing plan, including some billboards for next year."

"That'd be dope. Maybe I'll look into it, too. We'll rule OBX together."

Brick grinned. His affection for Marco had grown, thanks to Aspen. He was happy to call him a friend and didn't mind looking after him and the guys. "Sounds like a plan."

"Does Aspen still plan on leaving? Or is she gonna stay?"

Brick winced at Marco's bold question. "Not sure yet. We need to talk about it tonight."

"Well, after what she did at the support group, I'd say she wants to stay." Marco chuckled. "About time someone took down those ladies."

Brick cocked his head. "What are you talking about?"

"You're kidding. You didn't hear about what she did?"

His jaw clenched. Had Aspen been gathering information about him?

Did she plan to use these women's stories to rationalize why she wasn't going to stay? Sickness clawed at his gut, but he had to know. "What did she do?"

"Stormed the place to burn it down, man. I was out with the guys the other night, and this cool chick Kate, who works at Sunfish, was our waitress. I must've mentioned you because she asked if I knew you. I said yeah, we were friends, and then she told me Aspen came to the support group and bitched them all out and said to leave you the hell alone or she'd kick ass. Kate said she'd never seen anyone stand up for you before. Guess they took a vote to change their name to Bitches or something like that." Marco shrugged. "Aspen's fire, man."

Brick's entire being shook, and raw emotion surged over him in a tidal wave.

She didn't go there to gather evidence to leave.

She went there to blow up the group. To defend his honor.

Joy exploded through him. She was coming over tonight, and he'd be ready. He'd tell her the truth: that he was madly in love with her and wanted her to stay. With him. They'd work it all out: the book, the contract. Nothing mattered but them. She'd proven she wanted the same exact thing he did: for them to be together.

"Thanks, Marco. I gotta go."

"Anytime. Tell Aspen I said hello."

Brick rushed to his car. He had some errands to take care of before she arrived.

He was ready when she walked in.

Aspen's gasp of delight made him want to strut like old-school John Travolta. He'd raced to the floral shop and bought up a ton of Tisha's stock. Vases of wildflowers were spread around, and rose petals were scattered on the bed. He'd attempted to sprinkle them on the stairs, but Dug had tried to make dinner out of them, so Brick ditched that plan. He'd lit a bunch of candles and placed them strategically around the house, then dimmed the lights. Music drifted from the old boombox, giving off that tinny sound reminiscent of their beach dancing. The table was formally set with china and linen, with steaks, potatoes, and green beans. Champagne was chilling, and he'd put a strawberry in each crystal flute.

Brick wanted a certain mood to say all the things he'd been holding back.

She blinked, and he caught the sheen of tears in her cocoa-brown eyes. "Brick, this is so beautiful," she breathed, glancing around. "No one has ever done something like this for me before."

"Because they were assholes," he said lightly, giving her a kiss. Dug did his usual freak-out, and she dropped to the floor, petting and crooning to him in the way he loved. When she straightened, Brick's hands itched to grab her and touch her in all the ways she loved, teasing out those throaty moans that drove him crazy. But he was going slow tonight, though it would be hard. Her short dress bared her gorgeous legs, and he kept thinking about what was underneath.

Or wasn't.

Tamping down on his testosterone, he poured champagne and pulled out her chair. "I know you said you'd be hungry, so I figured we'd eat first, then take our time with after-dinner drinks on the deck."

"Thanks. I'm bleary-eyed from sitting and cranking out words. I try to get out for walks now, but I wanted to push today."

Brick read between the lines. Her deadline was approaching, and things weren't going well. His gut clenched as he wondered what would happen if she couldn't write the book she wanted. Hopefully, they could figure it out together tonight. "I used to think I'd thrive in a corporate atmosphere. It was all I dreamed about. Now, I realize my soul would have slowly withered. Maybe I'm more like my grandfather than I originally thought."

Her warm smile stole his heart. "Isn't it funny how certain paths lead us to surprises? How something terrible can become a precious gift? It's one of the things about life that fascinates me."

He cut into his steak, which was perfectly rare and tender. "You have the soul of a writer. I just wonder about something."

She sipped her champagne and sighed with pleasure. "What?"

Brick chose his words carefully. "You've expressed that the last two books haven't been fun to write."

Her face pulled into a frown. "True. There were rare moments, but mostly, it was painful."

"But writing the *Zany Zoo* stuff makes you happy."

She looked up in surprise. "Yes, but that's just a hobby. I use it to destress from the real book I'm writing."

"Aspen, I think those stories are amazing. They make me laugh, and I can't imagine there's not a market for those types of books. It hits perfectly—right between adult and teen. I would've been hooked. You have a wicked sense of humor, and those characters come alive."

He registered the puzzlement in her eyes. Had she really never thought of publishing *Zany Zoo*? She had notebooks full of treasure that she kept aside. Watching her struggle to piece together a sequel this summer that didn't make her happy frustrated him. He knew she loved writing. Brick just believed she was writing the wrong thing.

"I made a name for myself in the adult genre. I have a responsibility to give readers what they're asking for. My agent, publisher, fans…they all expect this book. *Zany Zoo* is a bunch of cartoons and fun stories. There's no money in it."

"I think you may be missing something more important.

"What?"

He smiled. "Joy. When you work on those stories, you glow. And giggle. When you write your so-called *real* books, you're unhappy."

She nibbled at a green bean and snuck Dug a piece of meat. "Writing is hard."

"I can imagine. Did you have this experience with the last two books you wrote?"

"Kind of? I think it's because I was in my head too much. When *Fifty Ways* made Book of the Month, everything changed."

"So, you wrote things for commercial success after you went viral?"

"Well, I wrote a story I was interested in and tweaked it for success. Wrote it to market. Nothing wrong with that."

"I'm not saying there is. When you wrote *Fifty Ways*, was that hard?"

"No. It was like the words poured out of me. Like therapy. I think back to that experience and believe it was a way to transcend my pain. Ryan had robbed me of my confidence and voice. I took it all back with that book."

Made sense. If he'd had writing talent, Brick wondered if journaling or creating a book about his experience with Anastasia would have freed him sooner. Which brought them full circle.

Because the reason she'd hired him was to give her the same type of painful experience she'd had for her first book. In Aspen's head, she believed there was only one way to write a bestseller. It was up to him to convince her otherwise. "I only wanted to point out that there may be other ways to explore your writing career. Writing stories that make you happy."

He registered her nod but knew it would take her some time to think about it and decide. Brick only wanted to see that type of fire in her day-to-day work. Aspen deserved to flourish, not cripple herself struggling with books she didn't really want to create.

Brick changed the subject, and they finished dinner. Dug got a few more pieces of steak, which made him snort, cracking Aspen up. Brick refilled their glasses with bubbly, and they moved out onto the deck to listen to the night music. They sat close, holding hands, and he played with her elegant fingers, their heads bent close. Peace settled over him. He had it all.

Grandpa Ziggy's home.

The tour company.

OBX.

His friends.

Dug.

And Aspen. The woman he'd fallen completely in love with. He'd gotten everything he never dreamed about, and it was everything he had ever wanted or needed.

"I heard what you did at the support group," he said quietly.

Her head lifted. She stared back at him with a touch of wariness. "How'd you find out?"

"Marco heard about it from Kate, a waitress at Sunfish."

She winced. "Yeah, she was there. Are you getting any backlash?" He frowned, and she rushed on. "I'm sorry if I embarrassed you. I just got really mad about you getting trashed all over town, and not one of those women had a real story to share. Plus, they admitted they didn't know anyone you slept with and supposedly destroyed. It was bullshit, and I wasn't going to allow it anymore."

His throat thickened, blocking his words. Brick stared at her, fiery and pissed off on his behalf. She'd charged into that group of women and defended his honor. It was the sexiest thing he'd ever seen, and his insides clenched with the need to tell her everything she deserved.

"Aspen, what you did was a gift," he finally said. "No one has ever stood up for me before, let alone taken the time to hear my side. You've been tearing down every damn part of my world since I met you."

She blinked. "Is that a bad thing?"

He cupped her chin and pressed his forehead against hers. His heart sang, and he wanted to take her to bed and demonstrate all the ways he adored her. "No. It's the best thing. You changed me, Aspen Lourde. I'm not the same man I was before you came, and I never want to let you go."

Her eyes widened, and he smiled.

"I love you, baby. Completely. I'm asking you not to go back to New

York. Stay with me."

Her breath caught. A wild flare of emotion lit her eyes, and as he waited for her to return the words, a tiny bubble of doubt seized his insides, clenching his gut. Brick ignored it. This was their happy ending, and he refused to allow his insecurities to ruin it.

He waited. A sob escaped her lips, and slowly, she pressed her mouth to his, trembling in his arms. He went to take the kiss deeper, but she pulled back. "I love you, too. I fought my feelings for a while, but I can't lie or deny the truth. I'm in love with you, Brick. But I can't stay."

Stunned, his hands dropped to his sides. Tears shone in her eyes.

"I have to leave, and I have to write this book, just like we both promised."

Shock barreled through him. He'd been so sure of her response; it took him a few moments to realize she'd rejected him. Even though she admitted to loving him.

Brick remained calm. She was scared, just like he'd been. With a little patience and understanding, Aspen would take the leap.

"I know how important this book is to you," he said carefully. "What if we can have both? You can still write the story as you need, but we'll stay together."

Misery etched the features of her face. "I signed a contract. I promised the world this sequel, but it's not working. Something's broken inside me, Brick, because I can't finish the story unless this relationship ends in heartbreak. Just like it happened that first time. I can't seem to connect with the words any other way."

Her explanation was the thing she'd promised from the beginning. But that was before they fell in love with each other. Wasn't their relationship stronger than a book? "What if you tried to write it anyway?" he suggested. "Maybe you haven't been able to finish because this thing between us is unsettled. A little more time or some tweaks? We can work this out."

"I wish we could." Her voice sounded choked. "I've been trying, but the book is failing. I can't do this, Brick. I'm so sorry."

As he stared at the woman he loved, Brick realized she had already made up her mind. Somehow, she'd convinced herself this was the only way to complete her book. She'd tied her pain to the story, and he was the casualty. Instead of fighting for their relationship, Aspen was retreating to her safe space, believing she had no choice.

His happy ending shattered, and Brick wondered if he'd recover this time.

He loved her.

This man, this extraordinary, gorgeous, kindhearted man, had fallen in love with her. It was a complete plot twist she hadn't planned on. Watching the shock on his face broke something inside her. His expression changed from open joy to distance. That wall slammed down between them. Aspen wanted to cry with grief, beg him not to pull away. She wanted to say that she'd stay, forget the book, and claim him.

But she couldn't.

Because he was right. She was unhappy writing this book. It was their story, twisted with fiction, but she couldn't get it right. Just like *Fifty Ways*, she had to experience the pain to connect with the story and write what she needed. The pages she'd sent her agent still lacked what a success required, and they both knew it. Aspen had ended the conversation with Nic and realized there was one thing left to do.

Leave Brick. Go home. And write her bestseller.

Fighting nausea, she watched as their love story crumbled into pieces to lay at her feet. He stood, backing away, and her heart broke at the coolness in his ocean-blue eyes. The same eyes that had brimmed with love and trust and happiness. She'd stripped it away and replaced it with pain.

How could she live with this? How could she push away the man she loved?

For a bigger purpose, her inner voice whispered slyly. *For the book you promised to write. He agreed. He was the one who changed the rules.*

"Did you know this when you came over tonight?"

Aspen pressed a hand to her stomach and nodded miserably. "I realized there was no other way. I can't write it like this, Brick. It's not working."

"So, you want me to give you the same experience as *Fifty Ways*?"

Her voice was a raw whisper. "It's what we both agreed on."

Brick flinched, and a hard laugh escaped his lips. "Yeah, well, at least you were honest. I was generously paid and agreed to a contract. I was stupid to think this was different."

"No! It was. I fell in love with you, too. I just don't know how to do this!"

His brow lifted in mockery. "Do what? Stay? Not write the book? Be in a committed relationship? What don't you know how to do, Aspen?"

"All of it. I have a life in New York. I have a book under contract. I was clear on what was needed, and yes, everything changed, but how can I walk away from all my responsibilities? From my life?"

His face was cut from stone. Ice shimmered in his eyes. "Obviously, you can't. Hey, at least you had a hot-girl summer. I'm sure you'll thrill your fans with the sequel, make a ton of money, and write more books from this experience."

Aspen jumped to her feet and took a few steps forward. "Don't. Please."

"Just remember this, baby. I didn't break your heart." He paused in the terrible, pulsing silence. "You broke mine."

"Brick—"

"I'd like you to leave now."

"But—"

The words snapped like a whip. "Please."

Aspen jerked back. The pain throbbed like a bruise in her body, but there was nothing left to say. She'd ripped off the Band-Aid, and the wound she'd created was an open, throbbing mess.

She left the deck and headed toward the door. Dug trotted after her, his tongue hanging from his crooked jaw, staring at her with adoration and hero-worship. Tears streamed down her face as she knelt and snuggled him one last time. "Take care of Daddy," she whispered.

He licked her cheek and regarded her with a touch of seriousness, then raced back to the deck.

Aspen gently closed the door behind her.

It was done.

Chapter Twenty-Five

Aspen hugged her sister goodbye and tried not to cry. "I'll text when I get back to New York," she said, her voice tight.

"I wish you didn't have to go." Sierra stared at her with worry. "Are you going to be okay?"

She smiled sadly. "No. But that's the whole point."

"What if there are other options? You love each other. Can't you try?"

Aspen had thought about it endlessly after she left Brick's house. How many times had she jumped in her car, ready to drive over and beg for forgiveness? Forget about the book and deliver an inadequate manuscript, refusing to care? Move to be with the man she'd fallen in love with and her sister?

All those choices flipped through her brain, but it always came down to one decision.

This was her opportunity to write a book that could be even bigger than *Fifty Ways.* The absolute agony of leaving Brick behind was already stirring and growing inside her, dying to burst out and onto the page. It was a familiar feeling and exactly what she'd experienced with her first book. Her readers deserved the best for this sequel, and so did Mallory.

It was easy to believe that Brick would always be her summer love. The one who'd inspired her and taught her so many new things. But her life was in New York, and no one sold everything to move in with a man she'd dated for two months. That stuff just didn't happen in the real world.

She did better by herself. Always had.

Though the look on Brick's face when she rejected him would haunt her forever.

"Better go. Love you."

"Love you back. Drive safe," Sierra said.

Aspen didn't look in the rearview mirror as she pulled away. She was too afraid she wouldn't be able to keep going.

Kane stood beside Brick, arms crossed over his chest. "You miss her bad."

Brick dropped the book and cursed himself for constantly flipping through its pages, reading what she'd written. He'd fallen apart after Aspen left. It had taken all his strength to show up for the tourists and keep moving forward. He was desperate to call or text or show up at Sierra's house, but his gut told him Aspen had to make the first move. She'd made the final decision. She was the one who'd left.

Brick had been hopeful until he came home and found a package on the porch. When he opened it, a copy of *Fifty Ways to Leave Your Lover* fell out. Signed.

It was real. All of it. Love, Aspen.

He'd read it again, looking for clues. A sign she was coming back. But he didn't find anything. And he knew she was gone for good.

"I'm worried about you, dude. Can I do something? Take you out to get drunk? Hook you up with one of the women dying to get into your pants?"

His laugh held little humor. "Nope. That's how I got in trouble before. Just want to be alone anyway."

"You need time. Summer is behind us, and you've got some exciting projects to focus on." His friend's voice was full of fake enthusiasm. "I'll help you fix up Grandpa Ziggy's house, and you're already booking out for the fall tourists. Plus, I'm putting together a new deal out here you may want to get in on. Some property."

"Is that what you've been working on when you disappear? Thought that mix-up in New York wouldn't let you do any further investments."

"The company went bankrupt, and I had to pay off debtors, but I'm starting something new."

Brick lifted his brow, curious. "You thinking of staying?"

"Yeah. I like it here. It's a different vibe. More relaxed. I needed a change. Plus, I missed you."

"What about what you left behind?" Brick asked. He knew his friend had ties and some family obligations to work out. Kane hadn't confided in him regarding all the details of what had gone down, but Brick knew he'd open up eventually.

"Working on it. But I'll be able to get my own place within the month."

"Great."

Kane studied him. "Hey, you ever think of going to New York and fighting for her?"

His chest squeezed. God, if he'd thought it would work, Brick would try. But she'd made her decision to leave not only OBX behind but also him. Would they be able to move forward once she wrote the book? Seeing their story plastered all over the shelves, in the hands of endless readers, knowing what she'd sacrificed to do it?

No. He couldn't bend that far. It would hurt too much.

"Better to respect her choice and move on."

Even though it seemed impossible. Even though he'd never love anyone like he did Aspen.

Dug whined, sensing his emotion. "Sorry, buddy. I know you miss her, too."

Kane sighed. "Okay. Then I think the three of us need a quiet night in. I'll pick up a six-pack, some Duck Donuts, and we'll watch all three *John Wick* movies. Sound good?"

Brick looked at Dug, who seemed to like the idea. "Yeah. But I thought you mentioned a date?"

Kane squeezed Brick's shoulder in comfort. "Bros over hos, remember? You're stuck with me tonight."

"Thanks, Kane."

Brick stared at the book and wondered how Aspen was doing in New York.

It was finished.

Aspen stared at *The End* on her computer screen. A mix of emotions hit her, some familiar, some brand-new.

Elation that she'd gotten to the end.

Pride that she'd written another book.

Sadness that the characters she'd lived with for the past few months were no longer hers.

Grief that she'd given up something real for something imaginary.

Pain that it was all over. Because now that it was, she realized she'd lost everything else that mattered.

She usually wept bitterly after finishing a book. The intense emotions were always too much, and tears helped release and move the energy. But there were no tears inside her. It felt like her body had become a dried-up husk. Whatever was there had been emptied into the sequel, which was still untitled and becoming a hot argument at her publisher.

It had been brutal, but since she'd returned from OBX, the words had flowed endlessly. Days morphed into nights. DoorDash turned into Uber Eats. Pj's became sweats.

And she kept writing.

But now it was done, and she had to deal with the fallout.

God, she missed Brick.

Knowing Nicolette was waiting impatiently for the manuscript, she did a quick look-over and tweaked some minor things. Then texted her agent.

It's done.

The three dots appeared immediately. *Send it now!*

Aspen attached it to an email and hit send. When her phone rang, she dragged in a breath and answered.

"Did you get it?"

"Yes. I can't wait to read it. Do you like it? Are you happy?"

She smiled as Nic peppered her with the usual questions. "I think it's really good."

"I knew the beach trip would help. Bella's going out of her mind to get her hands on this. The team is ready to launch as soon as we deliver. If it's as good as your first, get ready for your life to explode again. I'm talking TV, book clubs, signings, the whole works. You'll be on the road constantly for this one."

She remembered how the thought used to excite her. Finally feeling like a real, successful writer had fed her ego and soul. It had been everything she'd ever wanted or needed.

Funny, she'd worked so hard to get to this moment. Sacrificed so much. Yet she felt…

Nothing.

Her agent rushed on, not waiting for an answer. What author wouldn't want the dream? "Just tell me one thing. Does it have a happy ending?" Nicolette asked.

She half-closed her eyes, and her insides seemed to shatter. "No. The best stories usually don't."

Silence hummed over the line. "Okay. Well, I'm not sure how they'll feel about the sequel not giving Mallory the happiness she deserves, but I'll read it and get right back to you. I'm so proud of you, Aspen. I know this wasn't easy, but I think it's the best choice you could have made for your career. Your fans have been begging for this for a long time."

Why did nausea turn her gut at the idea of sharing her inner heart for the world's entertainment? This was exactly what she'd wanted. What she'd paid Brick for. She'd fallen in love, gotten her heart broken, and wrote a fabulous book. Hell, the emotions practically dripped onto the page because she cried many times as she wrote a scene, imagining herself back with Brick. How did everything get so confusing and messed up?

But honestly, what were her options? Return to OBX and beg for his forgiveness? Tell him she wanted to try for a real relationship even as her book was released, and she dealt with press and signings and lies about how the story came to be?

Would Brick always wonder if things were real when there was a bestseller between them?

The questions made her head hurt. "Let me know when you're done reading. I'd better go, Nic."

She disconnected. Prowled her apartment. She ordered her favorite Chinese takeout with the television blasting a popular new Hulu series. She drank wine in her comfy pj's, safe in her familiar cocoon and happy place. But nothing was the same.

Tears stung her eyes as she looked around. She missed her sister. She missed stepping out to walk the beach and being soothed by the rush of the waves and the sand between her toes. She missed helping Marco and the guys at the souvenir shop. She missed Brick and Dug so badly her entire body throbbed with pain.

Maybe she'd been wrong, and the book *hadn't* hit the mark.

Maybe Nic would hate it and cancel the contract. Then Aspen could run back and throw her arms around Brick and force him to take her back.

Maybe her publisher would insist on changes, and she'd refuse, rendering the contract null and void.

Maybe…

The next day, Nic called and told her the book was brilliant. She was making minor corrections and would send it straight to her editor. They'd argued about the ending, but Nic gave in, conceding to Aspen's stubborn refusal to change it. A happy ending wasn't in Mallory's fate.

Or Aspen's.

She thought about what would happen next. Her editor would give the final approval, finalize a title, and begin cover talks. The book would be rushed to copyediting and put up for preorder.

The blurb and teasers would be sent out. Marketing and PR conferences would begin around the long, shiny table, Zooming in staff who worked from home. A fat lunch with her agent and editor would be reserved at a five-star restaurant while they drank champagne. Endless interviews and podcasts would be scheduled, as well as a signing tour. Usually, that was a year out, but Aspen knew with this type of press for a spring launch, it would be twice as intense. She'd be back on top in a competitive industry that rewarded you as long as you were as perfect as your last book.

She had everything she'd ever wanted.

Aspen sat in her empty apartment and began to cry. Hopelessness curled within her. She wished Dug would come over and lick her face and Brick would gather her in his arms. She'd feel more complete than she did right now after her supposed great achievement.

Blinking through the tears, her gaze fastened on the notebooks on the coffee table. She got up and picked them up. Flipped through them. Began to laugh as the characters sucked her into their madcap adventures. Brick's words echoed through her mind, asking the question over and over.

Why don't you just write something you truly love?

Because it wouldn't work.

Because *Zany Zoo* wasn't the stuff she usually wrote.

Because it was too late. The real book had been written. The contract had been signed. And the editor was waiting on the final copy.

Because…

The excuses were endless and made all the sense in the world.

Still, Aspen wondered what would happen if she blew up the rules of the game and did what her heart wanted. She'd never have the strength, though. Better to return to her safe life, lean into her success, and try to enjoy it. Because if she did blow it all up…

She'd lose her advance, her contract, and her publisher.

She'd lose her agent.

She'd lose her niche in the industry and slide into oblivion.

She'd lose the respect of her peers, her fans, and the world.

But…she'd get Brick. She'd get a new life where she got to create new rules. She'd get her sister and friends. She'd get…

Everything.

The truth slammed into her. Aspen's heart pounded crazily in her chest, sweat dampened her palms, and goose bumps broke out on her skin. She began to shake from the inside out, seeing her future in a way she'd never imagined.

And then she began to laugh a bit hysterically as joy flooded her.

She needed to talk to her sister.

Sierra answered immediately. It took a while to try and make sense of her jumbled thoughts, but her sister calmly heard her out until Aspen collapsed in silence, awaiting her sister's opinion.

Sierra spoke carefully. "Having you here would be a dream for me, Aspen. But it's not really about that. You need to know if you blow it all up, Brick may not take you back. It wasn't about a book for him. It was his heart."

Aspen closed her eyes as the familiar pain battered her insides. "I know. I treated him like all the other women in his past because I couldn't see my own story. It was never the book. It was always Brick. He deserves to hear that, at least."

"If he can't forgive you, do you still want to move here?"

The raw truth of Sierra's words ripped through her. Could she settle in OBX knowing Brick would never be hers? It would be torturous, but her intuition screamed this was her new path. She may not know the twists and turns ahead, but Aspen needed to take a chance. "Yes."

A sigh spilled over the receiver. "Then do what you need and get your ass back home."

She laughed and hung up. Then called her agent and began the fight of her life.

Chapter Twenty-Six

Clad in sweats, his chest bare, and Dug snoring between his legs, Brick tipped back the beer bottle and stared sightlessly at the baseball game playing on the television. Kane was out doing God only knew what with the local women, even after he'd been warned. Brick wondered if they'd soon be starting a support group for him.

The bell rang.

He cursed, wishing he could play possum. Maybe the person would go away. But Dug jumped up and barked ferociously, sounding like he meant business. Brick shook his head. "Yeah, you're real scary, buddy," he said. He looked around for a shirt, but he'd left it upstairs, so the hell with it. The person would have to be shocked at him being half-naked. Hopefully, it wasn't a female bent on healing his broken heart.

When he opened the door, his entire body froze. He stared helplessly at the woman before him, wondering if he'd literally thought about her so hard he was seeing a ghost. Because for the last two months, he'd dreamed of this.

"Hi, Brick. Can I come in?"

He tried but still couldn't move. Dug kept barking like a maniac. Brick squinted and leaned a bit closer. Was he drunk? Had he fallen asleep? Was he hallucinating? There was no way Aspen was on his porch. It was one of those fantasies he'd spun where she appeared, begged for forgiveness, and told him she refused to publish the book because she loved him more than a bestseller. Shit like that just did not happen.

"Um, Brick? It's me. I know you're probably beyond angry and maybe even hate me, but can I please come in? I have to tell you something."

He blinked. Holy shit, this seemed real. With a shaky hand, he undid the latch, and she stepped through the door. Her scent was the same, like orange blossoms and sunshine. She wore jeans, a V-neck yellow T-shirt, and sneakers. Her hair was in a ponytail, but curls had escaped and lay against her cheek in disarray.

Damned if his gut didn't clench like he'd received a sucker punch.

"What are you doing here?" he asked in a high voice, barely able to register his reality. Dug jumped up and down, whining, and like she'd done so many times before, Aspen sank to her knees to cuddle and pet him, smothering him with affection.

Had he gone back in time in his messed-up head?

"I'm sorry I sprang this on you. I've been driving nonstop, and all I could think about was getting here. To tell you some things. Things I'm not sure how you'll feel about."

"Why aren't you in New York? Is Sierra okay?" Panic filtered in. "Are you okay?"

"We're all fine. I'm fine. Well, I'm not fine. I'm fucked up and trying to fix it, but only God knows if it's too late."

He shook his head hard. "Aspen, I'm really confused right now. I've only had two beers, but I feel drunk. If you're really here, and no one's hurt, then why? Why are you suddenly on my porch asking to come in?"

She rose to her feet and met his gaze head-on. Those beautiful cocoa-brown eyes were filled with such pain and regret it seared right through him. "I'm here because I made a terrible mistake. I made the wrong choice, and I'm begging for a do-over. I chose the book—this book I thought I wanted so badly. The book that would put me back on top and confirm I'm the bestselling author Ryan never believed me to be. I chose a life I created too many years ago before I met you, Dug, Marco, and everyone else out here. I don't want that life any longer, Brick. I don't care about anything but you. I love you with my heart and soul. And if you take me back, I'll choose you first every single time."

His head spun. "What happened with the book? Were you unable to write it?"

She shook her head. "I wrote it. My agent said it was perfect. I took what happened between us and created a story that had all the elements of a bestseller. But I changed my mind. I called my agent and pulled the book. Canceled the contract. I'm not publishing it."

Shock barreled through him. Was she telling him the truth? How could she have written the book and then refused to sell it? "Wait. Are you even able to do something like that?"

A laugh burst from her lips, and her eyes danced with satisfaction. "I just did it. Oh, sure, everyone freaked out bad. My agent wanted to call me a therapist, but after a deep discussion, she agreed to do what I asked. Nic got me out of the contract, and she's still keeping me as a client. I'll give back the advance, which I banked anyway. I'm done with my publisher, of course—my reputation won't be the best for a while—but I'm sure it will work out. Worse things have happened in the industry, and writers got second chances."

Only one question spilled from his lips. "Why?"

"Because I love you more," she said simply.

Brick stared at her. Since she'd left, he'd fantasized about this exact scenario but had woken up every morning to an empty space and the realization that she hadn't picked him when it mattered most. Aspen had stuck to the contract, even after she fell in love with him.

In that moment, all he wanted was to yank her against him and drag her to bed. Show her all the ways he'd missed her. Finally release all the hurt and pain deep within her body and forgive. The happy ending was right before him. Her eyes shone with hope. Her beautiful lips trembled as she waited for his answer. All he had to do was step forward and claim it. Claim Aspen Lourde for himself.

Until the truth hit him full force.

After they climbed out of bed, things would still be broken between them. There was no more trust. Brick could forgive, but he couldn't forget. And he couldn't spend his days worried about the next time she left or a new book she couldn't write because she was too happy.

God help him; it was too late. Even if he loved her.

Brick swallowed the lump of regret and retreated a few steps. The wall he'd cultivated over the past two months held strong as he remembered how she'd walked away. He couldn't live through that again. Better to keep things the way they were.

"I'm sorry, Aspen. It's too late."

His words rang through her hollow body, and it took her a few seconds to register his distance. While she was ready to blow up her life to give Brick one big, grand gesture, he'd been slowly healing and didn't want her back.

Shock vibrated in her bones. Had she really expected things to go smoothly? She wasn't living in a romance novel. This was real life, and it was messy. Ups and downs. The type of relationship she didn't understand but wanted to.

But yeah, she needed to be real with herself. Aspen had hoped that showing up at his front door, not publishing the book, and moving to OBX would be enough.

Apparently, this was no rom-com with a breezy, easy ending.

She fought back her grief at this new Brick Babel who looked at her with politeness instead of open hunger. The emotion he'd shown when he first opened the door had cooled. It was as if he'd retreated a safe distance and refused to come out.

He kept talking. "I appreciate you telling me all this. But you can publish the book, Aspen. You were always clear about what you wanted from the start. I'm the one who screwed up."

She took a desperate step forward, then stopped. "No, I screwed it up because I wasn't brave enough to take a risk. I got stuck on the goal of the stupid book and refused to see what was right in front of me. I'm not afraid anymore, Brick. I'll do anything to make it up to you."

It was the sadness in his ocean-blue eyes that told her she'd truly lost him.

"It's too late, Aspen," he repeated gently. "I can't go back to the way it was. I told you I loved you and asked you to stay. When you made your choice, something broke between us that we'll never get back."

Tears burned her eyes. "What if I gave you some time? Some space? We could talk and go slowly."

"I can't. I don't trust you anymore. Not with my heart."

The brutal words hit like shrapnel and broke her into pieces. She choked on the grief, wanting to crumble and cry and beg in front of him. But he didn't deserve that. She was the one who'd left and betrayed him. If the roles had been reversed, she would have felt the same.

Aspen had figured things out too late to save them.

"I understand." She knelt and kissed Dug on his bumpy head, then straightened. "There are no words to make this right. I think words are what got me into trouble in the first place. The wrong ones." He waited silently, the space between them more like miles than inches. "I can only hope that somewhere down the line, we can be…friends." Her smile was weak, but she battled through. "Because you're the most beautiful man I've ever met. Inside and out."

She turned to grasp the doorknob. "Aren't you going back to New

York?" he asked.

Aspen shook her head. "No. I meant everything I said. The book won't be published, and I'm moving out here. I want to be by my sister, around people I care about. But I promise not to bother you. If you don't want to see me, I respect your decision. I never want to hurt you again."

He didn't say anything, so Aspen did the only thing left to do.

She walked away.

Chapter Twenty-Seven

Brick stepped outside and dragged in a breath. With fall in full swing, the air was cooler. Tours had calmed down from the summer chaos, but there was still enough business to keep him busy. Which was good since he thought about Aspen every moment he wasn't.

Marco came out. The familiar scent of weed drifted from him, but his eyes were clear as he stood beside Brick. "We just sold half a dozen Boogie Boards to those dudes from Chicago. Full price."

Brick nodded. "Did you upsell the new Salt Water shirts in the matching colors?"

A grin curved Marco's lip. "Hell, yes. Business 101, just like Aspen taught." They both winced. "Sorry."

"It's fine. I'm glad she's still helping you with stuff."

Her name drifted on the wind and in his head like a melody he couldn't stop repeating. It had been a month since she'd stood at his door, begging him to take her back. And though he'd made the right decision, knowing she was floating around his town was beginning to drive him insane.

Brick constantly looked for her. He imagined catching glimpses of wild, dark hair, hearing her deep belly laugh, and smelling her familiar scent as he took great pains to avoid her. She allowed him the distance, respectful of shared spaces when he went out with Kane to the local bar. If she visited Marco, she parked in the back and went through the side door to avoid Brick's office.

It didn't matter. His mind was strong about his refusal to try again, but his heart didn't give a shit.

"You doing okay?" Marco asked gruffly.

"Sure. I'm running special tours for the holidays. Partnered with some local inns that offer weekend getaways. It's been lucrative. Profit is up and steady."

"I mean with Aspen."

Brick forced a smile. "It's for the best."

Marco made a noise that sounded doubtful. "Is it? I mean, I agree that she screwed up bad. But she literally left New York and refused to publish the sequel. You know, I begged her to read it. I'm desperate to see how Mallory ended up, but she said the book would never see the light of day. She ended up choosing you over the fans."

Irritation hit. "I know, Marco. But it doesn't erase her leaving me in the first place."

"Yeah. Guess you're right. I respect your decision, man. Especially if it makes you happy."

Brick ground his teeth and lied right through them. "It does."

"Good."

He was about to go inside and leave the painful conversation when a bright-pink Hummer screeched into the parking lot. Maleficent climbed out, dressed in leather pants and a fringed black top, her long hair in elaborate braids. "Babel. We gotta talk."

He held back a sigh. Marco got that dreamy expression on his face again that had nothing to do with the weed. "Hi, Mal," he said, eyes all starry with admiration. Once she stopped stealing Brick's customers, Marco had suddenly developed an awful crush.

At least he'd moved on from Aspen.

Maleficent gave him a sharp nod. "Hey. Listen up, I had dinner with Aspen the other night, and I think you need to give her another chance."

"Like you did with Ziggy?" he challenged.

She spit like one of the wild horses. "Hell, no! Ziggy was a cheating asshole, even if he was your grandfather. Aspen made one bad mistake, but she loves you. Do you know I begged to read the sequel and she wouldn't let me? Said the book would never be seen or read. Said it was a reminder of her biggest regret. Losing you."

Had she really said that? Brick had figured since she'd kept her distance as promised, she was moving on. He'd given her permission to publish the book, but she still hadn't. With another woman, he'd figure she was playing games to gain points, but he knew Aspen wasn't like that. She did what she felt and didn't give a crap about the pretense. Which meant…

She still loved him. Still wanted him back.

Brick clenched his jaw. "Yeah, I heard."

Maleficent blew out a breath. "Dammit, you're stubborn. I guess she was right. You need to learn to trust her again with actions, not words."

His heart squeezed. "She said that?"

"Yep. Well, better get going. See ya later."

"Bye, Mal!"

She gave Marco a strange look, nodded again, and took off.

"Think she'd go out with me?" Marco asked.

"I doubt she's Mrs. Robinson."

He cocked his head. "Who?"

Brick groaned. "Never mind. No, Marco, she's too old for you."

"Love knows no age or restrictions, man."

Brick huffed and went back into his office. He had to stop thinking about Aspen. He'd made his decision, and there was no going back.

Two days later, he got a text from her.

Sorry to bother you. Would you be willing to meet me for coffee tomorrow morning?

Heart pounding, he made himself wait three full minutes before responding.

Sure. 7am?

Thumbs-up emoji. *See you then.*

He'd meet her for closure. That was all. Brick was positive he'd be reassured that he'd done the right thing once he saw her and was reminded of what she'd done.

Brick briefly wondered what to wear, then smothered the thought.

"Hi."

"Hi." Her smile faltered as she hungrily took in his figure. His hair was mussed and windblown. Those stinging blue eyes were shielded. Excruciating pain hit her in waves because she was the one responsible for putting such distance between them. He'd once been open with his affection and free with his love. But she'd thrown it back in his face. Now, she needed to deal with the consequences.

Aspen tilted her chin up and fell back on her usual grit. The same perseverance that had her spending hours and weeks and years alone in a room, with only her thoughts and the blank page. That type of stubbornness would give them a second chance. Eventually.

Hopefully.

She'd spent the last month carving out space here in OBX and working on herself. Her sister's words about her relationship with Ryan kept circling her mind until she began journaling about that time in her life. The writing was different this time since it was for her eyes and not a book. Aspen began to see the type of expectations she'd put on relationships based on an affair with a teacher who took no care with her heart. Brick had shown her things could be different, but it had been easier to fall back on what she knew.

Experience brutal pain; write a bestseller.

Digging deeper, she realized it had actually been easier to think she wasn't good at relationships and was better off alone. By examining some of her beliefs and speaking with her sister, Aspen had begun to heal on a deeper level than just writing *Fifty Ways to Leave your Lover.*

Now, it was time to see if she could ease back into Brick's life. If he was willing.

"Thanks for meeting me. I ordered you a coffee," she said.

"Thanks." He retrieved the mug and took a sip. "How's Sierra?"

"Great. The store is thriving. How's Kane?"

"Great. He's doing less tours and starting a new business here."

"Great," she echoed. Aspen wanted to cry at the painful conversation, but that wouldn't help. Only actions would earn back his trust. "I volunteered to do some work with Judy. I like the idea of giving back."

A shadow of a smile passed his lips. "She's lucky to have you."

I love you.

I made a horrible mistake.

I'll never hurt you again.

Instead, she forced another smile and nodded. "You showed me a lot of what's possible here. I took it for granted, but not anymore."

He shifted in his seat. A stray lock of hair fell over his brow, and she itched to reach over and smooth it back. Cup his rough cheek and press her forehead to his. Longing reared up and flooded her entire being.

His gaze crashed into hers, and she allowed him to see it all.

Brick stiffened. Then focused on his coffee. "How's the writing?"

A small laugh escaped her. "Actually, that's why I wanted to see you. To thank you."

"For what?"

"For believing in me," she said quietly. Her fingers wrapped around her cup. "I sent the *Zany Zoo* stuff to my agent. She loved it. Said it was fresh and different. We're in negotiations now with some children's publishers."

Her heart warmed when she glimpsed authentic pleasure in his ocean-blue eyes. "That's great, Aspen. I always knew it would be a hit."

"Well, there's no guarantee of anything, but I'm happy to be writing something I'm excited about again. I never would've figured it out without you."

"Yeah, you would have. Eventually."

She shook her head slowly. "I was too attached to outcomes I didn't even care about. Fame in the book world. Success in my career to prove I was worthy. Ryan messed me up a little more than I realized. I see things better now."

"I'm glad." He sipped his coffee. "What about the sequel?"

"What about it?"

He gave her a level stare. "You should publish it, Aspen. It doesn't matter anymore for us. Your readers want the story. There's no need to hold back because of me."

Grief sank into her. "Yes, there is. I'll never share that book with anyone. It's a reminder that I lost you because I wasn't brave enough. It's a reminder that I will never do it again."

His gaze fused to hers. Shock turned to something more, but it was too early to see if it could be a beginning. She continued.

"I love you. I will always love you. But I'm not going to pull an Anastasia and stalk you or beg. But I *will* be here. Quietly waiting to see if you might give me another chance. And if not? I'll be your friend. And if we can't be friends?" Her smile wobbled, but she let him see her true emotion. "I want you to be happy no matter what."

He remained quiet, so she sucked in a breath and finished up. "Thanks for meeting me, Brick. I miss you."

She paused, but he seemed to struggle for words. Shoving down her disappointment, she got up from the booth and walked out.

She'd meant it. Brick needed time and space. He needed to see that she wasn't running away and that she'd always choose him.

He needed a reason to give her another chance.

Brick sipped his beer at the end of the bar and waited for Kane.

The clatter of glasses and chatter rose around him. The scent of burgers and fries filled the air. Some woman approached him, but he just shook his head, and she disappeared with a huff.

He thought about Aspen.

Two weeks had passed since their meeting.

Brick had reread all her books. Twice. He heard stories about how she was helping in her sister's store and making friends with the volunteers at the sea turtle rescue organization. He'd read a story online after a Google alert with her name pinged him. The article mentioned that Aspen had put an end to rumors that there would be a sequel to *Fifty Ways to Leave Your Lover*, and the book world was upset. They also said the famous author had moved to OBX and was apparently taking a hiatus from writing.

Slowly, as the days passed, Brick began wondering if his pride was blocking him. In a way, it was easier not to forgive. To hold on to the hurt and resentment and wear them like a shield. To have it all be part of his story, his mind spinning elaborate tales of betrayal and images of him being a stoic warrior, separate from love and mess and hurt.

Aspen was here. And she wasn't Anastasia. She was on her own journey, and deep inside, Brick believed she loved him.

So, the real question was: Could he take the leap himself?

A slap on the bar interrupted his thoughts. "Dude, you with me? I've said your name a few times."

He looked at Kane. "Yeah. Sorry, was just thinking."

"Therefore, the smoke."

Brick rolled his eyes. "Hysterical."

Kane grinned, ordered an IPA, and slid onto the stool. "You really denied that pretty redhead glaring at us?" he asked.

"Yep."

"Interesting. Guess she'll be an addition to tonight's support group."

Brick frowned. "That broke up months ago. After Aspen left."

Kane laughed. "Nope. They changed it to the Badass Bitches Club, but then Aspen joined as a member. You didn't hear?"

Coldness washed through him. No. No, no, no…

Kane continued. "Guess she's the leader now. Who knows what type of stories she's sharing about you? Meeting's going on tonight. Right now, as a matter of fact."

The roaring built up in his ears. He gripped his glass and swiveled his furious gaze to Kane. "Are you fucking kidding me?"

Kane shrugged. "Nope. Thought you knew. Why don't you go blow it up right now? They still go to that wine bar. Maybe you can put a stop to all the gossip—your reputation is killing my mojo here. No one wants to sleep with me because I'm your best friend."

Brick stumbled off the stool, his vision blurry. Aspen had betrayed him. Right now, she was talking about him to that group of women who'd tried to destroy him. How could she do this to him? Had the past six weeks only been a game?

He was about to find out.

"I'm going over there. I've had enough of this shit."

"Good plan. I'll buy your beer," Kane called out.

Brick stormed out and drove to the wine bar. Lifting his hand at the bartender, he headed to the back room where feminine voices rose and tangled in the air. He was about to burst in and lose his shit when he heard his name from Aspen's lips.

He froze.

"I don't know if Brick will ever forgive me," she said brokenly. "I keep seeing his face when I left. I had everything I ever wanted, and I broke his heart. Do I even deserve a second chance?"

Riley spoke, her voice cutting across the murmurs of sympathy. "Yes, you do. And you will get Brick back. We've come up with a three-prong plan which guarantees success."

"You've already done the first part. Give him space to miss you. The second is the apology tour. The third phase is to seduce him." Was that Lacey? A peek confirmed the petite blonde had spoken.

"I met him for coffee two weeks ago," Aspen said. "I apologized again, but I'm not sure it made a difference."

"What were you wearing?" another female asked. "Were you showing boobs?"

Brick pressed his lips together so he didn't snort.

Aspen gasped. "No! I can't use my body. It's not fair."

"Everything's fair in love and war," Riley stated. "Lacey's right. You need two more weeks of apologizing in various ways. Then you can move on to the fun part."

"Oh, send him handcuffs and a mask," Kate chimed in. "With a note that says you're sorry."

"That's ridiculous. What about a love poem? I've been practicing," Aspen said.

Groans rose in the air. "God, no. That's so cheesy," Lacey said. "What about crotchless panties?"

"I refuse to play dirty and use sex!" Aspen yelled.

"We're still talking about phase two of the apology. Crotchless panties with an apology note is fair game," Riley said.

"I love this man. I just wish I could convince him that I'll never let him down again."

Aspen's voice whispered across the room, rose to his ears, and buried itself in his heart.

In that moment, the ice broke, and the walls tumbled down. Suddenly, he realized that he not only loved her, he also forgave her because Aspen Lourde was his soulmate.

It was time to claim his woman.

Aspen released her innermost fear to the group, knowing they'd support her.

The girls had all reached out about changing the support group's name and asked her to join. Even Riley admitted that she was tired of blaming everything on Brick and wanted a clean slate. They'd named themselves the Badass Bitches Club and gathered to give support, drink wine, and be each other's cheerleaders. For the past month, they'd been doing journal work and sharing stories. Unfortunately, Aspen kept talking about Brick, so he still remained the main subject of their meetings.

She was about to steer the subject away from crotchless panties when Brick suddenly stepped from behind the wall and walked into the room.

Everyone stared in shocked silence.

Hands on hips, gaze narrowed, he took in all the members, then focused on Aspen.

Oh. God.

Those ocean-blue eyes blazed with raw emotion as he dove deep, forcing her to not only recognize but also accept everything he was about to give her. A small moan rose from her throat as sexual chemistry crackled in the air, and low murmurs vibrated through the room.

This man was a force to be reckoned with, and he'd come for her.

His voice was velvety smooth and made goose bumps break out on her skin. "I appreciate the plan you all came up with, but I'd like to speak with Aspen now. Alone."

Even Riley didn't fight. In a rush, they all jumped up and left, murmuring, "Good luck." And then it was just them, staring at each other in the vibrating silence.

"Brick—"

"I'd like to ask you an important question."

She winced. Her heart pounded wildly, and her palms sweated. "Of—of course. Anything."

He stepped forward, towering over her. His muscled body caged her in the chair. She swallowed hard and tilted her head back, his powerful, masculine presence pressing down on her with magnetism.

"Why did you want to skip the seduction phase?"

She blinked. Stared. "Huh?"

He placed a palm on either side of her chair, then leaned in. His spicy scent rose to her nostrils, and his carved lips stopped inches from hers. She melted into a puddle of want and hunger and confusion.

"That would have been my favorite part of the plan. Seducing me. Can we fast-forward to that portion?"

Hope flared. Her breath caught as tears burned her eyes and her body trembled. "Yes. Anything you want. Because you're the love of my life."

A half smile quirked his lower lip. "Good answer."

He slammed his mouth over hers, kissing her hard and deep. Her lips opened, welcoming him, urging him to take everything she had to give. He pulled her from the chair to wrap his arms tightly around her. "I missed you, baby."

"I'm so sorry," she whispered, cupping his cheeks, kissing his face. "Can you forgive me?"

"Yes. Because you came back. And you're mine."

Aspen sighed with pleasure, leaning into his hard strength, and knew she was home.

Epilogue

After her conversation with Nic, Aspen hung up the phone. Strong arms wrapped around her from behind, and she leaned against his hard chest, a smile playing on her lips.

"Any news?" he asked, his voice rumbly in her ear.

"We sold the first three books," she said with satisfaction. "*Zany Zoo* is an official series. They're not going to use my drawings, but I think a professional illustrator will do my characters justice."

"You did it. Congratulations." She turned her head, and he kissed her. "Did you get the terms you wanted?"

Pleasure speared through her. After months of submissions, they'd found the perfect publisher for her books. It wasn't one of the big five, but the terms were generous, and they had a stellar reputation for putting out books that consistently won awards and gained a solid audience. "I got to keep media and audio rights, and Nic negotiated a seven-year term. So, if they don't work out, I get them all back and can publish on my own."

"Smart. What about the sequel?"

Aspen sighed, still a bit unsure. "Nic had a conversation with my editor. She read it, and they want to offer."

"Why don't you sound happy?"

She got up and walked into his open arms. With a sigh of contentment, she murmured against the soft cotton of his T-shirt, "Because I'm still worried you'll regret it."

He tipped up her chin, and she fell into his ocean-blue eyes. A smile curved his lips. "Baby, you owe your fans that book. Besides, it's not our story anymore. Is it?"

She smiled back. "No, it's not."

"Then you're going to sell it and give readers a great gift. It's a beautiful book and meant to be in the world. Okay?"

Emotion choked her throat. "Okay."

"We have to celebrate. Call the gang?"

"Yes. We haven't seen everyone in a while."

"It's been an off month. I wanted to keep you to myself until the spring season began and we're both working nonstop."

"Oh, I wasn't complaining," she purred, leaning in for a second, deeper kiss. "I intend to have our own private celebration after."

He laughed, easing away. "You're killing me. Gotta run a few errands. I'll be back soon."

Aspen sighed with contentment, alone at her desk.

She'd done it.

It had been a difficult process. Brick had pushed her to publish the book, but after looking it over, she realized it wasn't right any longer. Too many things had changed, and Aspen didn't feel the story did justice to Mallory.

So, she'd re-written it.

The sequel was different from the original she'd written six months ago and walked away from. Aspen had been able to connect because Brick had taught her about real love, and Aspen no longer equated pain with good writing. The result was a book she was proud of and loved writing.

There was more space and breath within the passages as Mallory fell in love again and relearned how to not only stay true to herself but honor her scars without living in their shadow, as well. The previous pages were soaked in pain and growth.

With this one? There were more lulls and flow, ups and downs, and scenes of silence that Nic said she'd never read before in Aspen's work, bringing the emotions to a higher level. Plus, she'd changed the ending. Her fans deserved happiness and hope with Mallory's story.

So did Aspen.

With Brick's full support, Aspen had her agent handle the delicate negotiations. Now, she had a contract for a sequel worthy of publication and a new endeavor with her beloved characters of *Zany Zoo.* She lived in a place with family and friends and the man she loved with all her heart.

Aspen had created her very own happy ending.

Her life turned out to be the best book ever.

Are you ready for Sierra and Kane's story?
Read on for a sneak peek!

The Reluctant Flirt

By Jennifer Probst
Coming July 15, 2025

Just one night…

After discovering her husband's affair, Sierra Lourde flees to New York City for a little damage control—and a lot of wine. A tipsy night in a bar with a charming stranger seems like the perfect way to forget her troubles. No names, no promises, just one night to escape reality and regain her confidence. The next morning, mortified by her vulnerability, she flees without looking back. But who needs closure, right?

But one night changes everything…

Sierra has reinvented herself as the proud owner of Flirt, a trendy boutique in the Outer Banks. Life is good—until Kane Masterson, the man she left behind, walks back into town. And of course, he's now the developer whose big new project threatens to bulldoze her beloved shop. Kane needs this deal to save his career (and his brother), but Sierra's not about to let him demolish her hard-won success.

With sparks flying, sarcastic jabs turning into lingering looks, and a family wedding forcing them into close quarters, Sierra and Kane find themselves tangled in a battle of wills—and hearts. But now he has to choose: reclaim his career or risk everything for a second chance with the one woman he can't forget.

Sierra stood in line at Duck Donuts and figured one little treat wouldn't hurt. It had been a hell of a day with demanding shoppers, conference calls, and a lost shipment. It was either sugar or a margarita, and since she still had a long evening of work ahead, the nonalcoholic option won.

"Chocolate Coconut Dream," she said, stepping to the counter.

"Bad day?" Greta asked with a knowing smile.

"Challenging."

"I hear ya. Things can get hairy in here at breakfast rush hour." The pert brunette was the owner's daughter and learning the ropes. "I'll swing by to pick up my layaway tomorrow night. Gonna wear it to a party this weekend."

"No worries. It's safely tucked aside for you. I got some gorgeous earrings that match perfectly, so I put those away for you to check out."

"You're the best. Thanks, Sierra."

"Anytime." She swiped her card, picked up her donut, and headed out.

Then stopped short as she almost collided with a man on his way in, taking up all the space in the doorway and the air around him.

Kane Masterson.

Sierra froze. A fragment of her hoped if she stood very still and stayed quiet, he'd walk past her and pretend he didn't see her. After all, they'd been playing the game well for the past few months, and it was working.

Kind of.

Instead, he paused and let the door swing shut behind him. In the silence, their gazes locked, and within seconds, she was transported back to the night when everything had changed. The ultimate secret she'd confided in no one—not even her sister.

Dear God, he was perfect. Even sexier than she remembered, and she'd replayed every moment of their time together over and over, late at night, on the vulnerable edge of sleep. With her defenses down and susceptible to dreams, he visited her, even after all this time.

Thick, russet hair with touches of gold tumbled over his brow. His features were classic Irish but held a carved symmetry that fascinated a woman, urging her to look closer. A short, clipped beard hugged his lush lips, giving him an edge. But it was his eyes that had grabbed Sierra from the very first. A deep-set emerald, gleaming with both mischief and ruthless intelligence. His body was drool-worthy, lean and trim, muscled and elegant, clad in designer clothes that he wore on his terms. He was a man who claimed a room with his presence, radiating an aura of sensual masculinity that was hard to resist.

God knew she hadn't been able to.

"Sierra."

A shudder racked her. He uttered her name with an intimacy that wrapped around her as tightly as his smoky, erotic voice had once rumbled in her ear. She remembered the night they'd met at the bar. Aspen had been so intent on getting them together, and they'd both stared at the other, shocked. Kane had whispered her name just like he did now. But she'd panicked and pretended they were meeting for the first time as she introduced herself.

Of course, it couldn't have been pain she'd spotted in his eyes. Not after their agreement.

They'd been careful afterward. Spinning excuses not to be in the same room. If they were, Sierra made sure to drift around and stay with others. Never be alone with him.

Her luck had run out.

Sierra opened her mouth but couldn't say his name. It was just too intimate. Instead, she nodded. "Hello."

A tense silence fell between them. His gaze narrowed. "Still playing the silent game?"

Her brow arched. "I'm not playing any games," she said cooly. "I'm just getting a donut."

"Which one?"

She blinked. "Huh?"

"What flavor?"

His question came out as a demand, as did most things uttered from those lips. "Chocolate Coconut Dream."

"That's my favorite, too."

Her body softened from his low murmur. Her female parts buzzed with recognition and throbbed in awareness. She wished she could wipe out the memory of that mouth over hers, the way he demanded and controlled and gave so much pleasure. She'd shattered like glass, feeling alive for the first time.

Sierra cleared her throat and prayed her voice worked. "Goody for us. Before I dole out friendship bracelets, you'd better hurry. There's only one left."

He grinned slowly, and shivers raced down her spine. "Still mouthy, I see."

She couldn't do this. She'd combust and embarrass herself, and Kane was already the hottest bachelor the town was fighting over. She refused to go there. "Well, see you around."

Sierra squared her shoulders and pushed past him. Her arm brushed his, and his fingers suddenly shot out and grasped her wrist, stilling her. The familiar scents of clove and whiskey rose to her nostrils, an aroma that was twisted into her memory like wisps of smoke dragging her back.

"You can keep running for now." His thumb pressed into her throbbing pulse at the base of her wrist. "Until I'm ready to catch you."

She made sure not to show fear. Cranking her head around, she met his gaze head-on and slowly tugged her wrist away. "I'm not yours to catch," she said calmly. "Goodbye."

Sierra walked away with slow, careful strides. She wouldn't run.

But she felt his stare burning her alive with each step of her retreat.

Book Club Questions

1. Book of the Month focuses on Aspen's career as a writer and her drive for success at all costs. Could you relate to her passion and plan to pen another bestseller? Why or why not?

2. Aspen is afraid she is a one-hit wonder. Have you ever felt like this in your career or life? Discuss.

3. Brick's reputation in OBX creates conflict and drama. Did you sympathize with his plight? Do you think he should have tried harder to tell the truth and salvage his reputation?

4. There are many secondary characters in Book of the Month that bring humor and chaos. Who was your favorite and why?

5. Fifty Ways to Leave your Lover was Aspen's breakout bestseller. Would you like to read actual excerpts from this fictional book?

6. When Aspen returns and begs for forgiveness, Brick refuses to take her back. Did you agree with his decision? Did you think Aspen moving and refusing to publish the sequel should have been enough? Discuss.

7. Romantic comedy is a popular genre. What were your favorite scenes in the book that made you laugh?

Discover More Jennifer Probst

Christmas in Cape May
A Sunshine Sisters Novella

Devon Pratt loves many things in life. The beauty of flowers. The yin and yang of energy. The power of positivity in people. And everything to do with the Christmas season.

As a floral shop owner in the beach town of Cape May, she looks forward to decorating both the town and running the annual holiday party to benefit the local animal shelter. Too bad the new owner of her favorite venue is more like the Grinch than Santa. Working with him will be a challenge, but she's too full of seasonal cheer to let him annoy her, right?

Jameson Franklin hates many things in life. Crowds. Fake cheer. Ostentatious décor. And especially Christmas. The season is full of things he'd rather avoid, but since taking over the popular restaurant Vintage temporarily for his cousin as a favor, he's trying to play nice with the locals. Too bad the florist is insisting on overrunning his sacred space with blooms, dogs, and an endless positive persistence that pushes all of his buttons. But when too many heated confrontations lead to heated encounters, he begins to wonder what it would be like to love not only Christmas, but Devon Pratt.

Let the festivities begin.

* * * *

Something Just Like This
A Stay Novella

Jonathan Lake is the beloved NYC mayor who's making a run for governor. His widowed status and close relationship with his daughter casts him as the darling of the press, and the candidate to beat, but behind the flash of the cameras, things are spinning out of control. It all has to do with his strait laced, ruthlessly organized assistant. Her skills and reserved demeanor are perfect to run his campaign, but her brilliant brain has become a temptation he's been fighting for too long. Can he convince her to take a chance on a long-term campaign for love or will his efforts end up in scandal?

Alyssa Block has admired the NYC mayor for a long time, but her secret crush is kept ruthlessly buried under a mountain of work. Besides, she's not his type, and office scandals are not in her job description. But when they retreat to an upstate horse farm for a secluded weekend, the spark between them catches flame, and Jonathan sets those stinging blue eyes on winning her. Can she convince him to focus on the upcoming election, or will she succumb to the sweet promise of a different future?

* * * *

The Marriage Arrangement
A Marriage to a Billionaire Novella

She had run from her demons…

Caterina Victoria Windsor fled her family winery after a humiliating broken engagement, and spent the past year in Italy rebuilding her world. But when Ripley Savage shows up with a plan to bring her back home, and an outrageous demand for her to marry him, she has no choice but to return to face her past. But when simple attraction begins to run deeper, Cat has to decide if she's strong enough to trust again…and strong enough to stay…

He vowed to bring her back home to be his wife…

Rip Savage saved Windsor Winery, but the only way to make it truly his is to marry into the family. He's not about to walk away from the only thing he's ever wanted, even if he has to tame the spoiled brat who left her legacy and her father behind without a care. When he convinces her to agree to a marriage arrangement and return home, he never counted on the fierce sexual attraction between them to grow into something more. But when deeper emotions emerge, Rip has to fight for something he wants even more than Windsor Winery: his future wife.

* * * *

Somehow, Some Way
A Billionaire Builders Novella

Bolivar Randy Heart (aka Brady) knows exactly what he wants next in life: the perfect wife. Raised in a strict traditional family household, he seeks a woman who is sweet, conservative, and eager to settle down. With his well-known protective and dominant streak, he needs a woman to offer him balance in a world where he relishes control.

Too bad the newly hired, gorgeous rehab addict is blasting through all his preconceptions and wrecking his ideals…one nail at a time…

Charlotte Grayson knows who she is and refuses to apologize. Growing up poor made her appreciate the simple things in life, and her new job at Pierce Brothers Construction is perfect to help her carve out a career in renovating houses. When an opportunity to transform a dilapidated house in a dangerous neighborhood pops up, she goes in full throttle. Unfortunately, she's forced to work with the firm's sexy architect who's driving her crazy with his archaic views on women.

Too bad he's beginning to tempt her to take a chance on more than just work…one stroke at a time…

Somehow, some way, they need to work together to renovate a house without killing each other…or surrendering to the white-hot chemistry knocking at the front door.

****

Searching for Mine

A Searching For Novella

The Ultimate Anti-Hero Meets His Match…

Connor Dunkle knows what he wants in a woman, and it's the three B's. Beauty. Body. Boobs. Other women need not apply. With his good looks and easygoing charm, he's used to getting what he wants—and who. Until he comes face to face with the one woman who's slowly making his life hell...and enjoying every moment...

Ella Blake is a single mom and a professor at the local Verily College who's climbed up the ranks the hard way. Her ten-year-old son is a constant challenge, and her students are driving her crazy—namely Connor Dunkle, who's failing her class and trying to charm his way into a better grade. Fuming at his chauvinistic tendencies, Ella teaches him the ultimate lesson by giving him a *special* project to help his grade. When sparks fly, neither of them are ready to face their true feelings, but will love teach them the ultimate lesson of all?

****

Begin Again
A Stay Novella

Chloe Lake is finally living her dream. As the daughter of the governor, she's consistently in the spotlight, and after being dubbed the Most Eligible Bachelorette of NYC, both her career and personal life has exploded. Fortunately, her work as an advocate for animal welfare requires constant publicity and funding, so she embraces her role and plays for the camera—anything for the sake of her beloved rescues.

But when a big case is on the line, she's faced with the one obstacle she never counted on: the boy who broke her heart is back, and in order to gain justice, they need to work together.

Chloe swears she can handle it until old feelings resurface, and she's faced with a heartbreaking choice.

Will this time end differently—or are they destined to be only each other's first love—instead of forever?

Owen Salt fell hard for Chloe when he was a screwed-up kid in college, and spent the next years changing himself into the man his grandfather believed he was capable of. But when his career led him across the country, he knew he needed to leave the woman he loved behind. He's never forgotten her, but as the new darling of the press, now she's way out of his league. When work brings him back to fight for justice by her side, he swears he can handle it.

But he's never really gotten over his first love—and he wants one more opportunity to prove he's a man who's worthy.

Can Owen convince the woman who holds his heart to take a second chance on forever—or is it too late for them both?

For fans of Jennifer Probst's Stay series, *Begin Again* is book five in that series.

About Jennifer Probst

Jennifer Probst wrote her first book at twelve years old. She bound it in a folder, read it to her classmates, and hasn't stopped writing since. She holds a masters in English Literature and lives in the beautiful Hudson Valley in upstate New York. Her family keeps her active, stressed, joyous, and sad her house will never be truly clean. Her passions include horse racing, Scrabble, rescue dogs, Italian food, and wine—not necessarily in that order.

She is the New York Times, USA Today, and Wall Street Journal bestselling author of over 50 books in contemporary romance fiction. She was thrilled her book, The Marriage Bargain, spent 26 weeks on the New York Times. Her work has been translated in over a dozen countries, sold over a million copies, and was dubbed a "romance phenom" by Kirkus Reviews. She is also a proud three-time RITA finalist.

She loves hearing from readers. Visit her website for updates on new releases, and get a free book at www.jenniferprobst.com.

Discover 1001 Dark Nights Collection Eleven

DRAGON KISS by Donna Grant
A Dragon Kings Novella

THE WILD CARD by Dylan Allen
A Rivers Wilde Novella

ROCK CHICK REMATCH by Kristen Ashley
A Rock Chick Novella

JUST ONE SUMMER by Carly Phillips
A Dirty Dare Series Novella

HAPPILY EVER MAYBE by Carrie Ann Ryan
A Montgomery Ink Legacy Novella

BLUE MOON by Skye Warren
A Cirque des Moroirs Novella

A VAMPIRE'S MATE by Rebecca Zanetti
A Dark Protectors/Rebels Novella

LOVE HAZARD by Rachel Van Dyken

BRODIE by Aurora Rose Reynolds
An Until Her Novella

THE BODYGUARD AND THE BOMBSHELL by Lexi Blake
A Masters and Mercenaries: New Recruits Novella

THE SUBSTITUTE by Kristen Proby
A Single in Seattle Novella

CRAVED BY YOU by J. Kenner
A Stark Security Novella

GRAVEYARD DOG by Darynda Jones
A Charley Davidson Novella

A CHRISTMAS AUCTION by Audrey Carlan
A Marriage Auction Novella

THE GHOST OF A CHANCE by Heather Graham
A Krewe of Hunters Novella

Also from Blue Box Press

LEGACY OF TEMPTATION by Larissa Ione
A Demonica Birthright Novel

VISIONS OF FLESH AND BLOOD by Jennifer L. Armentrout and Rayvn Salvador
A Blood & Ash and Fire & Flesh Compendium

FORGETTING TO REMEMBER by M.J. Rose

TOUCH ME by J. Kenner
A Stark International Novella

THE MARRIAGE AUCTION 2 by Audrey Carlan

BORN OF BLOOD AND ASH by Jennifer L. Armentrout
A Flesh and Fire Novel

MY ROYAL SHOWMANCE by Lexi Blake
A Park Avenue Promise Novel

SAPPHIRE DAWN by Christopher Rice writing as C. Travis Rice
A Sapphire Cove Novel

EMBRACING THE CHANGE by Kristen Ashley
A River Rain Novel

IN THE AIR TONIGHT by Marie Force

LEGACY OF CHAOS by Larissa Ione
A Demonica Birthright Novel

On Behalf of Blue Box Press,

Liz Berry, M.J. Rose, and Jillian Stein would like to thank ~

Steve Berry
Doug Scofield
Benjamin Stein
Kim Guidroz
Chelle Olson
Tanaka Kangara
Stacey Tardif
Suzy Baldwin
Chris Graham
Jessica Saunders
Grace Wenk
Ann-Marie Nieves
Dylan Stockton
Kate Boggs
Richard Blake
and Simon Lipskar